Heir Undisputed

Hannah James

HEIR UNDISPUTED

ISBN 9798879182705

Written by Hannah James
Cover design by Neal Strydom

WARNING

This book is not suitable for readers under the age of 18.

'Heir Undisputed' is a paranormal romance novel that contains the following:
descriptive sexual content
violence
graphic killing
foul language
mentions of sexual assault
mentions of illegal drugs
references to fertility and/or pregnancy
grief/loss

Any and all sexual content occurs between consenting adults and may include but is not limited to edging.

'Heir Undisputed' does not contain any depictions of non-consent, dubious consent, or cheating between main characters.

'Heir Undisputed' is the second book in the Night Heir series.

Playlist

1. Lady Rich, Her Galliard – John Dowland & Nigel North (Chapter 1)
2. The Pretty Flounder Tavern – Scorewizard (Chapter 5)
3. Desire – Meg Myers (Chapter 6)
4. Murder In My Mind – Kordhell (Chapter 8)
5. On Top Of The World – Imagine Dragons (Chapter 12)
6. Teardrop – Massive Attack (Chapter 14)
7. Bad – Royal Deluxe (Chapter 21)
8. Death of Peace of Mind – Bad Omens (Chapter 22)
9. Hall of Fame – The Script feat. Will.i.am (Chapter 23)
10. Zitti e Buoni – Måneskin (Chapter 24)
11. Enjoy The Silence – Depeche Mode (Chapter 26)
12. Far From Home (The Raven) – Sam Tinnesz (Chapter 28)
13. The Only – Static-X (Chapter 29)
14. No Swinging in Your Walking – Black Cat Zoot (Chapter 32)
15. War of Hormone – BTS (Chapter 35)
16. Lovin On Me – Jack Harlow (Chapter 38)
17. Punch – Oliver Michael (Chapter 39)
18. This Is The Life – Amy McDonald (Chapter 42)
19. Everything Black – Unlike Pluto (Chapter 44)
20. Running up That Hill – Placebo (Chapter 49)
21. Džanum – Teya Dora (Chapter 51)
22. Oh Caroline – The 1975 (Chapter 58)
23. Moonlight – Kali Uchis (Chapter 59)
24. Lights Out – Mindless Self Indulgence (Chapter 65)
25. One of your girls – Troye Sivan (Chapter 66)
26. In The Stars – Benson Boone (Chapter 68)
27. The Death & Resurrection Show – Killing Joke (Chapter 69)

Available on Spotify: Heir Undisputed – HannahJames_Author

Pronunciation Guide

Names
Dr. Emmeline Woods – Em-muh-leen Woods
Katalina – Kat-uh-lee-na
Ljudmila - Lood-mee-a
Ionáthan – Yo-na-tan
Dionissia – Dee-oh-nis-see-ah

Russian Words/Expressions
Nuchka (nickname) – Nooch-ka
Lastochka (little swallow) - Las-ti-chka
('i' sound like the 'i' in switch)
Belka (squirrel) - Byel-ka
Solnyshka (Little sun) – Sol-nish-ka
Zaichonok (Little bunny) – Zai-cho-nok
Malyshka (Small/baby girl.) – Ma-lysh-ka ('y' sound is still kind of like the 'i' in switch)
Moya lyubov (My love) - Maya loo-boif (more mature way of addressing a partner)
Poshyol na hui (Fuck you) – Pa-shol na h-oo-i
Kiryusha (Diminutive) - Kiroosha (roll the 'r')
Izvinite (I'm sorry) - Iz-vee-neet-ye
Vanya (Nickname for Jonathan. Vanya is a nickname for a person with the name 'Ivan', which has the same root as 'John'/'Jonathan') - Van-ya (Like Tanya, but with a V)
Kirillovich (Older nickname, still used) - Kir-eel-a-vich (roll the 'r', the vich sounds like 'which')
Da (yes) - Dah
Nyet (no) – Nyet (like the 'yet' in 'yeti', just add an 'N' in front of it)
Spasiba (thank you) – Spa-see-ba
Pozhaluysta (You're welcome) - Pah-za-leesta ('z' like 'zhuzh')
Eniky beniky eli vareniki, eniky beniky…klets – Eh-nyi-ki be-nyi-ki ye-li var-yeh-ni-ki,eh-nyi-ki be-nyi-ki kl-yets

Czech words/Expressions
Na zdraví (to health, used as ‘cheers’) – Na zdra-vee

Greek words/Expressions
Agori mou – Ag-gôh-ri mo
Koritsi mou – Ko-ree-tsi mo

Romanian words/Expressions
Cochetă – Koh-keh-tuh

Places
Nyhavn - Nee-hown

Go on. Read it.

Good girl.

Chapter 1

Just like the forbidden fruit in the garden of Eden, I knew from the first moment I laid eyes on her that she was not meant for me. At the same time, I'd never been one to pay any mind to societal or moral constraints. I want what I want, and I always get what I want. And what I wanted was her... More specifically, I wanted what was in her veins and between her legs, even though I was well aware that I could easily obtain both elsewhere. I knew she had feelings for me, but that didn't mean anything to me. Neither did her marriage. Generally, I respected the institution that was matrimony, most often I even admired it, but hers was a fucking joke. That was the whole reason I wanted her in the first place: Spite. I knew she belonged to another. I simply didn't care.

But as she lay beneath me, drops of perspiration pearling on her lip, on her forehead, soft whimpers and moans tumbling over her trembling lips, her legs wrapped around me as I thrust into her, I realized yet again that it would take a lot more than a willing body to captivate me. I wasn't sure how long I would continue these visits to her chambers before I lost interest. If I were being honest, I started losing interest a long time ago…

Her physical appearance was not what had attracted me to her. Her height was but average, her build slender, and her dark hair anything but unique. Similarly, her face was not unattractive, but at the same time not particularly beautiful either.

True, her mind was brilliant, she was forthright, and very, very charming. None of that impressed me, though. In truth, the thing that had drawn me in was her foul temper and her unavailability. The thing that had originally kept me coming back was that sharp tongue, but I'd grown weary of her quips.

Once I had gotten what I wanted, I found her company tedious and all I wanted to do was get the fuck out of there.

"When will I see you again?" she wanted to know from where she was still in bed, the sheets draped over her naked frame. She smelled faintly of sweat… and roses… and sex. I wasn't too keen on the combination.

I offered her half a smile, "This I cannot tell you, milady."

She sat up and looked pleadingly at me, "Oh, but sir, you must."

Her neediness was becoming suffocating, but I thought it best not to voice it. I got up from the chair where I had been sitting after our tryst and strode over to her, putting my hands on the bed on either side of her, my face in her neck, "And why is that?"

"Because…" she breathed, "I deserve to know."

I wanted to laugh. *Mortal wenches can be so pathetic.*

Yet, there was one more thing I wanted before I would take my leave. Under different circumstances I'd have to play my cards right to get it, but not this time, not with her. She was… willing. Keen. Easy.

"Oh, do you?" I brushed my lips against her skin.

Her lips parted and she gasped, "I do. And besides… you must be starving."

I fought the smirk plucking at the corners of my mouth. A simple touch of my lips to her throat was all it took to titillate her. *Her and every other fucking mortal woman I'd ever taken to bed.*

I locked eyes with her, my fangs bared, "May I?"

She nodded and lay down on her back, offering herself to me, "Be my guest. My husband won't lay with me for at least another month."

As if I gave a fuck what her husband did or didn't do. I moved my head down, lower, lower, until I sank my fangs into her bare thigh. This was what I wanted all along: To feed.

She gasped, moaned.

I groaned inwardly, but I did my best not to let her see my annoyance. My mother always did say that my vicious tongue was a beast that I had learned to control well, but at times my face still required deliverance.

Had she felt pain? Was it pleasure? I do not know, nor do I care. All that matters is satisfying my thirst.

When I opened my eyes and sat up, he had disappeared just as quietly as he had shown up.
I smiled to myself, wrapping a cloth around the marks on my thigh. *He is always so secretive.*
I often thought of the night we met. The masked ball my husband was having that night was becoming quite the drag, and I was weary with the same conversations with the same people. It was then that I saw him. He wore a mask of gold upon his face, his black hair falling just over his collar, his body moving across the dance floor with powerful, almost feline grace.
And then he disappeared from the ballroom.

Later, I stepped onto the terrace for some fresh air, when a voice like warm honey materialized from within the ether and greeted me with a hushed "Milady…".
I turned to gaze upon who had addressed me, and a breath caught in my bosom. It was him. The masked man from the dance floor. When our eyes met, I was overcome with a feeling that adventure awaited. Those dark, mysterious eyes that seemed to know all the secrets that I kept hidden in the deepest parts of my soul.
I grabbed hold of my skirts and curtsied in greeting, "Good evening, Sir… Apologies, I do not know your name."
His head tilted to one side, "Are names of import, milady?"
A chuckle fluttered over my lips, "I suppose not, I was merely…"
He strode closer as I spoke and before I had a chance to finish my statement, his mouth covered mine. He kissed me and something ignited within my blood, and had my heart pounding a furious rhythm against my chest.
My husband's touch was bumbling and unsure, but this man... He knew exactly where to touch, where to kiss…
There were moments, though, when my guilt overcame me: I was a married woman, I knew that laying with him was adultery. And I knew he was not human. I had known since the first time he drank my blood. But I did not care, I did not fear him. I kept his secret, as he kept mine. I knew I should end it, but I did not know how to stop myself. With him I experienced pleasures that I never even knew existed.
And I didn't even know his name…

The wars in Italy kept me rather busy, but once things calmed down, it seemed as good a time as any to get my prick wet, so I decided to stop by her residence in London to pay her a visit.
But she was nowhere to be found.
I searched for her everywhere, yet I could not find her. I was baffled, I had no idea where she could be… until I found her tomb.
For a while I just stood there, staring blankly at her name on the inscription. I was still standing there in silence when her maid of honor approached me.
"Sir," she said cautiously, "My Lady wanted me to bid you farewell on her behalf."
I frowned, "What happened?"
She dabbed a tear from her eye with a white kerchief, "Her husband, sir, he had her executed."
My eyes widened, "Son of a…! Why?"
The maid glanced around to make sure that we were alone before she spoke, "He accused her of treason, sir, and... Adultery…"
I closed my eyes and sighed, "Bastard…" *The fucking hypocrite, he's the king of adultery.*
The maid continued, "There is one more thing you should know, sir…"
I gave her a questioning glance, "I'm listening?"
She shifted uncomfortably before she responded, "My Lady, sir…. Just before she was taken… she told me… she was with child, sir…"
I pressed my lips together, "Her husband's, surely."
The maid shook her head and her answer set an inexplicable weight down on my chest, "No, sir, she seemed sure it was yours."

I couldn't breathe. I needed to get out. I needed air.
I turned on my heel and left. Out the door. Out of the city. Into the woods.
East.

Chapter 2

Dr. Kole Brennan

In the eyes of the ancient Greeks, Delphi was the center of the universe. Nestled at the top of the holy Mount Parnassos, the people believed that the measurements of the Temple of Apollo at Delphi were created by Zeus himself, and it was one of the holiest places of their time. Thousands flocked there from near and far to hear the knowledge of the blessed Apollo through the mouth of the oracle. Though the temple was demolished by the Roman Empire, the true believers, the followers of the Sun God have endured, and we have been fighting evil for thousands of years to preserve the decrees of Apollo. And the greatest evil we have ever faced, our biggest enemy, was the cursed ones, the children of the Moon: The vampires.
The Infinites.
Evil has fought back and we have had to run from the darkness many, many times now. But no matter how dark the night, or how many of us were murdered by the cursed ones, the sun would always rise again. No matter how deep we have had to hide, we had always known that we had but to turn our eyes to the east and wait for the Sun God to shine upon us once more.

We have continued the traditions of old into the modern age, appointing a priest to interpret the will of Apollo unto the people.

Our newest priest, Aleixo Nikolaides, grew up in the House of Apollo, both his parents having been members since before he was born. But unlike them, he believed that the House of Apollo had to fight fire with fire, and that the only way to end the vampire reign was with a vampire of our own.
When he was chosen as the new High Priest, he wanted a geneticist on board so that the House could conduct their own research into vampire DNA and eventually produce their own vampire. That was how I found my way into the House.

And now, after many long years of struggling and failing, a new dawn was finally breaking for the House of Apollo. For the first time in a very long time, on the premises of what would be the brand new laboratory of the House of Apollo, there was peace, there was calm, and there was a glimmer of hope. Once we were done moving in, of course. We were still waiting for most of our equipment to be delivered.
Finally, here, at our new location, disguised as a genetic diagnostics service in Berlin, we might be able to continue our work, without fear of being discovered.
The move had not been sudden, and it had not been easy. It had taken a lot of planning. The priest first came up with the idea of relocating to another country not too long after we lost Hector, and since then so much energy and countless hours of searching had gone into finding a more suitable location for the House of Apollo. Our efforts became even more laborious when the Black Prince of Carpathia began actively searching for us. His hunt for us was absolutely relentless, and because of that, Aleixo came to the conclusion that our only option was to move our entire operation to a completely different country, out from under the Black Prince's nose.

"This was a good move," the High Priest pondered out loud.
"I fully agree," I nodded, "our old lab was really nice, but it was getting too hot," I continued.
Aleixo nodded in agreement, "Yes. Unfortunately, the Prince was getting too close for comfort."
"Hmm," I hummed.
"I had such high hopes for Hector," the priest declared wistfully.

I glanced over at the priest and I decided to come clean and confess the truth. It was now or never.
"Holiness…" I started carefully, "There is something that I have to tell you."
Aleixo turned to me, "You have my full attention, dear Doctor."
I sighed, "Holiness… Hector… wasn't as successful as we had led you to believe."
His eyebrows slowly raised, "Oh…? And how so?"
I took a deep breath before I lit a cigarette to calm my nerves, "Hector's transformation wasn't exactly… complete."
The priest tilted his head sideways, "This is not good news, Doctor. Surely you realize this? The Sun God does not condone deception. You're going to have to give me more information than that."
I gulped and continued, "Well… He was able to reach high speed, sure, but not for a very long stretch of time. And his healing was not up to standard either."
"I see…" Aleixo said, "How was his hearing?"
"Not great, Holiness," I confessed, "He could hear very well, but he got everything all at once. He couldn't isolate sounds."
"Hmm…" Aleixo pondered, "And I assume he had light sensitivity issues as well?"
I nodded, "He did. We tried the contact lenses, but they had no effect."
"Was there not a single moment that he functioned to some… modicum of normality?" the priest wanted to know. I wasn't sure what to make of the tone of his voice. Was it hope? Anger? Desperation?
I considered my answer very carefully, puffing anxiously on my cigarette before I responded to the priest's question. "Sure, there were a few. He did fairly well when he hunted. At least for a while," I replied.
Nikolaides was quiet for a long time, and I felt my stomach lurch and gurgle from the suspense. *This cigarette isn't really helping. I'm going to shit my pants.*
As charming as he could be, the priest had proven himself to be just as ruthless. I was aware of many loyalists that had 'taken their own life' after a failed mission, but I had a suspicion that the 'suicides' were not by choice.

Much to my surprise though, Aleixo smiled calmly, squeezing my shoulder, "Then it was the will of the blessed Apollo that Hector was eliminated."
I was speechless.
"Surely Hector was aware of his… limitations?" Aleixo took a deep breath and sighed.
I nodded, and he shrugged, "If that is the case, his death was due to his own arrogance. He should have known better than to try and take on the Prince by himself."
"Maybe he should have called for back-up?" I suggested, still hesitant.
Aleixo agreed, nodding his head, "Had he done so, he might still be alive today, and the Prince might never have discovered the dorms."
I shook my head, "I don't know about that. I had a feeling it was only a matter of time until he found the dorms. And once he did, I wasn't surprised when he found our lab. He's too smart, that one. And he's like a pit bull, he doesn't give up."
"Yes, his tenacity has proven to be quite annoying," Aleixo pondered.

A few moments of pregnant silence passed before it started to suffocate me, and I changed the subject, "Holiness, we need a better DNA sample, we need to improve the serum. Do we have no leads?"
Aleixo smiled at me, "Actually, dear Doctor, I very recently received word from an associate of mine regarding another skeleton. Based on the location of the bones, it seems possible that it belongs to a relative of the one we already have. An older relative."
A huge smile crept onto my face, "That sounds good. When can we get it?"

He put a hand on my shoulder, "Patience, Dr. Brennan. I have dispatched a team to meet with my associate."
I frowned. I wanted, no, I needed better results. I needed a win. "But, Holiness…"
He patted my shoulder in reassurance, "I know, Doctor. This matter is paramount to our cause. As such, it requires further conversation and investigation."
I was disappointed, but I nodded in acceptance, "Alright then. We will keep working with the sample we have for the time being."

The priest nodded and grinned. He handed me a can of beer from a cooler-box, “Raise a glass, Doctor. Let us drink to the truth.”
As I gulped down my beer, I allowed myself to believe. Maybe my work would serve a purpose after all.

Chapter 3

Christina

"Fuck? What do you mean 'fuck'?" I snapped.
Jonathan stood up from the chair and looked at me, at the tears running down my face.
"I don't…" he started to say but I cut him short, "You don't what? You don't think it's yours?" I knew I was being a bitch as soon as the words left my mouth and he narrowed his eyes at me, "Really? That's who you think I am?"
I took a ragged breath and sniffed, "No…" I knew he would never think that, but my lizard-brain was in control.
"Christina, darling," he said evenly. "Please listen to me?"
I glared at him through the tears, "Then talk."
He lifted a hand toward me, but I slapped his hand away and he winced, "I did not mean what you think I meant," he tried.
"Then what did you mean?" I sobbed.
"Honestly, nothing. The word just... slipped from my mouth unguarded."

My mind was absolutely reeling. *I'm probably in shock. Honestly, who could blame me?* Unplanned pregnancy was shocking. Even when you were in a loving relationship with a really great guy. It wasn't something I expected or planned for. Sure, I'd thought about the possibility of maybe one day. But not now. Not like this.
It felt like someone pressed the fast-forward button on a rollercoaster, and it was running and twirling and looping at double speed, and I was getting motion sick but there was no way off the ride.

The sluice gates opened and a spastic little cocktail of emotions came rushing through all at the same time: Anger. Panic. Frustration. Confusion. Concern.
I wanted to write down what I was feeling, process everything later, but I couldn't move. Then a new emotion reared its sniveling little head: Doubt.

Am I even going to be able to make a good, healthy decision in this fucked up situation? What about my studies, my dreams, my future? There's so much I still want to do with my life, things to do, places to see, and I just can't picture doing it covered in spit-up, with a baby on the hip. I'm not ready for this.
I knew I had to make a decision. The rest of my life was at stake.

I didn't have to keep the baby. There were other options. Or rather, one other option. Because abortion was out of the question. Nothing against it, every woman had every right to choose what she did with her body and her uterus. But in my particular situation, this baby did not ask to be here, it wasn't her fault, or his fault, that Jonathan and I weren't careful.
Adoption was the only way to go. Surely there had to be an Infinite couple out there who wanted a baby… That's to say if the Queen was going to be okay with her grandchild being put up for adoption. But could I picture myself going through the process? Could I do it? Could he? I had no idea. All I knew was that I was scared.

I tried to take a step beyond my fear, to visualize each of my options, to imagine what my life would be like with a baby in tow.
An Infinite baby.
What kind of father would Jonathan be? Would he even want to be a father? What if he said he wanted nothing to do with the baby? He did say he wasn't ready… Not that I was, but I kind of had less of a choice… Or… what if he wanted to keep it and I didn't?
I gulped.
Shit, this can't be happening.
My fear stole away every rational thought I had. And I freaked out.
"Is your life ruined now, Jonathan?" I half-yelled at him before my tears overwhelmed me completely.

Jonathan didn't respond. In silent fortitude, the pillar of strength I adored him for being, he simply pulled me into his arms, ignoring my struggles and protests.
When he wrapped his arms around me, all my fear, all my anger simply melted into oblivion as Jonathan held my head to his chest, stroking my hair.
"Christina," I heard him say softly, "My sweet, beautiful Christina. My life is not ruined, how can it be? I have you."
"But I'm pregnant," I sniffled, "You said you don't want kids, and you... You said 'fuck'."

He sighed, and kissed the top of my head. Then he gently pushed me back to sit down on the chair, and got to his knees in front of me to look me in the eye, "I know I did. And I apologize. You might not know this about me, but I can be a real prick sometimes."
I wiped my nose with the back of my hand, "I don't understand."
He forced a smile, "Then please, allow me to explain my dismal behavior," he said, his hands on my knees.
I nodded, wiping my tears from my face, "I'm listening."
He took a deep breath, "Many, many years ago, I was in a… vaguely similar situation."
I frowned. *He got a girl pregnant? Who? When?*
He pursed his lips and took another breath, "I was young and dumb and full of…"
"Cum?" I tried.
Jonathan wiggled his eyebrows and cleared his throat, "Arrogance."
I smiled a little bit; I didn't think he even knew the expression.
Captain Mysterious, always surprising me.
"What did you do when she told you?" I wanted to know, looking pointedly at him, "Did you say 'fuck'?"
He looked down at the floor for a moment, shaking his head, "Actually, I found out she was pregnant after she died."
"Oh, shit… That's horrible."
He shrugged, "I was a bastard; I wasn't all that upset that she died."
Clearly there was another side of him that I hadn't met yet, didn't know. *But I wonder about the girl...*
"Who was she?" I asked, but Jonathan shook his head, "Who she was is inconsequential."

I didn't know what to say to that either. I found it a little bit surprising that he considered a woman that would have carried his child inconsequential. It seemed so callous, so unkind. Not at all like the Jonathan I fell in love with.
He continued, "You must think me a monster."
"No, I …"
He went on, "I was. I wasn't proud of my… relations with her, so I didn't tell anyone. But the truth of the matter was that I had no feelings for her. And a child would have been…" he didn't finish his sentence.

He shook his head, then went on, "When I learned that she had been pregnant, it felt like the world was ending, like I couldn't breathe. And all I wanted to do was run."
I folded my hands in my lap, "Did you…?"
He nodded slowly, "I did. Like a spineless coward. I left the city, left the country, and I didn't return for several decades."
I sniffed, "Is that what you want to do now? Run?"
A kind smile across his lips, Jonathan cupped my face in his hands, "Not at all."
"Really?" I asked. *Shit, I really need him to mean that.*
"With you, I don't feel like everything is ending. I feel… I feel the opposite, actually," he said, his voice warm and calm and reassuring.
A smile found its way onto my face despite the tears. Jonathan's words gave me the one thing I hadn't realized I needed: Hope.

He leaned forward and kissed my forehead, my cheeks, my eyes, the tip of my nose, "Everything will be alright, my love," he assured me, "I swear."
"I believe you," I replied, "It's just…"
"What is it, darling?"
"I don't... I don't know if I'm ready," I admitted.
He nodded, pulling me into one more hug as he got to his feet, "I know."
"What are we going to do?" I whimpered.
He pulled back and looked me in the eye, "Let's make sure of our options first, shall we?"
"What do you mean?"
"I mean, before we start buying nappies and onesies, I think we should see a doctor."

I shook my head, "I can't."
He frowned slightly, "Why ever not, love?"
I looked down at the floor, "Because… I don't have insurance. I don't have the money."
He chortled gently, taking my face in his hands again, "My darling, money is of absolutely no concern to me."

This was something that I still struggled to deal with: His fortune. Having money was all well and good, but sometimes he seemed to be under the impression that any problem would simply go away if you just threw enough money at it.
Want to go to an exclusive restaurant? No problem. Just call them up.
Want to travel to another country? Sure, hop on your private jet.
Feel like walking on the beach? Great, just zip on over to your private island in your dad's helicopter.
He grew up so privileged, that sometimes he didn't understand the things that regular people struggled with. Like not being able to quit a job you hate because you need the money. Or, having to decide which bills to pay this month because you can't afford to pay everything. Or even something as simple as actually having to work a 9-5 day job, and doing your own laundry.
Because he had money. Lots of it.

Frowning, I stepped out of his arms, "It is to me. And I can't afford to go to the doctor."
He sighed, "Love… You understand that we can't simply go to a normal doctor, yes?"
I folded my arms, "Then where are we going to go? Is there some special vampire doctor?"
Jonathan chuckled, nodding in confirmation, "There is, actually."
My jaw dropped and I sighed, "I keep thinking nothing about your world can surprise me anymore. And then… boom."
He smiled, "You forget, you are my world."
I rolled my eyes, but I knew I was blushing.
Jonathan hugged me one more time, "And please, do not worry about money. We are in this together."
"Fine," I conceded, "Can I just ask one thing?"
He nodded, "Anything my lovely."

"Is it okay if I talk to my mom about this? Not about your… you know… Your Infinity, and all that. Just… this," I asked, pointing to my stomach.
Jonathan nodded, stroking my cheek with his thumb, "Of course, love."
I pressed a kiss to his lips, "Thanks, babe."
He tucked my hair behind my ear, "Do you want me to go with you when you speak to your mother?"
I thought about it for a moment, then I shook my head, "It's okay. It's probably better if I go alone."
"I understand. But if you need me, I will be just a phone call away," he reassured me.

I made us some tea, and then I sent him home. I felt bad that I woke him up in the middle of the night, and that he then flew more than six hours to be with me while I had a meltdown. He looked exhausted and he needed to get some sleep.
After he left, I spent the rest of the afternoon trying to practice what I was going to say to my mom.
I wished I could just tell her everything, just come out with the whole story, the entire truth in all of its unbelievableness, but I couldn't even imagine how that conversation would go. *'Hi, Mom, guess what? Jonathan's a vampire. Oh, and I'm pregnant with his vampire baby.'* Fuck my life.

After dinner, my mom was just done doing the dishes, when I decided it was now or never. There really was no easy way to say it, so the best way would be to just blurt it out and get it over with.
"Mom," I started, "I have something… difficult to tell you."
My mom looked at me in concern, "You can tell me anything, sweetie. What is it?"
I closed my eyes and took a deep breath before I spoke the words that I had been dreading to say out loud, "I'm pregnant."
My mom was speechless; she just blinked slowly at me.
I continued, "I know this isn't what you expected." Tears started to well up in my eyes, "You're disappointed in me, I know, I'm disappointed in myself, too. And you're probably upset, and I'm really sorry for putting you through this. And I…" a small sob cut my sentence short.

"How did this happen?" My mom wanted to know, "Didn't you use protection?"
I sighed, "We did, but... I don't know… maybe the condom broke… or came off… or something… I'm sorry Mom…"
Or maybe vampire sperm is just more potent... Probably have fangs too, chewed their way through the condom.
Without nothing more except a soft "Oh, honey", my mom pulled me into a hug, stroking my hair.
"Mommy?" I sobbed, "I'm scared."
She nodded, "I know baby, I know."
"I don't know what to do," I whimpered.
"Are you sure you're pregnant?" my mom asked.
I pulled up my shoulders, "The test was positive…"
My mom pulled back and wiped my tears, "What did Jonathan say?"
"He thinks we should see a doctor first."
She nodded in agreement, "He's right, you should."
I shook my head, "You know I don't have health insurance, how am I going to pay for that?"
"Surely he can afford it?" my mom countered, but I shook my head again, "No. I don't want to rely on his money."
My mom gave me a pointed look, "I think we are well past the Rubicon, sweetheart. I'm pretty sure he knows by now you're not after his money."
"I know, but…"
"But, nothing." she interrupted me, "That boy loves you, and he wants to take care of you, and I think we have now reached a point where you need to let him."
"Mom!" I was exasperated, "You didn't raise me like that."
"Oh, honey," she sighed, "I raised you as best I could, with the little money we had. Heaven knows I would have given you the world if I could afford it."
My eyes welled up with tears again, "Mom…" I sniffed. My mom put her hands on my shoulders, "Jonathan can give you everything that I never could. And I wish, I wish you would just let him do that."
"But Mom," I said, "you raised me by yourself, without a man's help. And... well… if you don't need a man's money, then neither do I."

My mom set two cups down on the kitchen counter and switched on the kettle, “The difference is that I had no other option. I had to get by. I had your grandma to rely on, but financially speaking I was on my own. You are in a very different position, sweetheart.”
I tried to swallow at the lump in my throat, but my dry mouth kept it from going anywhere.

My mom turned around and looked pointedly at me, “Christina, I’m not going to stand here and blow smoke up your ass. Raising you by myself was hard, you’re old enough to understand that. But if anyone had offered to help me, I would have gladly accepted the help.”
I looked down at my folded hands, listening to my mom. She went on, “Just on the other side of town, there is a boy that loves you very much, a boy that wants to help you and take care of you, and who just happens to be very well off. Don’t be stupid, and don’t be selfish. You didn’t make that baby by yourself - Jonathan has just as much right to be involved in that child’s life as you do. And if you really are going to have Jonathan’s child, but you won’t let him take care of you and your child, then you are a damn fool...”
Then my mom strode over to me and put her hands on my cheeks, “Remember: Only the strong ask for help when they need it.”

Jonathan

I knew I had to speak to my mother, but fuck, I was dreading the conversation.
I took a shower and a nap as soon as I got home after seeing Christina, and after feeding, I slowly made my way to my mother's room. I was fucking nervous. This was about to be a play-by-play reenactment of a past incident which she hadn't been too happy about at the time, and I couldn't help but wonder how she was going to react this time around. The previous time, vases were thrown and harsh words were exchanged, and I could only hope she would be calmer about it this time.

In the master bedroom, my mother was sitting on the window sill, looking out at the garden.
She turned her head and smiled at me when I came in, "Hello, darling boy."
I smiled at her. Dressed in faded jeans and a simple t-shirt, she looked so youthful that it was hard to believe how long she had been alive.
"Do you see anything interesting in the garden, Mother?" I asked as I sat down on the *chaise longue* in front of the window.
She glanced back outside and shrugged before turning back to me, "I was thinking about replanting some of the flower beds, a change of color might be good."
I just nodded.
After a few moments, I spoke again, "Mami…"
She swung her feet down from the window sill to look at me, "Oh dear. What have you done this time?"
I widened my eyes at her in surprise, "What makes you think I did something?"
She rolled her eyes before she got down from the window sill and sat down in an armchair across from me instead, "Jonathan," she said, "You only ever call me 'Mami' when you're feeling sentimental, or when you're in trouble. And judging by the creases in your forehead, I'd be willing to bet it's the latter."
I sat forward, my face in my hands and I sighed heavily.
"Case in point." she confirmed, then went on, "So tell me, what is it?"

I leaned back and raked both my hands through my hair, and I took another breath before I explained myself, "Christina is… Or rather, she might be… pregnant."

In silent disappointment, my mother got to her feet.
"Mami…" I said cautiously, and she spun around and glared at me, "You know…. For once in your life, I really wish you would just… keep it in your pants. Just for once. Is that too much to ask?"
I slowly got to my feet and bowed my head, "What's done is done. For what it's worth, I am sorry, Mother…"
She mumbled something in Greek, and I winced at the unflattering names she called me, "I'm not sure I deserve all that, but I suppose I'll take it…"
"I'm assuming the two of you have already taken a pregnancy test?" my mother sought confirmation.
I nodded, "Yes, we did, and it was positive."
Then she sighed and ruffled my hair, "Oh, you silly boy. It baffles me how you can be so smart, yet so dumb and irresponsible at the same time."
I chuckled ruefully and glanced up at her from underneath my eyebrows.
She gave me a small smile, "How is Christina? Is she alright?"
I rubbed my eyes, "She's terrified..."
My mother nodded understandingly, "I can't say I blame her."
She regarded me in silence for a moment, before she shook her head and took her phone from her pocket.
"What are we going to do?" I asked.
"Well," she said, dialing a number on the keypad, "First, I am going to call your father."
I frowned, "Why…?"
My mother looked meaningfully at me, "To tell him that his son is too horny for his own good."
I pressed my lips together and nodded. My mother went on, "And then I will call Dr. Woods."

Back in my room, I took a moment to consider the situation that Christina and I found ourselves in. This was my second brush with potential parenthood, but I was sure it was a first for Christina. The previous time I went through this, it took me days to breathe normally again after hearing the news. The fact that the woman had allegedly been pregnant with my child honestly upset me more than the fact that she was, essentially, murdered by her husband.
This time around though, the possibility of Christina carrying my child put a smile on my face, rather than panic in my heart, so I didn't know why I reacted the way I did, why I said 'fuck'. *Some sort of knee-jerk reaction, I suppose.*

Honestly, I would be very happy if we saw Dr. Woods and the doctor confirmed the pregnancy. Not that I wanted to trap Christina with me forever. But I truly loved her, and I would be happy beyond all logic if she were to have my child. Perhaps a little girl with her mother's beautiful eyes. The idea of raising a child was terrifying, but it was something that I would very much like to do with Christina. I could take on the world with her by my side.
At the same time, I would also be relieved if the pregnancy test turned out to be a false positive. I saw the panic in her eyes, and it was clear that a baby was not something that she wanted right away. And if she were pregnant, I would be very worried about her for the next however many months it would take for our child to be born.
But I supposed, ultimately, what it all boiled down to was that I would be satisfied with whichever outcome made Christina the happiest. Baby or no baby, my life was complete as long as Christina was in it.

Chapter 4

Christina

When I woke up that morning, I didn't need to check the calendar to know what day it was: We were seeing the doctor to find out if I was really pregnant. I was terrified, and my insides were all tied up in nervous knots.

Ever since I was little, I always hated going to the doctor. For anything. I hated the vulnerability of being examined and poked and prodded, and I wished I didn't have to go, but there was no escaping or postponing. Not this time.

While I showered and got ready, my tummy kept rumbling and turning, and I felt like I was going to throw up.

Then I got a text from Simon, telling me that he had arrived to pick me up and take me to the manor, so I took a deep breath and made my way to the front door.

"Are you ready, baby?" my mom asked from where she was sitting on the sofa in the living room.

I tried to smile, but it was as fake as a $3 bill, "Time to find out, I guess."

In the car on the way to the manor, I folded my arms across my chest, and Simon glanced at me in the rearview mirror, "Miss Christina?" he asked, concerned.

I faked a smile, "Yes, Simon?"

"Forgive me Miss, I don't mean to pry… But you seem worried. Is everything alright?"

Shit, if even Simon can tell that I am freaking the fuck out, then I must really look like crap.

"Of course, Simon. Everything's fine," I lied.
"Miss Christina, may I speak freely?"
"You can speak any way you want to, Simon," I urged him.
"Thank you Miss," he said, his eyes going from me to the road and back, "I've been your driver for quite a few months now, and I can tell something big is going on. Now, I don't know what's happening that has you so worried, but try to relax, Miss. Everything will be alright, you'll see."
I chuckled softly, "You sound very sure of that, Simon."
He nodded, a bright smile on his face, "Of course, Miss Christina. Master Jonathan will make it so."
I smiled. A real one, this time. Simon was so nice, always so formal, speaking to me like I was royalty. But he was right. As long as Jonathan and I had each other, everything would be okay.
And that was what I held onto when I arrived at the manor, and a nurse came to draw some blood to run tests, and I went with Jonathan to his room to wait for the doctor.

I could feel him looking at me as we sat on the sofa in complete silence. In an attempt to comfort me, he squeezed my knee, "It's going to be alright, darling," he said softly.
I flashed him my bravest smile, "I'm not worried."
He cocked an eyebrow, "I know you're nervous, I can tell."
I took a deep breath, trying to steady my nerves, "I'm fine."
He took my hand and kissed the back of it, "I can hear your heart pounding, love. And you're doing that thing you always do with your tongue when you're nervous."
I know I am, shut up. Before I could answer, the bedroom door swung open and a slender, bohemian-looking woman strode in, her white hair cropped short in a pixie cut, holding a yellowish-brown manila envelope in one hand. She looked to be about the same age as Alastair, but she had a spritely way about her, a sort of flourish in the way she moved that reminded me of a faerie or a wood-elf. I felt myself frown. *I know her... we've met... But... wh...?* Then I remembered: This was the same doctor that took care of me when I got roofied that time.

When she saw Jonathan, she held out her arms. He stood up from the sofa and greeted her with a hug.
"I always forget how tall you are," she said mid-hug.

"How have you been, doctor?" he returned the greeting.
She pulled back and squeezed his shoulders, then looked at me where I was standing awkwardly just behind Jonathan.
The doctor scanned me up and down, "You're even prettier than I remembered," and extended a hand to me.
"Christina, darling, you remember Dr. Emmeline Woods," Jonathan introduced us.
I smiled, shaking the doctor's outheld hand, "Nice to see you again, Dr. Woods."

Jonathan gestured back to the sofa, "Shall we?"
We sat back down, and the doctor wasted no time opening the envelope, "Yes, right, let's get to it, then," she said as she pulled sheets of paper from the envelope, "I ran a few tests, and I did not detect any traces of hCG in your blood, Christina."
The declaration took me by surprise, "Uhm... I… huh?" I stammered.
Jonathan cocked a brow, "My dear doctor, plain English please."
Dr. Woods chuckled at herself, "Apologies, dearies."
I shook my head, "It's fine, I'm not stupid, I know what it is," I snapped. *I probably sound really rude, but oh well.* "You're saying I'm... not pregnant?"
Dr. Woods smiled, confirming, "You are not pregnant."
"Huh…" I was confused, "But the test…?"
The doctor nodded, handing me the paper with my test results, "At-home pregnancy tests can be inaccurate, for any number of reasons. Stress can play tricks on our bodies."

Well, damn. After all my freak-outs and flip-outs, I wasn't pregnant after all. I had spent so much time in my own head, absolutely losing it over how I was going to react if I was pregnant, that I hadn't really given much thought to how I was going to react if it turned out that I wasn't pregnant after all. *But this is good, right? I hadn't wanted to have a baby, and now I wasn't going to have one. Good. Christina-1, Things that fuck up Christina's life-0.*

Jonathan pulled me closer, took my face between his hands, and kissed me. When he pulled back, he smiled and tucked a strand of hair behind my ear, "I told you everything will be alright."

He wanted to say more, but he was interrupted by his phone buzzing in his pocket. He pulled it out and glanced at the screen, then looked pleadingly at me, “Forgive me, my love, I need to take this.”
“Sweden?”
He pressed his lips into a thin line, “Regrettably, yes.”
I nodded toward the door with my head, “Business away, babe.”
He kissed my cheek and nodded a goodbye to the doctor before he headed out the door.

Dr. Woods shook her head as she watched him walk away, “Hard to believe he was such a tiny little thing when he was born. Now look at him, big lummox.”
I smiled questioningly at the doctor, “You were there when he was born?”
The doctor nodded, “I was. Delivered him myself. And since then, I've had to stitch him up more times than I can count.”
“So, does that mean you’re…?”
“A vampire?” the doctor finished my sentence for me, and replied with a fang-baring smile, “I am. But I’ve known Alastair since his mortal days. We grew up in the same village.”
“Speaking of which,” the doctor changed the subject, sitting back on the sofa, “How are you handling all of this vampire business, little one?”
Good question, how am I handling it?
I wasn’t sure how to answer that, but the doctor spoke again before I could, “Difficult question, I know. I, for one, was shocked, at first.”
“Amen to that.”
I still didn’t know how to answer, so I figured deflection was better than bullshit, “I’d like to talk about my options for birth control, if you don’t mind? I don’t think I can handle an encore of this.”
The doctor slapped her knees and sat forward, “Of course, dearie. Let’s see what we have…”

“So, you’ve known the Langdon family for a long time?” I asked Dr. Woods a while later.
We had discussed all of the available choices for birth control, and she helped me choose the one that would be best suited to me and my lifestyle.

"I have," the doctor confirmed, smiling at me, "Alastair was the one that turned me."
"And you said you delivered Jonathan?" I asked, and the doctor nodded, "I did. I helped Her Sovereign Majesty bring her first and only son into the world."
The doctor folded her hands in her lap and smiled at me, "If you have more questions, please go ahead," she suggested, "I want to help in any way I can."
"What's vampire pregnancy like?" I blurted out, "With Jonathan's mom, I mean. If it's okay for me to ask."
The doctor pondered for a moment before she answered, "It certainly took its toll, and her Majesty did her best to handle it with grace, but she still did not have an easy pregnancy."
"Despite her Infinity?" I asked. *That's... scary. I would have thought that Infinity would have made it easier.*
Dr. Woods nodded, "No pregnancy is easy. And carrying an Infinite child would certainly be no easy feat for a mortal body."
I milled the information over in my head for a moment. I was definitely not ready, "I don't think I want to know, then. Not right now, anyway."
The doctor went on, "With modern technology it might be a different ball-game altogether. But give me a call if you change your mind, then we can certainly talk about it."
I gave a quick nod before I changed the subject, "Dr. Woods, you said you knew Jonathan's father from when he was human?"
Dr. Woods smiled broadly, "I was the healer in our village."
"So, how did it happen that you turned?" I wanted to know. I was planning on asking in a more subtle way, but the doctor had responded so kindly to all my questions that I decided *fuck it.*

Fiona entered the room with a tray full of tea and cookies, and the doctor waited until she left before answering my question. I didn't understand why, Fiona knew more about the Langdon family history than I did. Probably doctor-patient confidentiality or whatever.
"I had wanted to be a healer ever since I was a little girl, and when I found out there was a way that I could continue helping people forever, I knew that that was what I wanted, and I asked him to turn me." Dr. Woods said.
"What was it like, turning?"

Dr. Woods studied my face for a moment before she answered, “Not fun. Is Infinity something that you want, Christina?”

Is it?

There’d been fleeting moments where I caught myself wondering what happened when someone turned, and what it would be like to live forever, and never get old. But the reality of it was so daunting that I didn’t dare to ask.

“I... I don't know…” I replied truthfully.

The doctor smiled kindly at me, “When you are truly ready to hear the answer, let me know.”

“I think there's a lot that Jonathan hasn't told me.” I said, looking up at the doctor, “You said you've had to stitch him up a lot?”

Dr. Woods chuckled, “Yes, he was reckless and irresponsible when he was younger. The times that he was able to actually walk into my clinic by himself were few and far between. Usually he was carried in, bleeding and nearly unconscious.”

“I know he's been injured a lot, I've seen the scars, but…”

“He never told you how serious his injuries were?” the doctor guessed, and I shook my head. The doctor pursed her lips and shook her head, “Of course he didn't, that rascal.”

I took a big gulp of cold tea to get rid of the patch of desert in my mouth, “He told me about the hunter…” I said.

Dr. Woods lowered her head and her voice became soft and low, “And he probably downplayed it, pretended like it was no big deal… We could have lost him that day.”

All of my blood froze in my veins, “What…?” I managed to croak.

Dr. Woods took a deep breath, but she poured herself another cup of tea before she replied, “We might be immortal, but we’re not indestructible Christina,” she began explaining, “Silver doesn’t burn, or kill an Infinite immediately, but if it hits the wrong organ, it can cause significant damage. Even death.”

Every drop of color drained from my face as I listened to the doctor, “I’ll never forget that day… Oh, that poor boy.”

She closed her eyes for a moment before she continued, “The sword pierced his lung, resulting in a tension pneumothorax. Katalina came to fetch me, and when I got to him, he’d already started to turn blue, the veins in his neck were severely distended…. The sword had barely missed his heart… he was losing blood by the second and he was in so much pain...”

Everything inside me was trembling.

Dr. Woods must have noticed the look on my face, because she suddenly forced a smile, and her voice brightened, “In any event, it was touch-and-go for a while there, but by the light of the blessed Moon, he managed to pull through.”

I tried to smile back in reply, but the mental image of Jonathan, injured and suffering, was going to stay with me for a while.

Chapter 5

Jonathan

There was a specific type of barbaric magic encapsulated by 1630's Germania, even in the cities. Something about the unsophisticated, unrefined villagers, the muddy streets, and unwashed wenches that resonated with me, that somehow spoke to my soul. For some unknown reason, the savagery of it all had a certain appeal.

As per usual, I had traveled to the region for one reason: If the grapevine had it right, ongoing unrest had been wreaking havoc in the area. The rumor mill had continuously been churning out interesting tidings of impending doom… Everywhere in the country. Now, if there was blood about to be spilled, that was exactly where I wanted to be.

And judging by the smell of death and decay that hung in the air, I would put money on the rumors ringing true.

This time, I brought my new friend along.

We met a couple of years ago when she was almost burnt alive in a witch-trial. She was still rather new to my world, but she seemed to be adjusting swimmingly.

At the time, I had really tried to understand the narrow minds of the villagers that nearly ended her life, but I simply could not comprehend their inflexible views of the world.

Surely everyone had their predilections when it came to the pleasures of the flesh.

Hers just happened to be the flesh of the blond girl she had been discovered in the barn with, something that I took no issue with.
I myself frequently bowed at the Altar of Venus, so I could understand her druthers. I honestly failed to see why the villagers could not.
Surely they had all ridden below the crupper at least once in their miserable lives.
And if they hadn't, they could now dance around their own maypole in Hell.

I glanced at my friend, bareback on the horse next to me as we rode through yet another tiny little shit-hole village on our way into the city. True, she was quite pretty, with her rich brown hair and her violet eyes, but I felt no attraction to her. She was my friend. She was fun, and funny, and she listened to all of my opinions and thoughts and freely shared her own. And as she wasn't interested in any part of my anatomy, she was never flustered by me.
From a rather young age, I'd become well aware of the effect my physical appearance seemed to have on most women, mortals more so than my own kind. Always strutting and tittering, trying to get my attention. Of course, it did make it easier in the event that I wanted to end up between a particular woman's thighs…
In any event, I found it refreshing to be able to have a simple, honest conversation with a woman without her constantly fluttering her eyelids at me.

Katalina

I didn't have to see him to know that he was looking at me, "What are you looking at?"
I spoke a different language when we met, but since I lived with him and his family, I very quickly learned Romanian, Greek and English from them.
He shook his head, "Nothing."
I chortled, rolling my eyes, "What are we doing here?"
He widened his eyes at me, "We are aiding, bringing peace to the region, of course."
I had certainly not come to know him as much of an altruist, and I scoffed at the notion, "Truly? And which side are we aiding?"
He pulled up his shoulders, "Whichever draws the most blood," he snarled in dark delight, spurring his horse on to a gallop.
Laughing, I followed him.

We hadn't been friends for all that long, but our friendship was easy, effortless, natural.
Whether it was because our personalities complement one another or because he saved my life, I supposed I would never be able to tell for certain. He was my friend. Even if the name I gave him wasn't the name that I got from my parents…
When he first pulled me from the flames a few decades before, I thought that I was hallucinating from the pain, or perhaps that Death had come for me: It was not possible for human beings to walk into fire like it was a stroll through the woods, or to have wings and incinerate screaming villagers with black flames from thin air. However, as I quickly learned, it was very possible if you weren't human, but a vampire. And a very powerful one at that.

The day he saved my life was the first time that I saw a glimpse of the power that he wielded, but it wasn't until we were attacked again in a different village and he lost his temper, that I saw the full extent of what he was capable of.

I was at his side when the villagers stormed us, pitchforks at the ready. It was my fault that they charged at us; I accidentally showed my fangs, but it didn't matter to him. He shoved me away, telling me to run.

To hide.

Not to look.

But I refused; I wasn't going to leave my friend by himself.

When he realized that I wasn't leaving, he just shrugged and turned to the advancing mob. Then, his eyes turned from black to the brightest blue. His body raised up into the sky, like some invisible hand was lifting him up, and those black wings that I had seen once before suspended him in the air.

As black fire rained down from the sky, the world around us seemed to vibrate with his power. I could feel it in my stomach, in the quivering in my insides. I could see it in the pebbles and stones trembling and skittering across the ground at my feet.

I'd never seen anything or anyone like him, and I dropped to my hands and knees in awe as he single-handedly flattened the entire village in a cloud of fiery black death and devastation.

Upon receiving tidings of the village's demise, his mother was furious. In her rage, she placed a damper on his mind, a limit on his power. Punishment, for losing himself, abusing his power, for taking the lives of innocents in the village. And to make sure that he never lost control like that again.

I was hiding in the house, sobbing in fear, as his cries of pain echoed down the hall. Until that day, I hadn't realized how powerful his mother was, and I was filled with a newfound respect for Her Sovereign Majesty.

When his anguished screams finally subsided, a suffocating silence descended upon the house…

Jonathan

When my mother let go of me, I was breathless in my rage.
I could feel the limit she placed upon me, like a steel band around my mind, restraining me, limiting my power. A constant pressure, a throbbing headache that I instinctively knew would never go away.
Raw, molten anger roiled through my veins, contorting my face and flaring my nostrils, "I am the Prince! What the fuck am I supposed to do now?" I shouted as I got to my feet, banging my fist against my chest and shattering the silence that had enfolded us.
"Do better!" my mother shouted back, her gray eyes flashing in anger.
I roared at her, and my father raised his hands and shot a pulse of energy from his palms right at me. It caught me off guard, knocking me to the floor. "Show some respect for your mother!" my father yelled, reprimanding me.
I jumped to my feet and stormed out of the room, "I'm fucking leaving!" I hollered as I went.
"Then go!" my mother bellowed after me, "Come back when you're done acting like a child!"
I glared at my parents before I slammed the door shut behind me and marched out of the house. On my way out, I stomped past my friend, "We're leaving."
"Where are we going?" she wanted to know, following me to the stables.
I glared back at the house, and snarled in anger, baring my fangs.
Then I looked back at her, "Far the fuck away from here."

"Are you alright?" my friend asked as we were leaving the city we lived in. I'd been quiet since we left the house, and I was grateful that she broke the silence.
I took a deep breath, "I will be. Just as soon as I have fed… or fucked. Whichever happens first."
So there we were, riding through the countryside on horseback, headed to wherever the most blood would be spilt.

After a few days of riding, we neared a city towards the center of the country, and I was glad that I took a moment to grab some extra coin, so we were able to stay at an inn, instead of having to sleep outside, or in a barn.
Innkeepers always assumed us to be husband and wife, a concept we found quite laughable, but we left it at that. Best not to cause a scene. People could be so damn conservative, as we both were well aware of.
We spent a few idle days and nights in various inns and pubs and taverns on the outskirts of the city, and oh, what fun we had, gorging ourselves on blood, ale, food, more blood, more ale, then swiftly moving on before anyone became suspicious.

One particularly boisterous evening, we noticed a pretty young girl circling us, eyeing us up and down. The innkeeper's daughter, we were told.
The girl's frizzy blonde hair was pulled into a tight bun and revealed a round face with soft, rosy-hued cheeks, her blue eyes with their long, thick lashes set high within their sockets.
There was something about her that I found appealing. Perhaps it was the intrigue all over her face when she looked at me. Maybe it was her demure smile. Maybe it was simply the way she smelled of freshly baked bread and mead and honey. Or maybe I just really wanted to get my prick wet and she seemed willing.
My friend turned to me, gesturing to the girl with her eyes, "What do we think of her?"
I examined the blonde up and down, "She looks… scrumptious…" I replied, and my friend chuckled.
We glanced at her, and then back at each other and grinned. We were, quite clearly, thinking the same thing.
I tipped my mug of mead toward my friend, then got up from my seat and strode over toward the buxom blonde, my eyes locked with hers, and took a seat closer to her.

Sure enough, it wasn't long until she came over to me, smiling and giggling, and I heard my friend chuckling to herself, rolling her eyes. I knew why: mortal women simply couldn't resist me. That had been the case for most of my life, ever since puberty ended and my face took on its adult proportions.

At first, the little blonde and I said not a word to each other and I wasn't even sure which language she spoke. I made sure to smile at her, though. Often. Specifically the crooked smile that my friend had pointed out made women giggly. When she finally spoke to me in the local language and offered me another drink, I did not decline. Similarly, a few more drinks later, when she asked me if I wanted to leave with her, I did not say no either. I did, after all, see the invitation coming.

I was, however, rather surprised when she asked me if my 'wife' wanted to join us.

An amused grin on my face, I turned to my friend where she had been sitting alone with a mug of mead and beckoned her over. I couldn't help but laugh at the surprised look on her face…

My friend and I had no idea where the little blonde wanted to take us. Once we stepped outside of the inn, she took a moment to look around, before she grabbed each of us by a wrist and dragged us with her to the barn just behind the inn.

She barred the doors behind us, then looked expectantly at the two of us. I glanced at my friend… she returned the look… And then she, very gently, pulled the young lady into a slow, tender kiss. I kept my eyes focused on where my friend's hands were slowly working the young dame's dress down and off her shoulders, exposing her perky breasts. I took a moment to admire the ample fullness of them, before I stepped in behind her, taking her peaked nipples between my fingers and pressing my lips to the side of her neck. She let out a moan and slumped against me, and my friend took the sound as an invitation to further undo the bodice on her dress. The young lady returned the favor and started relieving my friend of her dress as well.

Then she stopped and looked at me over her shoulder, "You don't mind, do you?"

I wasn't altogether sure what she was referring to. To the two of us sharing her? To her taking my friend's dress off? The answer was no to either. It wasn't the first time that my friend and I shared someone, and it certainly wouldn't be the last. It wasn't an activity that we sought out, but when it befell us, we never said no.

I wrapped my fingers around her chin and turned her head to kiss her, and she moaned into my mouth when my friend sucked a nipple into her mouth.

It didn't take all that long for my friend and I to have our willing companion completely bare before us, and we quickly followed suit. The young blonde then put down a blanket atop the hay, and I stood back as my friend lowered her down onto it.

I wrapped my fingers around myself, working my hand up and down my shaft as my friend stuck her fingers into the young lady's mouth before sliding those same two fingers deep into her cunt.
She cried out in pleasure, and my friend grinned at me over her shoulder.
"How does she feel?" I asked.
My friend pulled her hand back and plunged again, "Tight."
"Is she wet?"
In response, my friend picked up the pace and I grinned at the obscene sound of her fingers inside the little blonde, combined with the whimpers and moans that were spilling from her mouth.
I tightened my grip around myself, "Do you think that dripping wet little cunt is ready for my prick?"
When my friend nodded, I took the blonde girl by the hips. "Turn around," I commanded before I flipped her over and put her on her hands and knees in front of me. I dug my fingers into her hair and she moaned in desperate need as I pressed the head of my prick against her wet cunt. "Look," I directed her attention to my friend's naked body in front of her.
"I see. I want," she murmured, nodding her head.
"Be a good little slut and make her feel good," I ordered. Then I pressed her head down at the same time as I ploughed into her.

By the time we were done with the limber, nubile little blond, after everything we did to her, all of the positions we bent her into and all the angles we fucked her in, morning had rolled around and it was time to get out of town.
Quickly.

Before blondie's father came looking for her and discovered his daughter, undergarments hiked up over her arse, utterly spent and snoring between us in the hay.

Just before we slipped out of the barn, I glanced back at the sleeping, half-naked blonde and I grinned to myself. For most of the night, I only saw the arse-end of her. Or just the top of her head. For the rest of the night, her face was buried so deep between my friend's thighs that, for a moment, I almost forgot what she looked like. My cock had not been the first she'd ever had, she seemed too… adept. Oftentimes I didn't, but this time I made sure to stock up on prophylactics and I made sure to gather them and take them with me, as I would certainly be needing them again. It wasn't that I was afraid of syphilis; I was immune to venereal disease. What I was afraid of, was babies. I was not at all ready to raise any offspring…

"Did you ask her what her name was?" my friend asked me as we rode out of the village.

I shrugged, "No… But I think I shall call her 'Apples'."

Her rambunctious laughter startled her horse and it bucked her off, which made her, and me, laugh even harder. "Apples!" she cackled, "Very fitting. She did have lovely knockers."

I smiled at the notion, "Lovely knockers indeed."

My friend brushed the grass and dirt from her skirts, "Where to next?" she wanted to know.

"I haven't decided yet," I responded pensively, "Perhaps we could head Southwest."

She glanced curiously at me, "What is happening there?"

I shrugged, "Nothing that I know of. But there is something that I wanted to show you."

"Alright," she agreed, "Let's go then."

"It would take a while on horseback." I said, "Perhaps we could give the horses a break, and you could take us there?"

Katalina

My face froze: He wanted me to make a doorway, a portal.
When I turned, my power of Traveling manifested a few days after my body stopped healing for the last time. But it was a curse rather than a blessing. I'd been struggling to control it, and when I was able to get it to do a semblance of what I wanted, it drained nearly all of my energy, leaving me weak and depleted. So, most of the time I would rather just pretend like I didn't have it at all.
"I can't…" I denied, but he had already dismounted and led his horse to a nearby meadow, "Of course you can," he disagreed, "I have complete faith in you."
I stood next to my horse, unable to look him in the eyes, "Sire, I…"
"Rubbish," he cut me short, "Don't call me that. I believe in you. Now come on, don't make me wait."

When I looked up at him, he was smiling brightly at me, and I could tell that he meant what he said: He did believe in me.
Alright, then.
I nodded, "Where are we going?"
He grinned at me, "To the place where we met."

It took all of my concentration, but I did it: I managed to make a portal and we stepped through it, to the outskirts of the town where we first met. But upon our arrival, my memories of the last time I was there came flooding back to me, and I stopped in my tracks.
A kind smile on his face, he turned to me, "Are you alright?"
I just shook my head; I couldn't speak.
Still smiling, he stepped up next to me and took my hand in his, "I'm right here. I am your friend, forever. You never have to face anything alone again."
Nodding, I tried to put on a brave face and he squeezed my hand, "Come on. We'll go together."

Holding my hand, he led me deep into the woods outside the village. When I looked up, I knew why he had wanted to bring me here.

In the middle of the small clearing, at the foot of a massive tree, stood a small, inconspicuous headstone.
The epitaph was short and simple, inscribed with the words 'Taken too soon' in my native language, and underneath it, the year he saved me from the fire.
The headstone bore no name, but it didn't need to, I knew who lay there.
My heart broke into a million tiny pieces, and I dropped to my knees and I wept.
Greth.
My sweet little Greth.
Murdered, for loving a woman.
For loving me.
It was then that I knew: For this man, I would travel to the ends of the earth and back if he requested it.

His powers were limited to only a fraction of what he actually commanded, and I knew it would take years still for the pressure in his head to subside. Perhaps it never would, and he would have to learn to live with it.
But I would always know:
By blood and heritage, he truly was The Black Prince of Carpathia.
And my best friend.

Chapter 6

Christina

"How did the phone call with Sweden go?" I asked Jonathan that night as we were sitting across from each other in the enormous tub in his bathroom.
He pinched his one eye shut, "Things are still quite a mess over there, honestly."
I didn't like that response, "Does that mean you have to go back there?" I was silently praying he would say no.
He thought for a moment… Then he shook his head, "No, they can figure it out on their own. At least for now, anyway."
I grinned at him, "Good answer."
"I'd like to take you there with me someday. If you want to go, of course," he said.
"I'd love to."
I looked at him in silence for a moment until his expression turned curious, "Is something the matter, my love?"
The thought of him nearly dying reared its ugly head, but I shook my head, scooted over to him and put my arms around his neck, "I love you. "
Jonathan reciprocated my smile, "I love you."
"What did you and Dr. Woods talk about after I left?" he wanted to know.
I kissed the tip of his nose, "This and that, other options for birth control, things like that. I'm going on the pill. So we just need to keep using condoms for the next few days."
He grimaced, "I'm sorry that you have to do that, darling."
"Why are you sorry? Taking birth control is pretty normal for girls."

He nodded slowly, "I know. But I also know that the side-effects can be quite severe. I'd offer to get a vasectomy, but…"
"It would reverse itself?" I guessed, and he nodded, "I'm afraid so…"
I ran my hand through his hair, "It's okay. Thanks for the offer, though."
He half-smiled at me, "If there were some other option, for me to take pills instead of you having to, then I would have preferred to do that."
"Aww," I crooned, "You're sweet. You may have just earned yourself a blowjob."
Grinning, he shook his head and snaked his arms around me to pull me against him. When our bodies met, I pressed my lips to his. Jonathan returned my kiss before he pulled back and smiled at me, "Congratulations on not being pregnant, darling."
I beamed a grin back at him, "Congratulations on not knocking me up, babe."
I kissed him again, parting his lips with mine and I pressed my body tightly against his, wrapping a leg around him.
My tongue pressed to his, I moved a hand to his neck, down his chest, across his stomach, down. And when I took his dick in my hand, he pulled his head back and looked questioningly at me, and I nodded silently. I was full of all kinds of mixed emotions. For some reason, a small part of me was kind of sad, fuck only knows what that was about, but I was mostly relieved that I wasn't pregnant. And I knew that sex was what had gotten us into this mess in the first place, but in that moment, what I needed to get my mind off everything, was him.

He pushed himself up out of the tub, pulling me with him. Then he sat down on the edge of the sofa, and I sank down on top of him to sit on his lap, my legs on either side of his thighs, and he ran his thumbs back and forth across my nipples, sending a shiver scuttling down my spine.
"Jonathan," I said softly.
"Yes?" he responded, his lips against my jaw.
"Hang on…" I replied, letting my eyes dart all over his face.
He frowned, confused, "Is something the matter, love?"
I put one arm around his neck, the fingers of my other hand wrapped firmly around the base of his dick as I leaned closer to him and examined his face.
He looked questioningly at me, "Do I have something on my face?"

A breath left his throat in a groan as I tightened my fingers around him and moved my hand up and down the length of his dick.
I shook my head and winked at him, "Nope. Just checking if you cleaned my seat."
"Oh, darling, yes," he growled, "Yes, yes, a thousand times yes."
I put my hands on his chest and pushed him over onto his back, and he moved my body up so my pussy was right above his mouth.
He looked up at me, ten million devils dancing in his black eyes, and proceeded to absolutely devour me.
My mind went blank.
My head tilted backward, my eyes staring unseeingly at the ceiling, my back arched.
Jonathan's tongue caressed every part of my pussy, inside and out, and my body writhed and bucked at every lick, every circle, every flick of his tongue.
I was going fucking crazy, but his hands were firmly clamped around my thighs, and I was going nowhere until he was done. And he didn't stop until a third orgasm shook my whole body.
Only then did he move his hands from my thighs to my back and let me slowly topple backwards to catch my breath, smiling crookedly at me as he wiped his mouth and chin.
"Are you alright, love?" he wanted to know.
I nodded, still breathless. He sat up, but I got to my feet and pushed him back down, "My turn."

Jonathan

I saw her intentions written all over her face as she lowered her head, but she didn't have to do this. I was more than happy to have her come on my tongue and let that be that.

"Darling, you…" I started to say, but my sentence ended short as Christina wrapped her mouth around the tip of my cock.

She locked eyes with me, and as I watched her, she took all of me into her mouth.

"Fuck," I hissed through clenched teeth.

My eyes closed and I let my head roll back.

Moonlight have mercy, her mouth is so warm. Her tongue ran up the length of my shaft and flicked over the tip of my cock.

And then she sucked my cock.

Really sucked, and I groaned.

I was not sure how to describe what I felt, all the things that went through my mind as the back of Christina's throat pressed against the tip of my cock. I couldn't remember the last time anyone had that much of my cock that far down their throat.

When I felt suction again, another moan escaped from my throat, which only seemed to egg her on, and the sensation intensified.

I was half-expecting her to stop, to take a break. But she didn't stop.

"Burning fucking Hell," I cursed, and she just kept going.

And going.

And going, sucking, and licking my cock until I was about to come.

"Christina… fuck…" I tried to warn her, "Love, I… ah, fuck."

"Mm-hmm…" she hummed in response.

The vibration in her throat was my undoing, and I moaned her name as I came in her mouth. She continued to work my cock with her hand, coaxing every last drop of cum out of me and I shivered with pleasure as she swallowed everything.

"Uhm… fuck… wh… I…" I stuttered when she took her mouth off my cock and got to her feet, "Fuck."

She chuckled, "Look who's dropping f-bombs now."

I slowly turned my head to look at her, "So that's what you can do with your tongue… I've always wondered..."

She blushed slightly, "You sound… impressed… or something."

"Impressed?" I repeated and I let out a slow, rasping breath, "Woman, I am absolutely fucking enthralled."
"I don't know what you're talking about, I've gone down on you before, " she said to me as she started putting her clothes back on. I remained sprawled out on the sofa. I was going to need a moment.
I smiled, my eyes fixed on the chandelier above me, "I remember…." I stuffed a scatter cushion under my head and looked over at her, "But you've never done it like that."

∞

A little while later, we were back in my room after a trip to the kitchen for snacks, Christina curled up at my side on the sofa, and I was systematically eating my way through an entire sleeve of strawberry-jam-filled cookies.
"Talk to me, my love," I asked, "What is happening in your life? What has you so stressed?"
She tried to act innocent, "What do you mean?"
I gave her a blank look, "Try again, darling."
But she kept it up, "I'm fine, babe, really."
I held the same blank look on my face, "One more time."
She chuckled, "Jonathan, really, I'm fine."
"Actually," I said, the blank look still not leaving my face, "Keep trying, until I believe you."
"It's nothing serious," she insisted.
I shook my head and swallowed the mouthful of cookie that I had been chewing on, "Anything that makes you less than 100% happy is unacceptable. Tell me. What is it?"
Christina sighed before she toppled over and leaned her head against my shoulder, "It's everything. My studies, my job, my future."
I put my arm around her, but I didn't say anything. I knew my silence would prompt her to go on. It did.
"I don't know whether I should further my studies or not. I was thinking of applying to the PhD program, but I don't know if I would get in, and if I did, I don't know if I would be able to continue working, and if I can't work, that might mean that my mom has to take a second job again so we can pay all our bills. And urgh, my car, my fucking car," she groaned in frustration.
"Do you have a lot of bills to pay?" I asked.
She nodded, "A whole stack of them."

"Let me help you, please?"
Christina was my first and only girlfriend, in the truest sense of the word. I'd been involved with other women throughout my life, but what I had with Christina was unlike anything I'd ever experienced before.
I'd been wanting to help her and her mother in a real way ever since we started dating, but, according to my sister, I had the emotional intelligence of a teaspoon, and I had absolutely no idea how. I needed guidance.
I recalled one afternoon not at all long ago, when my mother was in the kitchen baking scones and I took my chance.

"Hello darling boy," she smiled up at me when I strode into the kitchen. "Hello, Mami," I smiled back. Looking around the kitchen, there appeared to be a good 40-odd scones already spaced out across the counters in various stages of cooling down and my mother was getting more eggs from the refrigerator.
"Are we feeding the first battalion?" I asked, and my mother laughed, "No, no, I just felt like baking."
I nodded slowly, "And who's going to eat all of these?"
She gave me a pointed look, "I'm certain you'll make a sizable dent."
She was right, of course, and I popped a still-warm scone into my mouth. My mother clearly hadn't been expecting me to eat the whole thing in one bite and she swatted me against the arm with the tea-towel that had been draped over her shoulder. "Could you at least try not to eat like such a barbarian?"
"Whatchu mean?" I mumbled, my mouth still full of scone. A few crumbs escaped in the process and my mother's jaw dropped in horror, "Jonathan Ambrose Langdon, do not speak with your mouth full, you were not born in a cave!"
In an effort to escape what I knew could very well be another tea-towel assault, I moved myself to the other side of the island she was working on. This time I waited until I was finished chewing before I spoke, "Do you need any help?" She shook her head, "I think I have it under control, thank you."
I nodded, and then hoisted myself up onto the kitchen counter to sit there. "The chairs in this house are not just for decoration," my mother said without even looking up from the batter.

I didn't reply. I just smiled to myself and hopped down from the counter to take a seat at the island instead. I sat there in silence, just looking at my mother, until she looked back up at me and smiled. "You look happy." she commented and I felt my smile broaden.
"Christina?" my mother asked and I raised my eyebrows in confirmation. My mother nodded approvingly, "I won't lie, I was very surprised when you told me that you had developed feelings for her, but I'm glad it finally happened. She's good for you."
I couldn't disagree, "She is. She makes me..."
"Nicer," my mother interjected and I chuckled, "I suppose she does."
"How is she?" my mother asked then, "I haven't seen her for a few days, I miss her."
I pulled another scone closer, "She's not been doing well, actually."
My mother stopped mixing and looked up at me, consternation written all over her face, "Why? What's going on?"
"They've been understaffed more often than not and if she can't find someone to stand in, then she covers the shift herself. She's also been rather stressed of late." I got up to get a plate, a knife and some butter. Under normal circumstances I'd simply drag the top of the scone through the butter and call it a day, but since my mother was in the kitchen, I had to rethink my strategy. "About what?" Celeste wanted to know.
I cut a scone in half and spread butter on it, "Everything, according to her." I ate half of it before I went on, "Her future, her studies, their finances..."
"Hmm..." came my mother's pensive hum. I went on, "I want to help, I just don't know how."
"Sweetheart," my mother said, "I was wondering..."
I ate the other half of the scone, "About?"
"Why is Christina working there? At that... quaint little place?"
I glanced sidelong at my mother as I reached for another scone. I somehow always forgot what a phenomenal baker she was. "Mami..." I said, doing my utmost to keep my tone gentle and unaccusing.
"Yes?" she met my challenge, and I cocked my head to the side, "Are we being snooty?"
She gasped indignantly, "I never! I was asking a simple question."

"Of course..." I didn't believe a word she said, but I decided to let it go. My mother was clearly not ready to do so, however, and she tried to defend herself, "I am simply of the conviction that our Christina has more potential than a dead-end job with zero growth opportunity."
I couldn't help but roll my eyes, yet I didn't respond; I simply changed the subject. "As I was saying, I don't know how to help my girl."

My mother said nothing as she took a tray of scones out of the oven and replaced it with a new one. She spoke again after she took the piping hot scones out of the baking tray and transferred them to a cooling rack. "You mentioned she was concerned about their finances?"
I nodded, "They have a substantial amount of debt, I'm afraid."
She looked questioningly at me, "And are you or are you not in a position to help? Financially speaking."
My hand that had been halfway to my mouth with another scone stopped in mid-air and I turned to look at my mother, "You know... I really should have thought of that..."

Since the start of our relationship, I had been hinting at helping her, but either Christina's pride or her ego would not allow me; she insisted on getting by without help. That stubbornness was one of the reasons I loved her. But that was exactly the problem, I loved her, and I wanted to make her life better, easier. Besides, what was the point of having money if I couldn't use it to help someone?

So, I decided to take my mother's advice to heart, "Let me help you," I requested and then I readied myself for another argument with my feisty little Gremlin.
"Yes, please?" came her soft answer.
"Darling, I know you want to help yourself, but..." I started, but I stopped almost immediately and I frowned at her. That was very unexpected, "Did you... did you just agree to let me help you?"
She looked up at me, the same vulnerable look on her face that she had the first moment our eyes met outside the escape room, "I did," she admitted, "I need help."
"You've been fighting me on this since we met. Why the change of heart?"

She wrinkled her nose, “My mom reminded me that it takes a strong person to admit that you need help.”
I nodded slowly and kissed her hair, “Your mother is a very wise woman.”

Chapter 7

Dr. Kole Brennan

I was speechless. I was so excited, my whole body was trembling. Finally, I had what I needed: The skeleton of the son of the first vampire. Or at least, part of it.
The priest's contact really came through. A skull belonging to Ionáthan Evangelios Adelphi, the oldest son of Ambrogio, born to a mortal Greek woman, was discovered… somewhere. So well preserved, it still had some of its teeth. And now it belonged to me, Kole Brennan. Actually, not to me, to the House of Apollo.
Who it belonged to was semantics. The point was, I could now finally continue my work; I could improve my serum. I had just finished unpacking the skull and the few bones that came with it, when there was a knock at thc door.

"Yeah?" I acknowledged, and I looked up when the door swung open. The man that stepped into the lab was familiar. I recognized him as one of the priest's personal guards, but I didn't know his name. Brown hair, buzzcut, heavily tattooed, the man now standing in my lab had military training. And a lot of it, I learned, as the guy who introduced himself as Hunter McCoy rambled off all of his stations and deployments in rapid fire.
"Uh-huh," I hummed, "And what do you want, soldier?"
"To serve the mighty Apollo, sir," Hunter responded, deadpan.
I chuckled, "I don't know how much a former SEAL can do in my lab…"
"I don't know much about science, doc," Hunter admitted, "But I know a whole hell of a lot about pain. And combat. And survival."

I chucked the empty containers that housed the skull and bones into the corner of the room behind me, "And how is that going to help me?"
Hunter offered his arm, "Test the serum on me. I can handle it."
I frowned, chuffed in disbelief, "You have no idea what you're saying."
I made a move to walk away, but Hunter stepped in front of me, blocking my path, "I do, Doc. I want in. I want to sacrifice my body for the glory of our generous god."
He was quiet for a moment, his jaw tense. Then he spoke again, "I volunteer for the procedure. For… whatever procedure you need to do. I want to be the Sun God's soldier. It's my calling. My destiny, I guess."
I examined him for a moment, and then a grin started spreading on my face from ear to ear, "Mr. McCoy…."
"Hunter," the soldier interrupted me, "Call me Hunter. Mr. McCoy was my father, and he was murdered by one of these bloodsucking beasts."
"What did His Holiness say?"
"I have his blessing to join your team, Doc."
I smiled, "Very well, Hunter. For the glory of Apollo, then."

Chapter 8

Jonathan

"When was the last time we did this?" I asked Kirill.
He dropped by unannounced, again, just as I was heading into the gym, so he decided to join me for a sparring session.
Since we first met, we'd spent a lot of time training together, and even though I was a lot older, and a lot faster than he was, I still enjoyed training with him. I usually won, which Kirill's competitive nature absolutely hated, but he liked to think that he gave me a run for my money.
He even won a few times, but only when I let him.

He took a moment to answer the question, securing the laces on his boots, "I not remember, my friend. Long time."
With Kirill distracted, I shoved him over and he fell on his arse onto the floor of the octagon and he looked up at me in surprise, "*Poshyol na hui*!" He cursed at me in Russian. Fuck you.
I cackled, "How the fuck does your English get worse every time I see you?"
In one motion, Kirill jumped to his feet and lunged forward, swinging at my face.
Laughing, I leaned back, out of range of Kirill's fist, and swung my foot up to kick him against the thigh.
He hawked up a bogey and spat onto the floor of the octagon, and I threw a punch that connected right in the middle of his chest, "Don't spit in my octagon, you fucking animal," I reprimanded.
Then I stepped away from him and walked away, and he leapt forward and dropped a dog shot to the back of my head.

I took the punch, but retaliated with a backhand slap and a kick to Kirill's ribs, "A sucker punch? Really?"

In response, Kirill launched a rather aggressive attack, a fury of swipes, slaps and punches aimed at my face, chest, stomach.
The last hit was an unexpected left hook that made contact with my jaw, and the metallic taste of my own blood trickled into my mouth. I wiped my mouth with the back of my hand, and Kirill grinned when he saw the blood.
I raised an eyebrow, "Kiryusha. That wasn't very nice. I thought we were friends?"
Kirill planted his feet shoulder width apart, his body turned sideways, his weight on his back leg. He put one hand behind his back, and raised the other to beckon me closer, "You want sorry?" he challenged, "Come get. I have sorry in fist."

Without warning, I grabbed him by the wrist and yanked him closer, slamming the heel of my palm right into his nose. Blood streaming from his nose, he dropped another curse in Russian. I balled my free hand into a fist and swung at his face, hitting his cheekbone and sending him reeling a few steps to his left. He quickly rebounded, leaping into a flying downward punch that I dodged, if only barely, and when his feet touched ground again, my knee hit him in the diaphragm, knocking the air from his lungs.
He growled back at me in contempt as he tried to recover from the blow, but I wasn't planning on giving him much of a chance. I zipped over to him, stuck a foot in behind his leg and shoved him over, slamming him down onto the floor, and bringing my fist down to his throat. I stopped my fist just short from crushing his windpipe, and, even though he had his teeth bared like a wild animal, he clearly knew it was over.

I extended a hand and helped him up, "You've gotten rusty, my friend." Panting, Kirill nodded, "*Da…*"
Then I swiped his feet out from underneath him, slammed an elbow into his back and threw him back down on the floor, his face right in the spot where he spat at the start of the session.
"Don't. Spit. In. My. Octagon," I snarled through gritted teeth as I used Kirill's face as a mop.

He shrieked helplessly, “Majesty, please! *Izvinite*!” Sorry.
I laughed as I let Kirill up, and he used his shirt to wipe the blood and spit from his face before he turned to me with a questioning look on his face, “Round 2?”
I cracked my knuckles, “If you really want your arse handed to you again, sure.”

After a total of 6 high-speed rounds and with a victory tally of me, 4, Kirill 2, both of us were out of breath and drenched in sweat, so we called it a day. As we went back to my room, I was laughing at another one of Kirill's bad jokes, and I nearly walked over Christina.

Chapter 9

Christina

I let out a yelp when Jonathan came barging in the door and almost crashed into me. I lost my balance and he grabbed me by the shoulders to steady me, “Shit. Sorry darling. I wasn't expecting you. Are you alright, my love?”

I slowly scanned him up and down. His sweat-soaked tank clung to every contour, every line of his perfectly toned body, his black hair equally drenched. I had never seen him like that before. My lower lip tucked itself in between my teeth and my pussy started yelling at me in Morse code. *Oh, shit, he’s hot.*

“Is this a bad time?” I asked.

I knew my man, and he knew me, and it took only one look for him to know what was happening in my head. I saw the slight twitch in his eyebrow as he locked eyes with me and turned his head to speak to Kirill, “Hey, you.”

“*Da*?” Kirill acknowledged.

“Get out,” Jonathan commanded.

Without a word, Kirill slinked out of the room and as soon as I heard the lock click, I grabbed the hem of Jonathan's tank top and peeled it off of his body.

I looked him up and down again, “Oh… fuck me…” I breathed, running my fingers down his chest and abs.

He smiled crookedly at me, “Is that a statement or a request?”

I wrapped my hand around his throat and pulled his lips to mine as he gripped my ass and pulled my lower body against his.

He moved his mouth from my lips to my ear, down to my neck, his hands slipping in under my t-shirt to deftly undo my bra and reach in under it.

I breathed him in. I didn't know why the faint scent of his sweat was such a turn-on, but my blood caught fire.

His fangs lightly scraped my neck and I moaned, which he took as an invitation to strip off my shirt and bra completely and toss them to the floor. The next item of clothing to go was my shoes and then my jeans, followed by his trainers and sweatpants, and he flung me down on the sofa.

“You haven't answered my question,” he reminded me, two fingers already deep inside me, his thumb drawing small circles on my clit, and I moaned again, “What question?” He took one nipple between his teeth, and then the other, curling his fingers rhythmically inside me, “What did you say earlier?”

“Fuck me. Fuck me.”

He grinned, “Ah, yes. But was it…?”

He was interrupted by the sound of me orgasming under his touch, panting and shuddering. *Fuck, I’m such a slut for him.*

“There's my good girl,” he smiled crookedly, “Was it a statement or a…?”

“Request,” I interrupted him again, “Always.”

Jonathan leaned over to kiss me, but I pulled away and got on my hands and knees, my back to him. I knew exactly what I wanted, and this was it.

“Oh? You want me to fuck you like this?” he asked, surprised.

I nodded eagerly, spreading my legs wider for him, “Yes, yes, yes please.”

He took a split-second to get a condom from the desk drawer, but then he was right back behind me.

I looked at him over my shoulder. I wanted to see the look on his face, and as he grabbed hold of my hips, pulled me closer and slid himself into me, I whimpered. *He feels so good inside me.*

He dug his fingers into my hair and pulled my head back, “Who do you belong to?”

“To you.” *Fuck, yes I do.*

He moved his free hand to the front of my body, shifting a finger down to my clit and he asked again, “Whose are you?”

I moaned the answer with every thrust of him into me, “Yours, yours, yours.”
With his next thrust, my arms buckled beneath me and I collapsed onto the sofa underneath him. He continued to plunge into me, and by the time that I climaxed again, Jonathan’s ending wasn’t too far behind, and he rammed himself all the way into me, his fingers digging into my hips as he came.

So there I was, stunningly fucked, sprawled out on my stomach on the sofa, my eyes following Jonathan as he got rid of the condom, put his boxers back on and crouched next to me, “Christina?” he asked, “Darling, are you alright?”
I clumsily wiped my hair out of my face and smiled languidly at him, “Is that what I get for dropping by unannounced?”
Grinning, he kissed my temple, “Yes, exactly.”
“Hmm,” I mused, “Watch me never tell you I'm coming over again.”
He laughed, “If you're willing and able to deal with the consequences, sure.”

I pushed myself up and turned to my side, “Sorry for interrupting, I didn't know that Kirill was here.”
Jonathan waved his hand dismissively, “Nothing to apologize for,” he said as he handed me my bra, “I would offer to help you put it on, but I'm afraid I'm better at taking it off,” he explained.
“That's okay, babe, I can manage. Thank you, though.”
“By the way,” I went on, “Technically, we don’t need to use condoms anymore… You remember I told you that, right?”
Jonathan pulled up his shoulders, “I don’t mind using condoms, darling. I just want to be inside you, that’s all.”
I sat up to put my bra back on, and out of nowhere… I fucking queefed. Loudly. More than once. There was nothing I could do to stop the air from leaving my body and I just sat there on the sofa, absolutely mortified, with my eyes pinched shut.
“Sorry…” I breathed an apology and I opened my eyes to see Jonathan grinning at me.
I grabbed a cushion off the sofa and buried my face in it. “Shut up.”
He laughed, “I never said a thing.”
I shifted the cushion down and peered at him over the brim of it, “Your face said enough.”

Jonathan leaned over and kissed my forehead before he got to his feet, "If you will please excuse me, I should really go take a shower. I reek."
I winked back at him and fluttered my eyelashes, "Don't be embarrassed, darling," I quoted his own words back to him, "You smell delicious."
He nodded slowly, "Yes… well… I put my foot right in that one, didn't I?" and I giggled.
He rejoined me when he was done, and he smelled so good but I had to resist the powerful urge to blatantly sniff him, because there was something I needed to talk to him about.

I knew my man, and he knew me, and that extended to more than just the physical aspect of our relationship. He knew all of my tells and ticks, and as soon as he came out of the bathroom wearing those damn gray sweatpants that distracted me so, he came over to me and took a seat next to me, "Talk to me, love. What is it?"
I tried to smile, but I knew it wasn't quite reaching my eyes, "Nothing babe, I'm fine."
He looked pointedly at me, "Darling, please, not this song and dance again."
I gave up; I needed to get this out, "Okay, okay… There's something that has been bothering me."
He slung his arm over the backrest, "I'm listening."
I turned in my seat to face him, "Just… How were you so calm about me possibly being pregnant?"
"Did you think I didn't care?" He raised an eyebrow. I shook my head, "I didn't say that…"
He inclined his head, "No, you didn't, but I'm rather sure you were thinking it."
I didn't respond. *I mean, I was a little…*
Jonathan took a deep breath before he responded, "Despite what you may have thought you saw on my face, it was not at all the same as what I was feeling on the inside."
"Really?"
"Really. I'm rather surprised you thought I was calm. Usually I have a hard time keeping my face and my emotions disconnected from each other."

I gave him a blank look, “You’re telling me you wear your heart on your sleeve?”
Smiling, he shook his head, “All over my face. My face is usually much more honest than my mouth.”
He took my hand and went on, “As I mentioned, I might want to have children someday, but when that pregnancy test showed two lines… Of course I was worried, the thought of bringing an Infinite child into this world is terrifying.” Then he looked up at me, “And I was afraid for you.”
I frowned, “For me? Why, babe?”
“It would have been the first time a mortal carried an Infinite child, at least to my knowledge, and I honestly have no idea what would have happened. When my mother was expecting me, there were no such things as ultrasounds and prenatal care, so she had a tough go of it.” Jonathan explained, “Regardless of technology, pregnancy is not easy, or so I’ve heard, and I would assume Infinite pregnancy even more so. Especially because you’re mortal. And you would have had to tell your mother about what I am, and about the child we were going to bring into the world, and I don’t know how your mother would have reacted to all of that.”

I nodded in silent agreement. Then, he looked up at me and cupped my jaw with his hand, “But I saw the fear in your eyes, I saw your panic, and I knew you needed me to be calm. So that was what I became.”
“Babe…”
He kissed my forehead, “Besides, there’s no need for both of us to panic.”
“I know, but…”
“Christina,” he interrupted me, “You are the most important person in my life. You are my entire universe. I will always put you first.”
Tears started welling up in my eyes.
He smiled lovingly at me, “I will be anything and everything you need me to be.”

“How do you feel now that I’m definitely not pregnant?” This was important, this I needed to know.
But he just sat there, looking at me, no reply.

Captain Mysterion's mysteriousness was not making me feel better, "Are you… disappointed?" I asked cautiously. He shook his head, "I'm happy if you are."

"Jonathan… Did you want to have a baby?" Fuck it, I took the direct approach. *I know I wasn't ready to be a mother, but... If he said yes... If he wanted to have a baby... Then there's a very real possibility that he's going to resent me for not being pregnant, and I don't think... shit, I know I wouldn't be able to handle that, and now he's just sitting there with that unreadable fucking look on his gorgeous fucking face and his silence is making me frantic.*

"Babe, please talk to me?"

The corner of his mouth lifted slowly into a crooked smile, "Sorry, love. I was imagining what you would look like, pregnant with our child someday."

I puffed out a sigh of relief and I chortled, "Please, I'll be so fat you wouldn't want to touch me."

His smile broadened, "I will always want to touch you. And I am endlessly fascinated by that concept."

"What concept? Me, fat?"

"Mm-hmm," he murmured his confirmation, "the bigger you are, the more there is for me to touch. And I can only imagine how stunning you'd look when you come for me…"

I blushed, and he pulled my head down to his shoulder with a wicked chuckle.

"So you're not mad at me for not being pregnant?" I asked when I lifted my head.

Jonathan blinked slowly at me, then he glanced down at my lips, "How about I answer that question in… interpretative dance?"

I frowned, "Huh? You want to dance?"

His eyebrow twitched, "Horizontally," he grinned before he pulled me astride him. *Oh, mercy be, he's already hard.* I just surrendered, "Fine. Dick me down, sir."

Chapter 10

The year was 1182.
Blood and chaos were all around me in the Byzantine Empire and I smiled to myself as the scent of it filled my nostrils, and screams filled the night air. This… this was living. Not stuck in the bloody house, bumping shoulders with upper-crusters and socialites. This was what I wanted: The freedom to go wherever the rumors of unrest and revolution took me.
I never cared who emerged as victors in battle, the struggles of mortal men were so horridly dull. I was there for one reason only, and that was bloodshed.

As was my habit, I started my day with the taste of blood and woman and wine still lingering on my tongue. I glanced over my shoulder at the naked woman, asleep in the hay behind me, my fang marks all over her legs and neck, and I chuckled to myself. How was she going to explain that to her husband? Then again, it was none of my concern. She could tell her husband whatever she damn-well pleased. I stretched, put my clothes back on, and I was gone long before she woke up.

And that was how I spent my days in times of war. I drank mead and ale from dawn to dusk, and when the world was bathed in moonlight, I hunted, drank as much blood as I could, and went to bed between the thighs of a different beauty each night.

In 1355 I did it again, this time in England.

The riots I chose to involve myself in lasted only for two short days, but I capitalized on it. I lost count of how many murderers, plunderers, rapists and rioters I hunted down and drank dry. A proper massacre, it was. Delicious, too.

But, as much as I wanted to rip apart and drain and kill everything that moved, The Laws of Night had to be obeyed, or I would suffer the consequences. As such, I had to pick my prey very carefully. Luckily, in times of war, the criteria was vast.

Times of unrest in the mortal realm made it so much easier to hunt and feed, and to hide the evidence in the aftermath of war. Not too many questions were asked about headless corpses and scorched bodies.

Discord in 1572 found me in France.

The French had such a flair for the dramatic, and every skirmish in France had its own special sort of flavor.

Oh, and the women… So naïve, so easily swayed.

I could play the same role in a different tavern each night of the week, and I knew I would never be leaving alone if I didn't want to. Even so, I did prefer some variety.

Sometimes I told them I was a traveling merchant, other times an aristocrat, or an actor. A few times I told some of them that I was a prince, and oh those special nights gave me a deeper understanding of what it meant to be 'royally fucked'.

One particularly drunken evening, I was leaving a tavern, planning to exchange it for another, but as soon as I stepped outside, sounds from an alley nearby stopped me in my tracks, The panicked voice of a woman, protesting, calling for help. And male voices, mocking her, heckling her desperate cries.

I knew what had to be happening in the alley, and my blood boiled. It was unacceptable.

I scanned the area, and when I was sure no-one was paying me any mind, I slipped into the alley, where I discovered a young woman being held by three very drunk men, all three grabbing and pawing and groping at her. They paid no mind to her protests, and kept ripping at her clothes. One of them was already unbuttoning his pants…

I felt a growl rumble in my throat. Mortal men were such absolute fucking pigs sometimes.

I sighed at the scene before me and switched to French. Even though my French was a far cry from perfect, I figured it was a better choice than any of the other languages I spoke, "Unhand the lady!"
One of the men looked at me, spitting on the ground near the woman before replying,
"Hah! She's a whore! This is what she wants!"

I sighed out loud before I zipped over to the disgusting, sweaty man at breakneck speed, grabbed his head and twisted, snapping his neck like a dry twig, and his companions screamed as his lifeless body dropped to the ground.
One of them lunged at me, right into my outheld fist and I laughed as my assailant fell to the ground. Useless…
The woman had backed up against the wall, and I turned to her and bowed, "Mademoiselle, you should go. Get yourself somewhere safe."
Nodding hastily, she muttered a brief 'merci' before she hiked her muddy dress up and sprinted out of the alley, and I chuckled to myself. She really was a whore, ladies did not run like that.
But I shrugged, it did not matter. Her chosen profession did not give these steaming piles of shit the right to violate her.
I turned back to the men. It was time to teach them some manners. Or rip them to shreds. Fun for me either way.

One of them lunged at me, knife in hand, swiping at me, screaming curses at me at every swipe.
It didn't take a lot of effort for me to relieve him of his knife and plunge it into his flabby gut, slicing him open from belly to breastbone. The disemboweled corpse dropped to the ground, and I turned my attention to the remaining attacker.
His eyes were wide, his hands trembling.
I lifted my chin and sniffed. Blood, death… and fear. The night air was rife with it. A glorious bouquet.
I beckoned the man closer, "Come on then. I don't have all night."
With a scream that, I guessed, was supposed to intimidate me, the man stormed at me. I simply stepped to the side, grabbed him by the throat and slammed him into the wall.
Digging my claws into his face and arm to hold him in place, I sank my fangs into the side of his neck, warm blood spurting into my mouth and onto my face.

I drank and drank, until the body was completely drained, before I stuck the blade that I took off the dead man in the mud into his neck, and slit his throat from ear to ear.
Satisfied, I wiped the blood from my face with my sleeve, and sauntered out of the alley, whistling to myself as I went.

A few blocks down the road, a small hand grabbed me by the elbow and pulled me into the dark.
I was very surprised to see the working girl from the alley, standing before me.
"Mademoiselle," I questioned, "Are you alright? Are you in danger?"
She smiled coyly at me and shook her head, "No, monsieur. I just wanted to thank you," she purred before she dropped to her knees in front of me and undid my trousers.
As she took my cock into her mouth, I closed my eyes, leaned back against the wall and I smiled to myself.
Vive le France…

Chapter 11

Christina

"Hold up," Devyn laughed, "That was it? 'Fuck'? That was the first thing he said?"

I nodded, "Yep, out of all the words that he knows, in all of the languages that he speaks, that was the one he went with. He said 'fuck'."

I was staying over at Devyn's apartment and we were sitting on her living room floor with a pizza and a few bottles of wine between us.

"Wow," Devyn mused, "so eloquent."

I groaned, "I know…"

"I mean… He's not wrong," Devyn said, "That was the thing that landed you in that position in the first place."

I snorted, "I know. Several positions, actually… In my defense, though, it's not my fault he's so damn good at it."

Devyn laughed, but she put her hand on my shoulder in empathy, "Girl, I am so sorry you went through that." She said, "Pregnancy scares are the worst, I know."

I smiled ruefully, "I remember."

She rolled her eyes and took a long sip of wine before she spoke again, "That sucked. But that's what can happen when you don't listen in sex-ed, and you take a Tinder date home."

I clinked my glass against hers, "No party without a party hat, girl."

"True that," Devyn agreed.

I finished my wine, "It was scary, but at least I'm not pregnant."

"What did your mom say?" she wanted to know.

"She was pretty chill about it, actually. I thought she would be mad at me, you know?"

"Maybe she secretly wants grandbabies?" she suggested, and I shrugged, "I have no idea. But she was really supportive."
"That's great," Devyn smiled, "I never even told mine what happened. She would have kicked my ass."
"Yeah… your mom scares me," I had to admit.
Devyn laughed, "You and me both. But anyway, I think Jonathan handled it really well."
I refilled our glasses, "I will drink to that. He was so supportive and understanding about everything. Then again, he always is…"

"Okay, so," Devyn changed the subject, "You just dropped another precious nugget of information about your mysterious man. He speaks more than one language?"
I winced inwardly. S*hit-on-a-stick, I really need to be more careful what I tell people about Jonathan.*
"Yes," I played it cool, "He is European, so…"
Devyn nodded understandingly, "That makes sense, then. They grow up multilingual."
I just nodded. *Me and my big mouth.*
"Speaking of Jonathan," she went on to say, "You said he was going to help you? Help you how?"
"Your guess is as good as mine. I hope he's going to help me sell my piece-of-shit car."

She laughed. I picked up another slice of pizza, and I changed the subject to a safer topic: Devyn's love-life. "Since you brought up the topic of boys, is there anyone new and interesting in your life?"
She gave me a shy smile, "No, but… I was wondering… Jonathan's Russian friend…?"
I gave her a sideways glance, "Kirill?"
She bit her lip, "Kirill... Is he single?"
I nodded in silence, and she grinned.
"Why?" I asked, "Do you like him?"
She wrinkled her nose and shrugged, "He cute."
I laughed, "Interesting…"
"Oh yeah?" she challenged, taking another slice of pizza, and I nodded, "Well, yes, because Jonathan said he was asking about you, too."

Her eyes widened, "Are you serious?" she shrieked, "What did he say?"
I giggled, "I can't do his accent, but apparently he was asking about my 'pretty friend with chocolate skin'."
Devyn's face wrinkled into what appeared to be an awkward smile, "Chocolate skin… I don't know how I feel about that analogy."
I grimaced, "I know. I had heartburn when I heard him say that, but we are talking about Kirill Sokolov, Mr. Unpredictable himself."
She sighed, "At least he's been thinking about me."
I nodded, "And he clearly wants to see you again… Maybe see more of your skin…"
Devyn shuddered, "That came out a lot more 'lotion-in-the-basket' than you probably meant."
I didn't know where the snort-laugh that escaped out my nose came from, but I buried my face in my hands in an attempt to keep it in. I failed miserably, and Devyn doubled over with laughter, shoving me against the shoulder.
"My point is," I said when I managed to stop laughing, "the man was clearly impressed by you."
My bestie squealed in delight, clapping her hands together in excitement, "Come on, child, hook us up. Double date, or something."
With a Cheshire Cat grin on my face, I clinked my glass against hers, "It's as good as done."
Devyn grinned from ear to ear, and she curled her legs under her and turned to me, "What can you tell me about him? Because, like, I only saw him that one time."
"And he made a big impression, apparently…"
Devyn sighed, "It's that jaw… I'm a sucker for a strong jaw. And the accent also helps. And then there's that… smoldering intensity…"
"Ooh, smoldering intensity," I mocked her. She rolled her eyes at me and opened another bottle of wine, "Okay, I'm going to change the subject now."

Devyn shook her head at me and handed me another glass of wine, "So after the whole almost pregnant thing, are you and Jonathan okay?"
We were fine, but keeping The Truth a secret from everyone was driving me crazy. I shot her a look that I thought was nonchalant, but Devyn knew me well enough to figure out that there was something going on.

She squeezed my shoulder, "Chris, if there's something that you need to talk about, I'm here. I can listen."
I closed my eyes and sighed, "I don't know how, Dev…"
She leaned her shoulder against mine, "Is this about you? Or Jonathan?"
"It's him…" I said into my glass of wine.
My friend was worried, "Is it bad?"
"It's just… Jonathan is…. He's dangerous." As soon as the word left my mouth I wanted to kick myself. *I should not have said that. Now she's probably going to think he's abusive or something and I don't need her or anyone else asking me questions that I am not able to answer.*

Devyn frowned, "To you, or…?"
I shook my head, "No, no, definitely not to me. He'd never hurt me. He just… he isn't normal. And I know what he is… I've known for a long time, I've seen… things… I just can't tell anyone…"
She twirled her glass of wine between her fingers, "Chris… I think I might know what's going on."
My blood ran cold. *Devyn knows? How?*
I was very sure I'd never said anything tell-tale. And that night at the club… Jonathan and the others would have been careful to hide the truth from her. So how did she know?
I gulped, "You do…?"
She nodded, "I think so…"
Oh, fuck. This is not good...
"Jonathan is…"
Shit. Shit. Shit.

Devyn guessed, "Jonathan's a mob-boss, isn't he?"
I stared at her in surprise for a moment… and I just rolled with it. Mob-boss was easier to explain than 'immortal vampire prince'.
I pressed my lips together, "How did you know?"
Her eyes widened and her face lit up, "Wait… Am I right? Is he?"
I gave her half a smile and I nodded, "How did you know, Dev?"
She took a big bite of her slice of pizza, "I don't know, I just guessed, with the money and the secrecy and the people he surrounds himself with.

Like Kirill, and that girl-boss that came with him to the club that night, and I just figured… He's the boss, and they have to be, like, his enforcers, or something. They both look like they take their coffee with a slice of murder on the side. And, I mean, Jonathan… dude is the living embodiment of death and danger."

I didn't know what to say, so I said nothing, I just took another slice of pizza. Devyn was so spot-on about the untamed trifecta that was Jonathan and his two best friends, it was actually scary.

She sipped her wine, smiling at me conspiratorially, "This should be a novel, or a movie or something," she said, "My Best Friend is Dating The Mob."

I could only laugh. If only she knew the truth. But at least she knows something, which was a fine start for me.

Chapter 12

Christina

I am probably the worst girlfriend in the world.
Ever since our run-in with potential parenthood, things in our lives had been really busy and just a little bit crazy, and the last time I told Jonathan that I loved him was… *Shit. When was it?*
Crap, probably when I first took the pregnancy test at my house. Or maybe it was that day we saw Dr. Woods…? Either way, it was ages ago. And I couldn't remember when was the last time, if ever, that I planned something special for us to do. Usually, he was the one doing all the planning. He always went out of his way to do nice things for me, and I just… Let him.
This time it was my turn.

One day after work, I was clicking around on the internet because I wanted to find something fun and exciting for us to do. Dinner dates were always nice, but maybe he would enjoy something more exciting. It didn't take me all that long to find it, the perfect activity, and as soon as I did, I texted him:
Babe, are you up for a date with me?

Not so long ago, after the umpteenth time it took him days to respond to a text, we had a serious conversation about it. I fucking hated it when people did that. I knew that my hatred of slow texting wasn't his fault at all, but as long as he wasn't aware of how much it bothered me, nothing would be changing in that department. So we had a conversation about it, and I told him how much it irked me when it took him days to respond to my texts.

He apologized, and explained himself: His mother, and his sister, and Kat had scolded him over the same thing many times, but he promised that it wasn't because he didn't care, he was just born in a different era. He was from a time of chaperoned outings and handwritten love-letters, and at times his phone was an annoyance. And, he freely admitted, women are better at adapting than men, so his mother and his sister, and even Kat evolved along with the changing times much better than he did. Despite all these things, he understood my point, and ever since we had that talk, he had really been trying to do better with his phone, especially when he was out of town. When he was busy he sometimes took longer to respond, but I haven't had to wait for days for him to get back to me. This time as well, his response to my text came rather quickly:
Always, darling.
What do you want to do?

I smiled to myself. *I hope he never stops calling me darling*. I replied:
It's a surprise.
Could you meet me tonight at 7?

After a few minutes of silence, he texted back:
Oh, and what are we doing?
Shall I pick you up?

I chuckled:
Curiosity killed the cat, Mr. Langdon.
That's okay, I'll meet you there xxx

My phone buzzed with his reply only a few short moments later:
But satisfaction brought it back, Ms. Miller.
See you tonight love xxx

I rolled my eyes at myself for grinning like the lovestruck little nerd I was.

I got to the meeting spot about 15 minutes early that night, and I felt a little bit silly, because as soon as I got there, I realized that Jonathan was immediately going to know what we were doing. *Damn his superhuman hearing. Whatever. He'll appreciate the thought.*

As I waited for him, I marveled at the fact that I still got butterflies in my tummy when I knew I was going to see him, even though we'd been together for… I frowned. *Shit. How long have we been together? Damn it, I really am the worst girlfriend in the world.*

After eight centuries, days probably blurred together for him, but what girl doesn't know how long she's been dating her man? Then again, maybe if your man is an immortal super-being, anniversaries are only celebrated every five years or something. Like, maybe there's some kind of different rule book when your boyfriend is an ancient vampire? Surely I can't be the first girl to date an Infinite. And if I am, then I am a pioneer, and I need to write a guidebook. Or a manual. Or something.

My inner monologue was cut short when I saw Jonathan's car pull up, and I could practically hear my heart applaud his arrival.

Fuck, I love this man. Supersonic hearing and all.

As he walked toward me, I couldn't help but stare at him. It had to be illegal for one man to be this hot.

There was something in the way he walked, a silent, unspoken power, a righteous confidence. His dark eyes looked right into my soul, and when he stepped up to me, all smiles and sex-appeal, I wrapped my arms around his neck, pressed my nose to his skin and breathed him in.

He returned the hug, "Are you sniffing me again?"

"You're lucky I'm not licking you."

He smiled and pulled out of my hug to kiss me hello.

Then he looked down at my shirt and read the print on it out loud, "Bite me," and he gave me a pointed look, "Darling, I love your shirt."

I looked down at it, "I knew you would."

He nodded, "I really do. Especially the glittery fangs. Very nice."

I giggled, and he took both my hands in his, "So what are we doing tonight?"

"Like you don't know."

"I have no idea, love," he denied, "Please tell me? The suspense is killing me."

I rolled my eyes at him and I chuckled, "You are so full of it. But whatever. We're going go-karting."

Jonathan touched the tip of his tongue to his top lip, "That sounds like a bloody good time."

I beamed a grin at him, "Really? You're keen?"

He nodded eagerly, “I am super-keen. I haven't gone go-karting in ages.”
He pulled me against him and cupped my face in his hands, “But tell me, is there any particular reason we are on a date tonight?”
I smiled up at him, my hands on his hips, “Because I love you, Jonathan Langdon. And I just wanted you to know that.”
He mirrored my smile, “I love you, Christina, very much. For a moment there I was worried I had missed our anniversary. When is it, by the way?”
I did my best to give him the least sheepish smile I could muster, but he wasn’t buying it, and I didn’t know how to lie to him, “I have no idea… I’m sorry… I really am the worst g…”
He ended my sentence with a shake of his head, “Don’t say things like that, love. Please?”
I frowned, “Say what?”
“I can't stand it when you speak ill of yourself. Even jokingly.”
I pouted, “I feel horrible that I don’t even know it's our anniversary, babe…”
He stroked my hair, “That’s perfectly alright, love. You’re not the only one.”
“So you also have no idea?”
He nodded, “I also have no idea,” he confirmed before taking my hand and starting towards the go-kart track. “We can figure it out later. Now come on. I have a need for speed.”

If anyone asked me, I would have told them that Jonathan’s legs were too long for the go-kart and I thought he looked very uncomfortable sitting behind the wheel. But the look of pure joy on his face as he sped around the track told me all I needed to know: he was having a great time, and it made my heart so happy to see him play like a little kid. As he won yet another race, he looked so youthful and so excited that I wished we had done this sooner. I always wanted him to be this happy.
After a few rounds around the track, I had enough racing for a while, but he started another race, so I went to the concession stand to get us some drinks and snacks.

As I stood in line, I heard an all too familiar voice behind me, “Hey, baby, how’ve you been?” and I shuddered at the sound.

I closed my eyes and sighed before I turned around to see…
My ex-boyfriend from university.
Owen North.
If I had to pick my top three worst relationships, my relationship with Owen would be all three.
It was fine for the first three months, but after that, things just got progressively worse. It started with him never texting me back which was where my hatred of slow texting was born from. It then progressed to him ignoring me even when we were in the same room and then to straight up verbal abuse. That mutated into 'cheating' and it's maddening cousin 'gaslighting'.

Devyn was the one who helped me realize that no matter how many times Owen promised he would change, a leopard couldn't change its spots. Owen North was a psychic vampire that drained me of my energy. But not, like, a real vampire.
I hated thinking about it, because it got me pissed off at myself all over again for staying with such a toxic mess of a guy for so long, but I promised myself: Never again. The next guy I dated, better treat me like the damn queen I was, or I was out of there. And lo and behold, enter His Eternal Majesty, Lord Jonathan Ambrose Langdon, an ancient vampire prince with an impeccable ass, a monster cock and nice manners, who called me 'darling' and held the door for me and massaged my feet when I was tired.

When I heard Owen's voice behind me for the first time in so long, I was expecting to see him in the same hipster-type outfits that he wore in university, so I was surprised to see him in a suit. I'd learned enough about men's clothing from Jonathan to recognize an ill-fitting suit when I saw one, but it was a suit nonetheless. The very ugly, very boxy suit reminded me just how stylish Jonathan was, and how well his clothes always fit him. Even his t-shirts fit him like they were tailormade. Well, a lot of them were, but still.

"Owen," I acknowledged, even though I wanted nothing more than to ignore him.
He leaned in for a hug, but I just stood there like a post; I really didn't want to touch him.

"You look good, baby," he smirked at me and I wanted to throw up in my mouth. *He still thinks the smirking thing is sexy. I mean, it is, but only when Jonathan does it.*
"I'm not your baby, Owen."
He wiggled his eyebrows at me, "You used to be…"
I stuck my tongue in between my teeth and my lower lip, "And then I grew a brain." I giggled on the inside. I learned that little move from Jonathan.
Owen ignored the jab, "We should grab some coffee some time, catch up."
I'd rather catch the clap…

My insides turned smoke on water when the scent of Jonathan's cologne and the warmth of his presence breezed in next to me, just as Owen asked me to have coffee with him. *Here we go. My amazing boyfriend is about to meet my very-much-not-amazing ex-boyfriend. This is either going to be spectacular, or an absolute train wreck. I cannot fucking wait.* I would have loved to know what was going on in Jonathan's head. To the undiscerning eye, he looked disinterested and unbothered, but if you knew him as well as I did, the anger and annoyance on his face was clear as day.

"Good to meet you, bro. I'm Owen," my moose-knuckle of an ex introduced himself.
Really? Bro…? Cringe.
"Jonathan," came the answer, totally devoid of any feeling.
"Are you from around here?" Owen asked.
Jonathan blinked slowly at him, "No."
Owen chuckled, gesturing towards the go-karts with his chin, "Did you have fun playing with the toy cars?"
I almost couldn't believe the arrogance. Then again, I totally could. My mom was right, Owen was never going to grow up.
He didn't give Jonathan a chance to reply before handing him a business card, "Tell you what, guy," he said, "If you're ever in the market for some real wheels, give me a call. I'll cut you a sweet deal."
Without a word, Jonathan sucked his teeth in disdain. He took the card from Owen but didn't even so much as glance at it before he crumpled it up in his hand, and I saw Jonathan's eyebrow twitch.

Owen needs to tread carefully. Jonathan didn't say anything, but his gaze remained fixed on Owen, almost burning into his skull.

In a show of staggering arrogance, Owen looked back at me, "Good to see you, baby," and he winked at me before striding off.
Jonathan just glared at him as he went, and he muttered something in Romanian under his breath.
I whipped my head back to look at him, "What was that?"
Jonathan was still glaring poisoned daggers at Owen, but he shook his head, "Nothing, darling, nothing at all. Who is that… delightful fellow?" he asked, sarcasm dripping from every word.
I groaned and pulled my shoulders in, "My ex-boyfriend…"
Jonathan tore his eyes away from Owen and looked down at me, "Dark secrets haunt us all… I shan't ask any questions, then."
I rolled my eyes at him, "Whatever, like you don't have any questionable exes."
He glanced back at Owen, "I really don't… Certainly none as greasy as that," he shuddered.

"What did he give you?" I asked Jonathan later between mouthfuls of fries.
"A business card. For his place of employment, I presume," Jonathan replied, showing me the wrinkled card.
I groaned, "A car dealership? What an idiot."
Jonathan shrugged, examining the card, "He seems to have a steady job. And at least he doesn't wear combat boots all the time..."

That was when I noticed the sullen look on his face, "Wait… Are you… Babe are you jealous?"
Jonathan peered at me over the brim of his soda glass, and for a fraction of a second, a lightning bolt of blue blitzed through his black eyes, "Should I be?"
My eyes widened and my jaw dropped and I shook my head in vehement denial, "No, of course not. Jonathan, I'm yours."
He just sat there, looking at me, not saying anything.
"Babe, come on?"
He tilted his head sideways, still not speaking to me, and I pouted, "Why are you looking at me like that?"

Jonathan blinked slowly, and as he did, the strange expression on his face was replaced by a smile that didn't quite reach his eyes, "If that greaseball touches you again, I will separate his head from his body."
I knew he was capable of it; I'd seen him do it. But this was completely unnecessary, "I don't understand why you're jealous. You have absolutely no reason to be. Have you seen yourself?"
His eyebrow twitched, "What does that mean?"
I gestured at him with open hands, "It means look at you, you're amazing. And you're gorgeous. And you make me happier than I ever thought it possible to be. I wouldn't touch another guy with someone else's 10-foot pole."
That did it. Jonathan threw his head back and laughed out loud. Seeing him belly-laugh, I figured he was pulling some kind of weird prank on me. But even though he was making it off as a joke, at the deepest corners of the back of my mind, I knew he meant every word.

Chapter 13

Christina

"How was your date with Jonathan?" My mom wanted to know the following afternoon. We were spending the day together, repainting the living room.

I shrugged noncommittally, but I smiled, "It was pretty fun. He's adorable in a go-kart."

My mom chuckled, "How did he make those long legs fit?"

I bent my arms and lifted my elbows up next to my ears, "Like this!" and my mom doubled over in laughter.

"It feels like I've known him forever," I said, dipping the paint roller into the tray, "and we haven't even been together for that long."

"Finding a kindred spirit, that feeling of your own heart beating inside the chest of the person you love, is a rare and beautiful thing," my mom smiled.

How is she always so right about nearly everything?

My mom probably saw the Major Cheeseball grin on my face, because she leaned closer and nudged me with her elbow.

"Oh, you'll never guess who we ran into?" I changed the subject.

"Uhm… Santa?" she guessed.

"Nope."

"The Boogeyman?"

I laughed, "Oh, so close. We ran into The Scourge."

My mom cringed, "Oh shit, Owen was there? Who let him out of his cage?"

"I have no idea, but he was there."

My mom poured some more paint into the tray, "So Jonathan met him?"

I nodded slowly, “Yes…”
She turned her head to look at me, “I’m guessing Owen was his usual embarrassing self?”
I pursed my lips, “He tried to sell Jonathan a car.”
My mom’s expression was blank for a second before she burst out laughing.
“That is absolutely mortifying,” she said when she managed to stop laughing.
I wiped my forehead with the back of my hand, “I would love to be a fly on the wall if Jonathan ever actually goes to whatever dealership Owen works at.”
My mom chuckled, “Do you think he would?”
I shrugged, “Who knows…? For some reason, though, I got the vibe that Jonathan was jealous.” My mom gave me a blank look, “Because…?”
“Your guess is as good as mine. I mean, Jonathan is just… better. No matter how you compare them, Owen could never measure up. He comes up short. In every way.”
She shot me a knowing look, “Really? Does he now? He comes up short?” *I obviously got my dirty mind from her.* I giggled, “Yes. By at least 3 or 4 inches.”
Paint splattered everywhere as my mom laughed so hard that she dropped her paintbrush right back into the bucket.

Later that night, when the living room was all painted, as I was stretched out on my bed, reading a book that Niki loaned me, I got a text from Jonathan:
Darling, could we meet tomorrow?

I did a quick mental walk-through of my schedule for the next day before I replied:
Sure babe.
I finish work at 3, we can meet after.
Is that okay?

No reply.
I was just about to get annoyed with him for forgetting about his phone again when he called,

"I am so sorry, love," he said as I picked up, "I was typing up a response when the manager of the Czech property called. No concept of business hours, that one."
I chuckled, "That's okay, babe."
He sighed in relief, "Oh, good. So, about tomorrow, will your mother be at home?"
I shook my head, "No, she'll be at school until late. Why?"
But he wouldn't say. He only said that he would tell me the next day. *Fine, whatever made his weird little heart happy.* I turned my attention back to the book that I was reading.

I wasn't usually into fantasy. Magical realms and Faeries weren't my genre of choice, but this one came highly recommended by Niki. The world-building was very impressive and it was a little bit spicy, and I was rather enjoying it. I did wish it was shorter and maybe a bit more spicy, though.

Sure enough, when I came home from work the next day, it wasn't long before Jonathan pulled into the driveway. I frowned when I saw that he brought his laptop with him. *Now I'm even more curious, What does he want to talk to me about that he needs his computer for?*
"I can see that you're curious," he said when he came into the kitchen. He started explaining as he set up his computer and we sat down at the kitchen table. "A while ago you asked me to help you."
I nodded slowly. I was still uncomfortable with the idea of him helping, but I decided to just let it happen. Maybe my mom was right, maybe it was time to swallow my pride and accept help when I need it.
He smiled, and held out his palms to me, "Tell me how."
"Oh…" he breathed in surprise when I jumped up from my chair and flung myself into his arms, "Thank you," I murmured into his neck, "Thank you."
He stroked my back as he held me, "Anything for you, my love. Anything, everything."
I kissed his cheek before I took a deep breath and sat back down, "Okay, the first thing I need help with, is getting rid of my car."
He had started typing something on his computer, but he stopped typing and looked at me with an amused look on his face, "Are you finally ready to admit that your car is a deathtrap?"

I chuckled, “Oh, trust me, babe, I’ve always known that. It was a piece of shit when I bought it.”
He smiled at me and shook his head, then he continued typing, “Alright,” he said, “finding a buyer should be easy. What would you like to do with the money?”
I thought for a moment, but I shrugged. I wasn’t grown-up enough to know the smart answer to that question, “I don’t know. Maybe a down-payment on a new car? Well, not new, but newer than this one.”
Jonathan tilted his head sideways for a moment, “That could certainly work. Or I could help you invest it?”
“Oh, yes please. That sounds very adult and responsible, I want to do that.”
Smiling, he nodded, “I shall get right on that.”
He clicked the computer trackpad a few times before he spoke again, “Next order of business…”
“Ooh,” I interrupted him, “Business? Are we having a meeting?”
He nodded slowly, “Yes, I’m here in my official capacity as boyfriend-slash-portfolio manager.”
I laughed.

“On to business then.” He went on, “If you do enter the PhD program, who would be financing your studies?”
“I took out a loan to pay for my undergrad studies,” I replied, “And I still owe a whole bunch on that. But, honestly, I’m not sure if I’m going to continue my studies right now. I might take a break and study again later. But I’ll let you know when I’ve made up my mind.”
He nodded understandingly, “That makes sense, love. You’ve worked very hard, you deserve a break.”
I wrinkled my nose at him and blew him a kiss.

Then he typed something on the computer, and looked back at me, “What is next? What needs to be paid?”
I stood up from the table and got a stack of documents from one of the drawers behind me and handed everything to him, “Here you go. This is all of our debt.”
A few silent minutes went by as Jonathan looked over all the statements that I handed him. Then he set them down on the table, “Is your student loan document also in here?”

I flipped through the stack of papers until I found the right one and showed it to him, "It's this one."
Jonathan nodded again, and without saying anything further, he turned to the computer and started clicking and typing away.
I let him work in silence for a few moments before my curiosity kicked my ass, "Babe… now what?"
He glanced over at me and smiled, folding his hands in front of him on the table, "Now, my love," he said, "I need to ask your permission for something."
I raised my eyebrows at him, "Go on?"
He picked up all of the statements, then looked at his computer and then back at me, "I would like to pay all of these accounts on your behalf."
My jaw dropped, "Even my student loan?"
He nodded his head once, "Even your student loan."
"The whole thing?"
Jonathan nodded again, "The whole thing."
"Holy fuck, how rich are you?"
"I'm very comfortable," he replied, smiling my favorite smile at me, "However, before I pay anything, I need your permission to do so. I really want to help, but I don't want to overstep."
A tear rolled down my cheek, and Jonathan reached over and wiped it away, "Is that a yes?"
I only nodded because my words didn't want to come out past the giant lump in my throat.
He stroked my cheek with his thumb before he turned back to his computer.

I just sat there, watching in awe as Jonathan paid off all of mine and my mom's debt, one bill after another. As he was making the payments, my eyes jumped to the available balance in his banking account and my eyebrows shot up almost to my hairline. Never, ever in my life had I seen that many numbers next to each other before a comma.
"Babe…" I asked.
"Hmm?" he murmured back, his eyes not leaving the screen.
I went on, "I'm sorry, I didn't mean to look, but shit that's a lot of money."
He pointed at the balance on the screen, "You mean this?"

I nodded, “When you said you were comfortable, you were not kidding.”
He shrugged nonchalantly, “You don’t need to fret about my financial status, darling. I have enough money, this is just what I managed to liquidate at short notice.”
I had no response to that.

A little while later he spoke again, “All done.”
My heart was so full, I was sure it was going to explode in my chest. I got up from my chair and went to stand right next to him, “Why are you doing this?” my teary voice squeaked.
He pulled me against him, and I rested my cheek against his head. “Because, my darling Christina, I love you,” he explained.
I wrapped my arms around him and pulled him into the tightest hug I could manage, “I love you. I love you so fucking much. Thank you for this. It’s my mom’s birthday on Saturday, and I’ve been wondering what to get her. This means more to me than you’ll ever know.”
Jonathan’s arms went around me, “I told you before, love, I’d move Heaven and Earth for you, all you have to do is ask.”
I pulled back to look him in the eye, “How am I ever going to repay you for this?”
He smiled, “Love me,” he said and I planted a kiss on the top of his head, “Too easy.”

Chapter 14

Alastair

When Celeste was very young, long before her body had reached maturity and she stopped aging, her entire family was slaughtered one night. She was the sole survivor, having escaped that horrible night with nothing more than the clothes on her back. Someone had saved her from the massacre and taken her away, where a friend of her father later found her and took her in. They settled in Florence, which was where she and I met. And every so often, when the anniversary of that awful night came around, she withdrew herself from the people around her and turned her thoughts inward. Now it was happening again. And every time I had to watch the love of my eternal life relive the pain of that night, my heart ached with her.

I took a seat next to her where she sat on a bench on the terrace outside our bedroom.
I didn't need to say anything, she could hear my thoughts, my concern for her, and she leaned against me, her head on my shoulder, "Forgive me, my love," she said softly, "I don't mean to make you worry."
I kissed her hair, "Nothing to be forgiven, my sweet."
She took a deep breath, "I miss them so."
"I know, love, I know."
She got to her feet and raked her fingers through her hair. I knew the gesture, knew that it meant she felt uneasy.
Staring out at the gardens, Celeste sighed, "I feel guilty. I should have done more…"
"*Mi stellina*," I tried to reassure her, "you were a child. What could you have done?"

She had a pensive look on her face, "I don't know… maybe I could have tried harder to find my little brother. He was just a baby, I…"
I went to stand behind my wife, hugging her to me, "You did your best, love. You searched for him, but you couldn't find him."
She released a shuddering breath, "I wish I could have at least buried them. They deserved that."
I kissed her cheek.
She turned her head and looked at me over her shoulder, "Will you say nothing?"

I looked at my wife, my beautiful queen. Even though a life of hardship and struggle has aged her, to my eyes she was even more beautiful now than the day I first laid eyes on her.
Seeing the light reflecting in her stunning gray eyes, I thought back to how hard it had been for us at first.

Afraid that whoever killed her family would find out that she survived and would be coming for her, we left Florence shortly after we were married. We packed up what little belongings we had and made our way to the Carpathian mountains.
The man she knew as her uncle had raised her in simplicity, and she did not have much. Coming from a small English village, neither did I. But I had friends, good friends, that were willing to help us get on our feet. Kind, honest folk that gave us shelter and food.
I worked the quarry, Celeste worked in the fields. We grew some crops to sell, and some to live on. The life we lived was hard, and very simple, but free. And all our own.

For as long as I lived, I would never forget the joyous day that my beautiful bride told me that she was carrying my child, and I vowed to always work as hard as I could to give her and our unborn child the best that I could.
When our child was born near the end of Autumn, a son, we named our beautiful baby boy Jonathan Ambrose, after Celeste's late father, Ionáthan, and her grandfather on her father's side, Ambrogio.
She promised herself many years ago, if she ever had children, she would teach them all the languages she knew.
And that was exactly what she did. Jonathan went to school in the little village near our cabin, where he learned to read and write.

At home, his mother instructed him in all the languages she knew until he could speak each one as fluently as his native language, just as Uncle had done for her, and I taught him hand-to-hand combat, swordsmanship and horsemanship, and we lived hand to mouth.

Then one day, when Jonathan was about 12 years old, a wagon loaded with trunks and wooden chests arrived at the cabin. The driver handed Celeste a rolled-up piece of parchment as servants offloaded the trunks, and she was shocked to learn that the man she called Uncle, her father's friend that had saved her, had gone missing one day, and never returned home, and that she was his only beneficiary.

We had never seen such riches. Gold, silver and gems to make your head spin. One trunk was filled with title deeds, for houses and mansions in countries that we had only ever dreamed of seeing. Finally, we were able to move into a warmer, safer house, to give our son the education that we had wanted to give him right from the start. So, we sent Jonathan to the best private schools, and hired the best tutors, and Celeste taught him the finer aspects of polite society and politics just as Uncle had taught her when she was young.
We did everything in our power so that Jonathan would one day be ready to take his place as the Undeniable, the Undisputed Son of Delphi.
For that was who he was, who he was born to be: the Sole Heir to the Genitori bloodline.

I took my wife's face in my hand, my eyes locked with hers.
Even now, so many years later, her beautiful eyes still bore the pain from the day her family was taken from this world, and all I wanted was to take the painful memories away from her, “I pray for the day that you will be able to forgive yourself for being the only survivor. That you may someday celebrate the miracle of your existence.”
Celeste closed her eyes and leaned her face into my hand, “Your prayers carry me, my darling.”

After a few moments of silence, she took a deep breath and forced a smile onto her face, “I think that’s enough moping for one day. Let’s spread some happiness, shall we?”

I mirrored her smile, “That’s my girl. What did you have in mind, beautiful?”
She went back into our bedroom to retrieve her phone from the bedside table, “Jonathan mentioned that tomorrow is Belinda’s birthday. So, I thought we could take her to dinner.”
I grinned, “Marvelous idea! Let me know where, and I shall make a reservation.”

Chapter 15

Christina

While my mom was still asleep that Saturday morning, I got her present ready. Jonathan had printed out all the statements of the accounts that he paid off, and I folded them and put them in a really pretty envelope that Niki handmade, along with the bottle of perfume that I got my mom. It was her favorite perfume, but she never bought it for herself. She always said that she would get it the next time we went shopping. She never did, though, and I knew it was because she felt like she couldn't afford it. So I used my bonus to get her a nice big bottle of it for her birthday.

I put the perfume and the envelope on the tray next to my mom's breakfast of cinnamon French toast, crispy bacon and a cup of freshly brewed coffee, and a cupcake with a candle in it.
Tray in hand, I went to my mom's room to wake her up, singing her the birthday song as I walked through the door.
She took a sip of coffee first, and then opened the perfume.
"Ooh, I'm going to smell so fancy," she commented, clutching the bottle to her chest. Then she picked up the envelope.
"Sweetie pie, what is this?" she wanted to know.
I grinned from ear to ear, "I'm not saying a word. Open it."
She looked like a kid at Christmas as she carefully opened the envelope and took out the papers inside it. When she saw what was on them, her jaw dropped and her hands started trembling, "How…?" she croaked, tears streaming down her face.
I pulled her into a hug, "Jonathan and I wanted to wish you a happy birthday."
"Jonathan did this?" she asked.

I nodded, and tears filled my own eyes to see the surprise and delight on my mom's face, "Oh, honey, why?"
I waved a dismissive hand, "Meh. Why not?"
My mom shook her head, closing the envelope again and holding it out to me, "No, Chrissy, I can't… I can't accept this."
I felt myself frown at her, "Why not, Mom?"
She wiped tears from her cheeks, "What do mean why not? This is too much, it's thousands of dollars… I can't… How am I ever going to repay him?"
I closed my hands over my mom's and gently pushed the envelope back to her, "That's the point, Mom, you don't have to."
"Chrissie-bear…" she tried to protest one more time but I wasn't having it, "Remember what you said: Only the strong ask for help when they need it."
"But… I didn't ask for this…" Miss Belinda clearly wasn't ready to give up.
So I hugged my mom one more time, "Doesn't mean you didn't need it."

My mom and I spent the rest of her birthday together.
We went to our favorite café for a cup of coffee, my treat. My mom was reluctant at first, but she finally let me buy her the slice of expensive artisan cake that she'd been eyeing for ages – carrot cake with cream cheese buttercream frosting and caramel rum sauce.
After leaving the café, we stopped by the bookstore and picked up a few books that we had both been wanting, and then we headed home to shower and get ready before Simon picked us up for dinner.

That night, at the dinner that Celeste and Alastair planned for my mom, we were all sitting on cushions on the floor in an Indian restaurant, the table practically groaning under the weight of all the food. Belinda and Celeste were laughing and talking, reminiscing about their childhoods.
I was grinning at the fact that the entire Langdon clan, in all of their European elegance, had their shoes off and they were all sitting on the floor, Alastair included.

And it was really cute how Celeste was telling my mom the mortal-friendly version of her childhood, though I knew she was deliberately being vague about the finer details.
Honestly, the truth would probably blow Belinda's mind.

Seeing my mom so carefree and relaxed made me really happy, and when we arrived back home late that night, she was still smiling from ear to ear. Jonathan insisted on driving us home himself and he walked with us right into the living room.
"Happy birthday, Belinda," he smiled at her. That big smile not leaving her face, my mom wrapped her arms around him and hugged him.
"Thank you," she said, "thank you so much. For everything. And please thank your parents for me one more time, this was so nice of them."
I was feeling left out, so I inserted myself into the hug. "You are most welcome," I heard my boyfriend say.

A while later, after Jonathan had gone home, my mom and I were sitting in our pajamas, sipping some tea. Normally we'd watch a chick-flick or something, but my mom looked so peaceful that I didn't even want to suggest it.
"Penny for your thoughts?" I asked softly. My mom slowly looked up at me from her tea, "I was just thinking. I'm glad you met Jonathan. He's a good man, and I want that for you. You deserve that.
That he definitely was. I smiled back at her, "How about you, Mom? Have you ever thought of getting back out there, maybe start dating again?"
She shrugged, "I don't know… Maybe… if I met someone worthwhile, I might consider it."
"Really?"
"I think so," my mom nodded and I cocked an eyebrow. *I've picked up so many expressions from Jonathan.* "What's your type?"
My mom grinned, "Filthy rich businessmen with giant… yachts… Does Alastair have any single friends?"
I laughed inwardly. *Uhm... yeah. Magnus, the Danish vampire.* But I just smiled at my mom. I knew she was kidding, she cared as little about money as I did, "I will let you know the moment I hear of one passing through town."

Chapter 16

Jonathan

I was watching Christina where she was sitting at her desk, scribbling something in her notebook.
I loved taking her out or going to new and exciting places together, but I was more than happy just being near her, either of us or both of us working on something. I particularly liked when she had work to do, because then I could just sit and watch her.
She was adorable when she was focused on something, and I hated interrupting her, but there was something that I'd been wanting to speak with her about.
"Darling, may I ask you something?" I said from where I was relaxing on her bed.
"Mm-hmm," she confirmed, not looking up from her work.
"Well," I went on, propping myself up on my elbow, "I was curious about your father…"

Silence descended upon us.

Christina stopped writing and looked up at me from the corner of her eye, and I once again felt like the world's biggest arsehole, "Should I not have asked?"
She turned to me with a pained smile on her face. I loved her smiles, but I wasn't too keen on this one. "It's okay," she said, "it's just… I don't really know what to tell you."
I tilted my head sideways, "What do you mean, love?"
She slowly got to her feet and retrieved a box from the bottom of her closet, setting it down on the bed in front of me.

She placed her palms on top of the box, “My parents got divorced before I was born, and my mom never told my dad about me, so I never met him. This is all I know about him.”
“Why is that, if I may ask?” I wanted to know as she opened the box and began taking out all of its contents and spreading it out on the bed.
“Long story… My mom thought that my dad was crazy because he believed that vampires were real…” Christina said. She gave me a pointed look, and I half-smiled at her. *Well...*
She handed me a newspaper clipping, “My mom said the main reason she left him was because my dad joined some cult called the ‘House of Apollo’ and…”
Shit.
Niki mentioned that Christina knew the name, but I had no idea that her father was connected to the House...? Have I met him? Fuck... I haven’t taken the lives of any mortals since I met her, but perhaps in the past.... Have I killed my girlfriend’s father? I felt my face turn ashen and she stopped talking mid-sentence, “Babe…?” she asked, concerned, “what’s wrong?”

I sat up on her bed and put my feet on the floor, staring at the clipping in my hand. It was time to come clean, and I took a few deep breaths before I responded.
“I know who they are.”
Her eyes widened, “What…?”
I put down the clipping and picked up a printed article, and she grabbed my forearm, “Jonathan, what do you mean you know who they are?”
I put my hand over hers, “Do you remember when you asked me about the bad guys?”
“Yes…?” she confirmed cautiously.
I gestured toward the papers on the bed, before I stood up and slowly strode over to the window, “It’s them. The House of Apollo. They’re the bad guys.”
“But…” she stammered, “I… mentioned it to Niki, and she didn’t tell me anything.”
I nodded, “I know. She told me that you had brought it up and she didn’t know what to say. We never meant to hide anything from you, we just…”
She smirked, “Are so used to keeping secrets you can’t help yourself?”

Harsh. But true. I dropped my head, “Something like that.”
I turned away from the window to face her and she gave me a sharp look, “Well, it’s now or never.”
I met her gaze, “The House of Apollo has hated my kind ever since the first of us came into existence. They believe us to be an abomination, a mockery of the power of Apollo, and they have been trying to exterminate us for centuries. The vampire hunter I told you about was one of theirs.”
She shifted uncomfortably, “Why didn’t you tell me?”
I rolled my neck, “Because I hoped that it would never come up, that they would never become an issue, and that I would always be able to keep you safe from this.”
She just looked at me. She was angry. I could tell from the way her breathing seemed to tremble, and how she kept folding and refolding her arms.
“I hate being excluded,” she said in a low voice.
I nodded, “I know.”
“Please,” she said, her voice still low, “stop keeping secrets from me. I don’t like it, I don’t deserve it… It hurts.”
I dropped to my knees and put my fist on my heart, “I am so sorry.”
She nibbled the inside of her lower lip before she spoke, “I mean it, Jonathan,” she said, “I can’t do this. I can’t do the secrets. Past experiences and… I just can’t.”
“I understand….”
She raised her eyebrows at me, “Do you? Really?”
I nodded. I did. Her hazel eyes on fire told me exactly how serious she was.
“Forgive me…” I requested, my voice equally low.
She raked a hand through her hair, “Okay, but… you need to start unpacking that vault of secrets in your head, because…”
She didn’t need to finish her sentence, I knew what she meant: Transparency was non-negotiable.
I nodded, “Whatever you ask me, I swear I will answer in honesty.”
Christina let out a sigh, “I wish you could just start at A and tell me everything there is to know all the way down to Z, but…”
I pursed my lips, “That’s over 800 years of A to Z, love…”
She ruffled her hair, “I know, I know… Okay then. Just… let’s start here. What else do I need to know about the House of Apollo?”

I got back to my feet and sat back down on the bed in front of her, "I have to tell you something…"
"Okay…" she said softly.
I put a hand on her knee, "The guy that drugged you at the club that night… He was a member of the House."
Her eyes widened, "How do you know?"
I rolled my neck again, "The tattoo on his hand, the lyre, that's the mark of Apollo."
She was quiet for a moment before she looked up at me with a questioning look on her face, "Why did he drug me? What did he want with me?"
I took both her hands in mine, "I'm not sure I should tell you that, darling."
She yanked her hands away with a force I didnt expect, "Fucking stop! No more secrets! I am not a child!"
My eyebrows shot up, "I am trying to protect you."
"I don't need protection, I need the truth!" she snapped.
I turned my head and looked out the window, "Darling… I don't know if you're ready to hear this…"
"It is not your place to decide what I'm ready for!" she countered. I recoiled a bit, but she was right; I promised to tell her as much as I could.
"You said you're an open book," she demanded then, "tell me the truth, Jonathan."
Fine.
I whipped my head back to her, letting my eyes go cobalt, "You want the truth? Alright then. Here it is: They sent that man into the club to find female test subjects to test a serum that was designed to turn mortals into vampires. That's what they've been busy with. They needed more human test subjects, and they were going to experiment on you. If it hadn't been for Devyn… The House of Apollo would have turned you into a fucking nascent, and I would have had no choice but to kill you."
I hated the sound of the truth in my own ears, and without waiting for her to respond, I stood up and strode out of her room.

Christina

My entire body was trembling. *I could have been a nascent... I could have been dead...*

It took me a few moments to recollect myself, but the sound of the front door closing snapped me back to reality. As fast as I could, I hurried out of my room, down the hall and out the door. I had to stop Jonathan before he left.

But I found him standing outside, next to the front door. He was leaning back against the wall, staring blankly at the sky.

"Going somewhere?" I asked him.

He turned his head to look at me, and he shook his head, "I just… needed a moment."

I went to stand next to him and for just a moment, I let the silence tumble over us. Then I took his hand, "So you know about the House of Apollo?"

He nodded, "I do."

"And they're not just a bunch of loonies, they're actually dangerous?"

He rolled his neck, "They are delusional, but they're also dangerous."

"Do you… Have you ever met my dad?" I asked.

"What is your father's name?" he wanted to know, intertwining his fingers with mine.

I looked down at his hand, "Anthony Sutton."

Jonathan looked back up at the sky for a few moments, and he shook his head, "I don't believe I have come across his name, love. But if I do, you will be the first to know."

"Christina…" my name was a litany across his lips, "Forgive me, please?"

"For what, exactly?" I wanted to know; I needed him to be clear. He stroked my hand with his thumb, "For not telling you sooner. I love you, and I want you to know everything, but there is so much to tell, I…"

"You don't know where to start?" I tried, and he nodded.

I lifted his hand and brought the back of it to my lips. He wanted me to know. That was enough for me, and I tugged on his hand to go back insidc.

Back in my room, I sat down next to him on my bed.
"I never told you this," he started to say, "Not too long ago, my father mentioned possibly leaving the city."
My jaw dropped, "Are you serious?"
He cleared his throat slightly, nodding slowly, "My parents got it into their heads that it would be better if our family left town. The House would follow us, and you and the rest of the town would be safe."
"What about me?" I asked, "Would you have just left me here, with nothing but my memories?"
He half-smiled at me, "You wouldn't have had any…"
"Oh…" I understood what he meant. His mom was a telepath, after all…
Then he chuckled, "We got into quite the argument about it, actually."
I pressed my shoulder to his, "Did you win?"
He gave me a sideways glance, "Of course I won. I always win."
After a few moments of silence, I stood up and walked over to look at a picture of me and my mom. The photo was taken on my 15th birthday, and I had such fond memories of the day. We went to the theme park, and we ate way too much, and we rode roller coasters until we both threw up. It was one of my favorite birthdays ever.

I turned to Jonathan, "What was it like growing up with your family?"
He peered up at me from underneath his eyebrows, "We have our ups and downs, and we argue, just like any other family, I suppose."
I sat back down next to him, "Right, but surely your life growing up was a lot different from mine? What with all the money and the luxury and stuff."
He frowned, "You seem to be under the impression that I was born into riches…"
"Well… yeah. Weren't you?"
He glanced down at the floor and he had a bit of a sheepish smile on his face, "No... I grew up poor, actually. Until I was about 12 or 13 my parents and I lived in a ramshackle little cabin in the woods outside of Brasov."
I had no idea that my jaw could drop that far, "Are you serious?"
He nodded, "I was born into simplicity, and my parents worked very hard to keep us alive. They continue to work hard, to this day. The money, the houses… That came later.."

"Huh…" I huffed, "Then I owe you an apology, babe."
Jonathan frowned, "Whatever for?"
I wrinkled my nose, "For some reason, I thought you were… privileged… that you grew up with a silver spoon in your mouth."
He shook his head, "Decidedly not, darling. It was definitely a wooden spoon."
"I had completely the wrong impression of you. I'm sorry…" I apologized. *I feel like such an ass, I completely misjudged him.*
Jonathan shrugged his shoulders in a dismissive gesture, "It's alright, love."
"Now I get it, why you want to help me…"
Jonathan put his hand on my thigh and pulled me closer to him, "Because I remember what it was like having nothing."

Chapter 17

I felt like I could scream.
I did it.
Becky Morgan, a lowly lab-tech.
I single-handedly extracted the DNA from the really old bones that Dr. Brennan gave me, and I combined it with the DNA we had extracted from the previous sample.
And it was perfect. Absolutely perfect.
I was sure the doctor would be overjoyed. Maybe the priest himself would come to congratulate me. Maybe I would get a festival in my honor? Ever since the first one I was invited to, I just thought that festivals were the coolest thing ever, with the music and the dancing and the wine… And I always secretly hoped that someday I would do something amazing enough with my life to have one in my honor. Maybc this was it, maybc this would bc my momcnt.
Practically jumping from excitement, I printed off the results and scuttled off to find the doctor.
I finally found him, smoking in the break room.
"Dr. Brennan!" I shrieked, "Dr. Brennan! I did it! We did it! It worked!"
A happy smile on his face, Dr. Brennan stood up from the bench he had been sitting on and took the test result from me, "Becky, you're a marvel!"
I beamed, "The two sets of DNA combined perfectly! The serum responded perfectly to all of the tests, and it's stable! We finally did it!"

Dr. Brennan smiled happily at me, his hand on my shoulder… before he whipped his other hand from his pocket and slammed the switchblade in under my chin.
Blood welled up in my throat; I gargled.
"Great job, Becky," Brennan said to me, "I'll be sure to jot your initials on a report… somewhere… maybe."
And he laughed.

Dr. Kole Brennan

I wiped Becky's blood from my hand with her lab coat before I let her lifeless body drop to the floor, and I stepped right over it on my way out the door. The glory would be mine alone.

The first thing I had to do was to share the news with the priest.

I checked the calendar first. By now I knew better than to just barge into the office.

The priest didn't seem to be busy, so I knocked on the door and waited until I heard the priest beckon me to enter before I turned the handle and pushed open the door.

Aleixo was sitting on a stool by the window, a thick joint of marijuana between his teeth.

"Dr. Brennan," he said through his teeth, and held the joint out to me, "Care to join me on a journey of enlightenment?"

Grinning, I took the joint from him and took a deep drag.

When I handed it back, I also passed the test results to him, "Holiness, we really did it. Our serum is perfect."

Nikolaides threw his head back and cackled maniacally, victoriously, "You never cease to amaze me, Doctor."

I shrugged nonchalantly, "By the grace of our blessed lord Apollo, Holiness."

"Is our soldier ready?" Aleixo wanted to know.

I had to think for a moment, "I believe so, yes. I think we can start soon."

Aleixo looked at the clock, "I was going to suggest that we start immediately, but I see it's close to midnight. Very well then, Doctor. Let's start in the morning, then we can all be bright eyed and bushy tailed and ready for a new dawn."

"Holiness..." I responded hesitantly, "I don't know about tomorrow... we might need to wait a while longer..."

"Of course, Doctor," Aleixo replied, but he seemed too high to really care, "Genius takes time. Tell me when you are ready."

I grinned at him, "I will. Glory to Apollo!"

Smiling, Aleixo took another drag of the joint and responded as he blew out the musky-smelling smoke, "Glory to Apollo."

Chapter 18

I had always wanted to fall in love. I thought of my parents, how they had loved one another before sickness took them two winters ago, and I wanted what they had. But, now that I was all alone in the small village, I no longer believed it possible. Not when I had known everyone my own age since birth.
Until she came to the village: Valentina.
With her long black hair, fair skin, eyes the color of honey and the smile of an angel.

I was a boy of only 17, she was merely 16, but I knew: She was to be the one meant for me.
Words could not express the way she made my heart feel, this beautiful, wild young woman that, out of all the young men in the village, chose me, for some reason. She made my heart beat faster with every touch. I loved holding her, kissing her, my Valentina, with her hair the color of raven feathers, my perfect little lastochka, my little swallow.

She was the first girl I had ever lain with, both of us fumbling and unsure, nervous and inexperienced. But it felt so right. And from the first moment that I slipped inside her, and she wrapped her legs around me, I knew I was done for. She had me under her spell, and there was no way to escape. And I didn't want to; she made me feel so alive.

For a while, for the first time in my life, I no longer felt like life had no point. How could life be meaningless, when I could spend my days kissing her underneath the trees, and making love to her in the long grass?

How could I be miserable when she weaved me wreaths of flowers in summer, and warmed my bed in winter?

But our happiness was to be short-lived.
When her father and brothers learned that I had plucked her most precious flower, they tore her from my arms, ripped her from my heart, and took her away from the village.
I thought they were gone for good.
Until one night. Her brothers came back to my house, dragged me from my bed and into the winter woods.
They beat me within an inch of my life, and then they left me there, tied to a tree in the snow, in nothing but my sleep shirt.

At first I was so cold, my entire body trembled and my teeth chattered so loudly I could swear it echoed through the trees. I felt so confused, but then I smiled – I could see my Papa, hear my Mama calling to me. Papa made a fire… It was so warm. But the fire was getting too big, too hot. I wanted to take off my sleep shirt and to cool down, but I could not move.
And then the world went black around me.

When I woke up, I thought that I was in the afterlife. An angel with violet eyes was smiling at me. I was wrong, I was still on Earth, but I was safe. I was saved.

At the back of my mind, I could hear my *lastochka* calling to me and I knew: I was going to be alright. I clutched her ribbon that I kept in the hem of my sleep shirt, to my heart, and looked to the moon, praying that maybe, just maybe she was looking at the moon too, and that she would be safe.

No matter how many years had passed, there were moments when my thoughts still wandered to her. I wondered what happened to her, what kind of life she had lived after she was ripped from me so cruelly. Thinking of her beautiful face, I couldn't help but smile. Despite the heartbreak I had suffered when I lost her, I was grateful to have known her, to have loved her, and to have had her love when I needed it the most. But, as much as I missed her from time to time, I knew that life had to go on.

I knew I had to say goodbye to my Valentina. I tucked her ribbon away safely, but left her smile in my heart. And I made a vow, swore to the light of the Moon, that I would live, live as long as I could, and as hard as I could. For her. For my *lastochka*.

I smiled, remembering what my new friends had taught me: *Carpe noctem, Carpe veritatem*.

Now, many years later, my heart still smiled when I thought of my Valentina, but new hope had appeared on the horizon.

I had only met her once, and only briefly, but I couldn't seem to get her out of my head.

Just like Valentina had been, she was unlike anyone else I knew. She was so spirited, unstoppable in her energy, like a stream carving its way down a mountainside.

I had so wanted to speak with her, but the night we met she had left before I had been able to spend time at her side.

Smiling to myself at the memory of her beautiful eyes, her radiant smile, deep in my heart of hearts I allowed myself to hope that, by some miracle of Moonlight, she could shine some light into the cracks in my soul.

Chapter 19

Christina

I can't believe my colossally shitty luck. This happens every single time. Just when I think it's going to be a good day at work, someone always calls in sick.

This time it was Michael, the guy that played the role of the concierge, 'Billy'. The news came to me via Neil, the 'Crimson Count' and Michael's best friend, "Mike said he's really sorry, Chris," Neil explained, "He just got the news last night about his aunt passing, he left for Florida early this morning."

I forced a smile, "I get it, Neil, life happens. We just need someone to cover for him, that's all."

"Right…" Neil said pensively.

So we stood there by the reception desk, scratching our heads, staring at the roster, trying to find a way to make it work.

"Hey," he said a few moments later, "what about that guy that covered for me when I was sick that one time?"

I frowned. Somehow I couldn't picture Jonathan in the concierge outfit for Billy, "I don't know…"

"Do you have his number?" Neil urged, "I can be Billy, and then he can be the Count, if he wants."

I mulled the idea over in my head. *Jonathan has been really busy lately, and I'm not sure if he'd be available on such short notice. And even if he were available, I don't know if he'd be interested. That, and I hate asking for help.* But my options were limited, so I punched his number into my phone.

"Hello, love," he said as he picked up, and I could hear the smile on his face.

"Hi babe. Are you busy?"
"Never too busy for my girl. What can I do for you?" he wanted to know.
"Could you stop by my work and help me with something?"
"Of course," he confirmed. "How can I help?"
"How would you feel about being the Crimson Count one more time?" I tried, "I'm short-staffed. I'll pay you, obviously."
"Oh, darling, I would absolutely love to, no payment necessary," I heard him grin, "When do you need me to be there?"
"Yay, thank you. As soon as you can?"

Jonathan pulled up at the escape room about 15 minutes later, and I laughed when I saw that he was carrying clothes on a hanger.
"Did you actually bring your own clothes?" I asked, pointing at the hanger.
He looked at the shirt and pants on the hanger and grinned at me, "Yes, I had to. No offense to your costume director, but the fit was a bit… snug."
I nibbled my lower lip, "Well, I wasn't complaining…"
His eyebrow twitched, "Shall I wear it for you tonight then?"
The fire in his eyes ignited my blood, "So I can rip it off you? Yes, please?"
He winked at me, and put his arm around my waist to tug me closer and kiss me hello.

"Damn, Chris," Neil said as he walked in from the staff room, already dressed in the concierge costume, "I didn't know you snagged the Count?"
A friendly smile on his face, Jonathan extended a hand, "I'm Jonathan, nice to meet you."
"Back at you, man, I'm Neil. I never thanked you for standing in for me last time, by the way," Neil shook his hand, introducing himself.
Jonathan waved a hand in dismissal, "It was no problem. I trust you are in good health now?"
Neil grinned, "I'm great. Are you ready to scare the ever-loving fuck out of some folks today, Count?"
Jonathan glanced at the name-tag on Neil's costume and nodded eagerly, "I most certainly am, Billy."

I honestly didn't know who was having more fun. Was it Neil, axing the door? Was it Jonathan, scaring the living shit out of unsuspecting patrons? Or was it me, watching them on CCTV?

I had to admit, with his hair slicked back, his face pale from the stage makeup, his black eyes flashing blue every so often, and his-very real-fangs on display, Jonathan was absolutely terrifying. *And very fucking hot.*

I'd never paid much attention to how Neil did it, but Jonathan's favorite tactic was to wait in a dark corner of the basement until the patrons were close enough. Then he stepped into the candlelight and opened his mouth and snarled at them, baring his fangs, and letting the stage blood run out of his mouth, down his chin. And as the patrons' blood-curdling screams echoed through the corridors of the basement, he grabbed the nearest patron and slipped back into the darkness. And, every time patrons ran away from him, screaming, I could see him laughing to himself, clapping his hands together in excitement. He was the cutest terrifying vampire ever.

Chapter 20

Dr. Kole Brennan

I was feeling a tad anxious. I was well aware that the priest had wanted things to progress sooner, but sometimes science took longer than expected.

But today was the day. Everything was ready for the serum to be tested.

Staring at the vial in my hands, regret flit through me for a brief moment. *Maybe I should have let Becky live longer...* She had been a good lab-tech, and she was quite smart. Maybe if I had allowed her to get more involved sooner, we could have had results quicker. Maybe I should have kept her around until testing was finished so if shit went south, I could blame it on her.

If anything went wrong now… I didn't want to think of what would happen.

I thought about a conversation I had had with the priest's associate a week or so ago.

Apparently, the prince's mother wasn't the only survivor of the Adelphi family massacre. They had good reason to believe that there had been a brother, only a baby at the time, who might have survived the attack. Living DNA would have been ideal, and the information had me excited at first, but the associate informed me that they weren't sure if the baby brother was alive or if he had also died.

This serum was my only hope. I wrapped my fist around the vial, closed my eyes and said a silent prayer that this was going to work.

Hunter

I'd been a soldier since I was 18 years old, and I'd been preparing for this day for a very long time.
I put in hours of rigorous physical and mental training. I read enough lab results and autopsy reports to know that the next step in the process would not be easy, and also very painful. But I wasn't afraid of pain. I was ready to use my body as a weapon for the glory of the Sun God.
I never forgot the day I became an orphan. My mom died when I was about 7, and after that it was just me and my dad. Until the day I came home from school when I was 10 and found my dad dead. Sometimes when I closed my eyes, I could still see my dad's body on the kitchen floor in a pool of blood, his eyes lifeless and unblinking, his face frozen in fear and horror, bite marks on his neck. The cops called it a 'burglary gone wrong' even though nothing was stolen. The M.E. said that he didn't know what to make of the bites on my dad's neck. They found black hair at the scene, but it didn't match anything in any database, and I spent years looking for answers, but I found nothing but dead ends.

Until the sacred teachings of Apollo showed me the truth: Vampires were real. Vampires murdered my father. And then I saw the surveillance footage of the Black Prince, of his rich black hair and I knew that this had to be the asshole that killed my father.
And now I finally knew that the only way to avenge my father was to become the very thing that had taken my father's life. And I was ready. Ready to become Apollo's vampire.

First, I was taken to the holy room, for a ritual to bless my body, and to prepare my mind for the transformation.
Then they took me to the lab and strapped me down onto a bed, my head and limbs secured to the bed with reinforced steel.
The lab techs hooked me up to an ECG machine, and lined up the morphine.
"Are you ready, Hunter?" Dr. Brennan asked.
I nodded as much as I could with my head strapped down, "Yes, Doctor. Let's do this. For the glory of Apollo."

A lab tech pushed a leather strap into my mouth, "Bite down on this." Dr. Brennan smiled as he sank the needle into my arm, "Alright then, soldier, here we go. For the glory of Apollo."

From the moment that the serum entered my veins, it brought with it harrowing, agonizing pain.
I bit down hard on the strap between my teeth, the pain contorting my face and pinching tears from my eyes.
But I didn't make a sound.
Even as every vein, every nerve felt like it was being scalded by red-hot iron.
Even as every single bone in my body snapped and shattered. From the stapes in my middle ear, and every single bone all the way down my body, to the femurs in my thighs, to the phalanges in my toes.

I could feel the jagged edges of the 206 broken bones in my body stabbing at my flesh within me.
Then I felt every fracture healing.
Only to break again.
And heal.
And break.
And heal.
The pain lasted for what felt like hours before my mind finally gave in and I blacked out.

I didn't know how long I was unconscious for, but when I woke up, the lights were so, so bright. And I was so very thirsty.
"Water," I managed to croak.
I couldn't see the face of the person resting the tip of the straw against my lips, but a few gulps in, I realized… what I was drinking wasn't water… It was blood….
I initially had some serious misgivings about the whole blood-drinking thing. I mean, I was up for many things, but I wasn't sure that drinking human blood would ever be one of those things, the whole idea was disgusting.
But I was so wrong… It was the most delicious thing I had ever tasted. I didn't want to stop, and I just kept drinking until I heard a slurping sound from the empty container.

I looked up at the ceiling but I regretted it in the same second that I looked. The lights were too much, "Can someone get the lights, please? It's too bright in here."
I heard Dr. Brennan's voice yelling at me from somewhere nearby, "Hunter can you hear me?"
and I winced at the volume, "Why are you yelling?"
Everything was so noisy. I could just barely make out the doctor's voice over the cacophony of sound that invaded my brain. Whirring machinery, fans oscillating at high speed, loud voices, some kind of drum beat pounding at different speeds… *heartbeats*?
At the same volume, the doctor replied, "I'm not, your hearing is amplified. Try to focus only on my voice, try blocking out everything else."
The doctor continued talking, yammering about some shit that I didn't care about, but I tried to do what he suggested, and I tried to focus only on his voice.
It seemed to work a little bit. The doctor's voice became just a little bit clearer, and the volume of the background noises faded a bit.
"Excellent," Dr. Brennan said, "Are the lights still too bright, Hunter?"
I carefully opened one eye, but I immediately pinched it shut again.
Dr. Brennan chuckled, "I'll take that as a yes."
One by one he forced open my eyes and slipped something into each eye.
When he was done, he let go of my face. I blinked a few times, and when the world came into focus, the lights were softer, less garish.
"What did you put in my eyes, Doc?" I wanted to know.
Dr. Brennan squeezed my shoulder, "Contact lenses, boy. Is that better?" he wanted to know as he removed the strap from my head.
I nodded slowly, "Much better, thanks Doc."
"You're welcome, soldier," the doctor said as lab techs started undoing the straps around my wrists and ankles, "Let's get you to bed, you need to rest."
"Doc, I'm fine," I said as I stood up, but my knees buckled and betrayed me.
Dr. Brennan pulled my arm across his shoulder, and put his arm around my waist, "I can see that. Here we go, bed-time."
I decided not to argue. Doctor knows best.

Chapter 21

Jonathan

As predicted, I very easily found a buyer for Christina's old car. Part of it I invested on her behalf, and the rest I had other plans for. I really wanted to get her a new car as a graduation present. That's what I needed the money from the sale of her old car for: to buy a new car. I had an inkling my girl wouldn't be all too happy if I bought her a car with my own money. She knew well I had enough, and buying her a car wasn't going to put a dent in my bank, much less break it, but that was not the point. Her money needed to at least be part of the transaction, and whatever makes her happy, that was what I was going to do. I enlisted the help of Belinda and Devyn, and thanks to their intel, I knew exactly which cars she liked, and which color she'd prefer. Devyn was the one who had informed me that Christina's birthday was also coming up, only a few days after her graduation, in fact, and I was still planning what I wanted to get her for that. She'd been dropping hints that she wanted to know when my birthday was, but I'd been actively avoiding the question; I stopped celebrating my birthday hundreds of years ago.

I was absentmindedly clicking around on the computer when Fiona approached my desk and put something down on the corner of it, "Here you go, sire," she said, "this was in your pocket."
"Thank you, Fiona," I acknowledged, before I glanced down to see what it was, and I had a bitter taste in my mouth when I recognized it. The crumpled-up business card that Christina's oily ex-boyfriend gave me. I'd forgotten about it.
Twirling the card between my fingers, I felt my frown deepen.
Ex-boyfriend...

I didn't like the lecherous look on that grease monkey's face when he looked at Christina.
And the way that animal called her 'baby' was enough to make me completely forget all manner of decorum and scorch the slimy bastard's face off.
I sighed out loud and tossed the business card back onto the desk. I had no right to be jealous of anyone from Christina's past, I knew that. I myself wasn't innocent when we met. But I simply could not help it, I detested the idea of another man touching her.

"Is everything alright, sire?" Fiona asked me from where she was standing just behind me, dusting off the bookshelf.
I cleared my throat and tilted my head, "I don't know yet…"
"Well," she mused, "if you don't mind me asking, sire…?"
"Not at all, Fiona. Go ahead."
"This… person... This Mr. North... Is he somehow connected to Miss Christina?" she guessed.
I raised an eyebrow and looked at her over my shoulder, "How did you know?"
Fiona curtsied, "Call it an educated guess."
She continued, "You know… my mother, rest her soul, used to say, 'If something isn't yours, don't touch it'."

For a moment I thought back to the night at the go-kart track. I hated the horrible, cheap-looking suit that he was wearing, and when he started flirting with her, jealousy burned in my gut like a fire-breathing dragon. My girl could handle her own, but the fact that this arsehole had the audacity to flirt with my woman, and worse, to try and hug her, made me irrationally angry.
The man didn't look like much. He was fairly tall, but shorter than I was, fair skinned with an angular face and thick eyebrows. He had greasy, dirty-blonde hair, and he seemed rather… unremarkable. But he was flirting with my woman. And he asked her to meet him for coffee. I didn't care that she said no, I was pissed that he had the gall to ask her in the first place.
I got to my feet and grabbed my car keys. *Fiona is right. Christina is mine.*
And perhaps it was time for Owen to understand that.

I called to tell him I was on my way, so when I pulled up at the dealership, I was expecting Owen to be waiting for me outside, and I was rather disappointed when there was no-one.
Shaking my head, I walked into the dealership, where I found him sitting at a desk near the corner. When he saw me he stood up and came over, hand already extended, palm down. Slimy prick apparently thought himself superior and it took a great deal of self-control for me not to laugh out loud, but I shook his hand nonetheless. I grimaced internally. He had the soft, squishy hand of an office dweller that had never done any sort of physical labor a day in his life, and had quite clearly never held a sword.
"Johnny, my man," he said, way too jovially for my liking
"It's Jonathan." I corrected him.
Owen ignored the correction and started walking backward toward the cars, "What are you looking for?"
I glanced around, and I honestly saw nothing that I liked, but I had just arrived, so I might as well take a proper look, "How about you just… show me what you have? We'll take it from there."

Owen nodded, and took me on a tour of every single car on the showroom floor, but none grabbed my attention. Christina deserved better than any of the vehicles they had on the floor. When we reached the last car, Owen let it slip that the cars were pre-owned, and I stopped dead in my tracks. Clearly I hadn't been paying attention, or I would probably have seen it on the business card, or on the sign outside.
I slowly turned my head to look at Owen, "I beg your pardon? Did you just say pre-owned?"
Owen nodded, still smiling, "Yes, but they've all been taken good care of, and…"
I held up a hand, silencing him, "Stop."
He chuckled, "Most of them have had more than one owner, so I'm sure even you can afford it."
A treacle of annoyance rolled down the back of my neck, "Choose your next words very, very carefully."
Owen opened his mouth to reply, but his boss came scuttling out of the office and intervened, "Mr. Langdon, sir, good afternoon," the boss said to me, "Please, step into my office, if you don't mind."

Owen

I waited just outside the door while Jonathan spoke to my boss in the office. I had no idea what they were talking about, but after a few moments, they shook hands, and they both emerged from the office.

"Owen, please escort Mr. Langdon to his vehicle?" the boss said, then turned to Jonathan, "Mr. Langdon, thank you for your time."

He nodded but didn't say anything before he turned around and started leaving the dealership.

I frowned. I really didn't get why I had to escort this dude anywhere, but I didn't have much of a choice. The boss has spoken.

Once outside, I turned to Jonathan, "Did you come to an agreement with my boss?"

But he didn't answer. He just pulled a car key from his pocket, and the lights on a nearby Cadillac Escalade flickered.

Douchebag.

"Enjoy Christina while you can, I'm coming for her," I snapped.

He had started walking toward his car, but he stopped dead in his tracks and turned back, "See, I was going to be civil, but now, on second thought, I don't think I will," he bristled and his tone sounded threatening.

I cleared my throat, "Are you her new boyfriend?"

He glared menacingly at me but didn't respond.

I glared right back at him, "I knew her long before you even met her."

He raised an eyebrow, "And I suppose you think that gives you some sort of claim to her?"

A sneer started curling around my mouth, "We were in love."

His eyes burned into mine, "What was, and what is, are two vastly different concepts."

"Yeah well, Christina is…" I started saying, but he cut me short,

"Christina. Is. Mine," he snarled and he emphasized each word. *She was mine first.*

I smirked, "She tastes good, doesn't she?"

"If I were you, I would shut the fuck up," Jonathan snarled, but I was on a roll, "Tell me, when you fuck her, does she still…?"

I didn't get a chance to finish the thought before Jonathan clamped a hand around my throat, "Watch your mouth, before I rip out your tongue," he scowled, and I could almost see the evil intent dripping from every word.

But I was not going to let myself be intimidated, "It's called freedom of speech, guy."

Jonathan's face darkened, "Don't push me," his voice rumbled, deep, dark and menacing. He glared at me with eyes black as night, and his accent was from another realm…

"Oh, yeah? What're you going to do?"

"Why don't you fuck around and find out?" he snarled at me.

I grabbed his wrist and tried to push his hand away, but he didn't budge. *Fuck, he's pretty strong.*

"If you don't let me go, I'm calling the cops," I warned him.

"Go ahead," he smirked. "Let's see how free your speech is after I make you eat your own tongue."

"You don't sc…" my sentence ended in a wheeze as Jonathan tightened his grip even more, "If I so much as sense you near my wife, I swear, to Heaven, and the light of the Moon: You will not live to see another day."

His hand around my throat was so tight I started to choke, "Do I make myself clear?" he asked.

Without waiting for a response, Jonathan let go, got into his car and left, leaving me on the sidewalk, gasping for air.

Who does this motherfucker think he is?

I yanked off my tie and stomped into the boss' office.

"What just happened?" I asked, "Who the hell was that?"

My boss pulled a face at me, "You're such a fucking moron. You seriously don't know who he is?"

I shrugged, "Some asshole."

The boss chortled at me, 'Yeah, an incredibly rich asshole, that just bought the whole fucking dealership."

That night at home after I stopped by the gym, I chucked another empty beer can into the trash as I replayed the conversation with that guy Jonathan outside the dealership.

I still couldn't believe that the boss sold the whole dealership to him just like that. *How rich is he?*
Who the fuck was this guy anyway? He had an accent, so clearly he isn't a local. And he did say he wasn't from around here. Where was he from then? England? No... couldn't be. Definitely a foreigner, though, with that accent probably European or something.
He said Christina was his wife. Did she really get married? I don't remember hearing anything about it. But I guess it is possible, it's not like we have any mutual friends.

Jonathan.
Something about him seemed... Vicious... And when he told me to stay away from Christina, his voice was... heavy... dark... There was something about his eyes that was really unsettling... Those dead, black eyes... And when he sneered at me like that, there was a moment that I could have sworn he had fangs...? Come to think of it... It looked like... Did his eyes change color? There was a flash of a second where it looked like his eyes turned blue...
I shook my head, cracking open another beer. *Impossible. No way.*
I clenched my teeth. *I don't give a shit what that arrogant asshole said, I am not going to let some rich fucker intimidate me.*
I crushed the empty can in my hand. I should never have let Christina go in the first place, but I was going to fix it. *Married or not, I'm going to get her back, if it's the last thing I do.*

Chapter 22

Christina

Sitting at the dinner table at Jonathan's house, I got the vibe that something was bothering him. He was a lot quieter and more reserved than usual, and for whatever reason, he was barely talking to me. He was stand-offish, cold, like I did something wrong and he was mad at me. Sometimes Niki was right about her brother. He really could be very surly.

Normally, dinners at casa Langdon were fun and full of jokes and laughter. Celeste and Alastair and Niki had been their normal, friendly selves, but Jonathan… This was the first time that his attitude stunk and he was making me feel uncomfortable sitting next to him.

After dinner, his parents went to bed, and Niki mentioned that she was going out. They were all probably running away before they got frostbite from Jonathan's frigid attitude.

So, Jonathan and I were left alone in the kitchen, standing on either side of the table, a thick silence hovering between us.

I tried to ignore it, but it was driving me crazy. "What did you do today?" I asked him, trying to break the tension, to start some kind of conversation.

Staring blankly at the table, he shrugged, "Not much, just a bit of shopping. You?"

I shrugged as well, "Not much. I went to work, I went home, and then I came here."

"Hmm," he acknowledged my response.

Clearly this was not working, and I sighed, "Babe, what is going on?"

He slowly raised his head to look at me, "How long were you and Owen together?" he asked out of the blue.

There it is.

Unbelievable. He's jealous.
Jonathan Ambrose Langdon, my gorgeous, 6-ft-2, sex-on-legs, vampire boyfriend is actually jealous.
I groaned in exasperation, "Are you kidding me?"
"I asked you a question, Christina," he said.
I chuffed in disbelief, "I am so not doing this here. We can talk in your room."
"Fine," he conceded, and without so much as looking at me, he stormed right past me and strode to his room.
Okay, that hurt my feelings. He'd never reacted that way before, but I was going to let it go. At least until we were in his room and we locked the door behind us. I'd rather not have the entire house hearing us argue.

In his room, as soon as I locked the door behind me, he zipped up to me and got right in my face, "Answer me."
I pushed him away and I took a step back, "Don't do that!"
He raised his eyebrows, "Don't do what?"
"Don't zoom in on me like that."
"Then stop ignoring me," he hissed.
"I wasn't ignoring you, Jonathan. You fucking ambushed me in the kitchen. And then you stomped off like a petulant child."
He gestured to the room at large, "Well, we're not in the kitchen now. So? Tell me. How long?"
I groaned, "You are so fucking demanding sometimes!"
He pursed his lips, "Yes, I am. And I am still waiting."
"A few years. Why?"
"Because I am your boyfriend, I have the right to know," he snapped. Then he asked, "Did you love him?"
Shit. I did at the time, "I guess…"
I folded my arms across my chest, "Urgh, this is so unfair. You've been with other women…"
"But I wasn't in a relationship. With any of them. For any period of time," he countered.
"Oh," I challenged, "so you were just fucking them?"
"Exactly. Empty, meaningless fucking."

I kept my arms folded, "Is that supposed to make it better? You fucked hundreds of women before you met me, but at least you didn't have feelings for them?"
He shrugged, "It is the simple truth."
Then he dropped a heavy sigh before he finished the thought, "Christina, I have lain with many, but I've never loved anyone. Until I met you."

"So you really are jealous," I said, and he nodded, "I am."
"You have absolutely no right to be jealous or mad or anything even remotely like that! It doesn't matter who I hugged, dated, loved or fucked: You have had over 800 years of whoring around…"
"Oh, so that's what you think of me?" He fucking interrupted me. Again.
My anger flared some more, "Don't fucking interrupt me! And if you acted like one, what am I supposed to think?"
He clenched his jaw, and for a moment he looked… hurt... but I was not done, "When are you going to get it through your thick-ass skull that I am yours and you are all I want?"
He let out a sigh, "I hate the thought of someone else touching you."
I mirrored the look on his face, "Same. But facts are facts, and we can't change the past."

Without a further word, he leaned back against the wall and shoved his hands into his pockets, and then he just stood there, looking at me in silence.
My turn to sigh, "Now what? Why are you looking at me like that?"
He tilted his head the other way, scanning me up and down, "I'm just wondering. How hard do I have to fuck you to completely erase that… that miscreant from your memory?"
A very sudden and unexpected heat blossomed between my thighs. Jonathan noticed, and the corner of his mouth twitched ever so slightly.
"How many times do I need to make you scream my name, until you forget that you ever had feelings for any other man?" he asked.
"Uhm…" I stammered, "When did you want to …?"
"Right now," Jonathan interrupted me and a moan slipped past my lips.

Jonathan lifted his chin and sniffed the air. Then he looked questioningly at me, a wicked grin starting at the corners of his mouth, "Wet for me already?"
My lips parted and I almost moaned again, but I pressed my lips together and clasped a hand over my mouth.
He slowly started walking toward me, his body moving like a predator stalking its prey.
As he walked, he stripped off his shirt and dropped it to the floor, "How long were you together?"
"Three years…"
"Hmm," he said darkly, "Then I guess you would need to come for me at least three times. Although… six times would be better. Six is a nice, round number, I think."
Whoo boy. He's never used this tone of voice before… My body responded before my brain could and I pressed my knees together, "Jonathan…"
He took me by the wrists and pushed me up against the wall, pinning my hands above my head.
I looked up at him, and he clamped his hand around my chin and kissed me hard, his tongue sweeping into my mouth to claim mine. Then he pulled away.

His eyes locked with mine, he released my chin, and he ran his hand all the way down my body.
Over my breasts, over my stomach, down to the front of my jeans. He stuck his hand in between my thighs and moved it up, "Hmm," he mused, "so warm."
Then he moved his hands to the hem of my shirt and stripped it off, and my breath hitched in my throat.
Jonathan stuck his knee in between my thighs and lifted me up, both my breasts in his hands and I couldn't have stopped myself from moaning even if I tried. A gust of heat shot down in between my thighs and I needed some kind of friction. *Maybe if I grind my pussy against him...*
As he kissed me again, he undid my bra, swept it away and dropped it to the floor.
He moved his mouth down to suck each of my nipples into his mouth before he got down on his haunches to take off my shoes and peel off my jeans.

Then he carried me up the stairs and laid me down on his bed.
He took one of my nipples into his mouth again as he took off my panty.
When he released my nipple, he sank a finger deep inside me. Hard and fast.
"I went to see your ex today," he said.
"Wh… why?" I gasped.
"To tell him that you're mine," Jonathan explained.

I whimpered as he curled his finger inside me and slowly pulled his hand back, before he sank a second finger into me, "I also told him if he ever went near my wife again, I'd kill him."
I had never been as wet as I was at that exact moment, and I didn't mean to moan as loudly as I did, "You called me your wife?"
Jonathan's eyebrow twitched and he plunged his fingers into me one more time, "Yes. You are mine. You belong to me."

"Where are you going?" I complained when he suddenly pulled his hand back and stood up.
He undid his belt buckle and for a moment I thought he was going to tie me up…
But he dropped his belt and jeans to the floor and got a scarf from his closet, "I want to blindfold you, if you're up for it," he suggested as he held the scarf out to me.
I had never done that before, but I trusted him, so I nodded, and he leaned over me and used the scarf to blindfold me.
I bit my lower lip. The scarf was so soft, and it smelled like him. It was tied pretty tightly around my eyes and head, and I couldn't see anything.
So I just lay there on his bed, stark-ass naked, panting in anticipation.
What is this man planning?

Without warning, he gripped my thighs and I gasped. His touch was fervent… passionate… deliberate as he moved his hands higher, and I felt his breath on my skin followed by the tip of his tongue, running up my thigh.
His hand moved in between my thighs, his fingertips caressing my pussy, teasing me.
Then his hand moved higher, and I felt his breath on my stomach.

Then my chest.
On my breasts.
The warmth of his mouth closed around my nipple, and I felt his teeth clamp around it, and my body arched to meet him.
But he put his hands on my waist and pushed my body back down with way more zeal and much harder than the way he usually touched me.
The warm feeling between my thighs intensified, and I could almost hear my soul screaming 'Hallelujah!'. *If he would just put his fingers…*
Like he read my mind, he moved his mouth to my other nipple and slipped two fingers back into me. *Yes!*
He pulled his hand back and gripped me in his hand, "This pussy is mine," he said before his fingers slipped back into me. "All mine," his voice rumbled.
He kept sliding his hand in and out of me again and again, fucking me with his fingers, until an orgasm shook my whole body.
"Come for me, there's my good girl," he murmured against my skin, the desire in his voice stoking the blazing heat between my legs, "Don't stop, Christina. Come for me."
He pressed his body down on mine as my orgasm ended and my body slumped beneath him. He pinned my hands above my head again and kissed me, and I could feel his dick pressing between me. My lower body squirmed against him, wanting more.
"Jonathan," I panted as he moved his mouth from my lips to my earlobe, to my neck.
"Yes?" he murmured, and I could feel his fangs grazing my skin.
But I didn't know what more to say, and every breath I drew was a gasp.
I still couldn't see what he was doing, but his body weight lifted from me and the next thing I felt was his tongue at the top of my thighs and I cried out at the unexpected pleasure.
His hands gripped my thighs and spread my legs wider. I really wish I could see what he was doing. But I could only feel him.

His tongue swept hungrily over every inch of me, tasting, licking, sucking my clit into his mouth until my body bucked against his lips, my orgasm ripping uncontrollably through me.
"Fuck," I heard him say, "you taste like heaven when you come."
"Babe, I'm so wet, please…"

His hands wrapped around my middle and he yanked my body down toward the edge of the bed.
"Jonathan, please?" I begged, "Take this blindfold off? I want to see you."
Wordlessly, he leaned over me and slowly pulled the scarf away from my eyes.
I gasped when I saw him standing by the bed. Magnificently naked, gloriously hard, cobalt eyes and fangs bared, and I reached for him.
He smiled crookedly at me, "Are you ready for me?"
I nodded, "Yes, yes, yes."
He rested his palms on the bed, looking intently at me, but he didn't make any further moves towards me.
"Please?" I begged, "I need you inside me."
His tongue flicked over his lower lip and he shook his head, "Not yet."
"Why?" I pleaded.
He grinned, running his hands slowly up my thighs, "I want to taste your pussy again,"
"Then fucking do it," I moaned. I was getting really impatient.
He locked eyes with me as he lowered his head, "My, my, is my girl greedy this evening?"
"Babe, please," I begged him, but he just smiled his crooked, devilish grin at me, shaking his head, "I want your pussy absolutely soaking wet for me before I take you."

A high-pitched sound screeched out of me as his fingers grazed my already sensitive skin.
Teasing. Coaxing. Making me squirm.
I felt his breath over my pussy when he spoke, "You are going to come for me one more time," he said before he pressed his tongue to me again.
My head tipped back and I moaned his name.
With every movement of his tongue, sparks and jolts of pleasure skittered through my body and I had no control over the way my body was writhing beneath him. Over and over, again and again his tongue flicked and caressed my pussy, my clit, until my body couldn't take it anymore and I came, and then he just kept going until I came again. Twice.
I was still panting, trying to catch my breath, when he slipped a finger inside me again.

"Ah, perfect," he grinned, "there's my girl."
"Jonathan, please?" I begged him again when he pulled his hand back, "I'm so wet, please."
"Really?" he teased, sliding his finger back into me, "Is that a fact?"
"Yes… fuck," I panted, nodding, "Majesty, please?"
He pressed his body down on mine, "Say it again," he growled.
And I obeyed, "Eternal Majesty, please."
"Say my name," I heard him order.
I felt the crown of his dick at the entrance to my pussy, and it took every ounce of my focus to heed his command, "Lord Jonathan… Ambrose… Langdon, please."
He snarled against my neck, and I felt the sharp tips of his fangs against my skin. Then he wrapped his hand around the base of my throat and held his lips against mine, "I love you," he said against my mouth.
My lips parted wider and a loud moan tumbled out as he slowly slid himself into me, "I love you," I breathed.
He plunged into me again, and then he pulled back and stopped, "Can you come for me again?" he wanted to know, and my breath quickened, "I… I don't know…" I managed to say.
That salacious grin again, and he chuckled, "Let's find out, shall we?"
His finger went back down to my clit, moving around and around in small circles as he drove into me, hard, until I climaxed again.
"Oh, darling, yes," he breathed, "Come for me."
I'd lost count of how many times he made me come, and I wasn't sure how much more I could take.

When he slowed down the pace and increased the intensity of each thrust, that was it for me.
The earth began to move once more. I got lost in the tectonic trembling of it, and I clamped my teeth down on his shoulder, holding the position as my body peaked one last time.
He gasped and cursed in Romanian and with my teeth still clamped firmly onto his shoulder, he came inside me a few short moments later, my name hissed through his gritted teeth.

"You bit me," he said a little while later where he had collapsed next to me, a look of surprise and wonder on his face.

I pressed my lips together and pinched my eyes shut, "I bit you…" I didn't know why, but I felt shy. *Is biting weird?*
"Wh… why did you bite me?" he wanted to know.
"I don't know… I think I saw it in a novel once, maybe… and it just… seemed like a good idea at the time."
He chuckled, rubbing his shoulder, "It definitely was. I'm just wondering what prompted it."
I blushed, "I really don't know what to tell you. Sorry, babe…"
He stroked my lips with his thumb, "It was rather kinky. You should do it again."
I blushed again, "If you liked it, then I certainly will."
After a few moments of silence, I spoke again, "Your room smells like sex now."
Jonathan burst out laughing, "I feel like I owe you an apology for not using a condom."
I shrugged, "That's okay. I'm on the pill, we're covered. Could you maybe just pass me a Kleenex, please?"
He inclined his head, holding out his hand to me, a little spark of mirth dancing in his eyes, "You can use my hand."
I laughed, shaking my head, "A Kleenex will do just fine."

But he insisted that he be the one to clean me up. It was, after all, his cum. At first I blushed at the notion, but he had his tongue all over my pussy moments ago, so him cleaning me up should really not be a big deal. Before he did, though, he bent my knees and spread my legs apart and just looked at me, his eyes scanning all over my pussy.
"Babe," I blushed, "why are you looking at me like that?"
He rolled his tongue over the middle of his lower lip and I heard him growl, "I have fantasized about this…"
"About what?" My face was scarlet.
He groaned, "I have always wanted to come inside you and fuck it in deeper. And this… Seeing my cum dripping out of you. Fuck…"
Shit I never knew that, and I pinched my eyes shut, "We're going to leave a stain on the bed…"
"I know," I heard him say, "but you have no idea how unbelievably fucking hot this is."
"Please, I'm a mess."
"Fucking beautiful…" he murmured before he started cleaning me up,

"Did you really tell Owen that I'm your wife?" I wanted to know after he had cleaned me up and we were in bed.
Jonathan smiled and nodded, "Yes, darling, I really did."
I blushed, "I like the sound of that."
Jonathan pulled me closer and kissed my temple, "I should hope so. I'm not sure why you sound surprised, though. I've called you that before."
Fair point, he had. I tilted my head up and looked at him, "You didn't buy anything at the dealership, did you?"
He looked down at me and nodded his head once, "I did, actually."
"Oh? What did you buy?"
He shrugged noncommittally, "Everything."
My jaw dropped, "Huh? What do you mean, babe?"
He intertwined his fingers with mine on his chest, "I mean, I bought the dealership."
I sat up in bed to look at him, "What?" I wasn't sure I heard him correctly, "So, you're Owen's... boss now?"
He smiled up at me, contemplating my question, "I hadn't thought of it that way. But I suppose if you put it like that, then yes. Your ex-boyfriend is now my bitch."
Shaking my head, I pinched his cheek, "You're such a jealous baby."
He cupped his hand over mine and raised an eyebrow, "Wait and see what happens if he dares to go near you again…"
"What are you going to do with it?" I wanted to know.
He shrugged. "Nothing at all, as long as he minds his manners and keep his eyes to himself."
"Or what? You'll fire him?"
Jonathan blinked slowly and nodded his head once, "That too."
I decided not to respond, so I changed the subject, "Okay, but are you done measuring dicks with my ex now?"
Jonathan chuckled, "Do I need to? Are you still not sure who the… bigger man is?" he asked, looking meaningfully at me. I gave him a blank look, "Did you really just ask me if you have a bigger penis than my ex-boyfriend?"
He nodded, "I did."
I blushed, but I didn't respond.
Jonathan grinned and pumped his fist in celebration, "Red means yes."
Honestly, men and their egos.

"I don't understand, though. Why does my relationship with Owen bother you so much?"
Jonathan turned his head to look at me, "You'll think I'm pathetic..."
I smiled endearingly at him, "Babe, never. Impossible. Tell me?"
He sighed, "I wanted to be your first everything."
My heart melted a little bit, "Jonathan..."
"I know," he rolled his eyes. "Impossible, and ridiculous. And potentially psycho."
"You're so obsessed with me... But that's probably the sweetest thing that anyone has ever said to me."
Jonathan kissed my forehead, and then he held me in his arms until he fell asleep.

Lying next to him watching him sleep, I couldn't help but smile: Jonathan called me his wife. Like how I called him my husband that night in Kat's club. It seemed like he'd also thought of a future together, and that was pretty fucking cool.
And if by some cruel twist of fate we broke up and he married someone else, he better be ready to have his wedding crashed, because I would be objecting. With a scene fit for Broadway, choreographed musical number and all, that was for damn sure.
But if he married me... I started daydreaming about what it would be like to really be his wife. To be Mrs. Langdon, to be married to the Black Prince, and I bit my lower lip. The rest of my life with Jonathan. What a concept...

∞

When I woke up the next morning, I was alone in bed. Jonathan left me a note on the pillow next to me to tell me that he went to the gym, and I thought it was really cute that he folded it into a little origami bat.
The fact that he was in the gym again was a little bit unfair though. My heart and my ovaries were going to combust if he got any sexier than he already was.
I stayed in bed for a few more minutes before I decided that I might as well get up and go take a shower.

As soon as I made a move, I immediately remembered that my poor pussy took a pounding the night before - I was sore. And when I got to the bathroom, I was shocked to see bruises, many of them, around my waist, on my hips and on my thighs. Inner and outer thighs.
I hadn’t even realized.
It made sense though, Jonathan was a lot less gentle with me than usual, but I wasn't going to complain. I liked it when he didn’t touch me like I was made of porcelain.
Oh well. My muscles are achy, but the bruises don’t hurt. Not too much, anyway, and they’ll fade eventually. Okay, they look kind of bad, but compared to his scars, my little bruises are nothing. And so what if my hooha took a beating and I have to waddle like a duck for a little while? I came like a fucking firehose, so let’s focus on that.
I finished my shower and I had just clipped my bra into place when Jonathan came back from the gym.
“Hey, lover boy,” I beamed at him.
“Good morning, beautiful,” he smiled back at me, “Did you sleep well… whoa,” he interrupted his own question and his face fell when he saw the bruises all over my body.
Concern clouded his face. He strode over to me and lightly ran his fingers over my bruised skin, “Christina… wh… Darling, did I do this to you?”
“It’s okay babe, they're basically hickeys, they don’t hurt,” I said dismissively.

The next moment, he dropped to his knees in front of me just as he had before. He put his hands on the floor and lowered his forehead all the way down until it pressed to the tops of his hands, “I am so, so sorry,” I heard him say, “I was too rough with you, I … I’m sorry,” he went on.
“It’s okay, really,” I assured him, running my fingers through his sweat-soaked hair. *Oh, mama, I love me some Sweaty Jonny.*
He sat up, his hand on his heart, and averted his eyes to the floor, “Forgive me?” he requested.

Standing in front of him in a bra and panty, I looked down at him where he was kneeling on the floor in the Infinite apology pose, and I shook my head.

He told me once that he could be a prick, but I wasn't seeing it... So far, all I saw was a really, really nice guy. Too nice, sometimes. I would love it if he grabbed me by the hair, smacked my ass and called me a good girl more often. And now he finally, properly manhandled me, had me moaning his name and begging for more, made me come more times than I ever had before in my entire life… and he was apologizing for it.

I shook my head. *Un-fucking-believable…*

I put my hands on my hips and sighed, "Babe, please don't do this?"

"What do you mean? Do what?" he asked.

"This teenage movie bullshit. 'Oh, I'm such a monster, look what I did to you'," I changed my voice and my accent to imitate him, "It's so fucking dramatic."

He was fighting a smile, so he clearly understood exactly what I meant. Even so, he remained on his knees, looking up at me, "I feel really bad about giving you those bruises, love, I would completely understand if you wanted to slap me. I'll take it, I deserve it."

I frowned at him, "There is no fucking way. Forget it. We had some rough sex and I ended up with some bruises, so what?"

He wrapped his arms around my legs, "I didn't mean to hurt you," he apologized.

I sighed softly before I continued, "You didn't hurt me, you marked me, now it's clear to see that I'm yours. But fine, I'll tell you what, If it'll make you feel better, you can make it up to me."

"I'm listening, my love," he replied, his arms still wrapped around my legs, "I will do anything."

I couldn't help but smile, "Get me the biggest breakfast you can organize, and we'll call it even."

Chapter 23

Christina

I couldn't stop smiling.
I was so proud of myself. I felt like screaming and singing and dancing all at the same time. It was finally the morning of graduation.
I fucking did it: I was graduating.
Jonathan had spent the night at my place, only a day after we had spent the night watching horror movies with Niki at his place.
I was beginning to get the idea that he didn't want to leave me alone. I wasn't complaining though, I loved waking up to that gorgeous face. I had purposely set my alarm a half hour earlier, because I was hoping for an orgasm or two before we had to get up, and I was really disappointed when I woke up to find the bed empty.
"Babe?" I said, but there was no answer. I huffed out a sigh before I looked around the room. His overnight bag was gone and I frowned. He really just upped and left me, on the eve of my graduation?
Nice. Day ruined.
I was about to get up and stomp to the bathroom when I noticed something on the pillow and I smiled: An origami bat.

I unfolded the paper critter to find a note from Jonathan inside,

My darling Christina,
You graduate today. Congratulations!
Enjoy this day, you earned every second.
See you soon.
Love, J

As I made my way to the kitchen to get coffee before I started washing up, I rolled my eyes a bit. Maybe I'd forgive him for abandoning me before I woke up after all. The moment I entered the kitchen, I stopped in my tracks.
Every conceivable inch of our kitchen was covered in flowers. Bouquet upon bouquet of sunflowers, roses, tulips, carnations and oriental lilies were spread out on every possible surface. Fifteen of them, to be exact.
My mom was standing in the kitchen beaming a smile at me so bright it rivaled the Bat-signal. "Start from the left," she said. I frowned, "What do you…?" But then I saw it: The flowers in each bouquet were arranged to form individual letters. C-o-n-g….
Congratulations.
Jonathan sent me fifteen bouquets of flowers that spelled out 'Congratulations'.
As I had been so many times before, I was speechless.

I drove to campus with my mom; all of our guests met us there. The commencement ceremony wasn't very long, we weren't a very big group, so I didn't have to wait very long for the Dean of the faculty to call my name to ascend onto the stage. The moment felt so surreal, I felt like I was flying.

The guests watched in hushed silence, like it was some sacred ritual that had to be revered. And when the Dean handed me my diploma, absolute pandemonium erupted from my loved ones.
Celeste and Alastair were cheering so loudly that people probably thought I was their daughter.
Kat couldn't be there, but she was watching, cheering, via video call. Niki was holding the phone, so she was doing her best not to jump up and down and shriek too much.
I was not at all expecting him to be there, but even Kirill showed up. My mom couldn't seem to stop crying, and I honestly wasn't sure who looked prouder: her or Jonathan, who hired a professional photographer to follow me around all day.
Dude showed up at my house at the crack of dawn, just after I discovered all the flowers in the kitchen. He wanted to get pictures of me getting ready, and once the ceremony ended, he aimed to take even more pictures.

Jonathan had me posing for so many photos that after a while, my face was starting to hurt from smiling so much.

When the photographer finally ran out of memory on his camera, everyone got into the stretch Hummer that Alastair rented for the day to take us back to the manor. When we pulled up, everyone piled out of the vehicle, but Jonathan held me back until it was just the two of us.
Smiling at me from ear to ear, he gently took my face between his hands and locked eyes with me. There was a warmth glowing in his eyes that made my everything inside feel warm and gooey, "I don't know enough words in any language to tell you how incredibly proud I am of you," he smiled at me, and I was pretty sure that if it weren't for his ears, his smile would probably have gone all the way around his head.
Returning his smile, I couldn't help but blush, "Thank you. For everything."
Jonathan's response was to pull my lips to his in a long, deep, hard kiss. When he eventually pulled away, he grinned at me, and I detected mischief in the atmosphere.
"I know that look," I said.
He wiggled his eyebrows at me, then he shook his head quickly, "You think you know, but in reality, you have no idea."
"Don't you mean 'actuality'?"
He chuckled, "Darling, English is by no means my first language."
I grinned back at him, "And yet your English is way better than mine."
He squeezed my hand, "I have a surprise for you. But you have to close your eyes, absolutely no peeking. Deal?"
I nodded, "Deal," and I covered my eyes with one hand while Jonathan took the other and, very carefully, helped me out of the Hummer.
He stepped in behind me, covering my eyes with both his hands, and used his body to usher me a few steps forward.
"Alright," he said, and I could hear the smile on his face, "Are you ready?"
"Yes, I'm ready," I giggled. I didn't want to rush him, but he needed to hurry up, my excitement was going to get the better of me.
He kissed my hair before he spoke, "I'm going to count down from five, and when I get to one, you can open your eyes."
"On one, or after one?"

Jonathan chuckled, "After one."
I took a deep breath, "Okay, okay. I'm ready."
"Here we go," he said before he started counting down, several other voices joining him, "Five… four… three… two… one…"
He slowly took his hands away from my eyes…
Someone popped the cork on a bottle of champagne, and when I fully opened my eyes, my jaw dropped, and tears welled up in my eyes.
On the driveway, in front of the massive fountain, stood a brand-new car with a huge purple ribbon on the hood. A pearl white mini-SUV.
"Congratulations, and happy graduation my love," Jonathan said next to my ear.
I turned around to face him, and he wiped a tear from my cheek, "Now, darling," he said, "today is a happy day, you shouldn't be crying."

I was not expecting this. He bought me a car? A brand new, never-been-driven-before car?
I was still baffled and reeling when I felt him put the keys in my hand. A voice in my head said 'Give it back', but I wasn't going to do that in front of everyone. So I said nothing, except, "Thank you," before I let him take my hand and lead me into the manor. He took me straight to the family dining room which was decorated with flowers and floating candles. My mom came over to give me a hug, "I am so proud of you sweetheart," she smiled. "Thanks, Mom," I accepted the compliment and returned the hug.

Once she was out of earshot, I walked over to Jonathan where he was standing by the chocolate fountain that Celeste had set up on one end of the table.
Without a word, I pressed the keys back into his hand.
"Thank you…" I whispered, "but I can't accept this."
"Why not love?" he wanted to know. I shook my head, "This is too much. I…"
He raised an eyebrow, "Was it not the car you wanted?"
I sighed, "It is, and it's the exact color I wanted as well, I just…"
The look on his face was kind and questioning, waiting for me to tell him why I was being so reluctant. I tried to explain, "I could have bought my own car, you didn't have to spend so much of your money on me."

He tilted his head to one side, "Technically you did buy your own car," he said, and I was even more baffled, "What are you talking about?"
He closed my hand around the keys and covered it with his, "I used the money we got when we sold your car."
My jaw dropped, "Don't you fucking lie to me."
He laughed, soft and low, "I am not lying, I swear."
My face wrinkled in disbelief, "My car was a piece of shit, there's no way it sold for enough money to buy the car in the driveway."
Jonathan tucked a strand of hair behind my ear, "The money from selling your old car was used to partially pay for your new car. But if you don't like it, we can exchange it for whatever other vehicle you want."
I was speechless for a moment, and then my words found me again, "I can't believe you bought me a car," my voice squeaked in tiny.
Smiling, Jonathan nodded and kissed my forehead, "You deserve it. You deserve the entire world, but I thought a car was a good start."
Who sent this man, seriously?

Chapter 24

Christina

Hanging out with Jonathan and his Infinite friends was quickly becoming one of my favorite things to do. Sure, I always had a great time with Devyn, but the vampires… They just lived life at a different speed, on a different level.
And oh, the stories they could tell. Especially when Kat and Kirill showed up with high percentage liquor. Which was every time.
For the immortals, pre-drinks started at around 60% alcohol and higher. I wasn't sure my body would be able to handle that, so Jonathan always made sure that they had enough regular stuff for me to drink.

It was the night after my graduation, and we were all congregated in the pool room at the Langdon manor. Devyn couldn't stay, she had a big presentation coming up that she had to prepare for, and my mom said she was too tired for drinks. I stayed, obviously. I didn't have a lot of friends from school, and I would much rather celebrate with my boyfriend anyway. At that point we'd spent about 72 straight hours in each other's company, but he didn't seem to mind. I certainly didn't either, and if he wasn't getting sick of me yet then I was for damn sure not going to ask him to take me home. Besides, Jonathan was the one that asked me to stay longer. So I was in, boots and all.
Kirill had poured them all a round of 69% rum, and a shot of vodka for me, when I had an idea, "Guys," I suggested, "is anyone up for a drinking game?"
Kat slammed her palm down on the bar, "Fuck yes! What are we playing?"

“Hmm,” I thought about it, “How about ‘Never Have I Ever’?” and nobody was more surprised than me when Jonathan whooped, “Yes! Good idea, love!”
Niki laughed, “Oh, shit,” she said, “This should be interesting.”
“Scared, *Belka*?” Kirill wanted to know.
Niki smiled very sweetly at him, “Fuck off, Kirill.”
Kat chuckled, “Kiryusha, don’t fuck with Bubby, she’s already kicked your lily ass once before.”
“Argh!” Kirill exclaimed indignantly before he slammed his shot of rum, “I was hungover!”
Niki blew him a kiss, “Don’t make excuses, own your bitchery.”
He could only sigh.
“Alright,” Jonathan started after he refilled everyone’s glasses, “Who would like to go first?”
“Pfft,” Kat huffed, “let’s spin the bottle and find out,” she suggested, and spun an empty bottle before anyone could protest.
The bottle spun… spun… and landed on… her. She laughed, “Guess I’m going first. Alright…” She thought for a moment, then she grinned, “Never have I ever… faked an orgasm.”
A few moments of silence passed… and I took a shot.

Kat laughed. Jonathan looked at me with a surprised, questioning look on his face, pointing at himself.
I blushed fire engine red and shook my head vigorously, “No, babe, never.”
He breathed a sigh of relief and winked at me.
Then it was my turn to spin, and the bottle stopped on Niki. She looked around at everyone for a moment, then she smiled, “Never have I ever had a threesome.”
Kat cleared her throat… and she and Jonathan took their shots. Kirill laughed out loud, and this time it was my turn to look at Jonathan in blank surprise. I pointed at Kat, and then at him, and back at Kat, and back at him, letting my face do the talking. Jonathan understood what I meant, and he and Kat both shook their heads vehemently, “No, no, fuck no,” Kat explained, “I love Jonny to bits, but eww,” she said with a look of disgust her face.
I looked at Jonathan, and he had the same look on his face. Kat went on, “Not… with each other, per se… Just… the same person… at the same time.”

Niki shuddered in disgust, "That is revolting, and you two perverts should drink again."
Kirill nodded, grinning, "Yes! Drink!"
Jonathan and Kat sighed, but they each took another shot nonetheless.
Jonathan looked at me and dropped his head for a moment before he spun the bottle. It stopped right back on himself, "Never have I ever… had sex with a coworker."
The only person drinking was Kirill.
I laughed, "What happened?"
Kirill shrugged as he refilled his own glass, "Alone, horny, and oops."
Then the bottle landed on me, and I was feeling brave, "Never have I ever... used handcuffs."
This time, everyone drank except me.
I looked over at Jonathan as he downed his shot, "Babe..?"
He had a sheepish grin on his face but he didn't say anything.
I looked pointedly at him, "Really?"
He shrugged, "I'd happily cuff you to something if you want…" he wiggled his eyebrows. I blushed and Kat whooped, "Bow-chicka-wow-wow."
The next question came from Kirill, "Never I had bad hairstyle," and a very chagrined Jonathan was the only one to take a shot. Niki burst out laughing when she saw my baffled expression.
"Oh-ho-ho, I will be right back. Christina needs to see this," she said before scuttling out of the pool room.

Jonathan looked like he knew where his sister was going. He groaned and lay his head on his arms on the bar, so I guessed it had to be him who had some kind of less-than-great hairstyle. I rubbed his back, "Aww, babe. I'm sure it wasn't that bad."
He pretended to sob dramatically, "It was. It was horrible."
While we waited for Niki, I refilled everyone's shot glass. I was feeling stupidly brave, so I joined them for a shot of 75.5% rum.
"Here we are," Niki said when she re-entered the pool room, and handed me a photo.
I examined the photo very closely before I burst out laughing: There Jonathan was, dad jeans in full force, with a tucked in white t-shirt, a black leather jacket, and a beautiful, shiny… mullet.
He looked up from his arms, and I had no idea that 900-year-old vampires could still blush.

Still laughing, I leaned in and kissed his temple, "Super rad, babe."
He chewed the inside of his cheek, shaking his head.

It was Niki's turn to ask the next question, "Never have I ever… Partied nonstop for longer than 24 hours."
Jonathan. Kat. Kirill.
I was enjoying the rum, so I finished my shot as well, "Someone knows how to have fun," I said, gesturing at the three empty glasses in front of the three grinning Infinites.
Niki laughed, "These two," she said, pointing at Kat and Kirill, "put a cocaine dealer out of business in the 80's."
I was shocked, "Was that before or after Jonny's mullet?"
Kat threw her head back, cackling with laughter, "During, actually."
Jonathan gave a tiny little groan, and I laughed again when I heard him mutter 'For fuck's sake…' under his breath.
Kirill poured up another round, "80's was good time."
"Hang on," I asked him, "this wasn't the week in Ibiza, right?"
He shook his head, "*Nyet*, Ibiza in 90's. 80's, lot of drugs."
I turned to Jonathan, "Do drugs actually affect you guys?"
Niki answered the question, "No, but that didn't stop Double K over here from snorting a dealer's entire stock. In one night."
Kirill chuckled, "Sad man, very confuse."
I looked at Jonathan, "Were you in on this?"
He pondered for a moment and scratched his head, "I don't think so..."
Kat shook her head, refilling the glasses, "This was me and Kiryusha, mostly. Portals are great for fucking with drug dealers."

I pressed my cheek to Jonathan's shoulder and he kissed my hair before I sat up again, "My turn," I said when the bottle landed on me, "never have I ever had to… use lube," I was running on alcohol and untold bravery, and the rum was making me feel like a pirate.
Kirill rolled his eyes and took a shot.
"Aww, Kirillovich," Kat crooned mockingly, "Do you need some tips?"
Kirill cursed at her in Russian, flipping her off with both hands.
He tried to get revenge with the next question, "Never I be arrested."
Niki and Kat grinned at each other.

"Russian Invasion of Czechoslovakia, 1968," Niki explained. Still grinning, Niki and Kat clinked their glasses together, "*Na zdraví*," they exclaimed in Czech before emptying their glasses.
"Did you go to jail?" I asked, but Kat shook her head, "No… the charges were... Mysteriously forgotten about…" she said, wiggling her fingers in the air and looking at Kirill with wide eyes. He winked and raised his glass to her.
Jonathan looked at me and his eyebrows shot up when he saw that I had also swigged my shot, "My, my," he said, surprised, "aren't you a dark horse. You got arrested?"
I shrugged, "Almost. My high school ex was being a dick, I punched him in the face, he called the cops." Smiling from ear to ear, Jonathan refilled my glass for me. I felt like I needed to explain, "He said he was going to hit me, so I beat him to it."
Kirill cheered loudly, "Yes! Nuchka! Beat shit out of asshole boyfriend."

To the next two questions about having sex in a public place and in a bathroom, everyone took a shot, but in response to Kat's question about having sex with someone more than twice your age, I was the only one to drink. My cheeks flushed bright red, and Jonathan grinned wickedly and kissed me.
Then, after my question about sexting the wrong person, Kat, Niki and Kirill needed a refill, and when Jonathan asked if anyone had ever sent a nude photo, me and Kat had to drink.
While the others talked about how many nudes Kat has actually sent, Jonathan leaned over to my ear, "I still have the photo, by the way," and I hid my face in his neck and blushed.
The last question came from Kat, "Never have I ever… been caught having sex," and she herself had to drink, and Niki looked pointedly at me and Jonathan until we emptied our glasses.
The next bottle of hooch the Infinites cracked open was a bottle of 88.8% premium vodka, and while Jonathan and Niki were talking about the first time they had it with their father in China, I took the chance to talk to Kirill. I had a date to organize.

"Kirillovich," I started, calling him by the nickname that Kat sometimes called him.

Jonathan explained to me once how the nickname wasn't grammatically sound, but since it came from Kat, they just let it go. Besides, Kirill didn't seem to mind, as he smiled at me, "Nuchka, what I can do for you?"
Smiling sweetly, I refilled his glass for him, "I heard from Jonathan that you have a little crush on my friend Devyn…"
Kirill started to smile, nodding slightly, "Very pretty friend, Devyn."
"Would you be interested in going on a double date? You and Devyn, and me and Jonathan?"
His smile broadened, and his eyes lit up, "Devyn want?"
I nodded, "She does."
The small smile on his face turned into a wide grin, "*Spasiba*, Nuchka." Thank you.
"*Pozhaluysta*," I replied in Russian, just like Jonathan taught me. You're welcome.

A few more rounds later, my body could no longer keep up with all of the alcohol and I fell asleep in an armchair in the corner.
I woke up from being moved, and I opened my eyes to see Jonathan, tucking me into his bed.
With the kindest smile on his face, he kissed my forehead, "Get some sleep, beloved."
I didn't know what incoherent nonsense I was babbling, but he chuckled and kissed my cheek before he pulled the blanket over my shoulders, and then he whispered something in my ear in Romanian.
I had no idea what he said, but it sounded sweet. Then sleep took me.

The next morning, I regretted every single decision throughout my life that led me to think I had big enough balls to take on the 75% rum the previous night: My head was throbbing.
Jonathan wasn't in bed next to me, and there was no note this time, so I had no idea where he was.
My tummy felt queasy, I was so thirsty, and everything was too bright, but I really wanted some water. I kept my eyes mostly pinched shut as I blindly made my way down the steps, hanging on tightly to the hand railing, to get a bottle of water from the mini-fridge.
I drank a bottle of water in one go and was sipping on the second one when the bedroom door swung open and Jonathan came in, still in his pajamas.

When he saw me standing there looking at him, his face turned pale and he stopped dead in his tracks: He was holding the tip of a blood-bag between his lips. He quickly spun around and turned his back to me.
"I didn't know you were awake," he said. He sounded so uncomfortable.
"Good morning, babe," I replied, a smile plucking at the corners of my lips.
He glanced at me over his shoulder but didn't turn around, "Good morning, darling."
"Sleep well?"
"Uhm… Yes, thank you. You?" he replied.
Poor baby, he was so uncomfortable, and I really wanted to milk it but I felt bad for him, so I ended his discomfort.
"Jonathan…" I started, "Babe… are you feeding? Is that a blood bag?"
He cleared his throat before he turned around, holding the bag behind his back, "Yes…" he said, not quite able to look me in the eye, and he sounded so guilty that I just wanted to hug him.
"Sorry, darling," he apologized, "I didn't mean for you to see…"
I finished my bottle of water and I dropped it into the recycling bin, "It's okay. Go ahead, finish it."
He produced an empty bag from behind his back, "I did…" he confessed, and I couldn't help but laugh; he was so cute.
He wiped his mouth, "And now you're laughing at me... Great."
I was still smiling because I realized that I could still see the blood on his teeth.
When he saw me looking at his mouth, his eyes widened and he lifted his arm to cover his mouth, "Excuse me," he mumbled, and disappeared into the bathroom.
And if I wasn't so hungover, I would have burst out laughing.

When he came back from the bathroom a few minutes later, the blood bag was nowhere to be seen and his breath smelled like mouthwash. But he still looked very uncomfortable, "I really am sorry about that." he apologized again.
I held out my arms to him, and he stepped in to hug me. I pressed my forehead to his chest and I groaned, "Please can we talk about this later? I am way too hungover for this conversation."

“Oh no, my poor darling,” Jonathan crooned. He got me some of the painkillers that he kept in the bathroom cabinet just for me, and some more water.

Then he scooped me up in his arms and carried me back to bed. I didn’t know if I was supposed to complain about him always carrying me everywhere, but I really didn’t want to, because I actually liked it. It made me feel so cherished. He tucked me in and he was about to leave, but I grumbled in protest and reached for him, “No go. Stay me.”

He chuckled, but he got back into bed next to me, “Darling, are you broken?” he asked, before he pulled my head onto his shoulder, and wrapped his arms around me.

I really wanted to answer him, but sleep was calling me way too hard.

Jonathan

We must have fallen asleep because when I woke up, it was early afternoon. I rubbed my eyes and reached for Christina, and I smiled at the adorable little sleepy sounds she made as she snuggled closer to me.
As I twirled a strand of her soft, dark blonde hair between my fingers, I admired every inch of her perfect face and I made a mental note that if I ever made it to Heaven, I would ask the angels what I did to deserve the love of this beautiful woman next to me.
I didn't know how long I lay there, just looking at her as she slept in my arms. Eventually, she slowly opened her eyes.
"Hello my lovely," I smiled at her.
"Hi…" she smiled sleepily, "How do you never have morning breath?"
I shrugged, "Perks of Infinity, I suppose. How are you feeling?"
Christina groaned and moved closer to me, "Like shit, honestly… I am never ever touching 75%-alcohol vampire devil juice again, ever."
I laughed, "Vampire devil juice… Very accurate."
She sat up in bed and moved up against the headboard, "I'm hungry… Are you going to feed me?" and I leaned over and kissed her arm, "Immediately, my queen. What would you like?"
She rolled her eyes, "You're so cheesy… Ooh… Cheeseburger. And fries. And…"
"And…?"
"A bubblegum milkshake. And coffee," she finished her order, and I smiled. *Moonlight hear me, I love this woman.*
She refused to let me leave the bed, so I used my phone to order our food to be delivered to the house. Fiona was a dear and brought it to the room for us.

Wiping the last of the burger sauce from her cheek with a napkin, Christina leaned back against the headboard, looking questioningly at me, "Are you okay?" she asked.
I pushed the empty take-out containers aside and propped myself up on my elbow, "I am… Although I do feel bad that you saw me earlier…"

"Ugh, stop," Christina grunted at me, and I frowned. I'd never heard her make that sound at me before, "What was that for?"
An annoyed look on her face, she folded her arms across her chest, "I don't give a shit about seeing you feed, I have literally seen you rip someone's head off like you were picking daisies."
I sat up, "I know, but…"
"But nothing, Jonathan," she interrupted me. "Yes, I admit, when I first found out what you were, I was freaked out. But I made a decision. And I chose to be with you, to love you, knowing what you are. You are a vampire, and you drink blood, big fucking deal. You don't have to hide it, or lie about it. About anything."
I felt the expression drop from my face as she continued, "Dr. Woods told me about the hunter, and you lied to me. You almost died, babe, how could you not tell me that? How dare you lie to my face about how bad it was?"
"You're scolding me…" I pouted.
She gave me a pointed look, "Yes, I am. Because Jonathan I love you, but I need you to stop sugar-coating everything. It really pisses me off."
I was floored. My words failed me and I just… sat there in silence, stumped. "Thank you, by the way…" I said after a while.
She smiled sweetly at me, "For what?"
"For choosing me."
She moved closer to me and cupped my face with her hand, "It was an easy choice to make."

"But babe," she went on, "If you need to feed, go for it. I chose your night. I chose your truth. I promise you I am not going to run screaming for the hills."
I smiled at her and I nodded, "Yes ma'am."
"Good boy," she said, and my eyebrow twitched. *Why do I like that…?*
She changed the subject before I could say more, "Speaking of blood… I was curious about something…"
"Yes…?"
"About… my blood…" she finished the thought.
My entire body froze, but she pressed on, "I wanted to ask… what does my blood taste like?"
I got to my feet and walked over to my closet, my hands in my hair.

I can't answer that. I haven't been able to stop thinking about her blood since the day I accidentally tasted it, and I can't talk about it. I shook my head.
"Jonathan?" she urged, "What's wrong?"
I walked back over to the bed and took a seat next to her. I pinched my eyes shut, "Darling, I can't talk about this. Not yet."
She nodded, "Okay…I don't understand, but okay. Sorry for asking."
I gulped, "I don't mean to hide anything from you, I just…"
Then I straightened my back and I recollected myself, "I promise, I will answer your question. Just... not yet."

Chapter 25

Jonathan

"Darling, what is going on in that beautiful head?" I asked Christina where she was sitting across from me in the jet.
On an impulse, I decided to take her with me to Copenhagen for a week. Partly because she'd been stressed and overworked and I thought she needed a break, but also because I wanted to show her the world. That, and if she was by my side, I knew she was safe.

I was my own boss, I came and went as I pleased, but it was more of a scramble for her, she had to take time off from work. Luckily her boss was a hopeless romantic, and when she told him that her boyfriend planned a romantic getaway, he was more than happy to give her the time off. He seemed nice, Christina's boss.
So we were on our way to Copenhagen, and we still had quite a few hours' flight time to go.
She was sitting in the recliner across from me on the jet, tilting her head from side to side, just looking at me, not saying anything.
Then she stuck the tip of her forefinger in between her teeth and a suggestive smile curled around her irresistible lips.

Just the look on her face was enough to drive me wild. To add insult to injury, she then uncrossed and repositioned her legs, and the first thing I noticed was the complete lack of underwear under her short skirt.
Fuck… After all this time, she still had no idea how much of a temptress she was.
Or, perhaps even better, maybe she did.
Maybe she knew exactly what those demure glances and come-hither expressions did to me.

When she looked me right in the eye and took her finger out of her mouth and ran the tip across her lip, I knew: She did know what she was doing to me.

"*Cochetă*," I said, my voice raspy.

"Yes, Your Majesty?" she responded, her voice sultry and seductive.

I slowly released a shuddering breath, "When, exactly, did you take off your panties?"

I was doing my best to keep my breathing even, but the sight of her bare-naked pussy under that skirt had already sent almost all of my blood rushing to my cock, and I had a hard-on that was fucking impossible to hide.

And she noticed, this enchantress of mine, which was why she stuck her finger in her mouth. *Sinful woman.*

She shrugged and swung her leg over the armrest of the recliner, giving me a full view of what was under her skirt, "I haven't been wearing panties all day…"

I let my eyes roam exactly where they wanted, and I did nothing to stop my fangs from lowering.

Christina giggled coquettishly, "Am I getting you all hot and bothered?"

I nodded, slowly flicking the tip of my tongue between my fangs.

When she kicked off her shoes and undid her ponytail, she also undid the last of my self-control.

"Come. Here. Now," I commanded, beckoning her over to me.

She gave me the most seductive grin I had ever seen, before she stood up from her recliner and strode over to me.

I pulled her down so she was straddling me and I had unrestricted access to the slick wetness waiting for me between her thighs. She kissed me wildly and passionately, running her hands down my chest and stomach before resting them on the front of my pants, right on top of my hard-on.

"Oh, Christina…. Fuck…." I hissed, and I felt my cock twitch beneath her hands as I slipped my finger inside her pussy. *Fucking soaked.*

And when she clamped her teeth down on the side of my neck, my patience for foreplay snapped in half, "I'm about to fuck you, fast and hard."

I picked her up and took her to the bedroom at the back of the jet and locked the door.
She stepped closer to kiss me, but I shook my head, "Fuck first, kiss later. Turn around."
She pressed her body against mine and reached down to take my cock in her hand, "Can I get a please, before you treat me like a common whore?" she murmured, "I'll do it, but shit, babe… Let's have a little… decorum here."
I chuckled, "I do apologize. Turn around so I can fuck you. Please?"
When she didn't turn around fast enough, I spun her around and bent her over the edge of the bed.
"Look at you," I said, motioning toward the mirror, "Look how stunning you are, bent over for me like this."
Her lips were parted, and her breathing came fast and ragged, but she didn't say anything.
Keeping my eyes on our reflection in the mirror, I slowly hiked up her skirt and caressed her arse with both hands, "This flawless arse…" I breathed, "And this wet pussy," I licked my fingers before I slipped two inside her and she moaned at the touch, "Perfect. And all mine."
She felt so fucking good, and my cock was begging to be inside her.
"Jonathan, please?" she pleaded.
I didn't need to be asked twice. I unzipped my pants and slammed my cock into her so hard that her arms buckled beneath her where she had rested them on the mattress and she toppled forward, moaning into the comforter.
"Do you want to watch me fuck you?" I asked as I started to pull my hips back.
She lifted her head out of the comforter and propped herself up on her elbows. Then she turned her gaze to the mirror, her eyes fixed on where my cock was sliding back into her, and she moaned my name.
"Look at that," I breathed.
Christina moaned and I pulled back, "There's my good girl," I groaned before I drove into her again.
"Babe… ah, fuck…" she whimpered.
"Are you ready?"
When she nodded, I put one hand on her shoulder, the other on her hip and I did exactly what I said I was going to do,
I *fucked* her.

Fast,
and hard.
Like the savage she awoke in me.
And I didn't stop fucking her until she fell apart all over my cock two or three times and she had to clamp her hand over her mouth to keep herself from moaning so loud that the staff would hear. When I finally came, I gripped her hips tightly and held her against me, spilling myself inside her until I had nothing left.
Then I pulled myself out of her and dropped next to her on the bed where she had collapsed and she now lay breathless, limp and unmoving. I grinned at her before I took her chin in my hand, "Am I too late for that kiss?" I wanted to know.
She was apparently unable to talk. The only response she had for me was a languid smile and a slight shake of her head.
When I pulled back from the kiss, she narrowed her eyes at me.
"Animal," she accused.
I laughed and I shrugged, "I did warn you."
She chuckled and I kissed her forehead, "Welcome to the mile-high club, darling."
She grinned, "Yay! Finally I get to check it off my bucket-list."
I smiled. She was so beautiful, and so innocent, and I couldn't decide if I should preserve that innocence or corrupt her absolutely.
"Probably not for you, but this was definitely a first for me," she said, and I frowned. She had a very specific image in her head of who I was, "Do you really not think this was a first for me?"
She shrugged, "I don't know. Honestly, no, not really."
I felt my eyebrows raise. Then I shook my head and got to my feet.
"What?" she asked, "Where are you going?"
"If you'll excuse me," I said, zipping my pants back up, "I'm going to speak to the pilot."
I started leaving the room, but she grabbed me by the wrist, "Jonathan, wait. Did I say something wrong?"
I turned back and glared at her, "You really do think I'm some sort of amoral man-whore, don't you?"
Her eyes widened, "I do not!"
I really wanted to believe her but at that moment I was having some trouble.
Christina sighed, "Babe, come on. Why would you say that?"

I shoved my hands into my pockets, "You just assumed that this could not have been my first time having sex in a plane."
"I just thought… you said you had lain with many…" she responded.
I wish it wasn't true: My past was one of promiscuity and debauchery, but I did wish that she wouldn't throw it in my face every chance she got.
I slowly paced to the bedroom door and back, "I have. But never here. I have never taken anyone onto the jet, or to the cabin, or to the island. No-one has seen the inside of my room, and I have never brought anyone home to meet my family. Except you."
Her lower lip started trembling, "Really?" she asked me in a small voice.
I nodded, "Yes, really. Christina, you are the first woman that I have ever wanted to share every aspect of my life with."
"I'm sorry," she whimpered, "I wasn't trying to be a bitch…"
There it was again, that little pouty face that I didn't know how to resist. I pulled her into my arms, because I knew that that wasn't her intention. And I should probably stop being so sensitive about it. After all, I used to be a bit of a whore…

"Seriously though, how is this my life now?" she said to me after we landed and a driver was taking us to the hotel where we would be staying for the week. Magnus offered us a wing in his house, but I thought Christina might be more comfortable staying at a hotel.
I looked over at her as she was staring out the window at the beautiful old buildings whirring past us, and I reached over and put my hand on her thigh. She kept her eyes on the buildings, but she put her hand over mine. "This is such a beautiful city," she murmured.
I had to agree. Copenhagen breathed Old World charm, and culture and history, and it really was beautiful.

The look of wonder remained on her face when we stepped into our hotel room.
"Wow," she breathed.
I smiled at her, unzipping my luggage, "Does that mean you like the room?"
Smiling at me from ear to ear, she nodded, "It's amazing. I don't even want to know how much this place is per night."

I chuckled, "If you don't want to know, I certainly won't tell you."
She took me by surprise when she skipped over to me from the terrace door and wrapped her arms around my neck to hug me. I returned the hug, my arms around her waist. I put my face in her neck and breathed in the scent of her skin. She smelled like sunshine and wildflowers.
"What are we doing this week?" she wanted to know when she pulled back.
"There are so many things to do and see here. Right outside our room is the second oldest amusement park in the world, so we can drop by there if you want. Or, I could show you The National Aquarium, or The Round Tower. We can also visit the Roskilde Cathedral, and Freetown Christiania. Or we can do something simple, like have coffee at *Nyhavn*."
She frowned, "And *Nyhavn* is what… exactly?"
I hung up one of my shirts in the armoire, "It's a 17th-century waterfront, Hans Christian Andersen used to live there."
"Interesting. And what is there in Christiania?'
"Marijuana."
Her eyes widened, "What?"
I nodded, "You heard me. You can buy cannabis there."
She giggled, "No thank you."
"I didn't think you'd be interested."

Our first night in Copenhagen, she didn't really want to do much. She was tired after the long flight, and I didn't mind. Any time with her in my arms was time well spent.
After brunch the next morning, we went for a walk down Strøget, one of the largest pedestrian malls in the world. It had a lot of high-end stores with some really nice clothes, but she refused to let me buy her anything. *Stubborn little gremlin.*
That night, I took her on a stroll through the breathtaking Tivoli Gardens, with its beautiful exotic architecture and historic buildings. I chose to take her there at night, because the thousands of colored lights created such a fairytale atmosphere. The look on her face told me that she felt it too: Magic and wonder.
She enjoyed the other sights and museums, but just as I thought she would be, she was captivated by *Nyhavn.* It was the only place that she wanted to visit almost every day.

I didn't mind at all, I could sit and look at her smiling face all day, every day, forever.
Our time in Copenhagen was quickly coming to an end, and we were having a late lunch at one of the many restaurants in *Nyhavn* when an email came through on my phone.
"Darling," I said as I read it, "I just received an email from a very important client of mine, and it is not good. I'm going to need to call him. Do you mind?" I asked, turning my head to her where she was sitting in the booth next to me.

She smiled at me and shook her head, "Go ahead babe. I like Business Jonathan, he's hot."
I chuckled, "Even in Danish?"
Christina winked at me and bit her lower lip, "In any language."
"Sinful woman," I breathed, "you're going to make me want to misbehave in public, aren't you?"
She took a sip of her Danish mead and shrugged, "Call your client."
And just as I thought, the moment that she heard the client answer the phone, she moved her hand under the table, and rested it on my knee. I turned my head slightly to look at her. She was silently sipping her drink, just watching the people passing by. Not even glancing at me, she slowly moved her hand up my thigh.

I felt the corner of my mouth twitch. *Sneaky little minx.*
Still not looking at me, she moved her hand higher up, right onto my cock, and I had to admit that I was having difficulty not groaning when she took me in her hand and squeezed.
Her hand moved to my zipper and she started undoing it. Even as more people passed by, as some glanced over at us, she kept going, but she gave me a quick look to gauge my reaction. *Oh, darling, I love this game*. I looked her right in the eye, and shifted my position, spreading my legs slightly to give her better access.

That finger of hers went back into her mouth as she slipped her hand inside my pants and gripped my cock over my boxer briefs. I smiled to myself when she squirmed. I was definitely getting hard and clearly, having my cock in her hand was making her just as randy.

I continued my conversation with my client, but I wondered where this new-found confidence of hers to fondle me in public was coming from. Perhaps the mead she was so leisurely sipping on was giving her a different kind of courage. Danish, instead of Dutch.

She innocently ate some more of her lunch. Then she gave me another quick glance before she pulled the hem of my shirt further down over my pants, and I felt my eyebrow raise. *What is she planning now?*

I didn't have to wonder for long. She undid my pants and stuck her hand all the way down my briefs, her fingers wrapping themselves around my cock.

Full-blown hard-on. Immediately. Again. Vixen.

I leaned over to her and nipped at her earlobe with my teeth, but she giggled and pulled away.

Regrettably, as I ended the call with my client, I realized that we were going to have to cut this little exhibitionistic display of affection short, "I knew you were going to make me want to do bad things to you."

She moved her hand up and down the length of my cock, then she bit her lower lip and looked at me from underneath her eyelashes, "Like what?"

I dug my fingers into her soft hair and pulled her head closer to my mouth so I could whisper into her ear, "Like dragging you onto my cock and absolutely fucking railing you, right here, in front of all these people."

She pressed her lips together and clamped her free hand over her mouth, but it made no difference; I'd already heard the little moan that she let slip out.

I put my hand over hers where she was still gripping my hard-on, and I let her feel my cock throb once or twice before I gently removed her hand and zipped up my pants, "I'm afraid we're going to have to continue this later."

She shrugged nonchalantly, but I saw how quickly she drank the rest of her mead.

I turned to face her and I put my right hand on my chest, "Darling, I am incredibly sorry, but I'm going to have to leave you alone for just a little while. I need to meet with the client I just spoke to, there's a problem that needs my attention."

She nodded at me and smiled, “Of course babe, no problem. I can keep myself busy, or I can call Kat.”
I nodded, “She’d be thrilled, she’s been bugging me to hang out ever since we arrived here.”
Christina grinned, “Then I’ll call her as soon as we get back to our room.”
She motioned to leave our table, looking questioningly at me, “Are you ready? Can you get up?
I gave her a pointed look, “Love… I’m all the way up.”
A rosy flush to her cheeks, she giggled. I winked at her, “But I’m going to need a moment…”

Katalina

"I am so happy that you called me," I said to Christina.

After Jonathan left to meet with his client, I went by their hotel to pick her up. She wasn't in the mood for dancing, so I took her to a cocktail bar. I didn't mind where we went, I liked hanging out with Christina. Jonny was a jam, but it was nice to have a change of pace and some female company.

"I had no idea you wanted to hang out with us, Jonathan didn't say anything," Christina said.

I rolled my eyes, "I'm not even surprised. He can be very selfish with you."

Christina smiled shyly.

I'm so glad Jonathan found this girl. She's really good for him.

"Did he say which client he was meeting?" I asked, but she shook her head, "No, he just said there's some kind of big problem that needs his attention, that's all. I don't even know how long he'll be gone for."

I took another swig of my drink, "I'm sure he's going to try to get back to you as soon as possible." That man was a fool for her.

She shrugged, "I don't mind, business is business."

"Speaking of business," I asked, letting my curiosity win, "please tell me you two finally shagged on the jet coming here?"

Christina blushed the same bright red as the low-cut silk dress that she was wearing, "Kat for the win with the very personal questions, everybody."

I tipped my head back and belly-laughed, "Judging by the shade of crimson your face just turned, I'm going to guess that you absolutely did. Sick puppies. Fucking finally."

Her jaw dropped, "What do you mean, finally?"

I took another swig of my drink, "He's been wanting to bang you in the jet for ages."

Christina hid her face in her hands, "I really shouldn't even be surprised that he discusses our sex-life with you, but shit."

I laughed again, "Only because I was pestering him about it. He just said no, but that he wanted to. He never goes into detail about you, he respects you too much for that. The only thing I know for sure is that you, apparently, give incredible head."

I didn't know that Christina's face could turn even redder than it was. But it could. And it did.
She turned her face away and downed the rest of her drink, and I cackled with laughter.
"Okay," she said then, clearing her throat as she turned back to me, "since you were the one that opened the door on personal questions, talk to me about that threesome you and Jonathan had."
I sighed deeply, "Oh, fuck."
She laughed, "You apparently did that already. And I want to know everything."
I took a deep breath, "We're going to need more booze."

Once the shots were lined up, I started the story, "This happened a very, very long time ago…"
"Before Jonathan and I met?" she interrupted.
I nodded vigorously, "Very long before that. Long before your great-grandparents were even born. It wasn't all that long after we met, so…"
Her eyes widened, "A very long time ago then, got it. Go on."
I took another shot before I continued, "It happened in Germany, and there was a pub, and a cute little blonde girl, and lots of booze involved."
Christina shot me a meaningful look, "A blonde? So he has a thing for blondes?"
I guffawed, "He probably does now, because you're blonde. But at the time, he just had a thing for vagina."
She covered her face with her hands and squealed with laughter. Then she looked up and teasingly swatted my forearm, "Katalina! That's disgusting!"
Giggling, I shrugged, "You asked."
Christina took a deep breath and another shot before she gestured for me to go on.
So I did. "Anyway, blondie had been eyeing us the whole night. She asked him if he wanted to leave with her, and if his wife - yours truly - wanted to join them."

She frowned in obvious confusion, "Wait, wait, wait… What the fuck? You were his wife?"

I shook my head vehemently. *Blessed Moonlight no, please.* "No, no, not like that. We were traveling together, and people were very conservative in those days, so we wouldn't be able to stay in one room because we weren't married, and for some reason nobody ever believed we were just friends. At the time we couldn't afford two rooms, so we just told innkeepers that we were husband and wife."
Christina considered the notion for a moment, then she nodded in acceptance, "Okay, I'll take it. So go on, you were leaving with blondie. Then what did you do?"
I cleared my throat, "Uhm… Her. We did her. In the barn behind the pub."
Once more, Christina covered her face, peals of laughter coming from behind her hands.

I went on, "Jonathan and I did not touch each other. I swear it to the Moon. But…" I gestured with my hands, trying to get Christina to understand, "Blondie was in the middle, and I had one end of her, and Jonny had the other. Like that… Not together... Just, at the same time. Jonny and I didn't bump nasties… We just bumped her nasty. Think of it as… Teamwork."
"Did you high-five each other at half-time and switch sides?" Christina giggled, her face still glowing faintly pink.
I laughed, "Exactly."
"Wow," Christina said when she stopped giggling, "if there are any more stories like that, I'm going to need so much more booze."
I laughed.
"I don't understand, though. Why could you not afford two rooms?"

I stiffened. I was not sure I should be telling Christina the whole story. Jonathan should be the one to tell her that part…
"Jonathan… was having some issues with his parents and he chose not to use the family's money at the time…" I tried to explain as best I could, "But you should rather let him tell you about it. It isn't my story to tell."
"He had a fight with his parents?" Christina tried to guess.

I sighed, “Something like that…” I couldn’t stop myself - I had to share this with someone. “Let’s just say there’s more to him than what you see now. He’s still pretty awesome now, but I do wish you could have seen him back then. He was glorious. But I’ve already said too much. I’m sorry...”
“Let’s have another round of drinks, shall we?” The smile that Christina plastered onto her face was obviously fake, but I had to leave it at that.

While we were waiting for our next round of drinks, a guy with light brown hair approached us.
I recognized him. I couldn’t remember his name, but I knew he was Infinite. He nodded at me, but he turned to Christina.
“You are stunning,” he said to her in Danish. “Can I buy you a drink?”
Christina smiled awkwardly at him; she didn’t speak Danish.
I tapped him on the shoulder, “You’re barking up the wrong tree, friend,” I told him, also in Danish.
He gave me a questioning look, “Why? Is she yours?”
I grinned, “No, but she is spoken for.”
The guy looked around, “I don’t see a boyfriend.”
I smirked and gestured toward the bar, “Go ahead then. Buy His Eternal Majesty’s wife a drink, see how well your night ends.”
The guy’s eyes widened and he gulped, “Excuse me…” he mumbled and disappeared into the crowd.
I burst out laughing.
Christina looked quizzically at me, “What just happened?”
I waved a dismissive hand, switching back to English, “He wanted to buy you a drink… until I told him you’re with Jonathan.”
Christina frowned, confused, “He knows who Jonathan is?”
I nodded, “Every Infinite knows who he is.”
“All hail his Majesty, then,” Christina quipped, taking a sip of her drink.
I glanced over Christina’s shoulder and motioned with my head toward the door, “Speaking of his Royal Darkness… Look who just walked in.”

Christina turned around and looked over to the door, and saw who I meant: Jonathan just arrived.

I laughed when the guy that had just wanted to buy Christina a drink mumbled a quick apology to an absolutely baffled Jonathan before scampering out the door.
Jonathan looked over at the bar and when he saw Christina, his dark eyes seemed to light up, and he winked at her. Then he and his guest, which I assumed to be the client that he had to meet, went to find a table.
Christina turned to me, frowning, "Did you tell him where we were going?"
I shook my head, "No, but he knows I like this bar, so he probably figured I'd bring you here."

Christina took another shot, then gestured to where he was sitting, "I'm going to guess that's his client?" and I nodded in confirmation, "I would assume so."
"Is this part of the client meeting? Going out for drinks?"
I nodded again, "Jonathan is a master of the subtle schmooze."
"Hmm," Christina mused, "he's a master of many things…" she purred suggestively.
I clapped my hands together eagerly, "Please indulge me, tell me more than I need to know."
Christina blushed but she slammed another shot before she answered, "He's a very cunning linguist…"
I pressed my lips together as hard as I could to keep myself from laughing out loud, but it was too late: A loud, almost maniacal cackle came tumbling over my lips and a few heads in the bar turned to look at me.

Christina and I both looked over to where Jonathan was sitting with his client. The client's back was turned to us, but we both saw Jonathan's eyebrow twitch when he heard me laughing and looked over at us.
"Five euros says he heard you," I wagered.
Christina giggled, "I don't even have 5 cents on me. But you're probably right. Freaking Superman hearing…"
Then she turned to me and leaned in, "You know Jonathan really well, right?"
"Unsettlingly well, according to him. Why?"
She glanced at Jonathan again, and then leaned back to me, "Do you know if he's into roleplay?"

I giggled gleefully and clapped my hands in excitement, “I think he is… But you should definitely find out for yourself.”
She grinned, “I am just about to. Do me a solid, order him a whiskey on the rocks?”

Chapter 26

Jonathan

I was quite surprised when a waitress brought me a glass of whiskey that I definitely didn't order.
She explained that it was from the blonde at the bar, and my gaze followed to where she was pointing… At Christina. When she saw me looking, she lifted her glass to me.
I lifted my chin in recognition and took a sip of the whiskey, wondering if the glass of booze had anything to do with what she just told Kat about me. I didn't mind, she could tell Kat as little or as much as she wanted to, just as long as she was happy with what transpired between us behind closed doors.
"I see you have yourself an admirer," my client asked, smiling.
I nodded, "It would seem so, yes."
He turned around and looked at the bar, "Wow, she is magnificent," he said when he saw Christina.
"She most certainly is."
I took another sip of my whiskey, then turned my attention back to my client; our meeting wasn't over yet.
A short while later, I looked back at my lady, and I frowned when I saw another guy standing next to her and Kat, talking to them. And Christina was smiling at the guy, laughing at whatever he was saying.
My client followed my gaze, "Oh no," he said, "looks like you have some competition."
"Apparently so…"
He smiled, "Go. I'm happy with our arrangements, I'll be in touch next week."
I bade the client farewell and goodnight, and turned my attention to where the man was still talking to Christina.

I was very tempted to tell him to get away from my woman, but Christina seemed to have a plan for the night.
I stood up slowly, abandoning the booth I had been sitting in and taking a seat at the other end of the bar.
From my new perch, I could more easily listen to the light-haired man's ham-fisted attempts at picking up Christina, and I really had to put in effort not to laugh out loud. The poor bastard was flirting his arse off. Kat kept looking at me over her shoulder, rolling her eyes at the idiot's sad attempts.
Shaking my head, I waved the bartender over and had him send Christina a glass of red wine.
When she accepted the drink and raised her glass to me to thank me for it, the man that had been talking to her, glared at me over his shoulder. He said something to Kat and Christina, and then came over to me, "Excuse me, what are you doing?"
I shrugged, "Buying the lady a drink, what does it look like?"
The man smirked, "The lady and I are getting along very well, and you are interfering."
I tilted my head, "I guess we'll have to see if the lady agrees with you on that, now won't we?"
The man snarled at me, "Fine. Let's see who gets to plow her tonight. May the best man win."

Anger knocked on the inside of my chest. *How dare this motherfucking cunt talk about my wife like she's a piece of meat? I'll tear his fucking head off.*
But I took a breath and forced myself to calm down. I didn't want to ruin this game that she started, "I always do," I responded.
I waited until the hapless hopeful rejoined Kat and Christina at the bar before I scribbled a note on a napkin in Danish:

You are worth every sin.

I waved the bartender over and handed him the napkin, together with a considerable tip, "Please pass this to the lady with the dark hair on the other side of the bar, ask her to read it to the beautiful blonde angel in the red dress next to her."
And then I waited.

When Kat read the note, Christina looked over at me and smiled, tipping her glass to me again.
The man next to them glanced over at me and cast me a dirty look.
I cocked an eyebrow. He can get fucked.
Christina got up from her chair and walked in my direction. *Fucking Hell, even the way she moves is magic.* She stopped next to me, scanned me up and down briefly… and then walked right past me, and went to the bathroom.
I was tempted to follow her… But I was having fun, and I wanted to see if she had any more surprises planned for me. So I waited for her to retake her seat at the bar next to Kat, and I patiently sipped my whiskey, listening to the guy trying to convince Christina to give him her number.
When he put his hand on her shoulder, I had to look away to keep myself from lunging at him and ripping his arm out of its socket. *If he doesn't unhand my woman in three... two... one...*

I turned back, and saw Christina smile politely at the guy before gingerly removing his hand from her shoulder, and asking him to leave.
I chuckled to myself when the guy simply dropped his head and walked away.
"I told you, I always win," I said when he walked past me.
"Fuck you," he sneered.
"I'd rather stick my cock in hot garbage. You can go fuck yourself," I sneered back.
Then I got up and walked over to where Kat and Christina were sitting, sipping their drinks.
I nodded at Kat, but I turned my attention to Christina, "Excuse me, ladies, sorry to interrupt your conversation."
"Not at all," Christina acknowledged.
I continued, "I thought I should introduce myself. I'm Jonathan."
"Nice to meet you, Jonathan," she replied, "I'm Christina."
I winked at her, "Lovely to meet you. And please, do remember my name."
"Why should I?" she challenged.
"Because," I replied with a grin, "you'll be screaming it later."
Then I walked away, smiling at the sound of Kat cackling with laughter, and I went back to my seat at the other end of the bar.

I ordered myself another glass of whiskey, and not too much later, Kat and Christina got up from their seats, getting ready to leave. Before they left, Christina came over and, without a word, handed me a napkin before she winked at me and left with Kat.
I kept my eyes fixed on her perfect arse as she sashayed out the door, then I looked down at the napkin.
It had the name of our hotel, and our room number scribbled on it, together with a note:

That shirt looks good on you.
I bet I'd look even better…

I bit my lower lip and grinned.
Cochetă...

At the hotel, I knocked on the door to our suite, and I waited a few moments before Christina opened the door, still in the figure-hugging red dress that she was wearing at the cocktail bar, her hair loose and her feet bare, a glass of wine in her hand.
"Good evening," I smiled.
She tilted her head sideways, "Hi… Jonathan, right?"
"That's right." I shoved my hands into my pockets and leaned against the doorframe.
"Would you like to come in?" she asked.
I shrugged, "Depends on if you're ready."
"Oh?" she asked, sipping her wine, "Ready for what?"
I undid the top two buttons of my shirt, "To scream my name in languages you don't speak."

Christina grabbed me by the front of my shirt and yanked me into the room, immediately crushing her lips against mine and I kicked the door shut on my way in.
My tongue pressed to hers, I gripped her by the waist and pressed her back against the door. She gasped when I raised her arms and pinned them against the door above her head.
I ran my free hand down from her waist and squeezed her arse. Then I moved my hand to the front of her body and up to her breasts.
She moaned softly when I lowered my head and my teeth nipped at her breasts through the fabric of the dress.

Her hips squirmed against me, and she tried to free her hands from my grip.
In response, I claimed her lips again and she moaned into my mouth.
When I pulled back from the kiss, I let go of her hands and looked her in the eyes, "How do you want me?" I asked.
"Deep inside me," she groaned, "no more games."
I chuckled, "Of course, love. But do you want me fast and hard, or slow and even harder?"
She ran her hand down my chest and gripped my cock through my pants, "A little bit of both."
I leaned my face into her neck and breathed her in. The scent of her… "I absolutely love that you're already wet for me."
Smiling flirtatiously at me, she unbuttoned my pants and stuck her hand into my briefs, just as she had done earlier that day at the restaurant.
I leaned forward, pressing my cock into her hand for a moment. I slipped the dress off her shoulders and she tugged her hand out of my pants to let her dress drop to the floor at her feet.
I looked her up and down, grinning at the red lingerie she had on, and pulled her tightly against me, "Darling, I don't think I've seen this naughty little ensemble before."
I slipped a finger under the strap of her lacy bra and slipped it off so I could have access to more of her skin and I pressed my lips to her bare shoulder.
"You wouldn't have. It's new. Kat and I went shopping a few weeks ago," she explained.
I undid her bra and chucked it to the floor and flicked my tongue over her nipples. She moaned, arching her back.
I carried her over to the bed and lowered her down on it, "Tell me something, love," I started before drawing her nipples in between my teeth.
She moaned again, "What?"
"Do you happen to know why a stranger apologized to me when I arrived at the bar?"
She chuckled, but her chuckle quickly turned into another moan when my hand went in under her red thong and I found my favorite sensitive spot between her thighs very quickly. She was trying to answer me, but I supposed my finger slipping into her slick warmth and then back to that fun little nub was making it difficult for her.

I slowly caressed her nipples with my tongue one more time, "I'm waiting, love…"
"Fuck…" she gasped, "He wanted... to buy me a drink…" she managed to get out.
"Uh-huh?" I urged her to go on, and I let her get a few more words out, "But Kat told him I was with you…" Before I slid two fingers all the way into her and her sentence ended in a moan.
I fucking love making her moan like that. Maybe it's time to up the ante...
I pulled my hand back and plunged my fingers into her once more before I stood up and knelt down in front of her.
"And tell me about the other gentleman, the one that was asking you so nicely for your number," I wanted to know between kisses to her inner thighs.
"He was flirting, but I wasn't interested," she panted.
"I didn't like it."
"I'm sorry, I…"
"Every time he said something that made you smile, or laugh," I cut her short, my fingers flitting around the edges of her thong, "I wanted to march over there and claim you, show him that you're mine."
"How?" She challenged me.
"I wanted to hoist you up on the bar, drape your legs over my shoulders and devour you. Like this." I said before I snapped the lacy strap of the thong and dragged her closer and right onto my waiting tongue.
She moaned a curse-word and raised her hips to meet my mouth, digging her fingers into my hair.
Then she pulled my hair… and I heard myself growl. *Fuck, she has no idea what she's doing to me.*
Perhaps I should show her.
I wrapped my arms around her legs to hold her in place and I unleashed myself on her completely.
I can never get enough of the taste of her on my lips, her scent in my nose, my tongue inside her, my fingers all over her.
She moaned my name when she came, and the taste of her changed on my tongue. So I did it again.
And again.

I would have loved to stay right there, on my knees, my face buried between her thighs until daybreak, but my cock was too hard to wait any longer - I needed to be inside her.
I positioned myself between her thighs and slid my cock into her and she gasped, wrapping her legs around me and pulling me deeper into her.
I needed to do that again. I adored sliding into her, feeling her open up to me and letting me inside her, but when I pulled myself all the way out of her, she groaned a complaint. *Don't fret, love, I'm just about to ram my cock back into you.*
With her own crooked little smile, she gripped me by the shoulders and rolled us over… But I misjudged how close to the edge of the bed I had placed her, and when she rolled us over, there was no more bed to roll onto and we went crashing to the floor. I pulled her tightly against me with one arm, using my other arm to break our fall.
I sat up when we hit the floor and took her face in my hands, "Are you alright, love?"
Her answer was to wrap her hand around my cock and guide me into her, taking me into her as deep as she could.
I groaned and lay back down on the rug next to the bed.
I looked up at her where she was sitting astride me, every inch of my cock all the way inside her, and I wondered if this would be an inappropriate moment to have immortalized on canvas.
She felt so good, and she was so beautiful, on top of me like this, riding me, fucking me, and I was sure my heart was going to explode in my chest. *I love this woman so much that it might really be the death of me someday.*

Smiling, she lifted her arms and slammed her hands down on my chest. It didn't hurt, but that untamed look on her face…. *Fuck.*
Her eyes not leaving mine, she scratched her fingernails down across my chest, over my stomach, and I groaned when she rocked her hips against me and I felt her soft warmth moving around my cock.
I shifted my hands up her body and ran my thumbs across her nipples, "Who's fucking who?"
"Make love to me?" she murmured, her hips still rocking against me, "No fucking."
I nodded and a quaking breath left my chest. Then I gripped her waist and raised my hips to meet her, matching her every motion.

Unhurried, I relished every sensation, every ethereal second of being with her as one.
And then, there it was - The heavenly moment her climax shattered around her, and her lips parted to moan my name, her back arched.
"I love you, Christina," I breathed, holding her hips as she bore down on me again.
I sat up, smiling at the look of surprise on her face when I toppled her over onto the rug and pinned her body beneath mine.
I leaned down and grazed the side of her neck with my fangs. She moaned, and I grinned to myself. She always seemed to enjoy that.
Then I pulled my hips back and slowly drove into her again.
The feeling of her warmth enveloping my cock, this has to be what Heaven is like.
I thrust again.
Magic.
Enchanting.
She is witchcraft.
My resistance crumbled when she said that she loved me. As I clutched her body to mine and came inside her, I silently swore to the Moon that I would never let this spell she had me under, ever be broken.

Christina

I woke up first the next morning and I wiped my hair out of my face. Then I turned over to look at Jonathan, fast asleep, his arm draped over me. When I moved, he pulled me closer to him in his sleep.
Careful not to wake him, I ran my fingers through his silky, mussed-up hair. I had no idea what possessed me the previous night that had me pulling his hair. Copenhagen seemed to be bringing out some kind of sexually deviant beast in me.
Oh well, he certainly didn't complain about it. It looked like he enjoyed having my hand down the front of his pants at the restaurant. And apparently I had a thing for exhibitionism, because I enjoyed it just as much…

Tracing the contours of his bicep with my finger, I smiled at the thought of the game we played the previous night. Devyn and I were talking about it a few days before I left for Copenhagen, 'Strangers-in-a-bar', and yes, having Jonathan chat me up in a cocktail bar was fun, but I really didn't like that other guy flirting with me. It made me really uncomfortable.

My eyes wandered over Jonathan's sleeping face.
This was all I wanted. Him. This beautiful, sleeping man next to me. My Infinite prince, with his dark eyes, soft lips, and possessive aggression. I saw the look on his face when that guy put his hand on my shoulder. Like Devyn said, the personification of death and danger.

I leaned in to kiss his forehead and I smiled when he mumbled something in his sleep.
It was our last day in Copenhagen and I was honestly a bit reluctant to leave.
This past week had been the most incredible experience. Just existing here, wandering through the streets, breathing in and experiencing the history, the culture, and the atmosphere of this vibrant city had to be among my top five favorite experiences ever. *And all of them have been with Jonathan.*

"Are you going to keep staring at me until I wake up?" he mumbled. His eyes were still closed, but he pulled me closer and held me against him.
I smiled and pressed my lips to his, "Sorry babe."
"It's alright love," he smiled, slowly opening his eyes, "I adore being stared awake by you."
Butterflies took flight in my tummy. There were so many facets to him.

Romantic Jonathan was sweet and thoughtful. Silly Jonathan was funny, like Tipsy Jonathan. Squiffy Jon. *I love it, it gets me every time.* Business Jonathan was assertive and sexy. Fresh-from-the-Gym Jonathan was an adrenaline charged animal. Then there was Dirty Jonathan… Now there was a panty-dropper if I ever saw one, a whole-ass sexual hurricane.
And then there was this, Early Morning Jonathan.
Early Morning Jonathan was just a different kind of gorgeous, with his hair all messy and that sleepy, lazy smile across his sensuous lips.
He snuggled closer for lazy kisses and cuddles, and I melted into his arms. It would be complete and utter bliss to wake up to this every day for the rest of my life.

Chapter 27

Belinda

"I'm exhausted, Mom," Christina said to me. It was really late, and we were sitting around the kitchen table, talking about what she wanted to do next. "If I'm being honest, I think I've always been an academic wreck."

"Yeah, you have," I agreed. At first, when Christina said she was tired I thought she just meant from her trip to Copenhagen, but I quickly realized that we were digging much deeper than that. "For a long time, I was actually really worried about you."

She frowned, "Why?"

"Well," I explained, pouring myself some more tea, "You were such a quiet, lanky little girl. You were so cute, your eyes always looked like they were too big for your face."

Christina rolled her eyes, "Thanks Mom, you paint such a flattering picture of me."

I laughed, "It's true, you were! And all you cared about was books, and reading. You were never interested in making friends."

She shrugged, "I still don't have many friends."

I nodded, "I know. But when you were little, I just wanted you to have a good balance, you know? Not all friends, and not all school. But nope. You chose the latter."

"I was such a little nerd," Christina said.

"You were a little bit," I agreed, chuckling at the memory. "You always started studying for tests and exams weeks in advance, and you always handed in your homework ages before it was due."

She nodded, "And I always asked teachers for extra homework after the other kids were gone."

My jaw dropped, "Really? How did I not know that?"

Christina shrugged, "Because I never told you. I did it all the way through middle school and high school."
"And I always thought your teachers gave you too much homework."
She grinned, "Nope. I asked for it."
See?" I pointed out, "I told you, you run on stress and donuts."
Christina smiled, "I know… but now… I don't know if I can keep doing it."
She was quiet for a few moments before she spoke again, "I really wanted to get my ducks in a row, to submit my resume and my application for the MA/PhD dual program, but…," she sighed, "It's too much, Mom."
"Did you get a look at the curriculum?" I asked, and she nodded, "I did. And I don't think I have it in me. Not right now. Maybe not ever. It's too many credits, too many seminars. I would have to attend courses and stuff abroad, and… No."
"That does sound like a lot to take on."
Christina helped herself to another cup of tea, "But I don't know what I want to do now."
"Maybe you don't have to do anything right now."
She pulled her mouth to one side, "I've never not done anything before."
"I know. Because we've always had a bazillion bills to pay. But now…"
"Hmm," she nodded, "Now we don't…"
I winked at my daughter, "Because a certain someone's rich boyfriend was a good Samaritan and dug us out of debt."
Christina grinned at me, "I know, he's a Shnookums."
"So maybe you could just enjoy having a Shnookums for a while?" I suggested, "Hang out with Jonathan, have some fun, go for a drive around town in the car he bought you, let your hair down."
She snorted, "Sounds like you're telling me to go be a trophy wife."
I shrugged, "Maybe I am. Relax. Live a little."

Christina

After saying goodnight to my mom, I lay in bed, thinking about what I could do with all of the free time I had now that I wasn't a student anymore. Maybe I could enroll in a few short courses, learn a new skill? Or learn a new language. It might be a good idea to try and catch up with the immortals.

Besides, my mom was right. Now that I finally had the time to relax, I should make the most of it and spend some time with Jonathan.

Maybe I could take him camping.

I turned on my side and I could see him in my mind's eye, how incredible he would look by the light of a campfire.

I dreamt of him that night, deep inside me, making love to me by the campfire, his hands and his lips all over my body…

I woke up horny, images from my dreams still swirling around in my head, and I instantly regretted not buying the vibrator I was looking at when Devyn and I went to that sex shop the other day. Mine wasn't working so well anymore. *I guess I could just use my hand, but I want more. Actually, I want Jonathan.*

Groaning in frustration, I grabbed my phone from the bedside table to text him. It was Saturday, and I really hoped he was up for camping:

Morning handsome
Are you busy this weekend?

His replies when texting were always so cheerful and happy, and they always made me smile:

Good morning beautiful
I don't have anything scheduled yet
Did you want to do something?

I kicked my feet under the blankets in giddy excitement. It still put me on Cloud Nine when he called me 'beautiful'. I texted back:

I thought we could go camping

I was about to expand on the topic when he called.

"Hi babe," I smiled into the phone.
"Good morning my lovely," his smiling voice said over the line, "where did you want to go?"
"Hmm…" I pondered, "I don't really know…"
"My father mentioned a few campsites," he replied, "shall I send them to you? Then you can decide which one you want to go to."
"Okay, sure," I said before I switched my phone to speaker so I could have a look at the campsites.
"Uhm… babe…" I stammered.
"Yes love?"
"These are all, like, really close to the mountains…" I countered. I wasn't afraid of ghosts or anything like that, but I'd heard stories about the things in the trees...
"I promise I will protect you," Jonathan assured me.
I contemplated the notion: Whatever was or wasn't in the trees, surely if there was someone who would be able to keep me safe, it was the Black Prince. *Alright then, beasties, bring it on.*

From there on out, Jonathan basically took over all the planning. He said he would take care of the tent, the firewood, sleeping bags and food, and that I only had to bring my clothes for the night. He came to pick me up late that afternoon, and we drove to the campsite.

The first thing he did when we arrived was to start a fire, and while I started offloading our luggage and the cooler box with all the food in it, I kept glancing over at him. He really did know how to do pretty much everything, and he looked so fucking good doing it.
When he was done setting up the pieces of wood in the center, he put some kindling on top, and just as he was about to light it, I hugged him from behind, "Are you going to use your own fire?"
He quickly glanced at me over his shoulder and then looked around to see if there was anyone else nearby. Using his power in public was probably risky, but after a quick scan of the area, he ignited a spark in the middle of his palm and dropped it right into the kindling.
I wondered again why his flames were black, but the sparks that sprang to life quickly put the thoughts out of my head, and I grinned, "My boyfriend's a bad-ass."
He chuckled, "You are absolutely adorable, do you know that?"

I planted a kiss against his back before I strode over to the cooler box, "Do you want something to drink?"
"Uhm…" he started to say, but I already opened the drinks cooler. I smiled when I saw the blood bags that he carefully packed in right next to the wine. I looked at the bags, and then back at him, "I always knew you weren't a beer guy."
Smiling, he shrugged, "Hence the wine."
"But darling, before we start drinking," he went on, "we really should put up the tent first."
"Oh, I'll do it!" I offered.
"Normally I would insist on doing it myself," Jonathan smiled, "but you seem really eager. So go ahead."

"I hope you remembered to pack enough food," I said a while later as we were sitting next to the fire. Jonathan slowly turned his head to look at me, "Are you still under the impression that I'm clueless?"
"No, I'm just asking."
He shook his head at me in mock frustration as he got to his feet, "I may have been born at night, but it certainly was not last night."
"Oh, please," I teased him, "you were born when dinosaurs roamed the earth." He was taking foil packets from the cooler and he laughed, "That makes you a panther, does it not?"
I just looked at him.
Jonathan put the last of the foil packets down on the camping table, shaking his head, "Excuse me a moment, I'm going to change into more comfortable pants."

I waited until he finished changing into a pair of sweatpants to go over to him.
I stepped right up to him, pushed him against the car, and pressed my lips to his.
A soft groan started to rumble in his throat as he pressed his tongue against mine, his hands on my waist, and I slipped my hand down the front of his sweatpants and took his dick in my hand. *Oh, I love how he feels in my hand, so smooth and warm.*
Then I pulled away and walked over to the table to get my wine and sat back down by the fire.
"*Cochetă…*" I heard him say, and I wiggled my eyebrows at him in response.

He cricked his neck to one side, "So you want to play… Alright…."
Then he changed the subject completely, "Are you hungry?"
I nodded, "I'm getting there. What's on the menu?"
He picked up a few foil packets and started bringing them over to the grill, "I thought grilled cheese hot dogs and corn on the cob would be a good way to go. Simple and easy."
"Sounds perfect!"
He winked at me, and arranged the foil packets onto the grill.
He started walking back to the table, when he suddenly crouched behind me and put his hand around my neck, his lips grazing my ear. I gasped in surprise. His hand around my throat was unexpected, but very welcome… as was the heat it ignited between my thighs. Now, he definitely had my attention.

His hand on my throat, his other hand under my sweatshirt, and he pinched and rolled my nipple between his fingers.
I caught my breath and leaned into his hand… But he stood up and walked away from me just as quickly as he had crouched behind me, and I squinted my eyes at him, "You're such a clam jam."
He tipped his head back and laughed out loud, "Is that the opposite of a cock tease?"
Nodding, I huffed at him through my nose. He winked at me, "Just taking a page from your book, darling." *Maddening, this man.*

I was ready with a smart answer, but he started taking the food off the grill, "Dinner should be about ready."
I went to stand next to him, making sure that my ass was next to his face as I bent over and pretended to readjust my boot.
"Is your flawless arse in my face for a reason?" Jonathan grumbled softly next to me, "Or are you just trying to unhinge me?"
A naughty smile on my face, I stood up and shrugged, "I have no idea what you're talking about, babe."
"Have it your way then…" he replied, nodding slowly and standing up. As he got to his feet, he ran his hand up my leg, from my ankle, over my shin, over my knee, right up to the apex of my thighs. His hand gripped my pussy for a moment and I moaned… before he let go and walked over to the picnic table, his face deadpan.
"You absolute…" I started saying, but I cut my own sentence short.

I left it alone until after dinner, so all I did while we ate was give him a couple of coy glances. But as soon he had cleared away the last of the trash, I pressed my body to his and kissed him again. He returned my kiss, pulling my lower body against his. I snuck my hands under his shirt, and as I bit the side of his neck, I scratched my nails down his back, smiling to myself when I heard him groan next to my ear.

But as soon as he reached under my shirt, I stepped away from him, "I'm going to get some more wine."

"Christina…" I heard him say as I walked away. I glanced over my shoulder at him, and I grinned. He was leaning over, his hands on his knees, trying to steady his breathing.

"You okay there, babe?" I asked. I was having so much fun teasing him.

"Woman…" he replied, "You…"

But he didn't say anything more, he didn't do anything more. After a while of him not making any moves to touch me, I was beginning to think that he got bored and he was done playing our little game. I really wanted him to touch me, but at the same time, sitting next to him by the campfire, my arm linked with his and my head against his shoulder, was pretty blissful as well.

It was so nice to just be there with him, enjoying the peace and quiet, with no other sound but his soothing voice and the crackling fire.

The wind started to pick up, and it was getting a bit chilly, so I wanted to change into my pajamas as well.

Next to the car, hidden from outside eyes by the tarp he had put up for privacy, I took off my bra and put on my sleep shirt. I was putting on sweatpants, and I had the elastic waistband only up to my knees when Jonathan suddenly stepped up right in front of me.

He pressed my body to the side of the car with his, and locked eyes with me.

Then he kissed me.

Hard.

I moaned against his lips and grabbed his shirt with both hands and pulled him closer.

He pulled his head back, and I gasped when he stuck two fingers in my mouth, shifted my panties aside and slipped those fingers deep inside me.

Once.
Twice.
And then he pulled his hand back and stepped away.
"Babe…" I complained, "Why? That was just mean."
He took my chin in his hand and made me look at him, "You started it."
"No, I... wh…" I tried to argue, but he didn't let me, "I certainly didn't grab my own cock."
And then he walked away from me.
It was my turn to lean forward and put my hands on my knees in an attempt to breathe again.
Where did that come from…? When did he start talking like that…? Does he really have no idea what it does to me…?
"Fuck…" I mumbled under my breath, and he looked at me over his shoulder, "Are you alright there, love?"
I watched him as he walked away, and I shook my head. This game needed to end.
I rejoined him by the fire, and I really was trying my best to behave, but my body was accusing me of all kinds of atrocities, and all I wanted to do was rip his clothes off.
Not all that much later, he suggested that we should get some sleep, so he passed me the lantern and gestured for me to go into the tent while he extinguished the fire.

When he finally came into the tent and lay down next to me, I couldn't take it anymore.
I moved in on top of him and kissed him with all of the fire that had been simmering inside me since I woke up that morning.
Jonathan returned the kiss and rolled over to pin me down on the ground. He held my wrists to the ground next to my head, and he spread my legs with his knee, bearing himself down on me, "Are you done teasing me?"
I nodded, my lower lip between my teeth. I was unable to speak; I could feel his dick pressing against my pussy.
Then he claimed my lips again, his hands skimming down my body.
He jerked my sleep shirt up over my breasts, and I gasped as he ran his thumbs across my nipples.
I loved that he was already hard, and I really wanted him to just rip my sweatpants off and take me.

All of a sudden, a gust of wind flattened the tent on top of us and I screamed, but I started laughing when Jonathan was already shaking with laughter on top of me, "I suppose that's Mother Nature's way of telling us to go to sleep?" he mused.

"I am so sorry," I chuckled, "apparently I suck at pitching a tent."

Jonathan stood up to fix it, shaking his head, "You pitched my tent just fine, love."

Blushing, I laughed.

Salacious.

But as much as I wanted to pick up where we left off, he fell asleep shortly after he got back in the tent, and there go all my fantasies about making love to Jonathan by the light of the campfire.

Shit.

Chapter 28

Celeste

My hands trembled as I held the letter. It arrived a few moments ago, and I hadn't opened it yet.
"My love?" Alastair asked, his hand on my shoulder, "What is it?"
I turned to him, my lips trembling as well, "Our son," I said, my voice but a whisper. "He sent a letter."
Alastair pulled me into his arms, and I leaned my head against him.
"Thank the Moonlight," he mumbled.
I clutched the letter to my chest, tears of joy and relief streaming down my face. We hadn't seen or heard from Jonathan since we had that big argument and he stormed out of the house after I placed a limit upon his power.

When he first left, his father and I thought he would be back in a day or so. But we both underestimated how stubborn our son could be. Days turned to weeks, weeks turned into months, months blended into years, and before I knew it my baby was gone for 70 years. And yes, when you lived as long as we did, years went by in the blink of an eye. Without my son, however, each day was eternal and the letter that had just arrived brought my half-dead heart back to life.

"What does it say, my love?" my husband asked.
I wiped my tears and sat down on the wooden chest at the foot of the bed. Alastair sat down next to me. I carefully opened the letter, and I started crying anew when I recognized my little boy's handwriting.

My dearest Mother and Father,

I hope that this letter finds you well.
Even as I write this letter, I still do not know what to say.
I have been wandering around between towns and cities and villages and farms, and I have come up with any and every possible reason why I cannot return home to you.
But as time has gone by, I now finally understand the true reason:
I am ashamed.
Ashamed of myself.
Of my immature and reckless behavior.

My beautiful Mother, I cannot begin to tell you
how much I regret the way I spoke to you before my departure.
I was rude, and disrespectful.
My actions were disgraceful. I deserved the punishment I was given,
and though I could not understand it then, I understand now.
You raised me better than to let my temper control who I am.
I can only pray to Heaven and the light of the Moon that you can find it
in your heart to forgive me.

Father, I admit that ever since I turned thirteen I have been disrespectful and disobedient towards you. I thought I knew everything, could do everything, and I did not want to listen to anyone. You have only ever wanted me to be a better person, a better man, and I regret the way I acted towards you. You are a man of honor and integrity, and I hope and pray that I might be blessed enough to someday be even half the man you are. And I pray that you may also forgive me for every wrong that I have done to you.

During my travels, I have learned the true importance of innocence,
the meaning of truth, and that revenge and justice are not the same thing,
to name but a few.
These years away from home have taught me a great deal,

yet every day that I have spent on the road, my heart yearned for my family, my home.
I hope that I may return there soon, if I still have a home with you.
I pray for this, yet I understand if your door is closed.

Forever your loving son,
Jonathan

"We must write him back immediately," I sobbed. I missed my son terribly. I just wanted to hug him and hold him for a while. Agori mou. Alastair nodded, tears in his eyes as well, "It's time for him to come home."
Nodding in agreement, I sprang to my feet to find paper and ink to respond to Jonathan's letter. I didn't even know for sure where I would send the letter, it bore no return address. Perhaps if we tracked down the messenger that delivered it, we could...
"It warms my heart to see that my letter wasn't tossed in the fire," Jonathan's voice suddenly sounded from the doorway.
I whipped my head up to the sound, "Oh! My baby boy!"

There he was, standing in the doorway. My only son. My little boy came home. He looked haggard and dirty, his clothes ragged and torn, a worn leather satchel in his hand.
But he was finally home.

My feet couldn't carry me to him fast enough, and I gasped in surprise when his knees buckled beneath him and he collapsed to the floor. I gathered him up and pulled his head into my lap and stroked his hair as he cried. Alastair came over and knelt next to us, wrapping his arms around us both.
"My boy," Alastair murmured, his trembling hand on Jonathan's back. I looked out the window at the sky, and I smiled when I saw the moon break through the clouds. How fitting for the Blessed Moon to shine upon the moment that her favored son returned home.

Alastair

"How are you feeling, sweetheart?" my wife asked Jonathan after dinner that night.
He'd had a warm bath and a shave, and he was sitting with us around the fireplace. Katalina had long since fallen asleep. I couldn't help but smile; his mother was clutching his hand as if he was going to float away if she let go.
We all knew what she was referring to: The limit she placed on him before he left.
He smiled at her and kissed her cheek, "It's still in place. But I'm alright, Mami. It took some time, but I got used to it. I think I would feel very strange if you ever lifted it."
She squeezed his hand, and he went on, "Perhaps it should stay in place. At least for now."
"How did you get by?" I asked, changing the subject, "Surely you ran out of money a long time ago?"
Jonathan nodded, kissing his mother's hair when she leaned her head against his shoulder, "Yes, so we had to work for money so we could buy food."
She cast him a curious glance, "Pray tell what kind of work did Katalina do? I would have loved to see that."
He chuckled, "She's rather handy with a shovel, that one. Although I think she might never forgive me for the calluses."
I nodded in understanding, and he elaborated, "Physical labor taught me some valuable lessons."
"Oh?" I prompted.
I had missed my son something fierce, but I was really glad to hear that he grew up in the time we spent apart, and that he learned something of value.

Looking at my first-born, I almost didn't recognize him. Gone was the defiance and arrogance of youth. The man sitting before me was no longer the capricious adolescent that let his temper get the better of him. No. This was someone I'd never met before. This was the true face of the Black Prince of Carpathia. Calm, focused, fair.
And I felt my heart swell with pride.

"Well," Jonathan continued, "I learned that food bought with hard-earned money tastes the best. And that it is not your title that determines who you are, but rather how you treat others.
But I think the most important lesson I learned was that family, be it chosen or blood, is one of the most important things we have in our lives, if not the most important. Your family will be the ones that tell you the things you do not want to hear, no matter how that might hurt your feelings, or make you angry. Your family does it out of love, to help you grow. To guide you into becoming the person that you are capable of being."

A while later Jonathan got to his feet. He looked exhausted, and he bade us goodnight.
"Sweetheart," Celeste said just before he left the den.
"Yes, Mami?" he smiled questioningly at her.
"Welcome home."

"He was such a small baby…" my wife's musings brought my daydreams to a gentle halt. I turned my head to look at her where she was curled up on the sofa next to me, flipping through one of our many photo albums. We didn't have photos of our son as a baby, only sketches, most of which had not stood the test of time. I knew our lack of baby photos was something that saddened my wife, so she tried to make up for it by taking as many photos as she possibly could in later centuries. We had quite a large number of photo albums filled to the brim with snapshots of Jonathan, Donika, Katalina, and even Kirill. 'Double K', as Donika affectionately referred to Jonathan's two best friends, had been part of our family since the day my son carried them over our threshold centuries ago, bleeding and barely alive. We nursed them both back to health, and my wife and I loved both of them as we loved our own children.

"He really was," I agreed, leaning over to see which snapshot she was looking at. It was a photo of the three of us, myself, my wife and Jonathan. My son's arms were wrapped around his mother who was doubled over with laughter at something he had said. I stood just behind my son, the biggest smile on my face.

Celeste rested her head against my shoulder and I pressed a kiss to the top of her head.
“Look at him now, taller than his father. I can’t believe he has finally settled down with just one girl,” my wife said then and I couldn’t help but laugh. Over the years our son had lived a rather colorful life, though he seemed to be under the impression that his mother and I weren’t aware of his promiscuity. When he finally stopped sleeping around and remained monogamous and faithful to Christina, we could hardly believe it.
“I’m concerned, though,” Celeste said.
“About what, my love?” I wanted to know.
“There are so many things that Christina doesn’t know about him,” she explained, flipping to the next page in the album.
I nodded in slow agreement, “You’re not wrong.”
She looked up at me, “I’ve been that boy’s mother for over eight centuries, and yet there are still moments where I have no idea what to do. I know that he loves her…”
“I know he does, and she loves him, too. That much is clear. And she knows his biggest truth, and she’s still here.”
Celeste turned back to the album, “But what of the rest…? She doesn’t know…”
I put an arm around my wife’s shoulders, “The rest of it is up to him to share with her. Our son’s life story remains exactly that: His.”

Chapter 29

Hunter

I had never, ever in my life felt as powerful, as fast, as ferocious as I did now.

Growing up in foster care, if anyone had ever told me that one day I would be a highly decorated soldier, and a vampire, I would have called them crazy.

And yet, here I was…

It was the first time that they were letting me leave the premises. Up until now, Dr. Brennan kept a close eye on me, only letting me outside the building for short periods of time. I understood that there had been many less than successful transitions in the past. But I wasn't one of them, and I was starting to feel like a prisoner.

I was fast, and strong, and it wasn't perfect, but my hearing had gotten so much better than it was at the beginning. I could isolate and focus on certain sounds so much more easily. It was the same with my sense of smell. At first, I smelled absolutely everything, and it made me sick more times than I wanted to admit. But now, I'm finally starting to get good at focusing on a particular scent and blocking most of the others.

I started the process when we first relocated to Europe and it has taken me weeks, even months, to get to this point, but Dr. Brennan finally decided that I was ready to leave the lab.

But as I walked down the streets, I honestly wasn't sure what I even wanted to do.

Wandering aimlessly, I soon found myself leaving the city, and heading into the forest.

I was pretty sure I was heading into some national park, but I was enjoying the scenery, and I was certain I could slip out of sight before any park ranger spotted me, if the moment called for it.

I hadn't gotten very far into the forest, when a very specific smell reached my nostrils. Fresh blood. Human blood.
I closed my eyes and breathed it in. The magical, inviting scent was coming from somewhere not far ahead of me, and my feet followed the trail by themselves.
A couple of hundred yards ahead of me, I found the source of the glorious smell. A hiker had cut her hand with her pocket knife, trying to cut off a branch.

Her light brown hair was braided into a thick plait at the back of her head and she had taken off her bandana to wrap it around her injured hand.
She looked up at me when she noticed me in the clearing and she smiled. She gestured to me and started talking to me in highly animated German and I had no idea what she was saying. I didn't speak the language.
My eyes traveled to her bleeding hand, and I felt the fangs in my mouth bare themselves.
I was still getting used to them, and sometimes they had a mind of their own, popping out whenever they felt like it.

When the girl saw my fangs, she screamed in terror and scrambled to her feet to run away.
I shook my head and I laughed. *She has a snowball's hope in Hell, I'm too fast.*
Her panicked screams escalated when I caught her and sank my fangs into her neck, and I groaned in satisfaction at the taste of her sweet, warm blood spurting into my mouth.
Fresh blood tasted so much better than the cold, bagged crap they gave me at the lab, especially if the blood came from a woman. I didn't know why, but women just tasted better.
I kept drinking long after her body had gone limp, only stopping when her body was completely drained of blood.

I wanted to just drop her right there, but I rolled my eyes as I remembered the doctor's admonishments of not drawing unnecessary attention. Then again, I could just leave her there.
I mean, there were wolves in the forest, after all.
And wild boar.
Those things will eat just about anything…

Chapter 30

Christina

The night that the nascent lunged at me in that parking lot haunted me more often than I wanted to think about, and the more I thought about it, the angrier it made me at myself.

Angry for being so completely useless, so utterly vulnerable, and so totally dependent on Jonathan's protection. I loved that he was physically more than able to protect me, but I wanted to know more, to do more, to be more.

I wasn't a complete idiot, I knew I didn't stand a chance of defending myself against a vampire, but I also didn't want to feel like a sitting, defenseless duck if anything happened to me and Jonathan or Kat or Kirill weren't nearby to save me. Kat had been teaching me Krav Maga, but I wanted to be able to do more than just defend myself. I wanted to fight back.

I originally thought to ask Kat, but then I changed my mind. I adored Kat, and she was a vacation for the soul, but I wanted any martial arts skills that I learned to be a surprise for Jonathan, and I knew there was no guarantee that Kat wouldn't let anything slip. The two of them had known each other for way too long for there to be secrets between them. They'd apparently had a few threesomes over the years which I didn't find weird, but because of the strength and depth of their friendship I was pretty sure Kat would have a tough time lying to Jonathan.

Besides, Kat's business has been booming recently, and her club has also been doing really well, so she's been busier than usual and I don't want to bother her.

I thought of asking Niki.
Jonathan's little sister was nearly just as much of a firecracker as his best friend, and
I had goosebumps all over when she showed me photos of her and Kat fighting in the Czech resistance against the invading Russian forces in 1968, so I was well aware that Niki was also quite the spark-plug.
But just like Kat, Jonathan knew his sister too well. He would know in a fraction of a second that she was keeping a secret, and Niki loved and respected her big brother too much to lie to him to his face, even if it was about something as innocent as his girlfriend wanting to surprise him with what she could do in close combat.
No, asking Niki to train me was out of the question. I also couldn't picture myself sparring with Celeste or Alastair, even though I knew they both had to be an absolute tour de force in a fight.

That left me with only one other option: Kirill. The guy was made of secrets. I was sure he would be up for training me, and if I asked him to keep it a secret, he would do that.
That settles it then, I'm going to ask the Beast from the East to train me.

Chapter 31

Jonathan

I had absolutely no idea what Christina was up to. I texted her, asking if she wanted to come over later, but she declined. Apparently she already had plans, and when she didn't elaborate, I didn't press her any further. She was allowed to have her own life outside of our relationship, and I supposed she didn't have to tell me about absolutely everything that she did every second of every day, even if I would be fascinated to know. But the fact remained that she was busy, and I was bored.

I strolled out of my room, walking idly down the hall, my eyes wandering over the pictures on the shelves in the hallway. I was especially fond of the photos of Christina with me and my family and friends that my mother added to the collection. I picked up one particular photo to look at: It was a photo of us on the balcony at the beach house, and I smiled at the memory. She looked stunning in the black bikini that she was wearing in the photo. Then again, she always looked stunning, in everything. *And in nothing.*

I put the photo back on the shelf and continued down the hall.
My mind wandered to Christina, as it so often did. She was the most beautiful woman I'd ever seen, but I knew that there were moments where she didn't feel quite as confident about her body. I recalled the look of insecurity on her face when she put on the black bikini, and how badly she wanted to wear a cover-up, even though it was just the two of us on the island. There was no part of her that wasn't utterly perfect, but she couldn't see herself through my eyes, so I was just going to have to work harder to make her feel as beautiful as she was.

I sighed. *Her skin... so silky soft and smooth to touch...*
I shook my head to clear my mind, and knocked on Niki's door.
"Come in!" she called out from inside, so I pushed open the door and peered around it.
Niki was sitting on the floor, her back against her bed, sketching something. She looked up at me when I came in.
"Hi," she smiled.
I strode over to sit down next to her, "Hello, Monkey."

Niki

I was surprised that my brother came into my room and sat down next to me.
Ever since he started dating Christina, he hadn't been around much. I didn't begrudge him his happiness. I loved Christina and I was really happy they found each other. But I did miss hanging out with my big brother.
We used to spend a lot of time together before he got a girlfriend, so I was genuinely happy that he came by. Even more so because he just called me 'Monkey'.

Back when I first joined the family near the end of the 18th century, the first nickname that Jonathan gave me was 'monkey' because I clung to everything. To our mother when I first arrived. To my pillow. To my bed. To a pillar in the foyer. To a tree. And he said I was so small, I reminded him of a pygmy marmoset monkey. Hence, Monkey.

I smiled at him and scooted closer.
Jonathan looked over at what I was doing, "What are you up to?"
I happily showed him my work, "A client from Luxembourg is getting divorced and she wants to reinvent her style, so I am trying to come up with a concept for her new bedroom."
He examined the sketch pad, "I do like the colors. I think the mustard accent wall you added here really warms up the room, and it goes well with the teal blue."
I gaped up at him in blank surprise, "Who are you, and what have you done with my brother?" He chuckled, "What is that supposed to mean?"
Clothing-wise my brother was very fashionable, but when it came to interior design, he was a bit of a dunce. His room always looked the same: Black, gray, and gargoyles.
I put down the sketch pad, "Where did you learn about color combinations and accent walls?"
He shrugged, "Comes with no longer being single, I suppose."
I smiled, "An increase of estrogen in your life seems to have done you a world of good."

Jonathan straightened his legs and stretched his back, “Do you want to do something with me today?” he asked.
“What did you have in mind?”
“I thought we could go ice skating,” he replied and my face lit up, “Really?”
He nodded, “Sure.”
I got to my feet, but I frowned at him, “You don’t even like ice skating all that much.”
He pulled up his shoulders, “But you do. Do you want to go?”
“Oh, yes please! Can we?”
He stood up and pinched my nose between his index and middle fingers, “Of course, Monkey, that’s why I suggested it.”
I clapped my hands together, and Jonathan chuckled, “You are very cute, but I call shotgun; I’m driving your car there.”
I agreed, of course, but I was so happy to be spending time with my big brother that he could have asked to drive my car off a cliff and I would have said yes.

Jonathan

When we pulled up to the ice-skating rink in Niki's red Mustang, bystanders quickly crowded around it to stare at it, and I shook my head. My sister's car was such an ostentatious piece of machinery that it garnered attention wherever she went.

Stepping out of the car on the driver's side, a passerby approached me, whistling low, his eyes locked on the car, "Dude… V8. Nice. How's the performance?"

I shrugged, "No idea."

The man pressed me, "Come on, you can tell me."

I pulled up my shoulders again, "I really have no idea…"

"V10, actually. And he really doesn't know," Niki chimed in from where she was standing on the passenger side of the car.

The man frowned, "And you do?"

I smiled to myself. Generally, Niki knew a lot more about cars than I did. It was an interest that she and our father shared, and her car was usually much flashier and a lot faster than mine.

Yet onlookers, more specifically men, usually assumed that the car belonged to me, and that she was just driving it.

"I do, actually," Niki retorted.

The man had the gall to challenge her, "Really?"

I laughed internally. Poor man had no idea he was about to get educated. Niki usually bided her time, waiting for the perfect moment to correct them. Which, apparently, was now. She let it fly, rambling off vehicle specs and performance stats that had the man's jaw halfway to the ground. When she was done, he had nothing to say, no witty retort, so she winked at him and blew him a kiss, "If you didn't catch that, I'm sure you can just Google it. Bye now," she said before I tossed her the keys and she sashayed away.

Chuckling, I fell into step next to her and gave her a high-five, "Nice job. Schooled his arse."

Niki laughed, "Misogyny is never going to fucking die."

There was a reason I took my sister ice skating: Her smile as she glided and twirled across the ice was heartwarming. I went around the ice for a round or two, but then I took a seat on the benches and watched my baby sister have her fun.

By the time she left the ice and plopped down next to me, she was red in the face and sweating, her hair clinging to her face in strands and clumps, but she was wearing the biggest smile I had seen on her face in a while.

“Thank you for this,” Niki said after a few minutes of us sitting in silence, watching the other merrymakers on the ice.

I clinked my container of soda against hers, “Anytime, Monkey.”

“I mean it,” she said, “This means so much to me, I… Well, to be honest, I’ve missed you.”

I cast a questioning glance at her, “You’ve missed me? What do you mean?”

She shifted in her seat, “You’ve not been around much, is all…”

My gut dropped; she was right.

“I’ve disappeared into my relationship, haven’t I…?” I admitted, and Niki nodded, “You have a bit... but I understand. You’ve never been in one, and I know you love Christina and you want to make her happy. I just…”

“Miss me?” I guessed, and she rested her head against my shoulder, “I do…”

I pressed my cheek to my sister’s head, “I’m sorry, Monkey,” I apologized, “I never meant to make you feel neglected.”

She gave me a small smile, “I didn’t say that.”

I kissed her hair, “You didn’t have to.”

Chapter 32

Christina

Ever since attending the costume ball, I'd really grown to love themed parties at the Langdon manor. Celeste and Alastair always went all out to ensure that everything at the party, from the decor, to the food and the music, was as authentic and true to the theme as possible.
This time, Celeste decided to have a James Bond-inspired casino night. Why? Because, why not. And, because according to her, her husband looked incredible in a tuxedo, and that was reason enough to make him wear one.

I was especially happy that my mom decided to join us this time around, and she and I had a lot of fun going dress shopping and getting ready for the party.
She looked stunning in the long, formal, gunmetal gray dress that she chose for the evening.
As we stepped out of the car and onto the red carpet at the Langdon manor, it was like we had just arrived at the Oscars, and when I saw the look of wonder and astonishment on my mom's face when we walked into the ballroom, I was even more glad that she decided to join.
Celeste had the entire ballroom outfitted to look and function exactly like a real casino, and my mom was completely transfixed.
Everything you could possibly think of finding in a casino, was there. From the flashing lights and mirrors that surrounded the slot machines, to stools and buckets of coins.

To the left of the slot machines were card tables and you could play anything you wanted, from craps and blackjack and poker to baccarat and roulette.
The atmosphere was buzzing with the crank of slot machine arms and the clink of coins falling into machines. Every so often an alarm would whoop loudly, announcing a winner, and everywhere around the casino were people laughing and talking and placing orders with servers, amongst a flurry of chips rattling in plastic buckets and cards being shuffled and dealt.

It was magical, and my mom's jaw hung wide open as she took everything in, "Is it someone's birthday?" She wanted to know, and I laughed and shook my head, "No, Celeste just felt like having a party." I didn't feel like gambling–I was never any good at it anyway–but my mom was quite keen to try her hand at the roulette table, so Jonathan escorted her there. He refused to let her bet any of her own money though, handing her an envelope full of cash instead. Guests got to keep their winnings, but every penny that the house won went to charity. Philanthropy for the win.

My favorite part of the night was, of course, Jonathan in a suit.
In keeping with the theme of the evening, he wore a very well-fitting black tuxedo, designed to accentuate his upper body's natural V-shape and broadened his shoulders to approximately the width of the Pacific Ocean. His suit trousers followed black tie tradition, with a silk stripe down the side that matched the silk facings on the jacket's lapels, and he really did look like a spy. Or a Bond-villain. I couldn't decide which was more appealing… Either way, I was wholly distracted by him, unable to really focus on what anyone around me was saying.
But I wasn't the only one having trouble staying focused. Every time I looked over at Jonathan, he was already staring at me. Clearly, I chose my outfit well:
A red, off-the-shoulder dress that hugged my body in all the right places, and had a very high slit almost up to the top of my left thigh.
My mom helped me style my hair into loose waves that hung down my back and over my shoulder, and I finished my look with a pair of sky high, strappy gold heels.

Jonathan seemed to be quite taken with my outfit, because he spent the night eye-fucking me from the other side of the room. It was a wonder the dress hadn't taken itself off yet.

My second favorite part of the night was the spy-game.
Guests that wanted to play, could draw a card from a black box in the foyer, and depending on what you pulled from the box, you were either an Agent, or an Operative.
Agents were each given a card with a set of missions to accomplish for the evening, their ultimate mission being to protect the world from the evil Operatives.
Then, among the Agents, certain players were secretly Operatives, who appeared and acted just like Agents, but they were actually double agents.
If you were an Operative, you also had missions to kind of keep up the appearance that you were an Agent, but your real goal was to try to make contact with your hidden contacts among the guests, servers and casino staff before the Agents could figure out who you and your fellow Operatives were, and stop you from taking over the world.

I was incredibly excited. I drew an Operative card and I was having an amazing time. I was absolutely built for this spy shit.
After completing another one of my missions, I received a reward from one of my 'contacts'. A small black box with a toy gun that fired water beads with red dye, and a holster. The gun was supposed to help me complete the next mission. Grinning to myself, I snuck away to strap the gun to my thigh, underneath my dress at the top of the slit. It was very well-hidden, but I could still easily reach it, and I felt like an international superspy.

Once I had the gun in place, I made my way back onto the casino floor.
I scanned the crowd for my mom, and I couldn't help but smile when I saw her, sitting at the bar, a big smile on her face and a very faint blush to her cheeks, talking to none other than Magnus Andreassen. Whatever he was saying to her, the Dane had my mom eating out of his hand.
I get it, Mom. Infinite men wield a different kind of magic.

I was just about to step into the ladies' room to use the bathroom and to reapply my lipstick, when a familiar voice sounded behind me, "Going somewhere… Operative?" the voice asked, low and dangerous, and my soul quivered at the sound.
Jonathan.
Fuck, he's an Agent. How does he know I'm an Operative?
I reached for the gun, but as always I completely misjudged how fast Infinites could move. Before I even touched it, he was right behind me, whirling me around to face him, and he grabbed my wrists and pinned me against the wall next to the bathroom door.

He flicked my dress aside and ran his fingers up my bare thigh. Then he pulled the gun from the holster and, like he'd been handling guns for years, he removed the entire chamber with the ammunition in a blur of high speed before slipping the gun back into the holster.
Then he kissed me, and his hand traveled higher up my thigh, under my dress.
His fingers gently caressed the front of my panties as his tongue pressed against mine. The anticipation had me breathless.
He pulled his head back, and moved his other hand up to my chest. He slowly ran a finger up the middle of my chest, in between my breasts, up to my collarbone, and then, very quickly, wrapped his fingers around the base of my neck as he pressed his crotch against me.
I could feel how hard he was, and the moan that escaped my lips echoed up the walls of the hallway we were standing in.
"Darling," he said huskily next to my ear, "what was that?"
I tried to press my body against him, but his hand at my throat limited my movement, "You're making me horny."
"Is that so?" he replied.
I nodded, "Yes. I can feel you… pressing against me… it's driving me crazy."
He leaned in and growled, right by my ear, his fingers still stroking the front of my panty, "Do you like it? Do you like having my cock, pressing against you?" he wanted to know, and I heard myself moan again.
Jonathan talking dirty to me was making me so wet my panties probably had a visible wet spot by now. I was unable to reply, so I just nodded.

Jonathan gave me a crooked smile, "Is your pussy wet for me?" and without waiting for a response, he simply pushed my panties aside like they weren't even there, and slipped his finger all the way inside me. My head rolled back and I gasped.

"Ah, darling, your pussy is soaking wet," he said against my skin before he kissed the side of my neck, "I want to fingerfuck you until you come for me," he murmured, "Would you like that? Would you like to come on my fingers?"

I whimpered.

"Are you ready, Christina?" he asked.

My knees were shaking and I nodded, and just as he pulled his hand back… the door to the men's room clicked and the handle started to turn.

Jonathan backed away from me just as quickly as he had stepped up to me, as one of the other party guests emerged from the bathroom. I wasn't sure if the guy was mortal or Infinite, but I didn't give a fuck. I ducked into the bathroom as soon as he started speaking to Jonathan in German; I had to escape.

I splashed some cold water on my chest and neck, trying to slow down my pounding heartbeat and calm my breathing. If the guest wasn't there talking to Jonathan, I knew for sure he would have followed me into the bathroom.

I looked at myself in the mirror and shook my head. One thing was certain:

This upgraded version of Jonathan, that grabbed me by the throat, talked dirty and took the c-word… this version of him was going to end me.

By the time I was calm enough to stick my nose out the door without worrying that other people would hear my heart freight-training in my chest, Jonathan wasn't in the hallway anymore, and I rejoined the party just in time to see Alastair announce the winner of the Agents and Operative game.

Great. After all that excitement and sexual tension, I lost the freaking game. Nice.

Jonathan's eyes found mine from across the room and he winked at me. I narrowed my eyes in response. *I'm going to get him for this.*

Chapter 33

Christina

"Are you nervous?" I asked Devyn.

She and Kirill were going on a double date with me and Jonathan, and I was getting ready with her at her place.

Devyn shrugged, touching up her makeup, "I don't know. I feel like it will be easier, you know? A double date, there's other people, we don't have to focus on each other all the time."

"That's true. Jonathan didn't say where we were going, but it will probably be somewhere fun."

Devyn started putting on her sneakers, "Bonus points if we're going bowling or something. Then I can skip the 'can-he-hold-a-conversation' phase, and jump straight to the 'is-he-sweet-or-psycho' phase."

I laughed. *Good old Kiryusha is very sweet, but I'm sure he's plenty psycho as well.*

"Your first date with Jonathan, were you nervous?" Devyn turned the question back to me.

I thought back to when Jonathan took me to 'Eclipse', and I smiled at the memory, "Not about being on the date, more like, going to an expensive restaurant. I wasn't sure if I was fancy enough."

Devyn grinned, "Quite obviously you were weighed, measured, and you were found perfect."

"I've been wanting to ask you," she continued, "How did you find out… you know… who he is?"

My mind froze for a second.

Most of the time, I tried not to think about the night that the nascent attacked me. *I don't think I'll ever be able to forget the sounds it made when it lunged at me, or the sound of bones breaking, or the sound from its throat when Jonathan...*

"I saw some stuff that I wasn't supposed to," I chose my words carefully.

Devyn's eyes widened, "I so badly want to ask you what you saw, but you probably can't talk about it."

I pressed my lips into a thin line and I shrugged, "Sorry Dev, can't."

"So, what happened? What did you do?"

I took a sip of water, "I bolted."

Devyn nodded understandingly, "Of course, you must have been scared."

It was really sweet of her to try and empathize, but she had no idea. I just nodded. Devyn just looked at me, but she didn't say anything. I took a moment before I went on, "It took me a while to process everything."

Devyn squeezed my shoulder, "I don't know if I'd be able to date a man as dangerous as Jonathan." The irony of Devyn's statement wasn't lost on me. She had no idea what Kirill was capable of. Honestly, neither did I, but Devyn had even less of an idea.

But Devyn calling Jonathan dangerous, immediately reminded me of what he looked like with his wings open and his fangs bared, and I could almost hear my body sigh. *He is dangerous, but he looks so damn good doing it.*

"I told you, Dev," I smiled, "He's not dangerous to me. Jonathan would never, ever hurt me." Devyn smiled knowingly, "But woe to the person that tries. Like, blue boy, at the club..."

My hair wasn't acting right and the chic, high ponytail I was trying to get in place wasn't ponytailing the way I wanted it to, but it was going to have to do because I was ready to give up. I was standing in Devyn's bathroom, trying to make it cooperate one more time when my phone beeped on the vanity in her room.

"Could you get that?" I asked Devyn. She was sitting on her bed, scrolling on her phone while she waited for me.

"It's your man," she replied, "he says they're almost here." I peered around the door. "You ready?"

She nodded, "Yes ma'am. Let's go."

As Devyn was about to open the front door, it occurred to me that I should confirm something with my best friend and I took her by the arm, "Dev? About Jonathan… I didn't tell him that you know about him being…"
"The mob?" Devyn completed the sentence, and when I nodded, she gestured that her lips were sealed.

We started at the bowling alley, confirming yet again that I was not good with balls. At least not the kind not attached to a body. Jonathan was though, obviously. So was Kirill. *Infinites... so unfair.*
Devyn, to her credit, was also pretty good, and at least we teamed up one couple versus the other, so Jonathan picked up where I was lacking, which was everywhere.
I never knew that Kirill was so socially… awkward. He was such a smooth talker at the manor, always witty, always cracking stupid jokes… but tonight, at this bowling alley, he wasn't saying much. He spoke when spoken to, but Devyn didn't seem to mind all that much. My friend seemed to be having a good time, despite the fact that her date was less than chatty.
The double-date also gave her a chance to chat with Jonathan. I knew she was cautious of him because of what she thought he was; I could see it in the uneasy smile on her face when he talked to her.

"So Devyn," Jonathan asked her, "Were you and Christina in any of the same classes?"
Devyn shook her head, "Actually no. I majored in economics."
Jonathan's eyebrows shot up, "Did you? That's interesting."
Aaand they were off. The two of them started talking about resource allocations and incentives, half of my brain shut off, and Kirill went to get a refill on our drinks. *Yay, my bestie and my boyfriend are bonding. If only I had any idea what they were talking about.* By the time Kirill came back from the bar, he glanced over at them and shot me a curious look, "Still talking?"
I grimaced, nodding, "Kill me now."

After the bowling alley, we moved to a games arcade. Devyn appeared to be more comfortable with him, and she challenged Jonathan to a motorcycle race, while Kirill dragged me to the skee-ball machine. *Damn it, balls again.*

Kirill then wanted to shoot zombies on one of the shooting games, and Jonathan was there for it. Devyn and I hung back and let the boys play, and I had to focus really hard to keep from laughing out loud when I saw Devyn's eyes widen at how Jonathan did not miss a single shot. If she wasn't convinced before that he was a mob boss, she had no choice now. *I am very sure my man has instilled some or other unworldly fear and deep and abiding respect into my friend's heart. It's a win-win, really.*

At the end of the evening we dropped Devyn off at her building. Kirill said that he also had to go, and he disappeared into the night.
Jonathan and I were sitting in his car in front of my house, and he turned his head to look at me, "I like Devyn, I can see why she's your best friend."
My eyebrows shot up to my hairline, "Oh, you like her, do you? Are you going to dump me for my best friend, huh?"
He leveled a blank look at me, "I'm not even going to dignify that with an answer."
I crossed my eyes at him, and changed the subject, "I think the date went well."
He nodded slowly, "They seemed to hit it off."
I turned sideways in my seat, leaning my head against the headrest, "I wonder if there's going to be a second date," and Jonathan pulled up his shoulders, "Maybe. If Kiryusha doesn't disappear first."
I smiled mirthfully, then I changed the subject, "Oh, I wanted to tell you. Devyn said she thinks she knows the truth about you."
Jonathan turned his head slowly and looked skeptically at me, "Really?"
"Uh-huh," I nodded, "I know, I had the same reaction."
His eyebrows raised, "Darling… if she knows the truth…"
I cleared my throat, "She thinks… that you're a mob boss."
"Does she now?" he asked.
I nodded in confirmation.
"How does she think Kirill fits into that scenario?" he wanted to know, and I pursed my lips for a moment, "She thinks him and Kat are your enforcers."
He leaned his forehead against the top of the steering wheel as he shook with laughter, and I giggled in my seat, "I know, it's funny."
"And you just let her believe that?"

I shrugged, "Of course I did. It's easier to explain than 'future vampire king'."

He shook his head slowly, "It sounds terrifying when you put it like that."

I leaned over and kissed his cheek, "It is what it is. Your Majesty."

Jonathan shook his head and chuffed. "Kirill the enforcer. That's rich."

I gave him a knowing smile, "I know, right? You're more than capable of handling your own business."

He lifted his eyebrows once in confirmation, "And I always do. Unless Kirill is bored."

That reminds me… "By the way," I went on, "Do you know whatever happened to the guy that drugged me? Like, did Kirill unalive him, or something?"

He cleared his throat and shook his head, "No, Kirill did not 'unalive' him. He is dead, but he apparently 'unalived' himself."

"Oh… That's kind of tragic."

Jonathan shrugged, "Doesn't seem like much of a loss to me."

Chapter 34

Celeste

"Man is the cruelest animal."
These words have been true since before they were spoken.
All throughout my long life, the worst suffering that I have seen human beings endure was not inflicted upon them by the hands of the Infinite, but by their fellow human beings.
Ever since I was able to understand, my father instilled upon me the Laws of Night, and I never had any difficulties discerning when to apply the First and the Second laws.
Innocence and Truth were easy to establish.
But, the Third Law was the one I had trouble with. Blood begets blood.

For a long time, I was under the impression that this Law was set in place by my grandfather so that we may take revenge upon those that had wronged us. That's what I wanted after my family was murdered and I was the only survivor: Revenge.
I wanted nothing more than to track down whoever was responsible for my family's gruesome deaths, and do to them what I, as a little girl of 11 years old, had witnessed them do to my father Ionáthan, my mother Dionissia, and my little sister Sophia. Moonlight knows, I never forgave myself for not trying harder to find my baby brother, Silas.

But when he took me with him to Italy, my father's friend, Uncle Dante, taught me that revenge would give me only temporary gratification, and that revenge was nothing more than a quick fix that spawned an endless cycle of retribution.

Justice, on the other hand, was not about retaliating or getting even. Justice sought to right a wrong, to restore the balance.
That's what I chose to bring about in the world: Justice.
The eldest of three siblings, I'd always had a protective nature, which only seemed to amplify after marrying Alastair and having Jonathan. So, when the prevalence of human trafficking came to our attention, we knew we could not let it stand.
His nature every bit as protective as my own, my husband and I started a new hobby:
The dismantling of every human trafficking syndicate we came across.

In the late 1700's, we were tracking a ring with suspected ties to the House of Apollo, which operated all across Slovakia and Austria and had extended its filthy claws into Italy.
It was there, in one of the seedier neighborhoods of Milan, that our investigation led us to an old rundown house. The house stood in sort of a composed way, as if it remembered having residents and now simply chose not to. A long time ago, the floors might have been a highly polished parquet, and while the walls stood firm, the window panes were mostly cracked or broken completely. What truly hinted at the horrors the building held was the odor. The stench of dust and death shrouded the atmosphere.
We searched every room in the house but found nothing. Then, Alastair heard something. I heard it too. A soft, shuffling sound, coming from the cellar.
Upon our descent into the dark, dusty cellar, I was horrified. Now abandoned, it was once a chamber of horrors. Some primordial evil hung in the air, clinging to the memories of unspeakable things that had been done to people in this space. Alastair cursed under his breath, and I was inclined to share the sentiment.

Movement in the darkest corner of the cellar caught my eye, at the edges of my peripheral vision.. I stepped closer and listened with my mind.
No words.
Only sounds.
Angry and afraid.

Then I spotted the source of the scuffling. In the corner of the cellar, chained to the wall, and sitting in her own filth, was a tiny, emaciated little girl, her hair the color of sunset, eyes the brightest green.
She saw me looking at her, and her little face contorted into the most ferocious snarl she could muster. She tried to lunge at me, but the chains around her wrists prohibited her from getting very far before she fell to the ground.
My heart broke, "Who would do a thing so vile, so evil, as to abandon this child here, in this squalid… hell-hole?" Alastair shook his head in disbelief, "The dregs of society, surely."
I pulled a sandwich from my shoulder bag and unwrapped it. Holding it out to the little girl, I got down to my haunches and slowly, cautiously, moved toward her.
The little girl was apprehensive, and she tried to back away into the wall, but there was nowhere she could go.
"It's alright, little one," I said as tenderly as I could in Italian, "Here, eat. You must be starving. What's your name, pretty?"
No response.
I tried asking in different languages: German. Russian. Slovak. Latvian. Ukrainian.
Still no answer, only angry, terrified snarls.
Then I changed tactics. Instead of talking, I spoke to her mind in song. In the lullaby that my mother used to sing to me when I was a child.

It seemed to work.
The little girl kept her eyes on me, but grabbed the sandwich and gobbled it up in two big bites. She didn't even chew, she just swallowed.
"Poor little princess," Alastair said softly.
Still singing the lullaby to the girl's mind, I inched closer. She snarled again, but I held up a reassuring palm, and quickly and easily broke the chains that had been holding her. She cowered against the wall, rubbing her raw, chafed little wrists.
I slowly reached for her, and she let me touch her arm.
She instantly pulled away at the touch, but then her body relaxed a little bit. I smiled and stroked her skinny little arm softly.
She still seemed apprehensive, but she moved closer to me.
Over my shoulder, Alastair handed me another sandwich to give to the girl, which she devoured just as quickly as she did the first one.

I still wasn't sure if she would be willing to trust me, but I had to try; I had to get this poor child out of the dark. I held my arms out to her.
In a leap that I was not expecting at all, she jumped into my arms, clinging to my neck like it was her only lifeline.
Alastair wrapped his jacket around the little girl, and I stood up, cradling the child against me.
"Now what?" I asked.
Alastair smiled kindly, and the next words he spoke reminded me exactly why I would love this man until the world stopped turning and time ceased to exist, "Now, we take her home."

Upon our arrival at our house in Florence, Jonathan was awaiting us in the foyer. When he saw the little girl in my arms, he had the softest look on his face that I had ever seen on my son, "What's this then?" he asked, "Who's this little princess?"
Smiling, he strode over and gently, tenderly stroked the little girl's auburn hair, "Hello, Monkey."

Despite our best efforts, it took the terrified little thing weeks to adjust. Most mornings she woke up screaming and wouldn't allow me or Alastair to touch her. She barely tolerated us giving her a bath and she snarled and scuttled away as soon as she had clothes on her body. The only person she seemed to be able to stand was Jonathan. As short as my son's fuse was at times, he could also be endlessly patient when he felt like it. Many a day he would spend hours upon hours, sitting on her bedroom floor reading to her, letting her do whatever it was that she needed to do.
We named her 'Donika', for the victory that she had achieved over the horrid hand that fate had dealt her, and for the light of the morning star that her rare and special little smiles brought into our lives.

"Mami," Jonathan wanted to know from me one morning over coffee, "I wanted to speak with you and Father about our little princess."
"What is it son?" Alastair urged.
Jonathan took a sip of his coffee before he went on, "It's been months and no-one has claimed her…"
I glanced at my husband and he gave me a tiny nod. Then I smiled at my son, "I'm glad you asked, sweetheart. How would you feel about officially and legally becoming a big brother?"

Jonathan's entire face lit up, "Really? You're going to adopt her?"
Alastair nodded, "That's the plan. We have the documents ready, we just wanted to check with our firstborn."
A small, shy little smile found its way onto my son's face, "I've always wanted to be a big brother."

Chapter 35

Devyn

One of my favorite things to do was to listen to music and dance. At high volume. All the way home.

I knew people were watching, but I didn't give a shit. The music from my wireless earphones drowned out the noise of the other commuters and the traffic, and carried me home on a river of sound. Down the sidewalk, across the street through the park, over the bridge that crossed the little stream, all the way to my building.

I was so swept away by the beat, so lost in the Korean lyrics even though I didn't understand them, that I didn't notice the figure following me, clad in black from head to toe, hoodie pulled up over their head, eyes locked on my every move, watching my every step. When I got to my apartment and unlocked my door, I still did not see the figure step up right behind me, until a hand clasped around my shoulder and turned me around, and by then it was too late, and all I could do was scream, right in the face of…

Kirill, and he put his hands up in surrender.

When I saw it was him, I put my hand on my stomach and breathed a sigh of relief, "It's you. Shit, I thought I was about to be murdered," I laughed awkwardly.

I took out one earphone and Kirill nodded slowly in comprehension, "Ah. Music. Of course."

I took out the other one as well and chuckled, "You thought I was ignoring you?"

He nodded, "*Da*, I see you go out, I call, I say 'Devyn, hello', but you no answer."

"So, you followed me?"

He thought about it for a moment, "*Da…* like creepy stalker."

"Can I get you anything to drink?" I asked him once we were inside my apartment.
Kirill shook his head, "No, no."
I turned to him, one hand on my hip, "What brings you by?"
He took a small step closer, "I don't know…"
My heart fluttered a little bit in my chest, and a droplet of desire trickled down into the pit of my stomach. There was something about his eyes, something wild and untamed, that was kindling for the fire within me. The curve of his lips was so inviting, and I found myself imagining his lips caressing unspeakable places all over my body.

I also took a step closer, decreasing the distance between us even more.
Kirill locked eyes with me, and stepped even closer, "Maybe I want kiss you."
I looked at his lips and then back at his eyes, "Maybe you should."
And he did.
I never knew that it was possible to lose every single shred of clothing so quickly.
Before I knew it, Kirill had me stripped down to naught but my skin, my body arched beneath his.
His touch, his kiss had me ravenous and by the time he slid into me, it happened in one smooth, delicious movement…

'Holy… shit," I breathed later.
Kirill was on his back next to me, both of us breathless.
"I think I need a cigarette," I said and he laughed, "You smoke?"
I chuckled, "No… but that doesn't mean I don't need a cigarette."
He got up to put his pants back on, and I went on, "Actually, I'm pretty sure the neighbors might also need a cigarette."
Smiling, he lay back down next to me and tugged me back into his arms to kiss me.

When he pulled back, he stroked my hair away from my forehead, "Devyn…" he started to explain, "I am not good boyfriend…"
I nodded slowly, "Somehow I knew that…"

He sighed, and I smiled a sad smile at him, “This was great, Kirill, but…”
“Friends…?” he finished my sentence for me.
I nodded in agreement, “Friends… with benefits?”
He winked, and leaned closer, “I show you benefit…” before his lips parted mine one more time…
After he left, I thought of taking a shower, but decided against it. I didn’t have any plans, and for the moment, I didn’t so much mind smelling like sex.
With a smug smile on my mug, I poured myself a glass of wine, plopped down on the sofa, and unlocked my phone to call Christina.

“Hi Dev.”
“I will give you three guesses, the first two don’t count. Guess who just got railed?” I started.
Christina burst out in peals of merry laughter, “It certainly wasn’t me. So, it had to have been you.”
“Ding! Give the woman a prize!” I whooped in celebration.
“Who did you bang?” Christina asked, still laughing.
I giggled, “Mr. Russia, of course.”
“What?” she exclaimed in surprise, “You and Kirill? Are you serious?”
“Hell yeah. I signed myself up for some Russian percussion.”
Christina laughed out loud again, “I am impressed. You shagged the Beast from the East. Well done, girl.”
“Thank you, thank you.”
“Was it what you were expecting?” she asked, and I shook my head, “No, it was more. Wilder. Savage.”
“Are you seeing him again?” Christina asked, but I just shrugged, “Doubtful. The sex was great and all, but I don’t think it’s going any further than that. Well, maybe different positions, but no further than sex.”

Sipping on my second glass of wine, I had to admit that I was a little bit disappointed that the connection I had felt with Kirill wouldn’t amount to much more than something physical. A relationship with him could have been interesting.

But it was probably for the best, I'd been planning on looking for work in a different city anyway. And my mom always told me: A broken man cannot be fixed if he doesn't want to be.

Besides, if a guy tells you he's not boyfriend material, it was usually better to listen to him. It was a warning, not a challenge.

Chapter 36

I have hated them from the first moment I laid eyes on them.
Such luxury.
Such riches.
They had everything. They have always had everything. Mansions, apartments, fancy cars. Never hungry, never wanting for anything. From the first time I saw them leave that gaudy monstrosity of a mansion in Florence, hatred blossomed in my heart. It grew from a tiny bloom, to a seething, bubbling black mass, coiling and reeling like an angry snake.

Every time they moved somewhere new, I was tempted to light the place on fire, to burn it down with them and all of their belongings and their servants in it. The thought of their screams always made me smile. Obviously they wouldn't die, but surely no servant of theirs would make it out alive. And the ones that did would make for a tasty snack.

Now, in their newest flashy mansion, I hated them even more. They looked so happy.
Especially him. The golden boy. The heir to the empire.
Look at him, breezing out of the restaurant as if the world belonged to him, whistling to himself as he goes.
I chortled to myself. Uppity son-of-a-bitch, thinking his money made him special.
Shaking my head, I glared at the scion, the crown-prince.
It should be me, I have just as much claim to the throne as pretty boy over here.

Anger flared in my heart again.
I blamed my idiot father.
If my father had spent even an ounce of his energy trying to give his son a better future, maybe there might have been hope. *Maybe we could have*... I cursed under my breath. Never mind. It was far too late for ifs and buts and maybes.
I'd always hated my father. Hated him for not finding the rest of the family, hated him for denying what he was: Superior. To everyone. Mostly, though, I hated him for the disgusting, sycophantic way he treated mortals. I spat on the ground at the thought.
Mortals.
What beastly creatures they were, primitive in their ways. They all had the same dull, bovine quality to them, which, to my mind, made them good enough for only one thing: Food.
Humans only served a purpose if they could be used for food, pleasure, or entertainment. In whichever order. They died so easily anyway, weaklings that they were.

And this family… They loved those sickening worms almost as much as my father did. They even married them, tainted the pure, consecrated blood of my forefathers with foul, mortal blood.
I hated that my own blood was tainted, but I vowed to never taint it any further by breeding with a filthy, disgusting mortal. It repulsed me enough that I was born from the body of one. So much so that I slit her throat as soon as I was able to hold a knife. How my pitiful father mourned her. I would never forget the sight of my father, weeping at her grave, cursing whomever took his love from him, and I remembered fighting the urge to laugh.

As much as I hated him, I cursed the day that my father left me, ending his own life, abandoning his only son to fend for himself. Oh, how I cried for my father, mourned him.
Until I woke up one day, and I decided that there was no point weeping over a father that had forsaken me and left me behind. I would forge my own path, make my own way in the world. And I would take absolutely everything that my father didn't have the balls to give me.
Soon it would be my turn, and I was going to take everything from them.

Everything that should be mine. I would be a better ruler than their precious prince, anyway.
I closed my eyes and sighed. I could see it: Me, sitting on the throne as King Triumphant, the corpses of my enemies at my feet, my golden-eyed queen at my side.

I opened my eyes to glare at the car speeding away from the restaurant.
And I knew exactly how to get it.
For the longest time, I thought those sun-worshipping lunatics to be of no importance, but after seeing what their little pet did in the woods in Bavaria, I changed my mind. They might be useful after all.

Chapter 37

Christina

Kat stretched out on the sofa and sighed.
I was sitting just across from her on the other end of the sofa in the family den and I chuckled inwardly at her groaning and grumbling.
"I feel like partying," Kat pondered out loud.
I looked up at her from where I was scrolling on my phone, "Could be fun."
Kat's face lit up, "Are you up for a bash?"
I shrugged, "Depends… is 'bash' code for something unspeakable? Or does it just mean party?" and Kat burst out laughing, "It just means party, Chrissie. The unspeakable happens later. Hopefully."
"In that case, why not? Jonathan's… in a meeting… somewhere. So sure, let's do it. When?"
Kat quickly replied, "Tonight."
I wasn't really surprised. By now I was used to Kat's impulsive decisions and spontaneity, so I nodded slowly. I was a little bit tired though. I had another secret martial arts training session with Kirill early that morning, followed by a Krav session with Kat, and I was actually looking forward to getting some rest. On the other hand, I hadn't really been out since we went to Kat's club in Prague, and I'd never been clubbing with Kat, so it could be fun, "And where did you want to go?"
"New York!" Kat beamed.
I frowned, "Sure… It's a long drive, but okay."
"Pfft," Kat breathed out her signature huff, "Ask Jonny if we can borrow his jet."

I mean, she could probably just open a portal for us, just Dr. Strange it, or we could take the jet. I didn't mind asking him, I was pretty sure he would say yes. But he was in a meeting with a new client, and I didn't know if he'd be able to talk. I decided it was worth a shot, "Okay, I can text him, let's see if he replies."
Hi babe, sorry to bother you
Kat and I want to go to New York
Can we borrow your jet?

He texted back almost immediately and my eyebrows shot up; I was expecting a longer delay:
582-222-8648

I frowned and showed my phone screen to Kat, "He just sent me a number?"
Kat looked at the screen and shrugged, "Pilot's number, I reckon."
I'm confused, "So… what do I do now? Do I just call up the pilot, like, 'Hi, this is Christina, fly us to New York?' Or how does this work?"
Kat nodded, getting up from the sofa, "That sounds about right, yes."
"I'll go get Niki," she said as she made her way out the door, "you call Devyn."

∞

A driver in a stretch limo picked us up from the airport and drove us to Kat's building. We entered the gleaming foyer of the luxury building where Kat's apartment was located, and Niki and Kat headed straight for the elevator. Devyn and I hung back, staring in awe around the lobby with its black and white tiles and walls, and accents gilded opulently in gold.
"I feel like such a movie star right now," I breathed.
Devyn only nodded.
"Are we going or not?" Niki called from the elevator.

As I was unpacking my suitcase to get ready for whatever club we were going to, my phone buzzed, and I smiled to myself when I saw Jonathan's name on the screen:
Have you arrived safely in NY?

I frowned. No 'darling', no 'love', no emoji… *Is he mad at me?*

I texted back:
Yes babe, I was just about to let you know
Got carried away, sorry
xxx

He didn't reply.
Well, that's disappointing. Oh, well. I tried to put it out of my head, and I went to take a shower.
When I finished my shower, I saw that I had three missed calls from him, so I called him back quickly, "Babe I am so sorry," I apologized when he answered, "I was in the shower."
"That's alright, darling," he smiled.
I sank down onto the bed and sighed in relief, "I thought you were mad at me."
"Of course not, love," he replied, "Why would you think that?"
"You didn't reply to my text."
"I didn't?" he asked in consternation, "I must have forgotten to press send. Here, I'll send it now. Check if you've received it."
My phone buzzed next to my ear, "Hang on, let me see," I said as I lowered it to take a look.
When I opened the message, it wasn't a text, but a photo.
Of him.
Sitting in the bathtub.
Halfway submerged.
Showing just enough skin to let me know that he was stark naked.
I pressed the phone back to my ear, "When did you take this?"
He chuckled, "Moments ago. I thought you might like it."
Obviously he's trying to torture me.

Jonathan changed the subject, "Have you ladies decided where you're going this evening?"
"Not yet…" I replied as I was getting my outfit for the night out of my bag, "Kat hasn't made up her mind yet."
"Alright," he accepted, "please promise me you will be careful?"
I smiled. I was so in love with how much this man loved me, "Are you worried about me?" I asked.
"Of course, I am," he replied immediately, "I love you."
"I love you too," I said back, "and I promise I'll be careful."

I had just hung up and put my phone back down on the bed when there was a knock at the door.
"Cover up what you don't want seen, here I come," I heard Kat's voice before she swung the door open and strode into the bedroom, "Are you almost ready?" she asked.
I made a face at her and glanced down at myself, "Does it look like I am?"
She shrugged, pulling a black leather corset top from her closet, "I don't know what you young people wear to the club nowadays."
I took my make-up bag from my luggage, "Have you decided where you want to go?"
She nodded and grinned, "Yes, but it's a surprise."
"I've been meaning to ask you," she went on, "what does Devyn know… about us? You know, me and Jonathan and Kirillovich."
I made a face at her, "Like you don't know. I'm sure Jonathan told you."
Kat giggled, "He did. I just wanted to hear it again… I'm his enforcer."

"Hey, you two!" Niki called out from the living room, "Let's go. Time's a wastin'."

Kat's idea to go clubbing in New York was inspired, and we should have done this ages ago.
The music was pounding, the drinks were flowing, asses were being shaken everywhere, and I was having a fantastic time with my friends.
My friends. It made my heart really happy to know that that was what I could call these three girls dancing near me. Devyn, Niki and Kat were my friends.

The issue with any club anywhere, was that 99% of the time, you would inevitably encounter some or other douche-canoe that would not take 'no' for an answer.
Enter Chad.
At least, he looked like a 'Chad', in his too-small shirt, approaching us like he had an icicle's chance in Arizona. I will give him props for perseverance, because he kept trying to dance with each of us in turn.
Poor Chad kept getting turned down, and when he approached me and put his hand on my waist…

Something in my mind clicked. I reverted back to the last training session I had with Kirill, and I bared my teeth, "Get your fucking hands off me!"

In a practiced automatic motion, I wrapped my fingers around his wrist, twisted his arm and pressed it to his back. He yelped in pain, "My hand! My hand!"

I sneered, "What's the matter, muffin? Is this the hand you beat your meat with? Touch me again, and I break it," I snarled at him.

I shoved him away into the crowd of clubbers, and when I turned back to my friends, Kat was the first to let out a loud whoop.

∞

When I woke up the next morning, the first thing I wanted was Jonathan. And then food. And Jonathan again. And then more sleep. I'd shared the bed with Kat, but she had already woken up, and the room was empty.

Her place was really nice. Huge and roomy, the walls of the bedroom were painted dark purple, with colorful calaveras everywhere. Very funky, very Kat.

I had another steamy dream about Jonathan, and I woke up horny again. *This dry-spell has to end. Fast. I am going fucking crazy.* To add insult to injury, I was very sure I was still drunk from the night before, which only intensified the horniness. Rubbing my eyes, I made my way out of the bedroom and into the massive open-plan living room of Kat's penthouse apartment.

Devyn was still fast asleep on the sofa where she had passed out, but Niki was nowhere to be seen. I remembered her and Kat mentioning that they were thinking of going to the sauna or the gym in the morning, so that was probably where they went.

I got myself a drink of water and went back to bed. When I unlocked my phone to see what time it was, I saw that I had a text message from Jonathan:

Good morning my love
xxx

Smiling, I curled up in bed and texted him back:

Morning handsome
How did you sleep?

My smile broadened when he called me,
“Good morning, darling. Did you sleep well?” he asked.
“I did, I dreamt of you.”
“Really? Was I naked?” he wanted to know.
“Very…”
“Interesting,” he replied, “sounds like your dream and mine would have had some fun together.”
“Oh? Really? How so?”
“Well, when I woke up this morning, I found myself… shall we say… rather inspired,” he replied, his voice sounding very sultry.
“What do you mean?”
He chuckled, “Check your messages.”
I opened the text he sent me and my eyes widened - It was a picture of his lower body, still in bed, the sheet pulled over a glaringly obvious case of morning wood.
And just like that I was wet. I bit my lower lip, “Wow, you could probably build a solid cabin with all of that wood. Do you… want to tell me about your dream?”
“Actually,” he said, “I’d rather show you… But I’m too far away to touch you the way I want to, so how about we play a little game of Jonny Says…?”
Red-hot desire blossomed between my thighs. “How does the game work?” I asked, and I could hear his grin in his reply, “Everything Jonny says, Chrissie does.”
Phone sex. Yes, please.
“Get your earphones, darling,” he suggested, “You’ll need both hands.”
When I had an earbud in one ear and the covers pulled up over me, he started,
“Reach in under your shirt for me.”
“Okay.”
“Take those beautiful breasts in your hands. Tell me how that feels.”
“Hmm… good… but I need you…”
He gave me a dark chuckle, “Now, I want you to take your nipples between your fingers, like I would.”
I gulped, but I did what he told me to. I closed my eyes, feeling the heat growing between my legs as I pinched and rolled my nipples between my fingers.

"Good girl," Jonathan's voice crooned in my ear. "Now," he went on, "keep one hand right there, keep rolling your nipple between your fingers."
"Okay…"
"Move your other hand down," he instructed.
I gasped, "How… how far down?"
"Touch your pussy for me," he said, and I moaned at the sound.
"Okay…" I said as I shifted my hand down between my thighs, "Now what?"
I heard him draw a breath through his clenched teeth, "Babe?" I asked, "Are you…?"
"Touching myself?" he asked, "Yes." *Ah fuck, I wish I could watch, that's so hot.*

Then he went on, "Slide your finger over onto that delicious little button there, and do what you would like me to do. Slowly now."
I moaned at the sensation. It felt good, stroking my clit, but I imagined that it was him touching me.
"Does that feel good?" he wanted to know.
"Yes…" I confirmed softly.
"Good girl, keep rubbing your clit for me," he continued, and my breathing sped up.
"Are you wet for me, darling?" his voice breathed into my ear.
"Yes… yes…" I whimpered. *I am, I fucking am, and the thought of him with his dick in his hand is just making me wetter and wetter by the second.*
"Oh, I wish I could taste you."
"Fuck… Me too," I whispered back.
"I need you to make yourself come for me, I need to hear you," he replied, "So, slip that finger inside you…"
I was about to obey, when the bedroom swung open, and Kat burst into the room singing loudly and very off key, "...Let's hear it for Neeeeew Yoooork!"
I hit panic stations, all hands on deck, and I ended the call and yanked the covers up to my chin.

Kat stopped in her tracks, and shut the door behind her, her eyes wide, "Oh… my… shattered… nerves! Are you and Jonny phone-fucking?"

She howled with laughter as all of the blood in my entire body shot up to color my face bright red, and all I could do was melt under the covers.

Fuck everything that is my entire life.

Jonathan

I was wholly and completely losing my mind.
The only thing on my mind was Christina. I hadn't made love to her in weeks, and all I could think of was her skin, her body, how her nipples felt in my mouth, what she tasted like, how she felt under my tongue, how her pussy felt; warm, slick and moist against my fingers, around my cock, the scent of her arousal, her moans of pleasure when I was inside her…
Our phone session this morning was going well until we were interrupted, by Kat, judging by how far off-key the singing was, and as the phone call ended, so did my hard-on.
And the only thing I could do to keep myself from going completely insane, was to pummel my frustrations out into the punching bag in the gym.
I was in there for a little over two hours, and even though I didn't feel like it was anywhere near enough, I didn't have time to do more. I had to take a shower and get ready. I had a brunch appointment with a very special lady.

I was quite happy that she agreed to meet with me, but I was nervous about the appointment, as this was not something I'd ever done before. I was so nervous that I nearly forgot to pick up the flowers that I ordered before I went to her house.

I thought a charming café or a restaurant would be the best choice, so that was where I drove us.
At the restaurant, I waited until the server brought us our orders to start our conversation, and I smiled at her and clinked my glass against hers.
"So," she started, "this was unexpected."
I shrugged, "I had to wait until Christina was out of town."
"Oh?" she enquired, "How so?"
I took a deep breath. *This is it, it's now or never.*

Belinda

My heart was thumping a mile a minute. When Jonathan called me to meet him for brunch, I was confused at first, even more so when he arrived at the house with flowers, this time a colossal bouquet of white roses.

I think I know what he's about to say. Or at least I hope I do. I really liked Jonathan. He was, by far, the best boyfriend that Christina had ever had. He was a good person. In everything Jonathan did, he was loyal and sincere, and he had integrity. And courage.

He made Christina happy. He made her laugh. She went in and out of each day with a big smile on her face. And he treated her with such respect, the way he spoke to her. Even when she wasn't around, he always acted with her in mind.

A while ago, when Christina was at work, he was helping me unload boxes of books that I was donating to the library where I used to work, and the poor little librarian was hitting on him like there was no tomorrow. I was watching from the doorway, I didn't think he knew I was even there, and I was about to step in and tell her that he was my daughter's boyfriend, but I didn't need to.

He flashed her a polite smile and asked what book she would recommend for his girlfriend. And then proceeded to hype Christina up so much that the librarian started looking a bit uncomfortable.

Not that their relationship was always moonlight sonnets and roses. They had their fair share of arguments. From what I could tell the one was just as stubborn as the other, but he even argued with her with reverence. Most importantly, he loved my daughter, and if he did want to marry her, I knew she would always be protected and well-cared for, and she'd never want for anything.

A small, shy smile on his face, he continued, "I am in love with your daughter. Deeply and absolutely. She inspires me to be a better man, a man worthy of her. I love Christina with every fiber of my being, every beat of my heart.

So, the reason I asked you to meet me today is because…"

I put my hand on my chest. I was right, I knew it, it's happening...

Jonathan went on, "I'm planning… hoping… to ask Christina to marry me, and I hope that I might receive your blessing to do so."

Chapter 38

Jonathan

"Hang on," Christina said, "Tell me again."
"Of course," I said, reshuffling the deck of cards. She looked up at me, and when she saw the amused look on my face, she threw a scatter cushion at me, "Don't fucking laugh at me!" she admonished.
I caught the cushion, still smiling, "I'm not laughing at you, darling, I promise."
She huffed at me out of her nose, "It's complicated, okay? Tell me again."
We were sitting on the rug in front of the sofa in my room, and I'd been trying to teach her how to play one of my favorite card games, but she wasn't getting it.
"Alright," I started, "Cards are ranked high to low, starting from Ace, then King, Queen, Jack, and then numerically, from ten down to two."
She nodded slowly, "Got it. And then…?"
I went on, "Each player gets twenty-six cards. At the start of the game each player is dealt eight cards, face down on the table in a four by two rectangle, and after that another eight cards face up on top of the face down ones. Before that, the non-dealer bids "high" or "low", and then after the face up cards are dealt, a hand of ten cards follows..."
I looked up at her. She was so focused, trying so hard to keep up, but I could see that she was already lost, and she looked so cute that I couldn't help but smile at her.
I had to confess - I was doing it on purpose.

She glared at me from underneath her eyebrows, then she pouted and folded her arms across her chest, "Please stop making fun of me?"

Shaking with laughter, I pulled her face into my neck, "I'm sorry, you're just so cute."
"You're being a shit," she murmured against my neck, and I nodded, "I know, I'm sorry."
I pulled back and kissed her temple, and I was going to suggest that we play something else when my phone rang. I frowned when I saw the caller ID: Magnus.
I looked at her, "Care to guess why Magnus is calling me?"
She shrugged, "Maybe it's nascent-related?"
I grimaced, "I hope not."

"My Lord," Magnus said when I answered the phone.
"Magnus, how are you?"
"I'm well, sire. Consumed by the investigations in Germany, but…"
"Hmm," I pondered, "Yes, the fully turned nascent. Any further progress there?"
"Nothing more than what we already know at this point, Majesty. But I will keep you updated."
"Alright," I accepted, and he continued, "I'm calling for a different reason today."
"I thought so."
"Yes, sire. Well, actually, I was wondering… is Lady Christina there with you?"
I looked at her, and she gave me a questioning look, shrugging.
I nodded, "She is, but why do you ask?"
"Well, sire… you see, the thing is… There is something that I wanted to ask her, and I thought it best to contact her through you…" Magnus stammered.
This is interesting. Magnus sounded very nervous, which to me, was a rather strange concept. Magnus was born around the same time as my mother, and he was, in my opinion, much too old to be nervous.

I handed my phone to Christina, "For you."
She frowned and mouthed *Me? Why?* but I just shrugged, and held out the phone for her to take.
"Hello, Magnus, how are you?" She greeted him, but she was still frowning in my direction.
"Lady Christina, I'm very well thank you, how are you?"

She pointed to herself and mouthed *Lady*? and I couldn't help but smile. She took the phone away from her ear and put it on speaker.
"Lady Christina," Magnus continued, "As you might be aware, I have recently become acquainted with your mother."
"Yes, my mom told me you met at the casino party."
"Indeed," Magnus gulped and went on, "And I find myself very much taken with your mother, she is… she is a remarkable lady."
She wrinkled her nose. Magnus gushing over Christina's mother was right up there with one of the sweetest things I'd ever heard.
"Lady Christina, I asked to speak with you because I respect your mother, and you of course, a great deal, and I… Well, I would like to request your permission to… to court your mother."

When the phone call ended, I looked over at her. I'd have loved to know what she was thinking.
She looked back at me, and she seemed a tiny bit flummoxed, "That was a very interesting conversation."
"What do you think of the idea darling?" I asked. She was quiet for a moment, "Did you know he was going to ask?"
I shook my head in denial, "I had no idea, love. I would have warned you if I knew."
"Good question, though, what do I think of the idea…?"
I moved closer to her, and I just sat there next to her in silence until she continued, "I want my mom to be happy. But… I don't really know him. What's he like?"
I tipped my head from side to side, "I've known him all my life, and he has known my mother for most of her life. He's a good egg."
"If he weren't, you and your family wouldn't have tolerated him for so long," she speculated. She was quiet again for a few more moments before she continued, "My mom has had a smile glued to her face ever since Bond-night. So… if Magnus will treat her right, then I have no problem with him 'courting' my mom. I'm worried about how she would react to him being Infinite, though. I mean, the circumstances were different, and I honestly don't know how well she would deal with it. I didn't take the news that well. Not initially, anyway."
A leaden silence shifted over us.
I started, "We never really talked about that…"

Christina

"About what?" I asked. The atmosphere suddenly became heavy and it was pressing down on my chest, and I wasn't sure I liked the direction the conversation was heading.
Jonathan raked his fingers through his hair and cracked his knuckles, "That night…"
"Oh…"
Yep, I was right. I don't like this.
"I try not to think about it," I tried to deflect, but he sent it right back to me, "You have to."
I sighed, "Why? I don't want to…"
Jonathan blinked slowly, his face an expressionless mask, "Christina, I killed that man. I drained the blood from his body. I tore his head from his neck. I burnt his corpse. And I enjoyed it."
Icy-hot fingers of dread wrapped around my heart.

That was the part of the truth I hadn't wanted to admit. I could never tell anyone, not even myself, about the pure, sadistic joy on his face that night as he ripped that thing's head off. Probably the same part of him that liked the taste of my blood, and wanted more.
I wasn't afraid of Jonathan; there was no part of the man I fell in love with that struck fear into my heart.
But even though he fascinated me to some morbid extent, I was a little bit afraid of the Black Prince. Of the unknown entity that dwelled beneath Jonathan's being, that sometimes peered at me through his dark eyes, and ever since Kat mentioned that he used to be more than what I saw now, I'd been wondering exactly how deep that darker part of him was buried away.

"Should I be afraid of you?" I asked.
He closed his eyes and rolled his neck, "Are you…?"
"Not of you… of…"
"Him," he finished my sentence.
I nodded, and a sad, half-smile snuck onto his face, "I haven't been him in a very, very long time."

I moved closer to him, and he looked up at me in surprise when I linked my arm with his. I needed him to know that I wasn't afraid of him, so I rested my head against his shoulder, "Can you tell me about him?"

Jonathan tipped his head back and wrapped his arms around his knees. Then he started, "That is a time of my life and a part of myself that I never speak of."
I put my hand on his arm, "You don't have to if you don't want to. But if you do, I'm here to listen."
He leveled his head, his eyes staring blankly ahead, "I don't recognize that... creature…"
"What was he like?" I knew for a fact I was heading into dangerous territory. But I wanted to know this man, who he is, and who he was, every part of him.
"Cruel. Hungry. Vicious," came his response.
"He was made of power and destruction," he went on to say.
"Anything and anyone he deemed unworthy of his time, he just… incinerated. And he was drunk on that power, on the havoc he wreaked. Because it just... felt so fucking good."
I said nothing. I sat there next to him in silence, and I listened.
He released a heavy breath, "One day, I lost my temper, and I wiped out an entire village."
I gasped, and his head whipped to me, "I know…"
"H… how?"
Jonathan summoned black flames into both his palms, "With this."

I kept my eyes fixed on the black plumes licking the air above his hands. They were actually quite beautiful, his flames, and they had an otherworldly quality to them that made them seem almost unreal. He closed his hands into fists and extinguished the flames.
Then he raked his fingers through his hair, "After that, my mother… limited me, my abilities. I was very angry at her for doing that, and yet again I lost my temper, and Katalina and I left. I was away from home for a very long time, several decades, but over the years I learned how to control my temper instead of letting it control me. I only returned back home many, many years later, when I was finally able to put aside the Black Prince, and just be… Me. Jonathan."

"You said your mom limited your abilities… What did she do?" I asked.
He rolled his neck, "I suppose it can be equated to something wrapped around my brain. Like a band, or a belt of some sorts, that prevents me from using my power to its full extent."
"Can you feel it? Even now?"
"I can, yes. I've gotten used to it, but the pressure in my head remains."
Wow... "Is that why you told me you don't like putting things on your head?"
He just nodded.

I stroked his arm with my thumb, and he put his hand over mine, "I am astounded that you are still sitting here," he said softly.
I frowned, "Where else would I be?"
He pulled up his shoulders, "I don't know. I would understand if you wanted to get away from me."
"We all have parts of ourselves that we don't like, that we don't want other people to see. But it doesn't change how I feel about you. I love you, there's nowhere else I'd rather be."
He didn't answer.
I pressed a kiss to his shoulder, "Do you mind if I ask something?"
"Not at all," he urged.
"Why are your flames black?"
He turned his head to look at me, and he flashed me a crooked grin, "I won them."
I motioned for him to go on, and he chuckled, "They used to be standard, regular flames, but I won a bet with Hades, and they were the prize."
I blinked slowly at him, "So… your black flames… are… from Hades?"

He extended the claws of his left hand and summoned another small spark into his palm, letting it roll around from one fingertip to the other, "*Ignis Infernum*. Hellfire. I used to be able to conjure it from the ether and just ignite the sky. Now, I'm limited to this," he said before he put out the flame again, "Kat told me what she said to you, in Copenhagen, about there being less of me than there used to be…" he said then, and I nodded, "She mentioned something about that, yes."

He pulled up his shoulders, “She’s right. The Black Prince could do a lot more than Jonathan can.”
“Do you miss being him? Do you want it back? The power?” I asked after a few moments of silence.
“No, I don’t want that darkness back in my soul,” he answered. Then he turned to me and cupped my face with his hand, “But if it means keeping you safe, I will embrace that darkness again.”
He ran his thumb across my lips, “Now I have a question for you…”
I kissed the tip of his thumb, “Go ahead…”
“With everything I just told you… the person I was, everything that goes with that… Do you still want to be with me?”
“Jonathan Ambrose Langdon,” I smiled at him, “Who you were, who you are, it doesn’t matter, I’m not afraid of you. Your bad temper doesn’t scare me. But if you’re asking me if I still want to be with you now that I know that you can summon literal Hellfire, the real kind, straight from Tartarus, into the palm of your hand?”
He nodded his head once.
I grinned and nodded, “Fuck yes.”

Chapter 39

Jonathan

Saturday morning saw me waking up incredibly early when my father strode into my room, whistling some happy tune.
“Come on, lazy bones,” my father called up from the living area, “Up you get.”
I propped myself up in bed and frowned at my father, “Because…?”
He threw a cushion at me, “Because you are getting sloppy and rusty and lazy. Now come on.”
I groaned, but I dragged myself out of bed anyway.
“Attaboy,” Alastair grinned. “Get ready, and I will meet you out front in ten minutes.”

It was still dark when we arrived at a large, open field. The area looked like it had been earmarked for development. The empty gravel plain had a stack of logs to one side, targets for shooting practice to the other, and nothing else for miles around.
I strode out onto the field and turned to my father, “What is this?”
My father gave me a self-satisfied smirk, “This is our new training ground. I know it doesn't look like much yet, but the shooting range and obstacle course are going up next week.”
I made a face, “Why do we need an obstacle course?”
He chuckled, “Because I’m looking forward to seeing you suffer through it.”
I shook my head, “My father, the sadist. So if everything is going up next week, what are we doing here now?”
From out of absolutely fucking nowhere, my father raised his hand and a blast from his palm hit me in the stomach, sending me tumbling backwards, and I landed flat on my arse in the dirt.

What the…? I brushed the dirt from my clothes and got to my feet, "What was that for?"
My father didn't respond. He held out his hand toward the stack of logs and one flew up from the pile, right into his hand. He chucked it at me, propelling it forward with another blast from his palm and it grazed my hair as I ducked out of the way in the nick of time.
Seriously, what the hell?
"Father! What is going on?" I asked again.
"A few years ago, that first blow would have barely reached you," he explained, "you would have reduced that log to ash before it even left the ground."
I glanced at the log that had landed to my right, and back to my father just as he sent another log hurtling at me, "You've gone soft."
I dodged it and I flicked open my palm to fling a black ball of flame at the pile of logs, but my father sent out another blast that wrapped around the logs, and the flame bounced off it and zapped back to my outheld hand.
"Weak!" My father accused.

Then he attacked.

He lunged at me, weaving in mid-air, readying a downward punch. I ducked to avoid the blow and moved myself out of my father's path of attack.
Quickly, before my father could respond with a follow-up, I let an uppercut rip that knocked him under his jaw and set his teeth clattering from the impact, stunning him. He was open for another attack, and I took the gap, swinging a kick to my father's stomach, doubling him over. But he followed up with an elbow jab to the chin and a knee to the groin, sending me tumbling, rolling across the ground.
Taking advantage of my back turned to him, my father leaned his weight onto his back leg and I heard him push himself off the ground towards me. His body shot through the air and his flexed foot collided with the middle of my back, and I fell forward and hit the dirt, face first. I used the momentum to push myself back up, springing off my hands, and throwing myself into a series of handsprings, building speed and momentum until I bounded off the ground and flung myself into an aerial spin, sending my body twirling and twisting through the air.

A blast from my father's hand disrupted my path, and I slammed into the ground, kicking up a cloud of dirt and dust and gravel as I went down.

I wasted no time and I whipped my head up, pulled my arm back and thrust my splayed hand forward, sending a concentrated stream of flame right at my father.
He slammed his hands together and spread them in front of him, blocking the roaring fire with an invisible wall of energy. His feet slid in the gravel as it pushed him backward, and I smiled in satisfaction. But he pushed back harder, and I was straining to maintain the stream of fire. Just as I was about to stop, my father shook his head, "Not yet, son! Hold it!"
So I grit my teeth and I held steady.

Suddenly, my father dove into a roll to the right, dodging the onslaught of flame and he launched blasts of energy, one after the other in rapid crisscross succession, right at me.
A quick scan of my surroundings told me that there was only one way to go: Up.
I bent my knees and propelled my body skyward, unfurling my wings to carry me higher into the air. My father didn't see that coming and he snapped his head up to look at me.
Hovering in mid-air, I cracked my knuckles as I contemplated my next move, but before I was able to do anything more, my father came hurtling at me from the ground, and swung a log at my head that I was too late to dodge. It hit me against my left ear, the force of the impact ringing in my head like the bells at Notre Dame, and I dropped, skidding through the dirt, my wings dragging behind me in the gravel as I went.

That fucking hurt. My reflexes were absolutely pathetic, my form dismal. *What happened to me?*
I sat up, clutching my ear, and my father strode over to check on me, "Are you alright my boy?"
I nodded, but I was half surprised to see blood in my palm. My father extended a hand to help me to my feet, and I brushed the dirt from my clothes, "When did I become such a complete fucking milksop?"

He laughed, “I don’t know. But let’s knock that namby-pamby little pushover right out of you.”
I nodded, shaking my arms out at my sides, “Agreed.”
My father leapt backwards, and beckoned me closer, “Once more.”
So we started again.

By the time dawn broke, we’d been at it for fucking hours, and I was exhausted.
Sweat was running down into my eyes, my t-shirt and sweatpants were drenched and clung to me like a second skin, and every time I took a step I could hear my socks squelching in my trainers.
The next moment, my body lurched forward and I vomited.
My father smiled endearingly and came over to me, patting my back. I straightened up and wiped my mouth on my sleeve, and I sank back to sit down on the ground, my arms resting on my knees. My father offered me a blood bag, which I gladly took and emptied as he sat down next to me in the dirt.
“Are you alright?” he asked me again.
I held the now empty bag in my hand and I nodded, but I didn’t answer.
My father and I sat in silence for a while, watching the sun split the night sky with rays of gold.
“This was unexpected,” I broke the silence. “How did you know I needed this?”

It was true, I did.
For the first time in a very long time, I felt… better. Good. Free. I hadn’t realized it until just now, but something inside me had become stuck, like a hawk in a bramble bush.
My father gave me a sideways glance, “I’m your father, it’s my job to know,” he said, “I also know that your tea-parties with Kirill, fun as they might be, are wholly insufficient. He’s no match for you.”
I smiled crookedly, “It is so much fun kicking his arse, though,” I commented, and my father chuckled, “Of course it is. But you mustn’t allow yourself to become lax. Especially not if you are going to propose to Christina and we are to potentially welcome another daughter to our household...”
I slowly turned my head to look at my father in surprise, “How did you know about that?”

My father ruffled my hair and got to his feet, “I told you, I’m your father, it’s my job to know.”

“What are your plans for this weekend?” he asked me as we were driving home.
“Do you remember Nathaniel and Lilian?” I asked, and he nodded, “Yes, yes, of course. I heard they got engaged. Your mother and I aren’t able to attend the engagement party, but I take it you and Christina will be there to represent our family? Along with Donika, of course.”
“I haven’t told Christina about the party yet, but I’d like to take her with me, yes.”
My father gave me a brief glance, “Has she been to London?”
I shook my head, gazing out the window, “I don’t believe so.”
He shuddered, “Horrid place.”
“It certainly is. Anyway, I thought I should ask her if she needs to go shopping for the party.”
My father laughed, “You like shopping.”
“No, see, what I like is taking Christina shopping.”
My father rolled his eyes, “Right, if you say so.”
We drove the rest of the way in silence, but gratitude covered my heart at how easily, how readily my father included Christina as a member of our family.

Chapter 40

The relationship between a child and a parent was supposed to be a beautiful and blessed one. From a child's birth, parents were instrumental in molding the child's life. They were supposed to teach the child values and morals, and guide the child in the right direction. A good parent should become a child's friend, guide, and teacher… Not tie them to a tree outside in the cold.
That was where I met her, outside a little village in Russia, and from the first moment I laid eyes on her, she captivated me.

Never before in my life had I met a mortal that I didn't want to obliterate on sight. But when her wild, honey-amber colored eyes locked with mine, I knew I was lost. I had to have her. But she was dying, and I couldn't let her go. So, I turned her.

She told me her story, about growing up with her stinking, alcoholic father and her idiot brothers, how her mother died when she was young and how she wished her father had died with her.
So, I did for her what any man would do for the woman he loved: I made her wish come true. We made love that night for the first time, bathed in the blood of her father, next to her brothers' lifeless corpses.

Oh, what a force of nature she was. A free-spirited, sexualized combination of the quintessential femme fatale, with a tough-girl kind of edge, and a generous sprinkling of crazy on top. Her supercharged feminine nature was raw and unruly, bound only by her whims. She was an unpredictable, self-aware, empowered woman unafraid to express and explore her sexuality, her wants, her desires.

Everything about her was dangerous. And her danger was what made me fall in love with her. Her tempestuous nature kept me guessing. One minute she loved me passionately, the next she hated me with the same intensity. She had a deep fear of being alone, and there were times she needed me more than she needed to feed. Other times, she was fiercely independent, and she'd stab me with a kitchen knife for opening the door for her.

Sometimes I found myself questioning if I should stay with her or just rip her head off, but then she impaled herself on my dick, and I remembered exactly where I wanted to be. Fucking her was always explosive and hedonistic, but she was too beautiful, too untamed, too much for one man. Her beauty needed to be shared. Others have to receive the blessing as well. To both of us, a monogamous, heteronormative relationship was stifling, and we thoroughly enjoyed sharing our bed with whomever was willing.

Out of all the things that she was, most importantly, she was mine. She was the only one I trusted, the only one loyal to me, and Hades help anyone who dared betray me. A young woman in Latvia learned that the hard way. She lied to us, and my golden goddess slit her throat. The last I heard the police still hadn't found all of her body parts.

This woman, this wild beauty with her raven hair and eyes like a sunset, was my queen. She was my most trusted confidante, my general and my best friend.
She hated this mortal-loving family as much as I did, hated what they stood for. When she found out that their precious little golden boy had a mortal beast for a girlfriend, she begged me to let her rip the girlfriend's little blonde head from her body.
But the time for that will come. And when it did, I would take my place as the true king, with my raven-haired queen at my side.

Chapter 41

Christina

"Is there a theme to this party?" I asked Jonathan from inside the changing room.
We were in yet another high-end women's clothing store, and I was trying on the dresses, blouses and pants that the shop assistant had pulled for me, while Jonathan was sitting in a comfy armchair near the changing room.

Friends of his invited us to their engagement party in London, and I was very excited. I'd never been to London and although Jonathan was telling me how it wasn't as nice as I might imagine it, I was still looking forward to going. The party was in a week or so, and because I was worried I wouldn't have anything to wear to the exclusive London club the couple booked up for their private party, Jonathan took me shopping.

"No theme, just a party," he replied, "I'm surprised, actually, Lilian loves to dress up."
"Ready or not, here I come," I announced before I stepped out of the changing room.
"That's not bad," Jonathan said about the dress I was wearing.
I looked at myself in the full-length mirror and then looked down at the dress. The short, sparkly pink dress came down to just above my knees, and the fabric had a lot of movement. It was cute, but I wasn't sure if it suited me.
Jonathan saw the look on my face and his eyebrow lifted, "Not your style?"
I wrinkled my nose, "No… Sorry babe."

He shook his head, “Nothing to be sorry for, darling. What’s next?”
I stepped back into the fitting room and changed into the next outfit. A mid-length cocktail dress in teal blue, “How about this?”
Jonathan scanned me up and down, “The color is lovely. But…”
“But…?”
“I’m rather certain my mother has a similar dress…”
That’s a no, then. I curtsied and ducked back into the changing room without a further word, and he laughed.
I scanned over the other items I hadn’t tried on yet… and I chose one I knew he wouldn't expect.

He was doing something on his phone but he looked up immediately when I stepped out of the changing room. When he saw me, he drew a breath through his clenched teeth.
I nibbled my lower lip. That was exactly the reaction I was hoping to get from the black leather pants, lacy red top and platform heels, “How about this?”
Jonathan’s eyes went from my face, to my breasts, my waist, my legs, and back up, and I smiled at the growl I heard rumbling in his throat. *I fucking love that growl…*
“I knew you would look stunning in those leather pants…” he grumbled huskily.
I winked at him, “You should see what I have on under them…”
He opened his mouth to say something, but snapped it shut when the shop assistant peered around the corner, “How are we doing here?’
“Everything’s fine, Charity, thank you,” Jonathan smiled politely.
Charity looked at me, “Ma’am, those pants were made for you.”
I knew a retail smile when I saw it because I had one of my own and I flashed it back at her, “Thank you.”
“Okay. Let me know if you need anything,” Charity gushed before she left.
I looked back at Jonathan, “What were you going to say, babe?”
He shook his head, “Something filthy and very inappropriate.” *Oh, mercy…*

It was time to change into the next outfit, but what I didn’t know was that it was also time to learn the struggle of leather pants. They clung like shit on Velcro, and I was hopping on one foot in the changing room, struggling to get them off.

"Do you need help, my love?" Jonathan asked, but he was just being a shit again because I could hear the laughter in his throat. I shook my head, "No, no," I denied, "I'm good."
No pair of pants was going to defeat me. Besides, if I let him come in, there was a very good chance that I was not going to let him keep his clothes on, and I didn't want to get us thrown out for lewd behavior.
The next outfit was also nice. Stylish, dark jeans and a slightly see-through black blouse.
I really liked it. As much as I wanted to be a dresses kind of girl, I was just more comfortable in a good pair of jeans.
"I like this," I beamed at Jonathan and he nodded approvingly, "Me too. I like the top."
I gave him a blank look, "Because you can see my bra?"
He wiggled his eyebrows. Shaking my head, I turned around to show him the back of the jeans, "What about the jeans? Does my ass look okay?"
"Darling," he replied, "that perky arse of yours looks good in everything."
I grinned at him, "Thank you, babe."

He winked, "Do you want to show me the next outfit?"
I looked back into the changing room at the rest of the clothes, and then back at him, "I really don't know if I want to try on everything here, I'm not feeling everything. Is it okay?"
He nodded, "Of course, love."
"Although…" I thought out loud, "I think there's one more I'd like to show you."

It was time to wrap up the shopping trip, I knew he was tired. He was up at 3 that morning to have a video conference with a client in France, so I wanted to keep the shopping session relatively short so he could go get some rest.
"How about this?" I asked him when I opened the curtain.
When he looked up and saw me, his jaw dropped. "Ohh, darling," he breathed, "why are you doing this to me?"
Ka-ching! Obviously, my matching white bra and panty set, with red and pink flowers and lace all over, and a pair of heels were a really good choice, judging by the look on his face.

Jonathan inclined his head slightly… Then he zipped over to me and pushed me back into the changing room.
He didn't even bother to close the curtain behind us before shoving his hand down my panty and slipping a finger inside me as I moaned against his ear.
But he suddenly stopped, pushed me back and closed the curtain.
I was confused for a moment, but then I heard Charity's voice, "Would you care for something to drink Mr. Langdon?"
"No, thank you, Charity. I think we're nearly done here."
He waited until Charity left before he stepped back into the cubicle and looked me up and down. He sighed softly and gently ran his hands all over me and I shivered.
Then he closed his eyes and took a deep breath, "I don't know how much more of this I can take…"
I frowned, "Babe? What do you mean?"
He opened his eyes and he had a look of longing on his face as he looked me up and down again, "All I have wanted for weeks now, is to make love to you. And every single fucking time, something gets in the way."
"I know…" I confirmed the sentiment, "I miss your body."
He pulled me into his arms and hugged me briefly before stepping out of the cubicle and going back to the armchair, "Is there something here that you like, darling?"
"A few, actually, but I can't decide which one I want."
Jonathan waved a dismissive hand, "We'll get everything then."

Chapter 42

Christina

I was having an out-of-body experience.
Being with Jonathan has been life-changing. Above and beyond being Infinite, he really was a global citizen. He had friends and contacts and apartments in almost every country in the world. On the plane on our way to London, he was talking on the phone with a friend of his in Tanzania, and I learned that he actually wasn't joking on our first date when he said he spoke Swahili. He really did.
Before I met him, I'd never set foot in a plane, much less a private jet. I'd never even left my city, and now I'd been to several foreign countries with him, possibly illegally, because I was not sure about the visa or passport regulations for traveling by portal.

And now, here I was, waking up in his apartment in Canary Wharf in London, and I couldn't believe the life I was living.
I was a little bit annoyed because I started my damn period a day or so ago. It was my own damn fault though. I had somehow gotten the dates of our trip to London wrong, and my last pack of pills ran out. I had a new one. On my nightstand. Where I left it. But whatever. It was my first time in London, and I was determined to have a good time regardless. *Aunt Flo can suck it.*
Sounds and the smell of fresh coffee drew my attention to the kitchen of the massive studio apartment, and I smiled. Jonathan was standing in the kitchen, waiting for the coffee to brew.
"Good morning beautiful," he smiled at me. *Shit-a-brick, look at him.*
I sat up against the headboard, "Morning handsome."
"Would you like to go out for brunch? Or do you want to just eat here?" he wanted to know.

I thought for a moment, “I won’t make the same mistake and ask you if you even have food in the house.”
He laughed, and I wrinkled my nose at him, “But maybe we could go out. I’d love some coffee first, though.”
Jonathan wanted to show me the view, so we had our coffee on the terrace.
Sipping my coffee, I glanced over my shoulder at the apartment and then back at him, “The view is amazing babe. And your apartment is gorgeous. It’s very different from your usual aesthetic, but it’s really nice.”
Unlike his room at the manor that was all dark colors and muted lighting, the apartment was bright and light and airy, with all the walls and furniture mostly white, and some shades of gray here and there. There were a couple of red decorations throughout the apartment, like a red vase on the coffee table, a few red cushions on the sofa, and some red coffee mugs. The only similarity to his room back home, was the gargoyles. Two small gargoyles sat on the mantelpiece, looking at the lounge set. No TV, though.
Jonathan put down his empty mug, “That’s what happens when you give your sister free rein.”
“Well, she included mini-Gar and mini-Goyle, so I think she did a pretty good job.”

I finished my coffee, then I went to the bathroom to take a shower and get ready for brunch. When I stepped into the bathroom, I stopped to stare for a moment.
Even the bathroom was gorgeous. One wall consisted entirely of a massive walk-in shower, with ceiling to floor Moroccan-style sea green fish scale tiles. It had two shower heads, and jets similar to the ones in his shower at home, and this shower had a bench.

“Babe?” I called over my shoulder.
“Yes, love?” he replied.
“If I’m not out of the shower in two hours, send a search party.”
Jonathan looked at me around the bathroom door, “What do you mean?”
I gestured at the shower, “Look at it, it’s fucking huge.”
Jonathan smiled and kissed my cheek, “I’ll always find you, love. Have a nice shower.”

We had brunch at a cute little café near the apartment, and then we spent the rest of the day, hand-in-hand, leisurely strolling around the streets of London.
I wasn't sure why Jonathan said that he didn't like London. From where I was standing, right next to him, in his arms, it didn't seem so bad.
The only thing I didn't like was how many women were blatantly checking him out, practically undressing him with their eyes, even with me standing right next to him.
After giving the umpteenth death-ray stare, I looked back at Jonathan to find him giving me an inquisitive look.
"What?" I asked.

He looked in the direction of the girl I was glaring at, "If looks could kill, she'd be a crime scene. What was that look for?"
"Hmph," I huffed, narrowing my eyes in the girl's direction, even though she was no longer there. Then I folded my arms and turned back to him, pouting, "You're right, London sucks."
He tucked my hair behind my ear, "Ten minutes ago you said you liked London. What has happened since then?"
"Too many women are checking you out," I complained.
Jonathan put his arms around me and pulled me in to kiss my forehead, "I hadn't noticed, love."
Is he kidding me? How can he not? They make it so fucking obvious.
"Are you serious? You haven't noticed a single girl ogling you?"
He shook his head, "No. I told you: There is no other woman that could ever compare to you."

Okay, that's a good answer. I stood on my tippy toes to plant a quick kiss on his lips, and he put his hands on my waist and leaned in to kiss me. I felt his tongue at the seam of my lips, and my lips happily parted to let his tongue sweep into my mouth. He tasted like more, and I pressed my tongue against his. His fingers dug into my skin and he held me tightly against him. I melted into his kiss, and I was fighting the temptation to slip my hand down the front of his pants. By the time he ended the kiss, my blood was on fire and liquid heat pooled at my core. *I want him so bad.*

“There,” he said when he pulled back. “Now everyone here can see I’m yours.”

I was unable to make mouth-words, and he smiled that stunning smile at me, “Come on, let’s go get ready for the party.

Chapter 43

Hunter

If anyone had told me that I would go to London on vacation one day, I would have laughed at them. If they told me that I would go to London on vacation as a vampire, I would have had them committed.

But now, there I was. In London. And I was a vampire. And I had underlings, people that obeyed my every command. It made me feel like a Drill Sergeant, and I absolutely fucking loved it.
I was their leader, their general, their god, because I was the one who chose them and, with Dr. Brennan's serum, made them the undead, indestructible soldiers that they were. It was by no means a large army, but having 20 vampires that did everything you told them to do was, in my opinion, better than 100 human soldicrs. Oh, thc havoc that 20 of them would be able to wreak.

Sure, His Holiness assured me that Apollo had given his blessing for my entire troop to hunt together, but I had a different strategy. The gracious Apollo said that we 'could', not that we had to.
The way I saw it, 20 hunting vampires would leave at least 20 corpses in their wake. Potentially more, if their appetites were anything like my own.
No. My guys were going to hunt on rotation. Only one at a time, each time in a different neighborhood, very far from the previous location. And they had to make sure that there was no pattern, no similarities. Luckily for us, that has turned out to be pretty easy. Out of all the places His Holiness has sent me and my subjects to, London was by far my favorite.

Every other neighborhood was a seedy, danger-ridden crime fest. From Crews Hill in the North, to Croydon in the South, the entire city of London was perfect for hunting.

However, the other thing London was full of, was vampires. Really old vampires. I found that out the hard way, when one of them caught and killed one of my guys. I knew it had to be a vampire that killed poor Edwin. No human I ever heard of had the power to rip a head clear off a body. After we found Edwin's beheaded body with his heart ripped out, we decided to lay low for a while.

Edwin's death was an unexpected and bitter loss for everyone. He was a good friend, a loyal soldier. He hadn't been a vampire for long, and he was just beginning to find his new identity in his new body when his life was taken. And for what? He didn't do anything wrong. He was hungry, so he fed. The city of London had more than 11,000 homeless skulking around, and it wasn't like anyone was going to miss the five he snacked on.

Besides, Edwin couldn't help himself, he was a vampire. None of us could. And we shouldn't have to, either. It was unfair and unreasonable to expect us to limit ourselves. We were too strong.

However, as much as everyone wanted to find the vampire responsible for taking Edwin's life, I forbade them. Whoever killed Edwin had to be a lot older and more powerful than we were.

For the next couple of months, we shifted our hunting grounds to other cities and other countries. I sent Ronan to Birmingham, and Andrew to Plymouth in the west. Then, a few weeks later, Sylvie begged for her chance, so I sent her across the water to Brussels, followed by Leigh to Eindhoven.

I kept a close eye on the news, and there were no reports about any of their prey; no-one had been able to make any connections between the deaths, so as far as I was concerned, things were going well.

Now, if only we had more troops.

Chapter 44

Christina

Walking into the luxury club in Soho that the couple had reserved, I once again felt like a celebrity. Valet parking, red carpet, staff and security treating us like VIPs. *I don't know if I will ever be able to get used to this.*

Once we stepped inside the club, I felt intimidated, though. Everyone was dressed so nicely, and I felt frumpy. I wasn't sure if my black leather pants and slightly see-through black blouse were fancy enough for the venue.

Jonathan must have noticed my insecurity, like he always did, because he squeezed my hand, "You are the most beautiful woman in this entire club."

I pressed my head against his shoulder. *Flattery will get him absolutely everywhere.* He kissed my temple and then led me through the milling party-goers to the bar to get us drinks.

"Babe?" I asked as I looked around at the other guests, "Is everyone here… Infinite?"

Jonathan looked around the crowd of people in the club and shook his head, "Not everyone, but mostly."

Wow.

So many people.

So many Infinites.

I had never seen so many Infinites gathered together in the same place, I hadn't even realized that there were this many.

Jonathan introduced me to a few people, but I forgot most of the names as soon as I heard them; there were just too many to remember.

A few drinks in, a very good-looking couple approached us where we were sitting on a sofa against the wall in one of the VIP lounges in the club. As the couple made their way to us, other guests were congratulating them, so I gathered that this had to be the happy couple. When they finally reached us, Jonathan greeted them both with a cheerful hug before he introduced them as Nathaniel Day and his fiancée, Lilian Griffith.

Nathaniel was tall, his light brown hair pulled up into a man-bun on top of his head, and he had a luxurious beard.

Lilian was gorgeous. She had full-sleeve tattoos down both her arms, a pierced nasal septum and her sleek black hair practically gleamed in the lights of the club.

They were a stunning couple. They didn't stay long, and soon excused themselves to go mingle.

After they left, Jonathan took my hand and led me to the dance floor. I loved dancing with him, I loved the way it felt when he held my body against him and we moved together. He was a way better dancer than I was so it was by no means in unison, but I felt so free in his arms. Sadly, my heels weren't as comfortable as the shoes he bought for me when we went to Kat's club, and I wanted to take a break. Besides, he was so sexy when he danced, his body moving like mercury, that I wanted to go sit down somewhere and just watch him. Maybe drool a little bit.

I was aware of other women on the dance floor looking at him, but this time I didn't mind so much. I get it, I really couldn't blame them for staring, my man was poetry in motion.

A while later, he checked the time on his phone, and told me to go take a seat and wait at the bar before he disappeared into the crowd.

I frowned. I had no idea where he was going, but I was happy to get off my feet.

Then the music slowly started to fade out and the flashing lights in the club dimmed.

A spotlight shone onto the stage, illuminating Jonathan.

I bit my lower lip for a moment. He looked so damn good in his dark gray suit pants and his black dress shirt.

He started moving toward the edge of the stage, and as he did my jaw dropped yet again when nearly every single person in the club turned to him… and bowed.

I was awestruck, and goosebumps erupted all over my body. They were all bowing to Jonathan.
They were paying homage to him.
Homage to the Black Prince.

I wondered why there was no microphone, but when he spoke, I realized that he didn't need one. His voice was… powerful… regal… and the rich, booming sound of it carried all over the entire club like he was talking into a megaphone,
"My brothers and sisters, Cursed Blood," he said, and the crowd cheered, "I want to thank each and every one of you for being here on this night, as we celebrate the one thing that binds us all, the one thing strong enough to break Apollo's curse…"
"Fuck Apollo!" someone in the crowd shouted and the crowd erupted into cheer again.

Jonathan laughed, then he motioned for the crowd to quiet down, and he carried on, "Please raise your glass, and if you don't have a drink in your hand by now, what the fuck have you been doing?"
The crowd chuckled, and he waited a moment until he saw enough glasses in the air, "A toast to Nathaniel and Lilian," he pointed to them where they were standing in the crowd and the spotlight panned to them.

All the guests turned to look at them, but I couldn't tear my eyes off of Jonathan. He was fucking magnificent. He saw me looking at him and he winked at me before he turned to Nathaniel and Lilian, "May your love grow and blossom. May it be old-fashioned enough to last forever, but young enough to evolve with the times. And may the worst day of each year together be better than the best day of the previous year. Carpe noctem…"
A shiver ran down my spine when the crowd echoed in unison, "Carpe veritatem."

After the toast, Jonathan dropped by the bar to kiss me and to tell me that he had a few people he needed to say hello to, and that he would be back to me as soon as he was done.

I didn't mind. I was completely surrounded by Infinites, but I wasn't worried; I knew I was safe. And besides, all the Infinites I knew were somewhere in the crowd. Throughout the night I saw Kat, Niki and even Kirill stopped by before disappearing again.

While I was touching up my make-up in the restroom, the door swung open and a pretty girl with platinum blonde hair came sauntering in. I recognized her. Jonathan introduced us earlier but her name was one of those I chose not to remember. *I feel like it was something with a B… Or an E maybe…?* When she saw me, she smirked and folded her arms across her chest, "Well, well, well, if it isn't the Prince's little human plaything."

I was so surprised at the snide comment that I didn't know what to say. When I didn't reply, the girl chuckled condescendingly, "How does it feel to have someone else's seconds?"

"Huh?" I heard myself ask.

"I had him first," Emery said.

Then my brain kicked into gear, "Oh, please. Jonathan used you as a cum-rag once and now you think you're special? Aww, that's really sad."

The girl snarled at me, "How about I show you how special my fist is in your face."

If this snaggle-toothed bitch thought I was afraid of her, she was out of her fucking mind. I didn't give a shit if she was Infinite or not. I squared up, "I've never started a fistfight, but you can be sure as fuck I'll finish it. Bring it on, Bitchy Spice."

"I'll fuck you up, Yankee skank," the girl stepped closer to me, and she balled her hand into a fist. This bitch was actually about to take a swing at me, and I was so ready to kick her skinny British ass. But before she could make any further moves, a door behind us in the restroom creaked open, and Lilian emerged from the cubicle, "Oh, fuck off, Emery," she said to the platinum haired-girl, "You're just jealous because you wanted forever, and His Majesty just wanted a quick fuck."

So that's her name. Emery. Stupid fucking name if you ask me. Emery pulled an ugly face. Lilian scanned her up and down as she washed her hands and shook her head, "Besides, out of all the broads he's shagged, your smelly cunt was probably the least memorable."

I snorted a laugh.
Lilian turned to Emery, “Tonight is not the night for you to be a raging bitch. Not at my engagement party. Behave, or go the fuck home.”
Emery spun on her heel and stomped out of the bathroom.
Lilian rolled her eyes and turned to me, “Are you alright?”
I nodded, “That was awesome. Thank you,” I extended a hand to Lilian, “We met earlier, I’m Christina, I’m Jonathan’s…”
“His absolutely everything,” Lilian smiled as she shook my hand, “I know. He’s been gushing about you for ages. And if you want to talk about awesome, look at you. Bitchy Spice? Fucking brilliant. I can see why His Majesty is so in love with you.”
“And don’t mind Emery,” Lilian continued, “Everyone knows she’s been in love with His Majesty since the 80’s, and he’s not interested.”
I didn’t want to know the answer, but I had to ask, “Did he really sleep with her?”
Lilian flashed me an apologetic smile, “Sorry, luv.”
“It’s okay, he was a man-whore, I know.”
Lilian burst out laughing.
I smiled, “Congratulations, by the way.”
She grinned, “Thank you! I am so excited!”
“Can I see the ring?” I asked, and Lilian gladly obliged.
It was a stunning ring. A vintage yellow and white gold ring, with a deep purple amethyst in the middle, and surrounded by small white diamonds.
“Wow,” I breathed, “it’s beautiful.”
Lilian giggled gleefully and grabbed my hand, “Come on, let’s go get a drink.”

We found our men standing at the bar, ten shots of something dangerous-looking lined up in front of them.
“There she is,” Nathaniel said in his thick Irish accent, smiling at Lilian, “There’s me bride.”
Lilian grinned and wrapped her arms around his neck and kissed his cheek.
Jonathan pulled me closer, my back to his front, and he wrapped his arms around me. Nathaniel gave Lilian a questioning look, “Emery seems right up to 90… What happened in the loo?”
She shrugged, “She’s away with the fairies, that one. And she was being rudc to Christina.”

He nodded understandingly, then he lifted up the first shot of his five out of the ten that they had lined up, “Alright then, Highness, here we go.”
Jonathan picked up a glass and clinked it to Nathaniel’s, “Sláinte!”

The rest of the night went by in spectacular fashion. The music was pumping, the drinks kept on coming, we danced, we laughed, and I had a fantastic time getting to know Lilian and Nathaniel.
But my feet were killing me, and it was almost 3AM by the time we arrived back at Jonathan’s apartment.
“Do you want to shower before bed, love?” he asked me as he unbuckled his belt and took off his boots.
I nodded, “I think so. If you don’t mind.”
Jonathan came over to me and pulled me against him, “Not if you don’t mind if I kiss you first.”
“I’ve been waiting all night,” I said, my voice going low.
He didn’t wait for me to say any more. He parted my lips with his, his tongue darting into my mouth to seek mine. My entire body practically purred against his, and he started to unbutton my blouse. I let him push my blouse off my shoulders before I unbuttoned his shirt.
When his shirt landed on the sofa, I put my hands on his chest and ran my fingers down and over his upper body like I was looking for a light switch in the dark.
Then I took a step back, “I need to go shower.”
He nodded, but everything on my body was sweaty and I wanted to get cleaned up, so I planted a brief kiss on his lips before I went into the bathroom.

Getting undressed was a struggle in and of itself. The leather pants clung pretty tightly when I first tried them on in the store, and now that my legs were warm and sweaty from dancing, they clung even worse, so when I finally had them off, I felt accomplished.

I was still annoyed at myself for messing so badly with my damn anti-baby pills. I was really hoping that this weekend in London would finally be the end of the dry-spell we'd been having. *I should have planned better...* But, oh well. My period should be over soon. I made sure to properly dispose of all unmentionables before I took off the rest of my clothes. The moment the last of my clothes fell onto the floor, the bathroom door opened, and Jonathan stepped in right behind me, his lips on my neck, my nipples between his fingers.
I gasped, my back arching, and I leaned my head back against him.
"Can you feel me?" he murmured against my skin,
I moaned. I absolutely could.
He was as naked as I was, and every hard inch of him was pressing invitingly against my ass. I couldn't stop myself from grinding my body against him.
He ran his tongue up to my earlobe, grasping my breasts firmly in his hands, and I moaned again.
I really wanted him, but there was something stopping me.
"Babe…" I panted… "We can't…"
"Why…?" he wanted to know.
I locked eyes with him in the mirror, "Because…" I said, trying really hard not to be embarrassed, "I'm on my period…"
"I know…" he murmured against my ear.
And my face flushed bright red, "Oh shit-a-brick. You can probably smell it, can't you?"
He moved his hands around to my backside and squeezed my ass firmly before he reached for my breasts again, "I can… But I still want to be inside you…" he replied softly, darkly.
I shook my head, averting my eyes, "No… it's gross…"
"Christina, darling, look at me," he said, and when I looked at him in the mirror, my every nerve-ending caught fire. His fangs were fully bared, and his eyes were a shade of blue that I had never seen before.
"Who are you talking to?" he asked, his eyes locked with mine.
"I know, but…"
"Do you really think blood bothers me?" he growled.

I sighed, and I didn't know who I should listen to:
To the throbbing heat between my thighs, begging to have him deep inside me?

Or to my brain, telling me that having sex on your period is gross and messy and a bad idea?

Oh, fuck, but that growl…

Jonathan ran his thumbs across my nipples, his fangs grazing my neck, "Christina, I want you…" he said softly, his dick twitching against my ass, "But I won't force you. I've waited for weeks to make love to you, I can wait a few days more."

He pulled his lips away from my neck, moved his hands away from my breasts, and he stepped back. My whole body felt cold and empty without his warm skin pressing against me and in a split-second, I decided who I was going to listen to. I turned to face him, "Fuck it. Take me. Just… take me."

With a questioning look on his face, he inclined his head, "Are you sure that's what you want?"

I nodded and flung my body against his, "Yes. Take me."

A salacious smile curling around his lips, Jonathan pulled me into the shower with him and turned on the water. He picked me up and pinned my back against the wall as he rammed his dick into me.

"Oh… Fuck!" my voice bounced off the shower walls. I was not expecting him to feel this good.

I mean, I knew my pussy would be more sensitive because I was on my period, but this… this was fucking insane.

Every stroke of him, pounding, thrusting inside me, pushed me closer and closer to the edge.

And when his thumb started drawing circles on my clit, that was it. My body arched in the sweet ecstasy of the orgasm that tore through my being.

Jonathan took my breasts in both his hands, "You are so beautiful when you come," I heard him groan again, and I dug my nails into his back.

"I love you," I murmured next to his ear, and he pulled his head back and looked at me, desire written all over his face.

He moved his hand back in between my thighs, "Say it again," he breathed, "say it as you come for me," and it wasn't long until another orgasm shook me. "I love you," I moaned.

Holding me against him, Jonathan drove into me until he came inside me, and then he just held me there, breathless and sated.

Slowly, he lowered me to sit on the bench, and he stepped in under the showerhead. I looked up at him and I couldn't help but be embarrassed to see him covered in my blood.

"Sorry babe…" I mumbled, covering my face with my hands, and I heard him chuckle, "It's alright, love," he said, "you don't need to be embarrassed."

Slowly, I peered at him from between my fingers, "Kinky bastard," and he laughed out loud.

"I love you," he said as he stepped out of the shower and gave me some privacy to get cleaned up.

"Okay," I said as I came out of the bathroom wrapped in a robe, "Now you have to tell me, no more excuses."

Jonathan was stretched out on the bed, and he flashed me a curious smile, "Tell you what, love?"

I stood in front of the dresser to put some lotion on my face, and I looked at him in the reflection in the mirror, "On the island, when I cut my finger… What did my blood taste like?"

He gave me a blank look, but I shook my head, "Nope, no dice, don't even try. Five minutes ago, you said, nay, you growled, and I quote 'Do you really think blood bothers me?'…"

I paused for dramatic effect, and Jonathan hid his face behind a pillow for a moment.

I made a beckoning motion with my index finger, "Spit it out. Tell me the truth."

He sat up on the bed, "Fine," he sighed.

He looked a little bit uncomfortable, but he pressed on, "It's hard to explain, really… Usually blood tastes, like, well… blood. But yours…" He stood up from the bed and strode over to me to stand behind me, "Your blood tastes like... life. Hope," then he chuckled, "I'm cheesy, I know. But you did ask."

"Why couldn't you talk about this when I asked you the last time?"

He raked his fingers through his hair, "I don't know. Perhaps I was worried that, if I talked about how delicious your blood is, it would make it that much more difficult to control myself."

"Is it difficult now?"

He ran a fingertip down the side of my neck, "It always is. If you knew the things I want to do to you…"

I shivered. I knew what he meant, but that wasn't what I was talking about, "Have you lost control before? Feeding…"
A shadow flitted across his face and he nodded.
I looked him in the eye in the mirror, "Do you think there might ever be a point where you would want to… feed… on me?"
He kissed my hair and shook his head, "As I told you before, I would never feed on you. Ever. But if you're asking if I would want to taste your blood again…"
His lips curled into that sexy crooked smile that set my insides on fire, "Fuck yes."

Softly kissing my ear, he wrapped one hand gently around my throat, and reached his other hand down into the robe and sought out my still-sensitive nipple.
I was unable to resist the power that he had over my body, and as I leaned into his touch, my lips parted.
Jonathan pinched my nipple between his fingers as he spoke softly next to my ear, "I want to be inside again. Will you let me?"
"You know…" I started as he untied the robe at my waist, "part of me wants to say no, because I really am on my period."
Jonathan growled behind me and scraped his fangs down the side of my neck, and my entire core and every shred of resistance I had just melted, "But you're so fucking fine, I can't decide if I should swallow your kids, or have them."
A wicked smile on his face, Jonathan gently turned me around and opened the robe all the way.
His eyes roamed all over my naked body before he swept me up in a fiery kiss.
"Jonathan…" I stopped him when he lay me down on the bed.
"Yes?" he replied before drawing my nipple into his mouth.
I moaned before I finished the thought, "No… no hands… please?"
Jonathan lifted his head and nodded, and kissed me very gently on the lips, "I understand love."
His lips moved to my jaw, to my ear, and then to my neck before he continued, "Just my cock, then."

Chapter 45

Christina

I woke up to Jonathan kissing my ear, his rock-hard dick pressed against my ass. As soon as I opened my eyes, his hand roamed in under my shirt.

"Good morning," I mumbled, rolling over onto my back for good-morning kisses.

"Mm-hmm, yes, good morning," he responded in barely a mutter before he shifted himself on top of me. He stuck his head in under my sleep-shirt and sucked one of my nipples into his mouth. My body responded before my brain did, and my hips shifted beneath him.

"Babe…" I breathed, and he lifted his head to look at me, "Yes, love?"

I didn't know what it was that I wanted to say, so I just looked at him. I hated comparing Jonathan to Owen, but it was the only reference I had. Owen never touched me when I was on my period. He barely even kissed me. I accidentally got some blood on my jeans once, and he completely flipped his shit and called me disgusting…

But when I looked at Jonathan and all I saw on his face was desire. For me... How was I supposed to resist that? *I mean, I probably could, but I really don't want to.*

"You want me?" I asked him, and he nodded slowly, "More than you could possibly imagine."

"Okay then…"

"But…?" he asked, and this time I shook my head, "But nothing."

That delicious crooked grin I loved so much appeared on his face, and without a further word, he tugged down my shorts.

I pinched my eyes shut when I realized that he was going to see e-ve-ry-thing when he took off my panty, but I was determined not to let it stop me. I kept my eyes closed, even when I heard my panties hit the floor next to the bed.
"Fuck my life…" I murmured.
"Christina, look at me," I heard his voice and I opened my eyes to look at him. He smiled, "It's alright."
"Promise…?" I asked. Jonathan nodded, "I swear, by the light of the Blessed Moon."
"Okay…" I breathed.
"Will you let me make love to you now?" he wanted to know.
"Yes…"
"The way I want to?"
"Yes, that's…"
"Without stopping me?" he cut me short. I pressed my lips together… but I nodded. "Can I keep my eyes closed?"
He nodded once, "Anything you want, love."
That was the last thing he said to me before I felt a finger sink into me.
"Oh fuck…" I groaned.
He pulled his hand back and added another finger.
"Fuckkkk…" I heard him curse under his breath, "Moonlight have mercy…"
I didn't get a chance to say anything more before I felt his tongue drag across my pussy and I cursed out loud, "Oh holy fucking shit!"
"That sounded really good. Keep going," he encouraged me before he pressed his tongue to me again. I wanted to look, because watching him eat my pussy was like my own personal interactive porno, but I kept my eyes closed.

Jonathan was showing no signs of stopping. He had an arm wrapped around my one thigh, the fingers of the other hand dipping in and out of my pussy while he devoured me like I was his last meal. I didn't even try to stop myself from moaning, or cursing or calling out his name. If the neighbors heard us, then so fucking what.
"Oh fuck, yes!" I cried out.
My clit was in his mouth, he had his fingers inside me, stroking back and forth, and I absolutely fell apart beneath his tongue. "Jonathan…!"

My body was still pulled taut from the orgasm that had just shattered me, but he was obviously not done. He didn't say anything, all he did was shift his body up on the mattress, and another moan tumbled over my lips when I felt the head of his dick slide into me.
"Fuckkkking hell…" he cursed again.
I finally opened my eyes to look at him. I didn't know what I was expecting to see, but there was only want and desire as he plunged into me.
"Jona… Ah, fuck!" I had only curse words left in my vocabulary box.
"Hang on…" he said before he pulled himself out of me. "What are you…?" I started asking but I stopped the sentence short when he growled, "Turn over."
I flipped myself onto my stomach, and I pressed my face into the pillow so I could moan as loud as I wanted when he lowered himself back onto me and slowly pushed his dick back inside me.

Having Jonathan inside me was always magic, and feeling every inch of him sliding in and out of me while my body was more sensitive than usual was beyond words. Even though another orgasm probably wasn't in the cards for me, that was perfectly fine. Because for the first time since we started sleeping together, I was not the only one making all the sounds.
He was holding my hips as he slowly drove into me, and with every thrust, Jonathan was moaning. He started off slow, taking his time with every shift of his hips, but after a few short minutes, it was like he started losing control. He started thrusting faster, and along with his speed, the volume of the sounds he was making also increased.
He sometimes let me take the reins in bed, when I made it very clear that it was what I wanted, but most of the time he was the one in control. And now, to feel and hear him losing control, and to know that I was the one doing that to him… Pure ecstasy.
"Christina…" he whimpered my name, "Shit… Oh f… Ah…" The last sound that made its way out of him was something that sounded Romanian before he lost control and came inside me.
Then his body went still on top of me, but he didn't get up immediately. Instead, he shifted my hair out of the way to press his lips to my bare shoulder, and then he remained there, motionless. I turned my head to look at him and I couldn't help but smile when I saw that he had his eyes closed.

After he pulled himself out of me and stood to pick my clothes up off the floor, I turned over onto my back. And then I just stared at the ceiling, trying to even out my breathing. I heard the water running in the bathroom, and I took a deep breath in an attempt to stop myself from cringing; he was washing my blood off him. *Let it go, Christina, he said it's okay.*
When he came back from the bathroom, I opened my eyes when he gently tapped the side of my thigh and said, "Lift your hips, love," before sliding a towel underneath me.
I was mortified, and I covered my face with my hands, "I got blood everywhere, didn't I?" I mumbled. He moved my hands away from my face and made me look at him, "I swore to you it was going to be alright, I need you to trust me."
I just nodded.

He lay down next to me on the bed, both of us still butt-naked, and I was just starting to relax when I felt something... twitch against the side of my thigh. As soon as I realized what it was, I turned my head to look at him. "Holy crap, you are insatiable. Are you seriously getting hard again already?"
He touched the tip of his tongue to his upper lip, "Sorry, darling. Am I being too much?"
I turned to my side to look at him, "We've been at it since last night, we just had sex, like, three and a half seconds ago. How are you this horny?"
Jonathan tipped his head back and laughed, "I don't know. It must be what you do to me."
A thought occurred to me and my jaw dropped, "Wait… Is it…? Babe!"
Jonathan frowned, "What?"
I chuckled in disbelief, "Are you extra horny because I'm on my period?"
For the first time since we met, Jonathan was the one to blush.
He wiped a hand over his face and clamped his fingers over his mouth before he turned his head to look at me, "You know what…" he mumbled from behind his fingers, "That very well might be it…"
"Jonathan!" I laughed at the extremely guilty look on his face, "You. Absolute. Horndog."

He jumped off the bed and scuttled back into the bathroom, and I laughed again when I heard the water running. "Are you taking a cold shower?" I called out.
"I need one!" came his reply.

∞

He had me take a shower while he made us French toast, bacon and a few links of some really expensive sausage for breakfast. I knew it was expensive because I had seen the price tag on the pack the night before, but I decided to just let it be. It was really good though. When I got out of the shower, I noticed that he had also replaced the sheets. *Nothing to be embarrassed over; he said he's got it handled.* He claimed that there weren't any stains on the mattress, and even though I wasn't sure that I believed him, I let it go. If he wanted me to trust him, then I was going to do that. Or try, at least.

"Tell me about Nathaniel," I wanted to know while we were having breakfast. Jonathan had a forkful of French toast halfway to his mouth but he froze and put the fork down. His eyes narrowed at me and he frowned, "Why do you want to know about him?"
I gave him a blank look, "You're joking, right?"
I pointed to the bed behind me, "After everything you've been doing to me since last night, all the ways you've bent me and fucked me, do you really think I have any interest in any other man?"
Jonathan kept his eyes narrowed… then he winked at me and grinned, "Of course not. What do you want to know?"
Fucking maddening. I rolled my eyes and shook my head, "When did you meet him?"
Jonathan thought back for a moment, "Around… 1920, I think. In Belfast."
"Wasn't that around the time of the Civil War?"
He nodded slowly, "About two years before, yes."
He looked like he didn't really want to talk about it, so I let it go, "He seems like a good time."
Jonathan chuckled, "I can never tell who drinks more, Nathaniel or Kirill."
"Did you meet Lilian around the same time as Nathaniel?"
He sipped some of his coffee, "No, I met her near the end of the 80's. And they met in the 70's.

They met in a similar way that we did, actually. Her university was running a course on vampire fiction, the guest lecturer didn't show up, so Nathaniel pretended to be the lecturer's teaching assistant and he swooped in and saved the day."
I smiled from ear to ear, "So I wasn't the only one that got Crimson Counted."

There was something I wanted to know, and I figured I might as well ask, "I was just wondering… What is it about... you know… blood… that… does it for you?"
He slowly blinked at me, and I went on, "Is it… the smell of it? Or... the taste…?"
"Love," he said, "I'm happy to answer you, but I don't want to make you uncomfortable."
I pulled up my shoulders, "Babe, you took off my pad and panty and tossed it on the floor. I don't know that anything you say now will make me so uncomfortable that I can't deal."
"Alright then," he conceded. "Are you talking about blood in general, or…?"
The pointed look I gave him was enough to make him understand that I was talking about a specific type of blood in particular.
"Ah," he said, "in that case… No, it isn't the smell or the taste. That is to say… I can't feed on it…"
"Because it's dead?" I interjected, and he nodded his head once before he went on, "Indeed. I think it's just the presence of it, the fact that it is there in the first place."
As explanations go, that's fine, I guess. Gross, but fine. If that's what he's into.

We ate in silence for a bit before he spoke again, "May I say something?"
I nodded, "Of course, babe, what's up?"
He glanced over at the bed before he looked back at me, "I know that everything that just happened was… outside of your comfort zone."
I widened my eyes, "No kidding."
Jonathan reached over and put his hand over mine on the table, "Thank you."
"For what?" I was a bit confused. *Is he thanking me for sex?*

He stroked my hand with his thumb, "For trusting me with your body, your life, after what I told you last night…"

Right. That thing he told me about losing control. I honestly hadn't even thought about that until he brought it up. It never occurred to me that I needed to be careful of him, or that he might not be able to control himself, and that he could end up hurting me, or worse… There's never been a moment where I was afraid of him. Something in his eyes when he looked at me made me sure that, no matter what, I was safe with him.

I smiled at him, "Loving you, and trusting you, are the easiest things in the world. When I'm with you, soul is home."

Chapter 46

Christina

With Jonathan away on business, this time in France, I used the time to ramp up my training with Kirill.
He'd also been really busy lately and wasn't around much, so I was happy when his schedule opened up unexpectedly and we were able to fit in an extra sparring session.

The first two rounds of the bout went pretty well, but midway into the third round, I completely missed the timing on a kick that I was supposed to block, and it landed against the left side of my face. Even though Kirill was by no means fighting at full strength, the impact still sent me sprawling across the mats.
"Nuchka!" he exclaimed, rushing over to me.
"Ow, fuck," I mumbled, sitting up and clutching my jaw.
Kirill was murmuring something frantic in high-speed Russian, and I had no idea what he was saying, but I assumed he was something between panicked and very sorry.
I tried to smile, but my jaw hurt, "It's okay, Kiryusha," I assured him as I let him help me up.
He shook his head vigorously, "No, no, not okay. Very not okay. *Izvinite*."
I patted his shoulder, "It's my fault, I fucked up."
He gently took my chin in his hand and examined my jaw, "Shit," he mumbled, "that look very bad tomorrow."

I refused to tell Jonathan what happened, but my mom insisted on taking me to the hospital to make sure I didn't have a concussion and that nothing was broken or cracked.

The ER nurse was convinced that I was a victim of domestic violence, no matter how many times I explained what happened, and she insisted that she had to alert the police. She would not believe my story, and kept a very skeptical eye on me, until I showed her the video of the bout. Good thing we recorded it.

The next day, the left side of my face was swollen and red, and it hurt. A lot. The redness then turned into a bruise that darkened to some spectacular shades of blue and purple. The bruising settled under my eye and at the bottom of my jaw, and it looked pretty bad. It did look a lot worse than it felt, though.

I declined all of Jonathan's FaceTime calls, because I didn't want him to see me like that. I was trying to buy time so the bruise could heal, but by the time he was due back from France, the edges of the bruise had just started to turn a yellowish-green. Even though it didn't hurt anymore, no amount of make-up or concealer would be enough to hide it from him…

When he arrived at my house and rang the doorbell, I felt my stomach drop. *The moment of truth.*

I was nervous about how he was going to react, but I couldn't just ignore the doorbell and pretend like he wasn't there. I was too excited to see him anyway.

So, I pinched my eyes shut and slowly opened the door.

As always, my heart did backflips when I saw him, but I didn't need to see myself to know what kind of stupid, sheepish grin I had on my face when I greeted him, "Hi babe, welcome home."

When he saw the bruise, the smile immediately fell from his face. He looked absolutely furious as he tenderly took my face in his hands to look at the bruise, "Who did this to you?"

"It doesn't hurt anymore, babe…"

"Christina," he cut me short, "I love you, but that is not what I asked you. Tell me who did this."

"Kirill, but…"

When he heard Kirill's name, his face darkened even more.

He let go of my face and took a step back, "He's dead. He's fucking dead," he said as he turned around and started walking back to his car.

Oh, shit.

I rushed after him to grab him by the wrist, "Jonathan, stop. Listen to me."

He stopped and turned back to me, and every inch of his 6-ft-2 frame was trembling with rage.

"Babe…" I said gently.

I had never, ever seen him this angry before.

Rage shadowed his face like a thundercloud, and he kept clenching and unclenching his jaw.

He was so angry that his eyes weren't even cobalt anymore. I didn't understand how it was physiologically possible, but, from corner to corner, his eyes were a black hole of barely-contained wrath.

I reached out to take his hands, and I was surprised that he had his claws out.

"You said to listen, so talk." he said through his fangs.

I glanced around the street. This was really risky, him showing his Infinity in public outside my house.

"I can see you're angry, but please let's just go talk inside? Not out here in the open."

He didn't reply, he just followed me back into the house in silence and as soon as we were inside, I started my explanatory rant, "Okay, so here's what happened. Kirill has secretly been teaching me hapkido, because I asked him to, because I wanted to surprise you with my amazing martial arts skills. We had a sparring session, and I fucked up, and I missed the timing on a kick and… wham…"

Jonathan cocked an eyebrow, "You don't need to cover for him."

Great. Stubborn ass thinks I'm lying. "I'm not, I swear. Babe, come on, please?" I pleaded, but his face remained dark and foreboding.

"Fine. Watch the video then." I shoved my phone in his hand.

He watched the video without saying anything, until the sound of the kick hitting me in the face broke the silence.

"Ohh, darling," he grimaced, "that was a solid hit you took."

He looked up from the screen, and I was very relieved to see his eyes back to their normal beautiful onyx and his claws gone. He smiled endearingly and took my chin in his hand to look at the bruise again, "Please tell me you went to the hospital?"

"My mom took me," I confirmed.

He lightly stroked my jaw with his thumb, "This must have really hurt."

I nodded, "Uh-huh. Like a son-of-a-bitch."

He looked me in the eye, "Was this why you didn't want to FaceTime me?"

I smiled guiltily and I nodded, “Yes… I looked like a blueberry for a few days.”
“Surely you were the most adorable blueberry ever.” Jonathan leaned in and kissed my bruised jaw, and then all over my face–from my cheek to my nose, my forehead, my eyes–before he carefully pulled me into his arms to hug me, “Did you sustain any other injuries that I need to be aware of?”
“Nothing serious, but I’ve had my fair share of bruises from training. I didn’t tell you about those, though. Sorry babe.”
He chuckled and kissed my forehead again, “Darling… I saw all of your bruises. I knew you were doing some kind of training.”
I stepped out of his embrace and my jaw dropped, “So you’re not even surprised?”
He cupped the right side of my jaw so as not to touch the bruise on my left, “I was. I am. But I figured there was a reason that you weren’t telling me, so I didn’t say anything.”
“Okay…Well, ta-da!” I said half-heartedly, “I learned hapkido.”
Smiling that heartbreakingly beautiful smile of his, he pulled me back into his arms, “You’re amazing, and I’m incredibly hot for you right now.”
I blushed, but I laughed, “You’re being a shit. Again.”
He took a small step back, “Well, this shit was hoping you would be keen on seeing a movie with him tonight? And then staying over. Please. I missed you.”

Chapter 47

Christina

"I'm just saying, strawberry is obviously your favorite," I said to Jonathan on our way to the car after the movie ended.

"Why do you think that?" he denied.

I looked blankly at him, "Are you kidding? Literally everything you ate tonight, with the exception of the popcorn, was strawberry flavored."

He was quiet for a moment, and I could tell by the look on his face that he knew I was right. But he shook his head in denial, "Strawberry just happened to be the best available option."

"Our first date," I countered, "you ordered strawberry tiramisu crumble."

"And…?"

I sighed, "Proving my point that strawberry is your favorite flavor."

"It is not," he denied.

I gave him a pointed look, "Really? Then what is?"

He wiggled his eyebrows at me, "You."

I laughed, leaning my head against his shoulder, "You're such a cheeseball."

He put his arm around me and held me against him, "Yes, I am."

We had almost reached the car when his phone rang.

"Hang on a second, darling," he said, looking at the screen, "it's Nathaniel."

"Oh, okay. Say hi for me, I need to pee," I excused myself and scuttled to the bathroom just around the corner, while Jonathan got into the car and answered the phone.

I wish I knew why he always chose to park in the basement parking lot.

And why are these bathrooms located exactly where they would be in a horror movie? Who builds a bathroom in a freaking alley? At least the ladies' room was closer to the start of the alleyway and not at the end of it, like the men's.

I had just left the bathroom when a hand from within the dark grabbed my arm and held me back.

For a moment I thought it was Jonathan, but I grimaced when I recognized the overpowering stench of cheap cologne, "What do you want, Owen?"

"You," he said, "I want you back, baby."

I pulled a disgusted face at him, "Stop calling me that. I'm not your baby."

He gave me a pleading look that repulsed me even more, "Don't be so mean. You used to be, once."

I rolled my eyes at him, "Yeah, 'once' being the operative word there."

"Come on, babycakes, we were happy together once."

"Urgh, Owen. Stop talking out of your ass. The unhappiest I have ever been in my life was when I was your girlfriend."

"I'm a better man now. If you just give me another chance, I can make you happy," he insisted.

"You're not hearing me. You have nothing that I want. Just... just go."

"How about you let me show you what I can do to your body? I know a trick or two," he said suggestively, and I felt like I was going to throw up in my mouth. "Eww," I chuckled in disgust.

Owen's lip curled into an ugly sneer, "You know what. Fuck this. You've turned into a real stuck-up little bitch, haven't you?"

He lifted up his arm. He was going to slap me. *Why is everyone trying to hit me these days?*

It was weird. Everything happened in slow motion, like I was watching a preview of what was going to happen before it did.

I saw his arm lift up and his hand move toward my face, and my body reacted, exactly as Kat taught me.

I brought my arms out–fingers extended, elbows slightly bent–and I raised my left forearm inside of his arm. At the same time, I lifted my right arm and slammed the heel of my palm up and into his nose, then I clenched my hand into a fist and I punched him in the throat.

When he dropped to the ground, coughing and gasping, I kicked him in the stomach, "Stay the fuck away from me, Owen."
I shook my head at him, and then I jogged back to the car.

Jonathan frowned when he saw me jogging toward the car, my face probably full of thunder and pissed-off-ness.
"Darling, what happened?" he asked me when I got into the car and slammed the door shut a lot harder than was probably necessary.
"Fucking Owen! Dickhole tried to hit me." I snarled. *Idiot.*

Jonathan went still and I could literally see the ice cold anger take hold of him, "Where is he?"
I gestured with my head toward the bathroom, "That way, somewhere. I throat-punched him and I left. He might be gone by now."
Jonathan removed the key from the ignition and handed it to me, "Stay here. Lock the doors. I will be right back," he said, before he, very calmly, got out of the car.
"What are you going to do?" I asked.
Jonathan smiled, but his black eyes remained dead, "I'm going to rip his fucking face off."
Before I said anything, he closed the door and strode off in the direction of the bathroom.
A very small part of me thought that I should probably stop him, before he really did kill Owen. But the other parts of me didn't give a shit; he did tell Owen not to come near me.
I locked the doors and curled my legs under me, and I shivered. I knew I was safe in the car, but basement parking lots gave me the heebie-jeebies.

Jonathan

It didn't take me long at all to find Owen, all I had to do was follow the stench of desperation. He was stumbling down the alley, rubbing his throat.

I welcomed the anger thrumming in my blood, and I started walking toward him.

"Did I not warn you?" I asked out loud, my voice thundering down the alley, "I told you if I ever sensed you near my wife, you would not live to see another day."

Owen's eyes widened when he recognized my voice. He tried to run away, and I laughed out loud at the sad attempt, "Just when I thought you couldn't possibly get any more pathetic…"

I didn't even need to engage my speed. It took me only a few strides to catch up to Owen, and I grabbed him by the shoulder. My face remained calm and expressionless as I spun him around and punched him in the face.

Blood spurted from his mouth as he staggered backward and fell to the ground.

I stepped over him and hoisted him up by the front of his shirt, then I slammed his back into the bare brick wall and pressed my forearm across his throat.

I sniffed the air and I sneered: Fear. Fear and piss.

Then I smiled, malicious and unkind, and I leaned closer to Owen, "Did you ever imagine that this would be how your life ended? In a filthy alley? Pissing yourself from fear?"

"P… please…" Owen begged, "Please don't kill me?"

"Why the fuck not?" I snarled, "It would be so easy. And so fun."

"I'm s… I'm sorry, I swear…"

"Babe?" Christina's voice sounded up from somewhere behind me. I kept my eyes burning into Owen's, but I turned my head toward her, "Yes my darling?"

“Can we go? I’m bored,” she asked. Bless this perfect angel. She was preventing me from killing him, but he needed to remember his place. I let out a hostile snarl that ended in a snap of my teeth right in Owen’s face, “Consider yourself lucky,” I hissed. “The next time I see you, you’re dead.”
I removed my arm from his throat, and he dropped to his feet and sank to the ground.
I rolled my neck, took a deep breath and turned around with a smile on my face as I walked back to Christina.
As we started walking back to the car, my arm draped over her shoulder, Christina looked over at Owen, still sitting on the ground in the alley, “Hey, Owen,” she called out to him, “watch your back.”

As soon as we reached the car, I pushed her up against the passenger door and kissed her with a fire I hadn’t felt since the time we were in London.
My lips and my tongue hungrily claiming hers, I shifted my hands from her neck to her breasts to her arse to the front of her jeans and back and up and down again.
Christina hooked her fingers into the pockets of my jeans and pulled me against her.
“Why did you stop me?” I asked before I took her earlobe into my mouth.
“You were going to kill him…” she breathed, and I nodded, “Yes, and I would have enjoyed it.”
She tipped her head to the side, “I know. I just didn’t think he was worth the effort.”
I took her hand, pressing her palm to my cock and she gasped.
I nibbled her earlobe again, pressing myself into her hand, “I am so fucking hard for you.”
She pulled her head back, panting, “Let’s go home. Now.”

We managed to keep our hands off of each other until we reached my room, but as soon as I locked the door behind us, I whipped off my belt, and slung it around her like a lasso to pull her closer.
She laughed, “Whoa there, cowboy.”
I smiled against her lips, “You know what they say, darling.”
“What do they say?” she asked in short breaths between kisses.

I pulled her shirt over her head and kissed her once more before I replied, "Save a horse, ride a cowboy."

She pulled down her jeans and yanked her panties down to her knees, then turned around and leaned over the back of the sofa, "How about you just ride me?"
Burning fucking Hell, I don't need a second invitation.
I wrapped my fingers around the back of her neck and rammed my cock into her, so hard that the sofa shifted forward and she lost her footing and stumbled.
I moved my hands to her hips to steady her, and I pulled back and plunged into her again.
She pushed back to meet me, and I slipped my hand to the front of her body, my fingers sliding in between the folds of her pussy. The sound of her moaning spurred me on, and I drove harder into her, stroking and teasing her clit until she climaxed.
I groaned. I could feel her orgasm, warm and wet, the inside of her pussy squeezing my cock, and my own ending came sooner than I would have wanted it to.
But I wasn't done.

I pulled myself out of her, and I made quick work of getting rid of the condom and hoisting up my pants before pulling her lips back to mine and kissing her.
I lifted her half-naked body up in my arms and carried her up to my bed, pausing only to whip off her jeans and panty and chuck them on the floor, somewhere.
Then I lay her down on the bed before me and shifted down her body, pressing her legs apart to take a long, lingering taste of her. She gasped in surprise, and I sighed in satisfaction: She tasted like sex and strawberries.
Then she draped her legs over my shoulders, her fingers twisted, tugging my hair, rocking her hips against my mouth as I ate her pussy until she called out my name in climax.

"I had no idea that that was a flavored condom. I don't even know where it came from," I said as I lay down on my side next to her.
She chuckled, "I bought it. You really didn't see the strawberries on the wrapper?"

I shook my head, “No… I grabbed whatever was in the box and stuffed it in my pocket before I left the house.”
“You really didn’t need to though…”
I nodded slowly, “Force of habit…”
She smiled, “I figured. But since strawberries are your favorite, I thought it was the best choice.”
I put my hand on her bare tummy, tracing little lines and swirls across her skin, “Why flavored, though? I might look like it, but I’m really not flexible enough to go down on myself.”
She laughed, “I bought the pack before I went on the pill, for in case I wanted to go down on you after we had sex. I’d prefer your dick tasting like artificial strawberries rather than latex.”
I smiled, “Trust me, love, I plan on never leaving you with enough energy after sex to do anything more than fall asleep in my arms.”
In response, she moved closer to me and snuggled up against my chest. We held each other, not a word spoken between us, and it wasn’t long before we both fell asleep as we were, half-way clothed, curled up in each other’s arms, barely moving until daybreak.

Christina

When I woke up, a part of me wanted to understand why I was having erotic dreams about Jonathan again, when he nearly banged my brains out right before we fell asleep.

Another part of me wanted to wake him up and tell him every juicy detail of the dream so he could re-enact it exactly…

Still thinking about the dream, my eyes remained closed as I let my hand travel down between my thighs, straight to my clit. I moaned softly and my hips started moving rhythmically along with the pulsating heat rising between my legs.

A creaking sound startled me and I opened my eyes.

Jonathan was sitting on a wooden bench by the bed, his lips slightly parted, fangs bared, watching me.

“Sorry…” I breathed.

He shook his head and whipped the covers off of me, exposing my body, my hand still between my thighs. My knees instinctively pressed together, but he reached over and ever so gently opened them back up. He looked down at where my hand was resting on my pussy, and he let out a shuddering breath, “Please,” he murmured, “don’t stop.”

I nodded and picked up right where I left off, my head tipping back into the pillow. I was too far gone to stop now anyway.

I heard Jonathan growl and it was like my body knew what he wanted me to do and just obeyed. My finger slipped inside myself, and I gasped; I hadn’t realized how wet I was.

I looked up at Jonathan, I wanted to see his reaction. His claws were digging into the wood, his resplendent wings spread out behind him, half-draped over the bench, his cobalt eyes fixed on the movement of my hand.

I can’t stop, I’m so close.

“Jonathan…” I breathed. I wanted to tell him

“I know…” he replied, his voice dark and hoarse, “Play with that beautiful pussy until you come for me. Don’t stop.”

I obeyed, and I kept going until I came and my mind went blank with pleasure, my eyes rolling back in my head.

When I looked back at Jonathan, he was standing at the foot of the bed in the faint morning light. He had taken off his pajama pants, every hard inch of him exposed. Still watching me, he wrapped his fingers around himself, his hand moving up and down the length of him.

I flashed him a feline smile, "Do you want to be inside me?"

His chest heaving up and down, he nodded slowly.

I bit my lower lip, spread my legs and beckoned him closer.

Jonathan knelt down on the mattress and sank down between my legs, his eyes locked with mine. He buried himself deep, deep inside me in a powerful stroke that shifted me up on the bed and had me crying out with pleasure.

I wrapped a leg around him to pull him closer as he drove deep into me, and I could feel his velvety soft wings brushing against my leg. Next to me, fabric ripped as he gripped the sheets and his claws shredded through the material.

His every thrust took my soul higher, and when he finally found his release, he snarled against my neck and the tips of his razor-sharp fangs pierced my skin. I yelped in surprise and returned the favor, biting into his shoulder as hard as I could.

When I let go, he pulled away, and as he turned his head to look at me, his face turned ashen.

"What's wrong?" I asked him, but before he could answer, I reached up to touch my neck where his fangs had punctured my skin, and I was surprised when I looked at my hand and saw blood.

I recognized the look on his face, but I wasn't going to let him go there. I tilted my head, exposing my neck to him. "It's okay," I reassured him, "go ahead."

Jonathan shook his head, but I dug my fingers into his hair and pulled his face down to my neck, "It's okay, I trust you."

I did my best to ignore the subtle flicker of what could only be fear. I did trust him, but this was probably going to hurt.

As his face came ever closer to my neck, I pinched my eyes shut, anticipating the moment when his fangs would sink into my flesh… and I gasped when I felt his tongue caressing my skin instead.

Instead of biting me, feeding on me, he licked the blood from my skin, and I heard him sigh. Then he buried his face in my neck, holding me tightly against him, clinging to me like someone was about to take me away forever.

And I savored it. I just lay there beneath him, the warmth and weight of his body crushing me into the mattress. I stroked his hair, his neck, and lightly scratched my nails over his wings, from where they emerged from his back, to as far as I could reach.

He shivered in my arms, and goosebumps raised on his shoulders and arms. I giggled, "Do you like that?"

"Hmm," he murmured in my neck, "you know I do."

I looked around the room and I frowned, "I realize that I should have noticed this earlier, but where did the armchair go?"

"I got sick of it, so I swapped it for the bench," he said.

"Okay," I accepted, "and what happened to your four-poster bed?"

He lifted his head out of my neck to kiss my cheek before he tucked away his wings and lay down next to me, "I replaced the bed-frame. It was time for a change."

I pressed my lips together and lifted up a few tattered strips of the sheets and showed them to him, "Well, now you need new sheets too, because…" I pointed at the shredded ribbons of fabric, and he chuckled, "Whoops."

He moved closer to me and draped an arm over me, his head on my shoulder, my arm around his.

"For the purposes of this conversation, because I know he would never, but what if Kirill had kicked me on purpose?" I asked.

Without a moment's hesitation, Jonathan replied, "I would have killed him."

I frowned, "Even though you've known him for years?"

He nodded, "How long I've known him would have had no bearing. If Kirill hurt you on purpose, I would have ripped his spine out through his throat. And he knows that."

I nodded slowly, "He was very worried."

"Hmm," Jonathan mumbled, "as he should be."

I smiled endearingly at him, running my fingers through his hair, "You're incredibly territorial over me, aren't you? Like, super protective."

He nodded, "I am. I can't bear the thought of something happening to you. The thought of you getting hurt… of someone hurting you…" he shook his head, "I just… I don't think rationally."

Jonathan tilted his head up and looked right into my eyes, "If anyone hurts you, there will be blood."

I knew he meant it. I could see it in his eyes, in the set of his jaw. And it made me fall in love with him a little bit more, "I know."
I lowered my head to kiss his hair before I replied, "You are amazing, and I am incredibly hot for you right now."
Jonathan laughed, then he readjusted his position a little bit, and he grimaced, "Yes, I definitely need a new sheet."

I had another question, "I'm curious… How did it happen that you ended up watching me…?"
He turned onto his side and smiled crookedly, "I went down to the fridge for… a snack… And when I came back, you were saying my name… and making all these delightful little sounds."
I closed my eyes and I could feel my cheeks glow from embarrassment.
Jonathan chuckled, "So I decided to take a seat and enjoy the show. I figured I was invited…You did moan my name."

We ate our breakfast in bed, and I had just settled into his arms for a snuggle when his phone buzzed on the bedside table.
"Oh, for fuck's sake," he complained as he looked at the screen. "My father's office in Prague. Why the fuck are they calling me and not him?"
He mumbled something to himself in angry Romanian before swinging his feet off the bed and switching to Czech to answer the phone.
Listening to him talk on the phone, even though he was still being polite, I could hear that he was annoyed with whoever was on the other end of the line.
It was astounding how quickly he could switch between languages. He just went from English, to Romanian, right into Czech, without skipping a beat.
When he ended the call, he turned back to me and he raised an eyebrow slightly, "Yes…?"
I sighed, "I feel so inferior to you sometimes."
His curious expression quickly turned into consternation, "Darling, no, why would you say that?"
He took my hand in his, kissing the back of it over and over.
So I went on, "I mean, you speak… How many languages? And I only know one."

He seemed to be waiting for me to go on.
I sighed, 'You don't get it, do you?"
He slowly shook his head, "I don't… I'm sorry."
I tried to explain, "You're just so… cultured."
"I'm not cultured, I'm snooty," he contradicted.
I ignored his comment and went on, "And well-traveled… "
"I have too much money," he added.
"And business savvy…"
"That's gluttony. I want more money…" he nodded.
I rolled my eyes, "And you're determined, and ambitious."
"Let's not forget stubborn," he said, "and very, very old."
I chuckled and he kissed my hand again, "My mother has been teaching me every language she knows since I was born."
"Okay, but how many college degrees do you have?" I wanted to know.
He shrugged, "A few, but darling, I've been traipsing the earth for eight centuries. I had to keep busy."
I smiled half-heartedly, "I know… Sometimes it just bothers me that I will never be your equal."
He inclined his head to one side, "Whoever said that you're not?"
I raised my hand, "Me. Because I'm not."
"Because you are so much more," he replied. I rolled my eyes in disbelief.
Jonathan sighed and ran his fingers through his hair, "Remember I told you that I didn't grow up with money?"
I nodded.
He continued, "What I did grow up with was a title, and expectations. I have always been 'The Prince'. From the time I was around 15,16, people have always just… done what I told them. Whatever I said, they obeyed. No-one challenged me, no-one said no to me."
"Wow… you must have really been an asshole," I said softly.
He chuckled, "And that, my darling Christina, is exactly why I am so in love with you. You are the only woman that calls me an asshole to my face. You scold me, you call me out on my bullshit." Jonathan moved closer to me and lay down with his head on my thigh, "And I love how you don't get flustered by me."
I leaned forward to look him in the eye, "Are you sure about that?"
He smiled up at me, "Really? You do?"

I ran my fingers through his silky soft hair, nodding, "When you first asked me out, I was hella flustered. And when you took me to the cabin… whoo boy."

He reached up and touched my face, "So that's why your heart was beating so fast. And here I thought you were just horny for me."

I smiled, "Obviously I was… but you seduced me. You and your charms."

He sat up and moved his back against the headboard and looked at me in surprise, "I beg your pardon? That is not how it happened."

I folded my arms and looked pointedly at him, "Then how did it happen?"

He raised his eyebrow at me, "Are you telling me that you don't remember how you mounted me on the sofa?"

I swung my leg over him and straddled him, "Did I do it like this?" I asked, grinding myself against him as I took off my t-shirt.

Jonathan bit his lower lip and nodded, "Exactly like this."

I put my hands on his bare chest. His skin was so nice and warm to the touch, "What happened next?"

Jonathan raked his fingers through my hair and down my back and I shivered.

A wicked grin on his face, he wrapped his hand around the back of my neck and toppled me over onto the bed, pinning my body down with his, "Let me show you…"

Chapter 48

Christina

"I have never done this before," I groaned.
I was at a day spa with Niki, in the middle of a scalp massage, and I kept getting goosebumps.
"Done what?" Niki asked.
"Spent the day at a spa, getting primped and pampered," I groaned again.
We were going to be spending the entire afternoon at the spa. The scalp massage was the first treatment in the full body package that Niki booked for us. I called Devyn to invite her along, but she didn't answer, so I went alone.
"Why not?" Niki wanted to know.
"Because I'm poor."
Niki laughed, "Well, after you marry my brother, we can do this as often as you want."
My jaw dropped, "Wait… what? Marry him? Wh… Niki, did he say something?"
Niki looked at me from the corners of her eyes, "If he doesn't propose soon, then he's a moron."
I rolled my eyes and smiled, "That's very sweet of you, Nix."
Niki smiled at me and blew me a kiss, "I really like you. I'd love to have you as a sister."
I blew a kiss back, "Aww, Nix. Me, too. I always wanted a sister growing up."

The spa day had more treatments than I expected.

It started with a back, neck and scalp massage, followed by a full body salt scrub. After the salt scrub, we were taken to a different room in the spa for a detoxifying body mask, followed by manicures and pedicures. Niki said the last two treatments would be a hydrating body wrap and a hot stone massage. But first… waxing.

"Do you have any preferences, ma'am?" the aesthetician asked me.

I was confused; I'd never had a wax, "Uhm… I don't know. Are there options?"

The aesthetician smiled, "Yes ma'am. Would you like a full Brazilian wax, or would you prefer a French bikini wax?"

My frown deepened, "I've heard of the Brazilian, but what's the French one?"

"Landing strip," Niki clarified from behind the privacy screen.

The aesthetician was still just smiling at me, waiting for an answer.

I tried to think quickly but I really didn't know, "I honestly have no idea."

"I've had both," Niki tried to help, "doesn't hurt."

"Which is better?"

Niki chuckled, "I'd go French. Although if you ask me, I'm rather sure my brother doesn't give a damn what your muffin looks like, as long as he gets to eat it."

I felt my face glowing bright red and I pressed my hands to my face in an attempt to suppress the snort-laugh that escaped through my nose.

I was really nervous about getting waxed, but I decided to treat it like every other new experience that I'd had while being with Jonathan, and just embrace it.

But the moment the aesthetician ripped off the first strip, she also ripped away all of my poise. I dropped the start of a curse word, and I was really grateful that the sound of Niki laughing drowned out the rest of the word that started with 'mother'.

When it was Niki's turn, I narrowed my eyes at her in passing, "You, sister-girl, are a fucking liar…"

The day continued to surprise me even more when I got a call from Lilian, inviting me to join her in New York the next day.

She didn't say why, but I decided to go anyway. We got along like a house on fire at their engagement party in London, so a trip to New York together could only be fun.

Jonathan was away at a construction site with his dad somewhere, so he arranged for the pilot to fly me to New York by myself, and he gave me the access code to his apartment on the Upper East Side. As I sat alone in the jet, sipping on a glass of champagne, I really did feel like a trophy wife, and even though I'd never say it out loud, I was starting to really enjoy this life. The freedom of not having to worry about the price tag…even though it wasn't my money, it felt good.

When I arrived in New York, I wasn't at all surprised that there was a driver waiting to take me to the apartment.

I also wasn't surprised that Jonathan's penthouse apartment was huge and absolutely gorgeous. It was clear that the interior design choices were his own. The apartment was all dark colors and stone finishes, and… gargoyles. Gargoyles everywhere. I chuckled. He really did have a thing for them.

My favorite room in the apartment had to be the bedroom. Dark gray everything, floor to ceiling windows, and the most breathtaking views on three sides. I sighed, imagining one day waking up to that view next to Jonathan.

Shit. Jonathan.

I forgot to let him know that I had arrived safely in New York, so I sent him a quick text before I headed back outside to go meet Lilian. I also texted Devyn, because she still wasn't picking up, and then put my phone away and got in the car.

The restaurant that I was meeting Lilian at was an upscale French restaurant overlooking a small park, and Lilian was already waiting for me when I arrived.

"Hello luv," she grinned when I approached the table and got to her feet to hug me hello.

"You look amazing," I complimented, and Lilian smiled brightly.

She was wearing a black t-shirt with three-quarter length sleeves, and a knee-length white skirt, and I loved that both of her legs were just as tattooed as her arms.

I glanced around to make sure that there was nobody within earshot before I asked, "I love your tats, but how did you get so many…?"

Lilian laughed, "I got inked before I turned, luv."

I giggled. Jonathan also called me 'love', but with Lilian's British accent it had a very different vibe than when Jonathan said it.

I wasn't sure which part of the UK her accent was from, but Jonathan told me she spoke like a Londoner.

"Okay, so," I asked her after the server brought us our meals, "What are we getting into today?"

"I needed a sidekick, I need to have a gander at some wedding dresses. I've shopped around London, but I wasn't finding what I wanted, so Nate sent me to New York so I can stop carping about it," Lilian explained, and I shrieked in delight, "We're going wedding dress shopping?"

Lilian shrieked back and nodded, showing me the business card of the dress shop we were going to.

I grinned. This was going to be fun.

At the bridal shop, a skinny consultant in a black pencil dress teetered over to us in her sky-high heels, a really big retail smile plastered across her face. She rambled through her entire 'welcome to our store, we will sell our soul to make you happy' spiel, and then she clasped her hands in front of her, "Which one of you beautiful ladies is our bride?"

Lilian raised her hand, "It's me!"

The consultant nodded and smiled acceptingly, then gestured toward me, "And who's accompanying you today?"

Lilian grabbed my wrist with both hands, "This is my maid of honor."

"Lovely. If you ladies will please follow me, right this way…" the consultant yammered on before she scuttled deeper into the shop, and I put my hand over Lilian's, "Lil… You want me to be your maid of honor?" I asked, tears in my eyes for some reason.

Lilian nodded, "Yes! I forgot I'm supposed to ask! But yes! Will you? Please say yes?"

I nearly cried, but I nodded, "Of course!"

The consultant brought five different dresses for Lilian to try on.

The first was a sleeveless, ivory-colored, A-line dress.

The dress was pretty, but Lilian didn't seem to like it. She wrinkled her face.

"No…?" I asked, and she shook her head, "No... I don't like the belt. Or the color, for that matter."

The next dress was a crisp white ball gown with spaghetti straps, a v-neckline, and layers and layers of tulle.

"How about this one?" the consultant wanted to know.
Lilian tilted her head from side to side, "I don't know…"
I agreed, "I don't know if white suits you…"
Nodding slowly, Lilian looked at the other dresses the consultant pulled for her, "Do you… Do you have anything in black?" she asked.
Grinning from ear to ear, the consultant nodded, "I was hoping you'd ask. I will be right back."
She took away all of the dresses that she had brought originally, and came back a little while later with arms full of black lace and tulle and chiffon. Lilian grinned like it was Christmas morning.
She tried on a black mermaid-style dress, but she said it was uncomfortable. Similarly, she didn't like the sheath dress because she said it reminded her of a negligee.
When she finally settled on a dress, I felt like crying; it was so perfect. A form-fitting gown with black lace sleeves, a skirt with layers upon layers of black chiffon, and a thigh high slit on the right.
It was alternative, fun, unexpected, and utterly, perfectly Lilian.

∞

"I have never, ever been in here," Lilian grinned early that evening as we walked into Jonathan's apartment.
I managed to convince her to spend the night at Jonathan's apartment with me instead of going to Nathaniel's place elsewhere in the city.
I smiled, "It was a first for me as well."
"Wow…" Lilian breathed in awe, looking around the apartment, "so this is how the Royal Family lives…"
I shrugged, "Yeah... In the jet on my way here…" I went on, but Lilian interrupted me, her eyes wide, "You flew to New York in His Majesty's jet?"
I laughed, "Lil, you can just call him Jonathan. He's not going to eat you."
Lilian widened her eyes, "Oh wow, I feel very important now."

"My life has certainly become very interesting," I said as we sat down on the sofa, each with a glass of wine, "Being with Jonathan…. Everything is new…"
"But dating an Infinite as a mortal is hard," Lilian added, and I couldn't agree more. "It is. Especially because you don't have anyone to talk to."

She nodded in agreement, "That was hard for me too."
"Did Nathaniel turn you?" I wanted to know, and Lilian nodded, "Yes, finally, in 1978, after 5 years of me begging him to."
"How did you find out his truth?"
Lilian giggled, "It was so stupid. We went for a stroll, and I fell and a rock on the ground cut my leg pretty bad," she lifted her leg onto the sofa and pointed to a scar on her shin, "There was blood everywhere, and I saw his fangs on accident."
"How did you handle it?"
"I threw a wobbly. Pounced on him like a wildcat and attacked him with the rock that cut my leg," Lilian said, and I couldn't help but laugh. Lilian went on, "I was gobsmacked. Took me a while to adjust to the idea." A tender smile appeared on her face, "But by then I was already done for, head over heels for the man."
"Been there," I responded, clinking my glass against Lilian's.
"How did you find out about His… I mean, Jonathan?" she wanted to know.
"A nascent almost attacked me, and he saved my life, wings and claws and all."
Her jaw dropped, "Whoa… That must have been aces. Bloody terrifying, of course, but still."
I smiled, "At the time it was just terrifying."
"And you couldn't talk to anyone about it?" Lilian guessed.
I nodded slowly, "Still can't. My friend is under the impression he's a drug kingpin…"
Lilian laughed out loud at the idea. I continued, "But I can never tell her the truth, that he's the Prince."
Lilian nodded, "My friends also thought Nathaniel was some kind of gangster, they were scared shitless of him."

I poured us some more wine, "Until your party, I don't think I fully understood the weight of who Jonathan is. Not until I saw everyone bowing to him."
Lilian nodded, "I'm going to be honest with you, at the beginning I didn't get it either. But after Nathaniel told me what he did for them in the war… Then I got it."
My eyes widened, "See, he doesn't tell me these things. He fought in the Civil War?"

Lilian shook her head, “He didn’t fight. He didn’t have to. Nathaniel said he descended upon them like the Archangel Michael, and just…” she imitated a bomb going off, “Obliterated.”
I had goosebumps.
Lilian shrugged, “That’s why I call him ‘Majesty’. That’s who he is, The Undeniable.”

Chapter 49

Kirill

From the moment I set foot inside the apartment building, I knew something was wrong.
The smell of blood hung in the air, like fog off a riverbank. The strong, overwhelming scent of it led me down a familiar hallway, and right down… to Devyn's apartment.
Something's wrong. The door isn't closed.
I used my sleeve to push open the door and slowly, carefully stepped inside.
What I saw made me sick to my stomach:
Blood.
Blood everywhere. All over the floor, on the kitchen counter, the sofa, and smeared on the walls.
"Devyn…?" I called out, but there was no answer.
I followed the scent, getting stronger toward the bedroom, and when I opened the door, an invisible fist knocked the wind out of me and I dropped to my knees:
Devyn.
Lying next to the bed on the floor, in a pool of blood. Her blood, that had flown out of the open wounds all over her body.
Her eyes were still open, but she was gone.

Someone screamed in anguish, cursed at the heavens, and it wasn't until silence descended once again that I realized that it had been me screaming.
And when I saw the mark of Apollo drawn on her forehead in her own blood, my anger flared up again. *Those fuckers. They killed her. And for what? For sport?*

I didn't know what to do.
So, I did the only thing I could: I called Vanya.

He arrived a few minutes later, but my scream had already alerted the neighbors. Someone called the police when they saw the blood, and I had to get out of the building.

Jonathan

I put a hand on Kirill's shoulder and closed my eyes to pray for Devyn's soul.
"It was those Apollo bitches," Kirill said. He gave up on English and was speaking Russian.
"The mark was drawn on her forehead?" I asked, and he nodded.
I contemplated the information for a moment, "I need to get in there, but…" I stopped talking when a police officer approached us.
"Officer," I acknowledged.
The police officer nodded, "Afternoon gents. Do you live in the building?"
I shook my head, "No, officer."
"So, you didn't see anything?"
I shook my head again, "No… Officer, what happened?"
The officer looked over his shoulder at the building and grimaced, shaking his head, "This whole fuckin' world is going to Hell in a handbasket, that's what."
He turned back to me and handed me a business card, "If you hear anything, or if you can think of anything, give me a call."

A familiar sound behind me made me turn around. Christina's car. She just pulled up to the building, "Fuck. She doesn't know."
She had texted me that she was on her way back from New York, but I didn't know that she'd be coming here.
She stepped out of the car and she smiled when she saw me, but she was obviously confused.
"Babe, hi," she greeted me with a hug, "what are you guys doing here?" she asked, pointing to me and to Kirill where he was standing a few yards away.
"Christina…" I started, but she was distracted, "Babe, I will talk to you in a sec, let me just go say hi to Devyn, this is her building…"
Then she frowned, "Why are the police here?"
I put my hands on her shoulders, "Christina…"
Her face paled, "Did something happen? Is Devyn okay…? Where…?"
I shook my head.

“Where’s my friend?” she asked, panic rising in her voice, “I want to see my friend, where is she?
I didn’t say anything, and the silence answered her question better than words could have.
“No…” Christina’s knees buckled and I caught her before she went down. “No! Devyn!” she screamed, and she tried to squirm out of my arms to get to the building, but I wouldn’t let go. “Devyn!” she screamed again.
I held her tighter, “She’s gone. I’m sorry,” I whispered against her hair, and I felt her tears falling on my arm.
“She’s gone…” I said again, and Christina’s body slumped.
“Devyn…” she whispered once more before she collapsed and pressed her face into my chest, and I was glad that she didn’t see the coroner wheel Devyn’s body out of the building on a gurney, zipped up in a dull black body bag.

I was well acquainted with Death. I understood the significance, the inevitability of it. I’d been around it, seen it, prevented it, and even brought it about more times than I cared to admit throughout my life. But no matter how many times I have had to deal with Death, nothing seemed to lessen the sting of it when it stretched its bony hand so close to home and hurt the woman I loved. Today, Death took away Christina’s best friend.
I looked down at Christina, stroking her hair, and I hated knowing that there was nothing I could do to ease her pain.
I took her home, and Belinda tucked her into bed. I stayed with her until she fell asleep, then I went back to Devyn’s apartment. Kirill wanted to join me, but I sent him back to the house.

I took a deep breath before I ducked in underneath the police tape and went into the empty, blood-smeared apartment and sniffed the air. There had definitely been a struggle in the living room. A vase was smashed against the wall, thrown from the other side of the room. The coffee table was crushed, an armchair turned over, some faint scorch marks on the sofa. Blood spatters against the wall in the hallway.
Devyn’s blood.
There was a lot of it, but I doubted that all of it was as a result of the struggle.

Whoever did this wanted to shock. They smeared blood everywhere after Devyn was already…
I followed the trail into the bedroom.
When I saw the pool of blood, I felt the same anger that Kirill had felt. So much sacred blood, an innocent life taken.
I closed my eyes for a moment, praying that Devyn's soul would find eternal rest and peace in the afterlife.
Then I got down on my haunches and sniffed the air again, and I frowned.
An Infinite was here, the scent was much too old to be nascent.
I sniffed again.
Two.
Two Infinites were in here. Old ones.
I could smell that Kirill was here, but the scent of the other two were stronger. They were here for longer. One male… the other female.
And at least one of them was pyrokinetic, judging by the scorch marks.
A pyro? That's impossible. Unless…
I slowly made my way back out of the apartment, careful not to disturb anything.
Kirill had told me that Devyn had the mark of Apollo drawn on her forehead. But that didn't make sense. The House didn't have any Infinites. They only had nascent, and nascent didn't have any abilities.
There was no Infinite that abided by the Laws of Night, that would have done this. Whoever did this, was guided by chaos.
This couldn't have been an Infinite.
Vampires did this.

Chapter 50

Christina

On the day of Devyn's funeral, the weather was perfect on purpose.
The sun was shining, and a light breeze was blowing.
I had no more tears left to cry. I cried everything out when Jonathan told me that a vampire killed my best friend.
He called them vampires, he said it couldn't have been any Infinite that he knew. I understood that the police weren't going to find much, I just wished that there was some way that I could explain it to Devyn's family, a way to help them understand this senseless loss of their daughter's life, and to help them find closure.
But there was nothing I could say to lessen their pain.

I looked around the church yard, but my eyes weren't really focusing on anything.
I went over to Kirill where he was standing by himself. I half-smiled.
He's wearing a suit.
"Nuchka," he said when he saw me approach.
"Hi," I replied, holding out my arms to hug him. He had to be having a hard time; he was the one that found Devyn. When he pulled back he just nodded, turned around, and walked to the far corner of the yard.
Poor guy.

My mom stepped up behind me and squeezed my shoulder, and I walked into my mom's hug. Magnus was standing next to my mom, and he put a hand on my arm, "I'm sorry for your loss."
Just behind my mom and Magnus, I saw Devyn's family.

I'd met them a few times over the years, and even though I wasn't that close with them, I wanted to pay my respects so I slowly made my way over to them.
"Mrs. Simms?" I said tentatively as I approached. Devyn's mom turned around and gave me a kind smile, "Oh, baby. She loved you so much."
That did it.
I thought that I was done crying, but tears ran down my face once again when Devyn's mom called me 'baby' and pulled me in for a hug. Then Devyn's dad hugged me as well, "You were such a good friend to my daughter. Thank you."
When I took a step back, I turned around and saw Jonathan.

He was just a few steps behind me. As he always was when I needed him. Right there beside me.
My feet moved by themselves, carrying me right into his waiting arms. He held me, stroking my hair, his lips against the top of my head, "I'm so sorry for your pain, darling," he said softly.
"I was a bad friend…" I whispered.
He put his finger under my chin to make me look at him, "No. Why would you say that?"
I took a shaky breath, "I didn't spend enough time with her…" I sniffed, "When I called her and she didn't answer I should have called again, I should have tried harder…" my voice broke and Jonathan pulled my head to his chest again, 'No, stop," he said firmly but gently. "This was not your fault. There was nothing you could have done."
"I could have gone to her, instead of going to New York…" I sniffled, "If I had just stayed in my lane, if I had gone to Devyn, then maybe…"
"Then maybe we would have buried both of you today," Jonathan ended my sentence.

The pastor delivered a beautiful sermon.
At least, I assumed it was beautiful. I didn't hear much of it. I was staring at Devyn's photo at the front of the church, next to her coffin. It was her graduation photo. She was so happy that day. I'd always remember that smile, so bright it should have had its own unit of measurement.

I didn't even know how it happened, but when the pastor asked if anyone wanted to say something, I found myself standing up and walking to the pulpit.

But once I was up there, it took several gulps and a few deep breaths before I was able to speak,

"Today, I have to say goodbye to my best friend, Devyn, the kindest soul and the most vibrant heart I have ever known.

She was always the strong one, and aside from being my best friend, she was also a sister to me. And I knew I could always count on her, no matter the hour.

Everyone who knew her, loved her, and anyone that didn't, needed to get their head examined, because she was amazing."

My voice cracked, and I wiped my tears with the back of my hand.

I closed my eyes and gripped the sides of the pulpit, and I felt Jonathan's arm circle my waist. He was holding me up. I opened my eyes and looked briefly at him before I squeezed his arm and turned to the coffin, "Dev, I am crippled without you. You're leaving us all lost in the dark without your light."

I sniffled, "But, hey, you go get some rest, okay? I'm not mad. I'm just sad. But like you said to me once, how are we going to appreciate the sun if it never rains?"

Chapter 51

Christina

Everything feels heavy.
My head, my body, my heart, my soul. And all I wanted to do was stay in bed. I wanted to sleep for weeks and weeks and wake up when the hole in my chest felt smaller and hurt less. I wanted to be alone, but Jonathan wouldn't let me, so I was staying with him at the manor.
I didn't want to scroll social media anymore, because all I saw were posts and funny pictures that made me think of Devyn. She would have been the first person that I would have sent them to.
And Devyn was gone.

The pain in my chest was a living thing that moved and breathed with me. I didn't want to eat, because anything I ate would just be fuel for the pain, and it would just keep getting bigger and stronger and more intense.
I wanted to cry, but the tears wouldn't come anymore. There were moments when one or two teardrops escaped and ran down my cheeks, but that was it. My sadness and my grief stayed locked-up in my chest, because what was the point? No amount of grief or screaming or crying would change the fact that Devyn was murdered in her apartment, and that she lay there for who knows how long until Kirill found her.
No amount of talking about it was going to change anything about the fact that my best friend died, scared and alone.

I knew what Jonathan said to me at the funeral was true, that if I had been there with Devyn, both of us might have ended up dead, but that didn't really make me feel any less guilty for not being a better friend to Devyn in the final days of her life.

All I did was look at the photos of Devyn that I had on my phone.

All I could do was sit in the dark of Jonathan's room and think about my best friend.

I didn't want to wash up or brush my teeth or take a bath, but Jonathan went to so much trouble to bring me to the bathroom every morning to wash my face, and he ran me a bath every night, and I didn't want to tell him 'no' and throw his kindness back in his face. Maybe I'd wake up one morning and feel like I can breathe on my own again.

Jonathan

For the first few days after Devyn's funeral, I let Christina be.
If she wanted to stay in bed all day, I let her.
If she wanted to spend the day in Niki's library, she could.
If she wanted to sit on the sofa in my room the entire afternoon, that was fine.
But I didn't want grief to consume her, so by the start of the second week, I wanted to do something to help her.
So I put on my training gear and got hers ready, and I waited on the bench by the bed for her to wake up.
"Hi," she mumbled softly when she opened her eyes.
I got to my feet and leaned over to kiss her, "Morning, love."
Then I grabbed the edge of the covers and opened them.
She frowned, "Babe, no. I don't want to get up."
I shook my head, scooped her up in my arms and lifted her out of bed, "Well, today you are. You're getting up and moving, whether you want to or not," I said as I set her feet down on the floor.
She folded her arms across her chest, "Please, I don't want to do anything."
I handed her her training gear, "I love you, but I don't care. You have ten minutes to put that on and meet me in the octagon."
She looked at me incredulously, "And if I don't?"
I started down the steps, "Then I will come back here and dress you myself."
I really would, so I was glad that she started putting on the gear that I gave her before I left the room and went to the gym.

She finally arrived at the octagon about fifteen minutes later.
"You're late," I said, "I said ten minutes."
"And I said I didn't want to get up," she replied.
I pulled up my shoulders, "Well, you're up and you're here, so get in."
"Jonathan…" She said, "I really don't want to be here right now."
I held my arms out at my sides, "And I really don't want you spending another day in bed. So…"
Christina rolled her eyes, but I shook my head, "Darling, you need to climb in here, before I come back down there and put you in."

She groaned in annoyance, but climbed into the octagon. Once inside, she gave me a questioning look, "Now what?"
I held out a pair of hapkido gloves to her, "Here, put these on."
She groaned, "No…"
"Christina," I said sharply, "I will not tell you again."
She frowned and glared daggers at me, "Excuse me? I'm not one of your subjects, do not talk to me like that."
I gave her a similar look, "Stop whining and do as you're told."
She grunted in anger and slapped the gloves out of my hands.
"Good! Get angry," I said, pointing at the gloves on the floor. "Pick them up, put them on and hit me."
"You're out of your mind," she denied, "I'm not going to hit you."
"Why not?" I challenged, "Would you rather just go back to bed and mope over your dead friend? Maybe blame yourself some more?"
Christina's jaw dropped and angry tears filled her eyes, "How dare you!" she yelled as she picked up the gloves and threw them at me, "You have no idea what I'm going through!" she screamed and threw a punch in my direction. I raised my hand and her fist hit the center of my palm.
"Again!" I yelled back, "Hit me!"
"This is your fault!" she screamed, punching again, "I lost my best friend because of you!"
"Really?" The accusation was unfounded and I knew she didn't mean it, but I needed her to react, to feel, "Tell me how!"
She threw another punch, "Your kind did this! A fucking vampire killed my friend! She's dead. Devyn is gone. My best friend is dead. Dead!
Dead!
Dead…"
She kept punching, screaming the word until it got stuck in her throat and turned into a guttural, keening wail and she collapsed into my arms, sobbing.
I sank down onto the floor of the octagon with Christina in my arms, stroking her hair as she cried. I hated seeing her in pain like this, but she needed to feel, to cry, and to grieve the loss of her best friend, and not just ignore the pain and hold back the tears every time they threatened to overtake her. I'd seen her blink away the tears too many times.

"It's alright, my love," I said softly, gently rocking her back and forth. "It hurts, I know. But you can't ignore the pain, or it will consume you later, trust me. Let it in, feel it. And let it out."

"You don't know how I feel," she sobbed.

I stroked her hair, "I do, love, I do. I've held friends as they breathed their last. Death has been a constant companion of mine for almost nine centuries, I've lost more friends than I can count. I do know how you feel."

I held her until her tears subsided, and when she eventually sat up, I kissed her forehead and wiped the tears from her face.

Then she opened her eyes and looked at me, "You're a shit," she accused me tearfully.

I kissed her forehead again, smiling at her, "I know I am."

"And you're an asshole."

"That too," I nodded.

She sighed and leaned her head against my chest, "I'm sorry… for what I said. It's not your fault." I just wrapped my arms around her. I knew that.

"How's Kirill doing?" she asked and I shrugged, "I honestly have no idea," I said, "he dropped off the face of the earth again."

She lifted her head and looked questioningly at me, "You have no idea where he went?"

I shook my head, "No… This is his way of coping. He'll resurface at some point."

After a few moments of silence, she spoke again, "Can you promise me something?"

"Of course."

"When you find the sons-of-bitches that killed Devyn, please, promise me you'll make them suffer?"

I nodded, "I'll find them, I swear. To Heaven and the light of the Moon."

Chapter 52

Christina

After spending a little over three weeks at Jonathan's house, it was time for me to go back to my own house.

Sitting in the back of the car as Simon drove me home, I tried to think of a way to thank Jonathan and his family for being so kind and supportive, although I was pretty sure there was no gift that they would actually accept.

Jonathan helped me recognize my pain and grief, helped me understand that it was important to feel the pain and to not let it turn into helplessness. He gave me time to grieve, but he didn't let me wallow in it, which I absolutely would have done if he didn't physically drag me out of bed.

When he wasn't around, Celeste was there for me. She always made sure that I ate–usually too much. In that sense, Celeste reminded me so much of my own mom. She was so kind and nurturing.

Niki's idea of helping was to distract me by taking me to art exhibitions, playing pool with me, or just telling me ridiculous stories from growing up with Jonathan as an older brother.

He never really talked much about his childhood, so I had no notion of what he was like growing up. Pretty much everything that Niki told me came as a surprise. He was so calm and collected most of the time, that it was hard to believe that he was such a troublemaker when he was at school. He was a lot older than Niki, so they were never in school at the same time, but each time Niki enrolled in a school where he used to go, there were always urban legends that Niki knew were based on her brother's exploits. Of course, there was never any proof that he actually did anything, but their parents knew…

My favorite story was the time he was so proud of his little sister when her and Kat were arrested in the Czech Republic, that he had t-shirts printed with Niki's mugshot.
And he still had the t-shirts.

Even Alastair helped to distract me from my grief. He taught me a few tricks about growing bonsais, and even though I was probably never going to use the information, I appreciated him taking the time.
I smiled to myself. I was always going to miss Devyn, and I would always be grateful to have had such a wonderful best friend. But as much as I was going to miss her, I also knew that Devyn wouldn't want me to grieve forever. She'd want me to live my life as best I could. On purpose.
So that was exactly what I was going to do.

When I got home, I took my luggage to my room, and then I went to find my mom.
I found her in her room, reading a book by the window.
"Hi, Mom," I smiled as I peered around the bedroom door.
She looked up from her book and grinned when she saw me "Chrissie-bear!" she beamed, "Welcome home, wayward citizen!"
I hopped over to her to hug her hello before sitting down on the edge of the bed, "Did you miss me?"
My mom closed her book and nodded, "Of course I did! The house was eerily quiet without you."
I smiled, "I missed you too. So, I came up with a plan for us to spend the rest of this weekend together. If you don't already have plans with the handsome Mr. Andreassen, that is…" I teased, and it delighted me to see my mom blush like a schoolgirl.
"I hope you're okay with it," my mom asked.
"With what? You dating Magnus?"
She shrugged, "With me dating, period."
I threw my arms around my mom for another hug, "Of course I am, Mom. I just want you to be happy."
She returned the hug, "I promise I am, especially now that my little girl is back home."
I pulled back and took her hands, "About my plan for the weekend, I thought we could do some pottery painting. Celeste told me about a great little studio in town.

Then tonight we do a movie marathon, you can choose the movies. Tomorrow morning we're going to the Farmer's Market, and then I want to take you to lunch. How does that sound?"
My mom stood up out of her chair, a wide smile on her face, "That sounds perfect!"
"Yay! Then let's get going."

Just as I had hoped, the weekend with my mom was precisely what the doctor ordered.
The studio that Celeste recommended was even better than she had described, and my mom and I left with a couple of really pretty vases. We needed some new ones anyway.
For our movie marathon, my mom wanted to do Bad Movie night, and she chose a few truly horrendous titles. I'd almost forgotten how much fun it was critiquing movies with my mom and making up our own bad dialogue.
When the alarm went off early that next morning, I almost regretted saying that we should go to the Farmer's Market… until I saw my mom dressed and ready to go. Obviously, seeing her so excited, there was no way I could cancel.

And I was glad I didn't. It was a lot more interesting than I thought, and I didn't realize how many unique products were available in our area.
For lunch, I really wanted to take my mom somewhere nice, so while she was talking to a jam vendor about their preferred methods of bottling jam, I texted Alastair to ask if it would be possible to get a table at that restaurant where he took me that one time. I was impressed when he was quicker to respond than his son:
Of course, dear one.
Your table will be ready when you arrive.
Lunch is on me.
Have a lovely day with your mother.

At the restaurant, my mom couldn't get enough of the interior of the place.
"Honey," she gushed after the waiter escorted us to our table, "how did we get a table? This place is really exclusive!"
I shrugged nonchalantly, "I know people…"

My mom laughed… until she saw the prices on the menu. Then her eyes widened, "Christina, sweetie, no, we need to go. These prices…"
I waved a dismissive hand, "It's okay, Mom. I've got it."
Her eyes widened, "Honey, I know you've been working a lot but this place is way out of our price range. How is it that you 'got it'?"
I smiled secretively, "Easy. I'll just use my card from the bank of TrophyWife."
My mom laughed, "Oh my gosh, I've created a monster."

Chapter 53

Celeste

I found it suspicious that Jonathan asked me to meet him in his father's study while Alastair was out of town. Once I went inside, he locked the door and motioned toward the desk for me to sit down.

"Alright," I said once I took my seat, "what did you want to talk to me about?

He took a seat across from me at the desk and started piling files and folders and documents onto the desk, "I want to bring you up to speed on what's been going on."

I nodded apprehensively, "Very well…"

He took a deep breath, "The House of Apollo appears to have gotten their hands on our family's DNA and they have used it to make their own vampire."

My face paled, "What…? How…?"

He shook his head, "I don't know, Mami, not yet. The man that drugged Christina told Kirill that they made a serum, but he didn't know how they did it."

I was shocked. I could hardly believe my ears, but I motioned for him to proceed.

"I don't have conclusive proof, but I have a suspicion that the House has relocated to Germany. There's been a lot of deaths in Europe lately, and it seems like they started in Germany. Three hikers were murdered in a local forest. Their deaths were made to look like predators had attacked the hikers, but I'm not convinced that was what really happened."

He gave me a moment to look over the autopsy reports of the three German victims before he went on. "The House seems to have completed a full transformation, and I think their little lab rat has been hunting, and making more vampires."
I raised my eyebrows, asking for clarification. He pointed to a stack of reports, "Murders across Europe, too random to have no connection. The randomness is too specific. Look, Eindhoven, Brussels, Birmingham, Plymouth, London. There have been several murders in London, either in dangerous neighborhoods, or vagrants."
"So, they're either practicing or feeding," I thought out loud.
He nodded in agreement, "The attacks all appear to radiate from London; they seem to have chosen it as their hunting ground. Lilian mentioned that she took down a nascent that killed five homeless in one night."

I made a move to stand up from the desk, but Jonathan wasn't finished, "Mami, how sure are you that you were the only survivor the night our family was attacked?"
My jaw clenched, "I have nothing to convince me otherwise. Why?"
My son knew he was treading into dangerous territory, "The vampires that killed Devyn…"
"Kirill said that he found the mark of Apollo at the scene," I said, switching to Greek.
Jonathan sighed softly, "You're angry, I understand, but I had no intention of upsetting you. And I know what Kirill said. I know what he found, I was at the scene, but I don't know that I'm convinced that the House did it. That has never been their modus operandi," he continued, "The vampires that killed Devyn were much too old to be nascent. There were two, I could smell them, and one of them was a pyro. You know as well as I do that only Genitori descendants have that ability."

Jonathan glanced down at my hands. I followed his gaze. My claws were slowly appearing, "My family would never do such a thing."
"No-one is accusing your family, Mother. But the beasts that murdered Christina's friend were not Infinite. They were savages that do not live by our code," my son said.

I slowly stood up from the desk, my arms folded, and paced to the window, "I searched everywhere I could…" I started, "that night. In the fire and the chaos. I tried to find my family, to save them," my voice started trembling, and Jonathan got to his feet and came to stand next to me.
I leaned my head against my son's shoulder, "I found them, Papa, Mama, little Sophia… but I…" my breath was shaky, "I didn't find Silas. My baby brother was gone. I wanted to search more, but one of the servants grabbed me from the dirt and took me away… and I… I didn't find Silas."
Jonathan wrapped his arm around my shoulders and hugged me, "So even though it is improbable, it is possible that my uncle survived that night?"
I nodded, tears welling up in my eyes, "When I was finally able to go back there, so many years later, it was too late…"
I lifted my head and turned to look at Jonathan, "And now you seem to have an uncle, or perhaps a cousin running amok in the world."
Jonathan kissed my cheek before he turned to leave the study.
"Sweetheart," I said as he was about to leave, "They have to be stopped. And they broke the Laws of Night. So, when you find them: Bring the noise."

Chapter 54

Christina

I wasn't sure why I woke up early on Monday morning, but since I was up anyway, I thought maybe I could have breakfast with my mom before she went to work.

"Morning, Mom," I smiled sleepily when I came into the kitchen.

My mom didn't answer. She was staring at the newspaper, her eyes wide in what appeared to be shock or horror. I wasn't sure which it was, but I didn't like it.

"Mommy?" I asked, worried, my hand on my mom's shoulder.

Her eyes not leaving the page, my mom pointed to an article, "Honey… have you seen this?"

"Seen what, Mom…?" I leaned in to read the article and the first line made my skin go all clammy and cold,

'The body of Owen North, a local vehicle salesman, was found dead in an alleyway, completely drained of blood….'

I didn't read any further than that and I sank down in the chair next to my mom, "Holy shit." She nodded slowly, "You can say that again."

I waited until my mom left for work, then I brushed my teeth and changed my clothes, grabbed the newspaper and jumped in my car.

I had no idea how I got to the Langdon manor so quickly, and I didn't disregard the possibility that I may have skipped a few red lights on the way.

Oswald opened the door for me, and I marched up the stairs and straight down the hall to Jonathan's room.

He was still in bed when I flung the door open and yelled, "Did you do this?"

The sound of me yelling at him must have startled him, and he sat up in bed.

He glanced down at me in disbelief where I was standing by the sofa, newspaper in hand, tapping my foot impatiently at him, "Well?" I prompted. He stood up out of bed and zipped down to me.

He came right up to me, his body about an inch away from mine, "Don't tap your little foot at me, Christina. What are you talking about? Did I do what?" he asked ominously.

I pointed at the article in the paper, but he didn't even look, "What is that?"

"Owen is dead, Jonathan," I exclaimed.

"Tragic," he replied emotionlessly, "How is that my problem?"

I whacked him across the chest with the rolled-up newspaper, "Did you do this?"

His eyes darkened, "Did you really just hit me with a rolled-up newspaper? Like a dog that pissed the carpet?"

I didn't answer; I just whacked him again.

Suddenly, Jonathan picked me up under his one arm like I was a puppy, carried me up the stairs at Infinite speed and flung me down on the bed.

He dropped down on top of me on the bed and pinned my wrists down on either side of my head.

He leaned in really close to my face, fangs bared, and he spoke through his clenched teeth, "Do. Not. Accuse me."

My eyes widened, "Are you threatening me?"

"No," he growled, before he ran the tip of his tongue all the way from my earlobe, across my jaw, to my chin and then kissed me roughly, "I'm advising you."

He let go of my wrists and stood back up, "I didn't touch him."

I propped myself up on my elbows, "Did you send someone?"

Jonathan frowned at me incredulously, "Are you seriously asking me if I put a hit out on your ex?"

"Did you?" I demanded.

He scoffed in disbelief. I got to my feet and shoved him against the chest, "Answer me, Jonathan!"

He looked up at me from underneath his eyebrows and cricked his neck to one side, "Christina, I swear, if you push me like that again…"

I raised my eyebrows, "Then what? Huh? What are you going to do?"

Before I could blink, he put my wrists together behind my back and held them there with one hand and kissed me again, his tongue aggressively seeking mine.
Then he took my chin in his hand, “I am going to drag you across my lap and spank you.”
I gasped and my thighs pressed together at the thought.
He grinned, “Are you horny for me already, so early in the morning?”
“Spank me?”
Jonathan scanned me up and down, “Don’t kink shame me, darling, you have no idea what goes on in my head when I see you.”
I shouldn’t let him do this. I’m not sure if it’s on purpose or not, but it doesn't take a genius to figure out that I'm not happy, and now he’s distracting me with sex. At the same time though…
“What if I wanted to know…?” I challenged… and pushed him again.
He inclined his head, “As you wish,” he replied.
In one swift movement he put his foot up on the bed, draped me over his bent knee and spanked my ass three times. Then he spun me back to look at him. My jaw slacked in surprise, but without breaking eye contact, he stuck two fingers in his mouth before he shoved his hand in under my skirt, yanked my panty aside and sunk those same two fingers inside me.
I moaned, and he immediately covered my mouth with his other hand, “Shh,” he whispered, “my parents are awake and the door isn’t locked.”
“Shit…” I whispered, “We should lock it first.”

His tongue rolled across the middle of his lower lip and he shook his head, then he pulled his hand back and sank his fingers into me as deep as he could go, “No, I already have my fingers inside your pussy, and you feel really fucking good, so I’m not stopping. I think I’m just going to finger your pussy, and you’re going to have to come for me quietly. Can you do that?”
I nodded. I could hear my own wetness when he drew his hand back and plunged his fingers into me again, and again, and when he started pressing and rubbing circles against my clit with his thumb, it drove me right over the edge of rapture. He grinned at me in wicked delight as my back arched in ecstasy, and I clung to him to hold myself upright, but not a single sound escaped my lips.

When my body relaxed, he withdrew his hand, “Good girl,” he said before sticking his fingers in his mouth.

“Hmm,” he mused, “delicious as always.”

Oh, fuck me.

He reached for me to pull me against him, but I held up a hand, “Wait.”

Jonathan eyed me skeptically, “Why…?”

“Because I don’t want to go to bed with you right now.”

He shrugged, “Who said it had to be the bed? I’ll just fuck you against the wall.”

It took a lot of willpower for me not to give in to him and just let him do what he wanted to my body.

Jonathan pulled me back against him, his lips right next to my ear, “Protest all you want, darling. I know your pussy wants my cock.”

As right as he was, I was not going to give him the satisfaction of admitting it, and I rolled my eyes at him, “Oh, please, just because you made me orgasm doesn’t mean…”

He gripped my ass, “Doesn’t mean what?”

I put my hands against his chest and pushed him back, “Jonathan…”

He immediately let go of me and took a step back, “Do you want me to stop?”

I didn’t reply, and he lifted my chin so I looked him in the eyes, “Would you like me to stop?”

Having him so close to me, inches away from his warm skin, I was trapped under his spell again. My body betrayed me, as it always did where Jonathan was concerned, and desire pooled in the pit of my stomach.

“No…” I whispered.

He looked at me in silence for a moment... then zipped to the door to lock it and came right back to me.

I gave him a pointed look, “Can I at least take my shoes off before you jump me?”

He didn’t answer; he only gestured for me to continue.

When my second shoe dropped to the floor, he stepped closer and traced the line of my jaw with his finger.

He smiled, “Am I making you nervous?”

I shook my head, “Not nervous, horny…”

I looked him up and down. My eyes stopped at his lower body for a moment, then I looked up at his face, "Is that a gun, or are you just happy to see me?"

Jonathan toppled me over onto the bed and pressed himself against me, "That's what happens when you burst in here and you start shoving me around."

I put my hands on his lower back and pulled him closer, "Please stop talking and kiss me."

"Yes ma'am," he replied before he pressed his lips to mine.

His tongue against mine, I could feel him move my skirt up and pull my panties down.

He sat back on his knees to grab the hem of my shirt and whipped it off over my head.

When he looked down at me, he smiled, "No bra this morning?"

"I left the house in a hurry."

He drew a breath between his clenched teeth, "Aren't I a lucky boy."

Jonathan lowered his head to the top of my skirt and, very lightly, very softly, kissed my bare stomach. I gasped, and he inched higher and higher until his lips and his teeth found my nipples. My back arched, pressing my body closer to him. He held my body against his, his tongue flicking across my nipples until I moaned in need.

His teeth still clamped around my nipple, he reached down and ran his hand up the side of my thigh. When he reached the top of my leg, he moved his lips to my throat and his hand shifted to my inner thigh. My leg wrapped around him as his fingers softly caressed me, and I moaned when he slipped the tip of his finger inside me and I heard a growl rumble in his throat.

Then he kissed me again.

"Jonathan," I mumbled.

"Yes, love?"

"Why do you still have your pants on?"

Chuckling, he got to his feet, "How inconsiderate of me, terribly sorry," he said, dropping his pants to the floor.

I sat up and took my panty all the way off, and I got to my feet to press my body against his and kiss him.

Jonathan pulled his head back and gave me a once-over, "You know… The way your skirt is sitting right at your waist… It reminds me a little bit of a bondage harness…"

As I kissed him in response, I reached down and wrapped my fingers around the base of his dick.
He groaned, and I shoved him onto the bed and straddled him.
I leaned over and kissed him, and he dug his fingers into my hair.
"Are you ready for me?" I asked against his lips.
He nodded his head once, "You never have to ask, love. If you want my cock, take it. Fuck me."
My eyes locked with his, and with my hand on his chest to steady myself, I guided him into me, gasping as he filled me.
"Ah, fuck…" I heard his voice rasp.
He wrapped his hands around my waist as I pressed myself against him, taking him as deep into me as I could.
Jonathan sat up, holding me tightly against him, "Take your time, darling," he breathed against my skin, "I'm not going anywhere."
And I tried, I really did, but I needed him, needed to feel him. Desperately, critically. And there was nothing I could do to stop myself from riding him at a faster pace than I knew was possible, until my entire body drew taut and I came apart on top of him.
Jonathan toppled me over and pinned me beneath him, and as much as I tried to have him take me faster, harder, he slowed me down. He took both my wrists in his one hand and pinned them above my head, forcing me to yield to him, to his slow, lingering, deliberate touch that transported me to a different plane of existence. To a world where nothing else existed, but him, and me, and this moment of having him inside me.
And as he found his release deep inside me, I felt alive again, for the first time in weeks.

Still resting on top of me, he lifted his head and smiled at me, "Good morning, by the way."
I laughed, "Morning, handsome."
He pressed another kiss to my lips before he stood up to put his pants on, then he sat down on the edge of the bed and looked at me.
"You need to stop distracting me with sex when you know I'm upset with you."
"Is that what you think I was doing?" he asked in a low voice.
I gave him a questioning look, "Wasn't it?"
He shook his head, "Not intentionally, no. But I can see why you would think that."

I shrugged, "That's what it looked like, so…"
He put his hand on his heart, "That was not at all what I was trying to do. I am sorry."
"Okay, thank you," I accepted his apology. Then he went on, "Now, to answer your question, no. I did not kill your ex, nor did I send a hitman to do it."
He was quiet for a moment before he said, "Although I was very tempted."
I nodded in acceptance and sat up next to him.
He took my hand and kissed the back of it, "As much as I would have wanted to get rid of him, there's been too much death around here lately; I wouldn't have done that to you."
He tucked my hair behind my ear, "And I'm sorry if it sounded like I was threatening you."
I shook my head and bit my lower lip, "I didn't dislike it…"
"Duly noted…"

I leaned against him and rested my head on his shoulder, "I'm sorry too, I didn't mean to accuse you. I was shocked when I saw the article that Owen was killed and…"
"It's alright," Jonathan said reassuringly, "I did say I was going to."
"How did he die?" he wanted to know.
I gestured with my head to where the newspaper had fallen to the floor, "Exsanguinated in an alley."
He nodded slowly, "In that case I really can't blame you for suspecting me. But if I had killed him, there would have been no corpse left behind. I clean up after myself."
I stood up from the bed to find my shirt, "Jonathan…" I said tentatively, "I'm going to level with you here. I'm getting paranoid."
He frowned, "About what…?"
I couldn't quite look him in the eye, "About… being with you."
"Christina…" he breathed, "Please, don't…"
I looked up and saw the fearful look on his face, and I realized what he had to be thinking to put that expression on his face. "Babe, come on, no. You need to stop thinking this way. I just had you dick-deep inside me, I'm not breaking up with you," I quickly corrected him, and he sat forward, his face in his hands, and breathed an audible sigh of relief.
"Thank the Moonlight," I heard him say.

It was heartbreaking how quickly he assumed that I didn't want to be with him anymore, as if that was even remotely possible. *I mean, how would I breathe?*

I stepped back into my panty before I sat down next to him on the bed. Jonathan lifted his head from out of his hands and looked at me, waiting for me to continue.

I took a deep breath, "I just have this… feeling of… impending doom, like something bad is going to happen. But at the same time, I know that even if something bad does happen, I will be safest if I'm at your side… Even if you are the harbinger of death."

Jonathan's face fell, "That's what you think I am?" and the hurt in his voice was really hard to hear.

"I'm not trying to hurt your feelings, babe," I went on, "But you said it yourself, death is your constant companion. I already lost my best friend… now my ex is dead…"

I released a fluttering breath, "I'm scared, Jonathan."

"Of me…?" he asked, worried.

I moved my hair away from my neck and shook my head, "No, not of you. Never of you. Of something happening to my mom. After losing Devyn… My mom is all I have left. If anything happens to her…"

I turned to face him, "I need my mom to be safe."

Jonathan nodded, "She will be, I swear. I've already increased security at your house."

The cold feeling of dread that had been holding my heart eased up and melted a little, "Really? You have? But… I didn't see anything. Or... anyone, for that matter."

He nodded, "You're not supposed to. But they are there, I swear. Between Magnus and myself, your mother is well-protected. Nothing and no-one is going to hurt her."

"Okay, but that's at the house. What about when she goes to work? Or to the store? What happens then?" I wanted to know.

He tilted his head to one side, "You're very good at underestimating me, aren't you?"

I blushed and he tapped the tip of my nose with his forefinger, "Darling, I swear, you mother is looked after and protected, 24 hours a day, 7 days a week."

I leaned over and kissed him deeply, "Thank you," I said when I pulled back.

He smiled, "Anything and everything for you, my love."
I forced a smile, and he frowned, "Oh… that was fake. Would you like to try again?"
I chuckled, "You know me too well."
He nodded, "Likewise. Now tell me, what else is bothering you?"
"I can't help but think…The vampires that attacked Devyn: What if they're the ones that killed Owen, too?"
"That is entirely possible, love," he replied.
"Who are they? What do they want?" I asked.
He sighed, stroking my hair, "I have my suspicions about who they are and what they might be planning, but I'm not certain. And I need to be sure before I say anything. For now, all I can tell you is that we are using all of our resources to track them down. I will find them. And I will stop them. I realize that that might not be good enough, but that is the best I can offer you right now."
He was right, it wasn't enough. But I trusted that he was giving me as much as he could. He always did.

Chapter 55

"I hate Germany," she complained, grimacing as she glanced around the square where we were sitting. We were having lunch at a charming little restaurant surrounded by lovely old buildings, and mildly interesting people milling about, but the look on her face spoke of soul-crushing boredom.

"I know," I retorted, "You've been saying that for eons."

She pulled an ugly face at me, "Then why are we here?"

"I told you already, I'm not telling you again," I said. *She's driving me crazy with her constant nagging.*

"I want to go home," she said.

"Then fucking go!" I snapped at her.

She sighed impatiently and folded her arms across her chest, "You're so impatient."

I took a deep breath, "Because you are driving me crazy, *solnyshka*." Little sun.

She locked her honey-colored eyes with mine, "I thought you loved that about me. *Zaichonok*." Bunny.

I put my hands over hers, "Of course I do, *malyshka*." Baby girl.

She smiled sweetly at me as she slowly pushed the steak knife from the table into the side of my thigh, "Then don't fucking snap at me," she hissed before jumping to her feet and storming off.

I winced as I pulled the knife out of my leg, glancing around to see if anyone had seen her stab me.

No-one seemed to be looking, so I left the blood-smeared knife on the table with the money for the bill and stormed after her.

I followed the heady scent of her perfume and found her a few blocks away, smoking a cigarette under a lamppost.

She glared at me as I approached, and she blew the smoke in my direction.
“Fine,” I sighed, “Sorry.”
She said nothing. She took another drag of the cigarette, blowing the smoke in my face.
“*Malyshka*, please,” I begged.
“Tell me again why you need me,” she demanded.
I held out a hand and she offered me a cigarette from the pack she was holding.
“Because a king is nothing without his queen,” I said after lighting myself a cigarette.
She leaned closer to me and licked the side of my face, “And don’t you fucking forget that.”

∞

“You know what I keep thinking of?” she said to me later.
She was sprawled across my chest, her feet hanging off the side of the bed.
“Of what, my queen?” I wanted to know.
She cackled before she answered, “How that girl screamed when she saw you standing in the door.”
I laughed, “Wasn’t it so funny when she threw that vase at your head?”
She cackled again, “As if that was going to do anything.”
I sighed and stroked her hair, “I just wish she’d put up more of a fight. She screamed, she ran, she died.”
She nodded, “I agree. She gave up so quickly, it was boring to watch.”
I reached for the cigarettes and lit one for each of us, “That guy in the alley by the gym was more fun.”
She burst out laughing, “I don’t think I have ever heard a man scream like that.”
I joined her laughter, “Pathetic. But an easy snack.”
She grimaced, “I didn’t like him, he tasted like dust.”
“Food is food, my queen. You needed to feed,” I tried to appease her.
“I know,” she pouted, “but that feisty girl tasted so much better. Why couldn’t we have just gone after her little blonde friend, hmm? *Moya lyubov'*?” My love.
I grabbed a fistful of her raven hair and yanked, “Not her! I told you! Fucking listen to me for once!” I yelled.
She slapped my hand away and slammed her elbow into my crotch.

As I lay on the bed, twisting and writhing in pain, she put her clothes on and left.

I woke up in the middle of the night to her going down on me, and I sighed at the sensation.
My queen always came back to me. She was my destiny.
I looked up at the mirrored ceiling, enjoying the sight of her head bobbing up and down in my lap. The future King and Queen.
We had taken a few days' vacation in our hotel room, but we had to get going soon.

Good things came to those who took it without asking. And the time had come for me to take what I was owed. And I knew where to start; I knew where the House of Apollo stationed their little secret lab. I'd been keeping tabs on their feeding frenzy in London, and as much as I appreciated the vigor and the effort, they need to do better. I didn't know much about them, only what my father told me before he died. The slave that saved him told him about our enemy, how the House of Apollo had been seeking our end since the days of my ancestors.
The way I saw it, why beat them or join them, when you could rule them? The loyal disciples were in desperate need of a real leader, and I was eager to meet my new subjects. But maybe the meeting should be postponed.
Maybe we needed to drop by the hunting grounds in London first…

Chapter 56

Christina

For the first time in my adult life, even though Jonathan and I hadn't been together all that long, I really felt like I was in a healthy relationship. I knew I could rely on Jonathan to be honest with me, as much as possible, and I trusted him with my entire life. He told me once that his mom had said that I made him a better person. I didn't know whether that was true or not, but being with him was definitely making me a better person. He had me thinking about my future, the kind of person I wanted to be. He taught me a little bit about how stocks and investments worked, and I felt like I finally knew how to be more financially responsible. I no longer felt like the naïve child I was when we first met.

He was the most selfless lover I'd ever had. He always put my pleasure before his own, and despite him being so much more experienced than I was, he always made me feel special, like I was the only woman he'd ever been with.

And even though he was the Infinite crown prince, our relationship didn't have an imbalance of power, and he never, ever lorded his status over me. Actually, I mentioned his title way more often than he did.

I'd learned so much since we started dating, and I felt like I was a better person for it.

On top of the fun things like a few new curse words in other languages, the main thing I learned was that, sometimes, it was okay to rely on people and that not everyone was going to let me down.

Not all that often, but it did happen once or twice that a random guy asked me for my number or my Snap. One guy pretended not to see Jonathan sitting right next to me, and handed me his number on a piece of paper.
I frowned as I took it from him, "And this is what, exactly?"
He winked at me, "Those are my digits. Call me."
Before I had a chance to respond, Jonathan gently took the paper from my hand, ripped it up and tossed the shreds onto the table, "She doesn't need your number, wankstain." My eyes widened a bit at the insult. *Never heard him use that one before. Wankstain? Hah! Nice.* He went on before the guy had a chance to say anything, "She already has mine."

So it wasn't that Jonathan was never jealous, because he definitely was, but his jealousy was never toxic, and it never scared me. And I never doubted his faithfulness to me. I never had to. We talked about it once, about my relationship with Owen and all the times he cheated on me and gaslit me to the point where I was starting to doubt that I ever saw the photos and the texts on his phone. That, or he twisted it so it was my fault...
After listening to me recount all the times I got my heart broken by Owen, Jonathan looked fairly pissed. But then he cupped my face in his hands and said, "I am not Owen."
I smiled, "I know. That's why I love you."
He went on, "If I ever see him again, it will be his last day on Earth."
"Babe..." I said softly, but Jonathan's face remained unyielding, "Justice be done."

Examining his handsome features, I smiled.
His perfectly golden skin, his silken black hair, those obsidian eyes that knew the contours of my soul, his soft, sensuous lips that kissed away my every fear, my every insecurity. This beautiful man was my lover and my best friend and I was genuinely happy with him.

"Why are you looking at me like that?" he asked me.
His warm, honey-caramel voice snapped me back to reality; I hadn't realized that I'd been staring at him.
I shook my head, "Nothing, babe. I was just thinking about some stuff."

He looked skeptically at me, "Right…"
I laughed, "I promise. I just got lost in my head for a moment, but nothing's wrong."
He pulled me closer to him where we were sitting on the sofa in his room. I swung my legs over his and rested my head against his chest. As he hugged me, I pressed my nose to his chest and breathed in the scent of his skin.
"There you go," he said, "sniffing me again."
I smiled flirtatiously at him, "Only because your shirt is in the way of me licking you."
He sat back and widened his eyes in pretend surprise, "Then I'll have to take it off immediately," and I laughed at him.
He tilted my chin up to kiss me and then smiled at me, "I had an idea."
I was just sitting there, tilting my head from side to side, examining his face, not really registering what he was saying.
"Darling…?" he said questioningly when I didn't answer.
I snapped back to reality again, "Sorry, babe."
He cupped my jaw with his hand, his eyes narrowed in concern, "Where's your head today, love?"
I looked him in the eye and grinned, "Somewhere under your clothes."
He rolled his eyes.
"What?" I asked in mock exasperation, "It is not my fault you're this hot."
Jonathan blushed a little bit, then he cleared his throat and changed the subject, "As I was saying, I had an idea."
I nodded, "Yes, take your clothes off, great idea."
He put his face in my neck and chuckled, "I'm serious," he said.
I nodded eagerly, "Me too."
Jonathan sighed, "I'm going to try again. I think we should go away somewhere for a few days."
"Ahh," I nodded, "and then you take your clothes off. Yes, even better."
Jonathan shook his head, "If you could just be serious for two minutes…"
I giggled and kissed his cheek, "Sorry babe," I apologized, wrapping my arm around his neck and squeezing him.
"Where do you want to go?" I asked him when I pulled back.
He pulled up his shoulders, "I don't mind. You can decide."

I was quiet for a moment, thinking about it, then I smiled, "Can we go back to the cabin?"

He mirrored my smile, "You want to go there again?" and I nodded, "I do. It was our first trip together, and I just… I really liked it there."

Jonathan kissed the tip of my nose, "It is a done deal then. Vermont it is."

"Can we drive there this time?" I asked hopefully. I'd secretly been wanting to go on a road trip with him, and maybe this could be it.

But he shook his head, "It's too far, love. It's about an 8-hour drive."

I grimaced, "Ohh… No, the jet sounds better."

I was really happy that Jonathan canceled all of his appointments and meetings for the weekend, and I was even happier that he was letting me help him pack and prepare for the weekend. Usually he did all the packing and prepping himself, and I figured it was probably difficult for him to let someone help him, but I was glad he was letting me in.

He was upstairs inside the closet looking for something, and I was downstairs, packing some things into the cooler box when I noticed that he hadn't packed himself any 'snacks' yet.

"Babe?" I called up to him.

"Yes my darling?" he answered from inside the closet.

"How many blood bags do you need?"

He didn't answer. Instead, he emerged from the closet and peered down at me, "Woman…" he said slowly.

I was confused at his reaction, "What, babe? You haven't packed any, so I'm just asking."

He nodded his head slowly, "Exactly… You're asking."

My eyes darted from side to side, and then back to the cooler box and I shrugged, "I am very confused right now."

Suddenly, I heard him growl and my eyes flew back to him, "Easy there, tiger. What was that for?"

His tongue flicked over the middle of his lower lip, "This is the first time that you've anticipated my… needs…"

"I know…"

"And I am very turned on right now…" he said

I blushed bright red and I laughed, "Can you please just tell me how many?"

He held up three fingers as he growled again and winked at me before disappearing back into the closet.

Chapter 57

Christina

We arrived at the cabin early that Friday afternoon, and I smiled when I stepped out of the car: It was exactly as beautiful as I remembered. When we went inside, I took a deep breath and sighed contentedly, "I love this place."

Jonathan stepped up behind me and hugged me to him, "I love you."

I snuggled into his hug, smiling wider, "And I love you."

He kissed my temple before he went back to the car to fetch more of our luggage. When he came back inside, just before he went upstairs with our bags, he pointed to the sofa, "That's where you mounted me."

I laughed and followed him up the stairs. In the main bedroom, he set the luggage down near the dresser, and I pointed at the bed, "And that's where you swiped my vam…" I corrected myself, "Sorry, I mean my Infinite v-card."

Jonathan laughed, "You wanted to say vampire, didn't you?"

I pressed my fingertip to the tip of my wrinkled nose and giggled, "Sorry…"

He lightly smacked my ass, "Maybe I should cuff you to the bed and fuck you like the savage I am. Then you can call me a vampire all you want."

"Did you bring handcuffs?" I asked.

"No," he denied, "but I'm very innovative; I'll use your bra."

I gasped, and he grinned at me before going back downstairs.

After a light snack, we went for a drive and just enjoyed the scenery. On a whim, Jonathan suggested we go on a wine tour, and we ended up leaving with quite a few bottles of wine.

We had dinner at a restaurant of my choosing, right next to one of the lakes in the area. It wasn't very fancy, or very big, but the seafood they served was incredible.

Back at the cabin, I went to change into my pajamas while Jonathan poured us each a glass of wine from one the bottles that we just bought and started a fire in the hearth.

"I should get a real job," I said as I stared into the fire. We were sitting on the soft rug in front of the fire, our backs against the sofa.

He turned his head to look at me, "Do you know what kind of job you want?"

I shook my head as I sipped my wine, "Not really. I've been having a blast working part-time and just living, but I need to start contributing to society."

"Hmm," he pondered, but he didn't say any more than that. Then he reached over, lifted my leg and draped it over his.

I smiled at him sideways, "Before you met me, how long were you single?" I asked.

He pulled up his shoulders, "Technically all my life."

"Okay," I corrected, "how long were you celibate?"

Jonathan raised his eyes to the ceiling to think, "About… twenty…"

"Weeks?" I interrupted and tried to guess, but he shook his head, "Years. Give or take a few."

My jaw dropped, "Are you serious? You didn't have sex–with anyone–for more than 20 years?"

Jonathan laughed, nodding his head. I was still gaping at him, "Then by the time we slept together, you must have had some serious blue-balls. Babe!" I put my hand on his shoulder, "Why didn't you pin me against the wall sooner?"

Jonathan stroked my thigh with his fingertips, "I handled myself just fine, and your touch was enough for me."

I ran my fingers through his hair, "Do you like it when I touch you?"

He gave me a shy smile, "Yes…"

So I scooted closer to him and draped my other leg over him as well, "In that case, I will touch you as much as physically possible."

"That reminds me…" I kissed his cheek before I stood up, "I have a surprise for you."

I came back with a small, dark brown bottle with a white cap and Jonathan looked apprehensive, "You should know, cyanide gives me terrible gas," he joked, and I rolled my eyes, "Why would you think this is cyanide?"

He shrugged, "There's a clandestine little bottle that smells of almonds. In my experience, that's cyanide."

I sat down behind him on the sofa, "Scoot."

"My, my, aren't we bossy this evening," he smiled, but moved forward nonetheless, "There, I scooted."

"Shirt off, wings out please?" I went on. He turned around and looked questioningly at me, "Darling, what are you plotting?"

I twirled my index finger, motioning for him to turn around.

Jonathan took off his shirt, and he had to lean forward to open his wings without knocking me off the sofa.

I couldn't help but gawk; I had never seen his wings from the back like this before.

"Can I touch them…?" I asked cautiously. Jonathan nodded, "Of course."

Softly and carefully, I ran my fingers from his back, along the dorsal edge of his wings, over the talons at the top, all the way to the tips. From this close, his wings reminded me of a manga demon, or a bat. They felt leathery, but they were so soft.

"This blows my mind…" I murmured, "Do they have, like, bones inside?"

Jonathan shuddered as I ran my finger across the other wing, and he shrugged, "I'm not too sure. They might." He reached up and pinched the top of one, "Here, feel that," he said. I moved my hand to where he was showing, squeezing the top of his wing, "Oh, yeah," I agreed, "it does feel like it."

His full wingspan was massive, maybe seventeen, eighteen feet, and my jaw dropped. His back muscles flexed as he unfurled his wings and they trembled as he opened them all the way, stretching them out on either side of him. He groaned, and I frowned, "Are you okay, babe?"

He nodded, "I don't use my wings much these days, so the muscles in my back have a hard time when I open them. I get really stiff. I should fly more."

So he uses his back muscles to move his wings. Wow. I never considered the physiology of how they work.

"Then it's a good thing I brought this clandestine bottle of mine," I smiled. "Would you like a massage?"

"Uhm… You mean, a wing massage?" Jonathan asked, and I nodded, "Yes, a wing massage. Back massage, too." Jonathan tilted his head to one side… then to the other side… again… and again, and I laughed, "What?"

"I… I don't know what to say," he admitted. "No-one has ever asked me if I wanted a massage before. People generally don't really touch me…"

The admission hurt my heart: He was touch-starved. That was why he always wanted me to touch him. The very idea of no-one touching him was baffling to me, when I could scarcely keep my hands off him. *I mean, jeez, look at him.*

I leaned forward and planted a gentle kiss in the middle of his back between his wings, "Would you like one now?" He nodded, and his reply was small and quiet, "Yes… please… that sounds really nice…"

Jonathan

I had to clench my teeth to keep myself from moaning.
I was enraptured, and I didn't know what to do with the exquisite feeling of Christina's hands, massaging my back and stretching my wings. Her every touch was feather-soft, and sent wave after wave of tingles, sparks, and shivers up and down my spine.
Her hands on my skin, on my wings triggered something within me, and by the time she was done and I tucked my wings away, I felt... emotional, and I didn't even know why.
I heard Christina close the bottle of massage oil and felt her hand press on my shoulder as she leaned over to look at me. She was just in time to see me wipe tears from my eyes.
She jumped to her feet and knelt in front of me, my face between her hands, "Jonathan?" she asked, concerned, "My love, are you crying?"
I sniffed loudly, pinched my eyes shut for a moment and cleared my throat, "I have no idea why..."
She threw her arms around me and flung her body against me, "I love you," she said, her fingers dug into my hair.
I held her to me, breathing her in, "I love you, too."
She pulled back and pressed her lips to mine.
I raised myself onto my knees, taking her with me. I wrapped my arm around her and slowly lowered her onto her back on the rug.
She ran her fingers through my hair, "Don't be sad, please?" she asked.
I smiled, "How can I be? Look at you," I said before I reclaimed her lips.

Returning my kiss, Christina scratched her nails down my back. An unguarded growl rumbled in my throat as I reached in under her t-shirt and brushed my thumb across her bare nipple.
Moonlight bless her for almost never wearing a bra.
She lifted her hips to press herself against me, and she moaned. *I'm already hard.*
"Jonathan," she breathed, reaching for my pants, "take me, please?"

But I wanted to touch her more, feel that incredible slickness waiting for me between her thighs, and I wanted to bury my face there and taste as deep inside her pussy as my tongue could reach.

I had her nipples between my fingers and my lips against her neck, "Darling, it's too soon."

She shook her head, pushing my pants down over my hips, "I'm ready, take me."

Fuck... My beautiful, wild woman. She's driving me fucking insane.

I lifted her shirt all the way up and drew a nipple into my mouth as I shifted her pants down and off, chucking them onto the sofa behind me, giving myself access to every inch of her. I caressed her soft, warm pussy, and she moaned when I slipped my fingers inside her.

"Please?" she pleaded.

It kills me when she begs for my cock like that.

I lifted my head to look her in the eyes, and I reached down to guide my cock into her warmth.

As I slid into her, I sighed at the witchcraft of being inside her. Her body fit me so, so perfectly.

She was made of Moonlight, just for me.

Chapter 58

Christina

"I hate you," I said to Jonathan early that next morning.
Peppy asshole woke me up sometime before dawn, and we were hiking up a nearby hill to watch the sunrise.
He chuckled at me over his shoulder, "That's alright, I'll fix it later."
"This better be worth it," I complained. I had been sleeping so well. I went to bed a very satisfied kitten, well-fed and thoroughly sexed, and I was having such a great dream when he woke me up. "Don't complain so much," he said as we walked. "Have I ever taken you somewhere that you didn't like?"
"No…" I admitted with a sigh, "although this is shaping up to have some potential."
He laughed, "You'll see when we get there, trust me."

When we arrived at our destination, as much as I hated to admit it, he was right.
Standing near the top of the hill with Jonathan's arms wrapped around me, watching the sun peek out from beneath its star-splattered indigo blanket to flood the sky with amber-gold, made the hike worth every step.
"Do you still hate me?" Jonathan asked, kissing my temple. I chuckled and shook my head, "No… you fixed it."

We stood atop the hill for a while longer, watching the day break through the scattered clouds, Jonathan's arms still tightly wrapped around me.

I didn't know how long we remained there, and after a while I turned around to look at him. "How long are we going to stay up here?"

He raised his hand to cup my jaw, "As long as you want."
"Hmm…"
"You're bored, aren't you?" he smiled, but I shook my head, "I didn't say that."
Nodding, he raised his eyebrows at me, "You didn't have to."
I gave him a coy little smile, and he stroked the side of my jaw with his thumb before he went on. "We can go back if you want," he said, and I didn't need a second invitation. "Okay!" I smiled before I immediately walked past him and started heading down the hill, and I grinned at the sound of him laughing behind me.

"I have an idea," I said to him over my shoulder as we made our way down.
"I'm all ears, love."
"Last one back at the cabin has to do the dishes," I suggested. "You want to race?" he asked and I nodded. "Uh-huh," I confirmed, "but no superhuman abilities allowed."
"If you're sure you want to lose, then…" he started to say, but I cut him short with a very quick "Get-set-Go!" before I took off running down the side of the hill.
I knew I was bluffing myself. He was way fitter than I was, and with those long legs there was no way I would ever beat him to the cabin, but that wasn't going to stop me from trying.
My hiking boot skid across some gravel and I heard Jonathan behind me, "Careful, love."
"Bah!" I countered, "Don't try and distract me with your charm."
"I wasn't trying anything, that was genuine concern," he replied.
I picked up the pace a bit, "Bullshit. You're trying to distract me so you can… Oh fuck," my own curse-word interrupted me when I was too late to miss a stone and I stepped right on it. My left foot must have been angled wrong in the step, because as my boot came down onto the stone, my ankle rolled outward, my knee buckled beneath me and I went down.

Jonathan was right next to me before I even knew what was happening, scooping me up into his arms before I hit the dirt.

"Ow…" I heard myself whine. He carried me over to a nearby log and gently set me down on it before kneeling in front of me. "Let me see," he instructed, already taking my left foot in his hand. He was being very careful, but I still winced when he took off my boot.
"Can you move your foot?" he asked as he peeled off my sock and tucked it into his pocket.
"I think so…" I replied. He cupped my heel in the palm of his hand and slowly, gently rolled my foot in every direction. It hurt a little, but not bad.
"It doesn't look like you sprained it…" I heard him murmur. "Does it hurt a lot?"
I shook my head, "No, it's okay. Just feels a little stiff."
Jonathan bent over and pressed a kiss to the top of my ankle, "There. All better," he smiled at me before he put my sock back on. It looked like he was about to get up but I stopped him, "Can I have my boot back please?"
He shook his head, "I think we should leave the boot off for now." I frowned, "So, what? I'm supposed to walk back to the cabin in one boot, one sock?"
Both his eyebrows went up, "Who said I was going to make you walk?"
I shot him a blank look, "Were you going to carry me?"

He opened his mouth to answer when a pair of hikers came up the path. Looked like a husband and wife. The woman saw me sitting on the log, Jonathan kneeling in front of me with my boot in his hand and she nudged the man next to her in the ribs to direct his attention to us.
"Hello there!" the man smiled as they made their way to us, "Do you folks need a hand?"
I flashed them a polite smile, "We're just enjoying the scenery. We're fine, thank you."
"Kind of you to ask," Jonathan agreed, and the man nodded in his direction. "You two have a good day now."
"Bye!" the woman waved before continuing on their way up the hill.
Jonathan waited until they were out of earshot before he spoke again, "I was actually going to fly you back to the cabin, but…" he looked in the direction where the hiking couple had gone, and I nodded in understanding, "Too many witnesses?"

"Indeed," he agreed before he stood up. Still holding my boot, he tucked one arm underneath my thighs and the other behind my back and lifted me up. "So yes, I am going to carry you."

Back at the cabin, Jonathan put me down on the sofa and propped my foot up on a cushion on the ottoman. "I'll be right back," he said as he put my boots down by the door next to his.

"Babe…" I tried to protest, but he wagged a dismissive index finger at me, before heading to the kitchen. He returned moments later, a pack of frozen peas and a tea towel in hand and I rolled my eyes. "Jonathan I'm okay, I promise. I don't need ice."

He ignored my objection and wrapped the tea towel around the peas before placing it carefully on my ankle.

I loved him for taking care of me, but I pouted. Concern flooded his face, and he immediately crouched in front of me and put his hand on my calf, "Are you in pain darling?"

"No…" I denied, "I wanted to make us breakfast."

He gave me a gentle smile as he stood back up, "Next time."

I kept the ice pack on my ankle until it was time to eat, but after that there was nothing Jonathan could say or do to convince me to put it back.

"What are we doing today?" I asked him as I started clearing the table. He tried to take the cutlery from me but I clicked my tongue at him and yanked the forks out of his reach.

"Hey now feisty," he jabbed, and I stuck my tongue out at him. He shook his head at me before answering, "I thought we could go exploring a bit, but your ankle…"

I sighed loudly. Then I hoisted my right foot into the air and hopped a few times on my left. "My ankle is fine. See?"

Jonathan put his hands up in surrender, "Alright then, you win."

We got ready slowly, as there was nothing and no-one rushing us. I wanted to wash my hair, and when I was done he helped me dry it.

"Would you like me to braid it for you?" he asked, and I felt my eyes widen, "You know how to braid?"

He nodded, "I used to braid Niki's hair all the time when she was little. I still do, from time to time."

"Huh…" I huffed, "Seriously, what is there that you can't do?"

"I told you, love." he smiled, "baking and Swahili."
I just smiled back at him in the mirror. "Let's see what you can do then."

He leaned over and pressed a kiss to the top of my head before he started braiding my hair. I closed my eyes to the feeling of his fingers lightly grazing my scalp, his hands in my hair, as he gathered it all together to braid it. *I've never had this before.* No boyfriend has ever played with my hair, much less braided it for me. I had asked my ex once, just to play with my hair, and he scoffed and asked me if I thought he was 'a nancy boy'. *Ignorant ass, I'm so glad I dumped him.* By the time Jonathan was done. I had a neat, practically perfect fishtail braid, and I was even more impressed with him. "Mr. Langdon, you're a man of many talents."

We took the day slow, starting off with a leisurely stroll through a market in one of the small towns in the area. As we went from shop to stall to vendor, I made sure to keep one hand on Jonathan at all times. On his forearm, on his elbow, on his stomach, his back, his chest, or sometimes I just tucked my hand into the back pocket of his jeans. When we sat down for lunch at a small restaurant, I moved closer to him so that my foot touched his leg where he sat across from me at the small table. He didn't say anything, but the small smile on his face when my foot grazed his leg, told me to do it again.

"You can decide what we do next," he said to me near the end of the afternoon, "Do you want to go horse-riding…?"
I gave him a skeptical, sideways glance, and he continued, "Or would you rather go on a carriage ride?"
"Do both options really have to involve horses?" I asked.
Jonathan raised his eyebrow, "Are you afraid of horses?"
I grimaced, "Maybe…"
"Alright," he conceded, "then maybe the carriage ride is a better idea."

Even though I was still scared of the massive beast that was pulling the carriage, the scenery made me forget about the creature…
"This is nice. I like this," Jonathan said pensively as the carriage took us along a dirt path with the most incredible views of the hills and forest that surrounded us.

He leaned his head against the top of mine, and I felt all warm and fuzzy inside. I snuggled closer to him and nodded, “Me, too.”
Then I sat up and moved my head so my mouth was close to his ear because I didn’t want the driver to hear. “Do you like this because it reminds you of your childhood?”
Jonathan crossed his eyes at me for a split-second, but then he nodded, “The good old days.”
“You are so ancient,” I said softly before I snuggled back into his chest and enjoyed the tranquility of where we were.

“What’s for dinner, by the way?” I asked him as the ride was nearing its end.
“I thought maybe I could cook us something,” he suggested.
I nodded, “Okay. I’ll help.”

Jonathan

When we arrived back at the cabin, Christina poured us some wine and got the ingredients for dinner. While she was doing that, I briefly took a seat at the table to respond to a text message from Niki. She'd been texting me the whole day, and I figured the only way to get her to stop was to just reply and tell her to leave me alone. For now, at least.

When I looked up from my phone, Christina had her arms folded and she was frowning, tapping her foot impatiently at me, "I thought you said you weren't working this weekend?" she scolded. I locked my phone and raised both my hands in surrender, "I wasn't working. My sister texted me."

"Oh," she smiled, "What did she say?"

I glanced at my phone.

I can't tell you what she said… I can't tell you the truth. Not about this. Forgive me my love.

"She wanted to know which vineyard we went to yesterday," I lied.

"Oh, okay," Christina accepted my fib. Then she handed me my glass of wine, and a blood bag, "Here you go," she said as she sipped her wine. My eyebrows shot up, "Is it snack time?"

She shrugged, "I thought it might be. I was with you all of yesterday, and I know you didn't feed. And because I don't know when the last time was that you did feed, here you go…"

I let out a content sigh and smiled at her, "I love you so much, woman."

She winked at me and blew me a kiss, "Love you too. So," she continued, giving me a chance to rip open the bag, "lobster mac and cheese. I've already preheated the oven like you said, what's next?"

"Cook the pasta," I responded out of the corner of my mouth, the tip of the blood bag still between my lips.

"How do you do it?" I asked her after I disposed of the empty bag.

"Do what?" She wanted to know where she was standing in front of the stove, keeping an eye on the *cavatappi* pasta so it wouldn't boil over.

"There I was, casually feeding, and you didn't even blink," I replied.

She chuckled and flicked her hair over her shoulder, "What can I say? Hashtag amazing."

∞

While I was doing the dishes after dinner, she came to stand behind me and wrapped her arms around me.

“Hello, beautiful,” I smiled.

“Hi gorgeous,” she replied between planting kisses all over my back and ever so slowly, she stuck her hand into the waistband of my sweatpants. *Cochetă…*

I looked down at her hand, and then turned my head to look at her over my shoulder, “Actions have consequences you know.”

“Really?” she played coy, and moved her hand lower, “You don’t say…”

“Christina Elodie Miller…” I warned her, “If you grab my cock, Moonlight hear me, I am hauling you upstairs and fucking you.”

So, of course, that was exactly what she did: She shoved her hand into my briefs and wrapped her fingers firmly around my cock.

I groaned as I slowly dried my hands on a kitchen towel before I turned around, “Don’t say I didn’t warn you.”

At Infinite speed, I slung a squealing and giggling Christina over my shoulder and zipped up the stairs and into the bedroom with her.

Chapter 59

Christina

When my feet hit the floor, I bluffed myself into thinking I'd be able to escape, but I kept underestimating how fast he was, and every which way I tried to run, Jonathan blocked me. In a last-ditch effort, I tried to feint a sidestep to try and run past him, but he grabbed me around the waist and flung me down on the bed, and something in his demeanor changed.

The look on his face turned from smiling and playful, to something much more physical… carnal.

He just turned into a predator, and I was his prey.

Oh… fuck. Me.

I sat up on the bed, my lower lip drawn in between my teeth.

"Don't bite your lip like that," Jonathan breathed.

"Why…?" I asked.

He took off his shirt and dropped it to the floor, "Because it makes me want to."

He immediately made good on his word, leaning in to kiss me and drawing my lower lip in between his teeth.

Before he pulled away, he gripped the hem of my shirt and hoisted it over my head, then got back to his feet and stripped off my pants.

His eyes ran all over me, from my bare torso to my light pink panty, to my legs, and back up to my breasts, and he sighed.

"What?" I asked. Sometimes, when he was looking at me like that, I wished he would just tell me, *verbatim*, what was going on inside his head.

"What a sight you are," he smiled crookedly. "But what shall I tie you up with if you're not wearing a bra…?"

A flicker of panic flashed through me.

“Are you really going to tie me up…?” I wasn’t sure if I was comfortable with the idea of being tied up…
“Not if you don’t want me to,” Jonathan said, inclining his head to one side, his warm, soothing voice halting the intrusive memory that reared its ugly head.
I shook my head a little bit, and he nodded, “Then I won’t.”
He leaned over me and grazed the side of my neck with his lips, “I will never do anything that you’re not comfortable with.”
“Thank you…”
“But I will do anything and everything that gets your pussy wet.”
Fuck.
“Are you still going to fuck me like a savage?”
He chuckled darkly, “Do you want me to…?”
I tried to answer, but his fingers found my nipples, and I was unable to speak.
“Lay back for me,” he suggested.
Then he picked his shirt up from the floor and used it to blindfold me, and my body tensed up at the sensory deprivation.

“Relax, darling,” I heard his soothing voice say close to my ear. I tried to, but his fingertips, lightly caressing my skin, were making it very difficult.
“I can hear your heart pounding, but there’s no need to be nervous,” he reassured me.
“What are you going to do?”
I gasped when he shifted my panty aside and I felt his tongue caressing my pussy.
“I’m going to make you come.” he said against my tummy, “Eventually.”
“But,” he continued, “I want you to tell me what you want me to do to you.”
“I… I can’t,” I denied, shaking my head.
He palmed my breasts, and I moaned when he caught my nipples between his fingers.
“Why ever not?” he asked.
“I… I’m shy…” I said softly.
He moved his hand down to the front of my panty, cupping my pussy and pressing the heel of his palm down right on top of my clit.

"Surely that can't be true…" his voice crooned, "I've watched you rub this pretty pussy until you made yourself come for me."
My breath caught in my throat again.
"I'm quite sure you can tell me what you want me to do to you, when you want my cock inside you," he finished the thought.
"Fuck, babe, when did you start talking like this?"
"Like what?" he wanted to know.
"These words you're using…" I tried to explain.
"I think I might know which words you're referring to, but for the intents and purposes of tonight's… activities, I'm going to need you to say them. Out loud." he teased.
I knew I was blushing but I pressed on, "When you use words like… 'cock'… and…" I felt my blush deepen, "And… 'pussy'…"
Jonathan ran his palms across my nipples again, "What about it?"
I moaned, "I like it."
"And I like it when you moan like that," he replied.
I took a deep breath.
Okay, Christina. You have a latent whore in your heart, you know that, just let her out, you got this.
I pinched my eyes shut and gave him my first instruction, "So make me moan again."
He let out a low whistle, "Yes, ma'am. Tell me how."
"Your teeth, on my nipple," I replied, and another moan escaped my lips when he did exactly what I said.
"Your hand on my other nipple," I said, then quickly added, "Please?"
Jonathan flicked his tongue over my nipple and I heard him chuckle, "No need for please. I am here to worship at your altar. Your every wish is my command."
My breath quickened, "Take off my panties…" I panted, "And touch me."
"Where would you like me to touch you?" he urged.
"My… my pussy," I blurted out quickly.
He did as I asked, shifting my panty down to my knees and I sighed as his fingers started exploring me.
"What do you want me to do next?" he asked, and I could feel his breath on my skin.
I wanted to answer, but all I could think about was Jonathan's fingers stroking my pussy. My whole body was tense and trembling, and all that came out was a whimper.

Jonathan softly stroked my thigh, “It’s alright, my love,” he said gently, “it’s alright. You can tell me what you want. I will give you any pleasure your heart desires.”
I shook my head. “Can’t…”
“Can I help you…?” he offered.
“Yeah…”
“Would you like to feel my tongue on your pussy?”
I nodded, “Fuck yes, yes.”
“Yes, your highness,” he complied, slowly peeling off my panty all the way and letting it drop to the floor.

I was going to protest him calling me ‘your highness’ but my brain stopped working, and every nerve-ending in my entire body became solely focused on where his hands and his lips were going. With a gentle but firm movement, he pushed my legs open, gripped my ass, and lifted my hips to meet his mouth. All the tension and anticipation left my body as he made me submit to him, slowly, gradually, insistently and with gentle but purposeful flicks of his tongue, Jonathan coaxed my body right to the very edge of orgasm… and then he stopped.
And he did it again… and he stopped.
Over and over.
“Fuck!” I exclaimed in frustration, “Why do you keep stopping?”
He chuckled wickedly, “I said I was going to make you come, eventually.”
I was panting, and I felt his body on top of mine, his knee between my legs. He had taken his pants off, I could feel his legs against mine, but he was still wearing his boxer briefs. He softly nibbled my earlobe, then moved his lips down the line of my jaw and until he reached my mouth.

Jonathan

I parted her lips with mine, slipping my tongue into her mouth, and she wrapped her arms around me and returned the kiss.

My lips not moving from hers, I pulled the shirt off of her eyes and moved my hand back down between her thighs.

I was planning on making her come soon, and I was going to make it a good one, so I wanted to see the fire in her eyes when her orgasm ripped through her.

"Inside, please?" she murmured against my lips

"What, love?"

"Your fingers… inside me… please?" she panted.

I gently pulled her lower lip in between my teeth as I did what she asked, and slipped two fingers into her. *Ah, fuck, her pussy is soaking wet and my fingers slid right into her. Fuck, yes.*

She put her foot over my leg and pulled me closer, clinging to me as I fucked her with my hand, my fingers sliding in and out of her wet pussy, until her body began to arch and tighten underneath me… and then I stopped.

"Jonathan! Fuck! Why?!" she cried out. *Oh, does my good girl want to come for me?*

I smiled crookedly at her, "Not yet, love."

She lay panting beneath me, her lips parted, with a look of desire on her face that almost ruined my self-control completely.

My only option was to break eye contact with her and take her nipple into my mouth.

But I couldn't help myself, I had to sneak another peak at my woman. Her eyes were fixed blankly on the ceiling, her hips squirming and writhing beneath my touch, and Psyche and Aphrodite had nothing on her.

"Do you want to come for me?" I asked, and she nodded vigorously. I applied some pressure to her clit with my thumb and she began to pull me closer, her fingernails clawing at my back, and I slipped my fingers back into her.

I knew she was close to orgasm. I knew the look on her face, and I was about to stop, but she grabbed my wrist so I couldn't withdraw my hand any further.

"Don't you fucking dare," she panted. "Don't. Fucking. Stop.... Jonathan," she moaned my name as her orgasm took her.

In silent delirium, her legs straightened and pulled taught, her lips parted wider.

She was so beautiful in the throes of her ecstasy that all I could do was stare at her, "Come for me, darling," I breathed. "Come for me hard."

When her body relaxed, I leaned over her and wiped her hair from her face, "Are you alright, love?"

She nodded, breathless. I stroked her cheek as I kissed her gently on the lips.

"Are you done?" I asked her when I pulled back.

She shook her head, "No, I need you inside me."

"Which part of me?"

She rolled her eyes, "You know which part."

"Humor me," I insisted. *Fuck, please say it.*

She blushed crimson red and closed her eyes, but she did it; she said it, "I need your cock."

I winked at her as I took off my briefs and I lowered myself down onto her but she stopped me, "I… I want to see you. Your wings. Fangs too. Everything."

And I smiled.

This.

She had no idea how much it meant to me when she asked this of me, to know that she trusted me that much to want to see every aspect of my physical being when I was making love to her.

"Gladly," I complied, baring my fangs and unfurling my wings before I lowered myself between her legs. I released a breath as I slowly sank my cock into her and she wrapped her legs around me.

I lost all concept of time, all notion of who and where I was as I thrust in and out of her, and all I knew, all that mattered was her warmth enveloping me.

"Jonathan, come inside me," she breathed next to my ear, "come for me."

I wasn't expecting to hear that at all, and I groaned at the invitation. And when she sank her teeth into my shoulder, it pushed me right over the edge, and I fell apart inside her.

"Woman, you'll be the death of me," I murmured next to her ear when I had withdrawn myself from her and collapsed next to her, "and I'm immortal."

She was too drained, too spent, to laugh. All she could do was smile and chuff, once.

I stood up and put my sweatpants back on, then turned to her, "Would you like some water? Or hot chocolate?"

She nodded, "Hot chocolate."

I winked at her and went down to the kitchen.

Chapter 60

Jonathan

When I came back with two mugs of hot chocolate, she was standing on the balcony, dressed in my underwear and my shirt, gazing out at the night sky.

"You look really good in those," I said, gesturing at the briefs, "you should keep them."

She didn't say anything, she just smiled at me in reply.

As she sipped her hot chocolate, I regarded her in silence. Something was bothering her.

"Darling?" I asked her after a while, "Is something the matter? It appears you have something on your mind…"

"Are you into BDSM?" she blurted out.

I was taken aback for a moment, "Wow. As questions go, that one was really unexpected."

She turned to me with a million questions in her eyes, "Are you?"

"May I ask what prompted this question?"

"I've just been thinking. You knew every implement in Kat's dungeon at the club, you've mentioned tying me down, handcuffing me, and spanking me several times now, and just the other day, you said that my skirt reminded you of a bondage harness… You definitely have a primal kink, and I'm pretty sure you'd be into bloodplay, which is fine, you're Infinite, I get it, but the other stuff… I need to know. Are you into BDSM?"

I raked my fingers through my hair, "When you lay it out like that, I sound like a pervert."

She sighed, "I didn't mean it like that, I just… I just want to understand."

I turned my face toward the forest, "I wouldn't say I'm 'into' it. But I would be lying if I told you I've never dabbled. And yes, I did enjoy it somewhat."

Christina gulped, and her face was pale, "Is that... Is that what you want? With me?"

I shook my head, "No. All I want is you. Just you, exactly the way you are."

"I just don't want you to feel... unfulfilled with our sex-life," she said softly.

Again I shook my head, "I don't feel that way, I swear. All I want is you," I said again. "As long as you allow me to be cock-deep in your wet pussy, I don't care how I get there."

She blushed bright red, "You and your filthy, ancient mouth..."

I set the empty mugs down on the dresser, and pulled her into my arms, "If you want me to, I will be more than happy to tie you up and spank you. But only if that is what you want."

She wrapped her arms around my waist, "Any other kinks I should know about? Knives? Fisting? Anal? Anything...?"

I laughed. A great, roaring laugh that echoed out into the night. *The joy she puts in my heart is indescribable.*

I looked up at the moon, and then down at the woman I love in my arms, and I knew.

This was it, this was the moment.

"Christina," I started.

"Hmm?" she mumbled.

I lifted her chin so I could look her in the eyes, "I love you. I love you more than I knew it was possible for me to love someone. And I would be honored, blessed, if you would let me show you how much, every day, until the end of time."

I pulled something out of my pocket and handed it to her, "Open it."

Her hands were shaking, but she opened the small, black, velvety jewelry box, and when she saw what was inside, she clasped her hand over her mouth, "Is this...?"

I nodded, and I smiled at her, "You are unlike anyone I have ever known. You're everything that I never knew I needed. Will you please do me the unparalleled honor of becoming my wife?"

"You're asking me to marry you?" her voice cracked from behind her hand.
I tucked her hair behind her ear and I nodded, "I'm asking you to marry me."
"And I know," I went on, "I know it's a big ask. Huge. So, if you want to think about it, or talk about it, that's fine. You don't need to answer me immediately."
I held out my hand for the jewelry box, but she closed it and held it to her chest, "I'll hang on to this, thank you very much."
I smiled and kissed her forehead, "Of course."
And then she said nothing.

In complete silence, she walked back into the bedroom and put her pajama pants on. She still didn't say anything as she left the room and headed for the stairs.
I raked my fingers through my hair and scratched the back of my head. I had wanted to get down on one knee, but clearly, not doing that turned out to be a rather prudent decision. I had no idea where she was going or what was going on in her head, but I didn't want to pressure her, so I let her be, and I lay down on the bed, interlocking my fingers on my stomach.
"Are you coming or not?" Christina called from downstairs a few minutes later.
Frowning, I got up off the bed and went downstairs to the living room, where she was sitting cross-legged on the sofa.
"What were you doing up there?" she asked me as I came down the stairs.
I gave her an apprehensive look as I sat down one seat away from her, "Giving you space, and time to think…"
She returned the look, "But you said we could talk about it… So, let's talk."
I indicated toward the bedroom with my thumb, "Could we not have talked upstairs?"
She shook her head, "No, because upstairs is where the bed is and in…" she glanced at an imaginary wristwatch, "Exactly five minutes from now, I would probably want to jump your bones again. Ergo, the sofa is the safer option."
I nodded understandingly, "Alright. Well, is there anything you want to ask me?"

"So many things. A whole fucking Pandora's box full. And not just about the future," she said.
I nodded, "Go ahead, love."

After a few moments of silence, she started, "Tell me about Emery."
I cleared my throat and my eyebrows knit together, "Have you been holding on to this one since London?"
She looked pointedly at me, "Maybe. For some reason I just remembered how she accosted me in the bathroom at the club, and I thought I should ask."
My frown deepened, "Accosted?"
"Yes…"
I inclined my head, "Was that why you called her Bitchy Spice? And a cum-rag?"
Christina nodded, "She should be glad that's all I said."
I raised an eyebrow, "What did she say to you, exactly?"
She lifted my hand and played with my fingers, "Something about sloppy seconds, and that I'm nothing more than a human plaything to you."
Actions have consequences, Emery should know that by now. And if she's forgotten, perhaps she was in need of a reminder. A bubble of anger popped in my gut, but then Christina looked up at me and smiled, "Emery can say whatever she wants about me. I was just…"
"Jealous?" I asked, and she nodded, "Yes. I was."
I looked at her in silence for a moment and she raised her eyebrows at me, "What? Am I not allowed to get jealous over your past dalliances? Is that privilege reserved for you alone?"
I stroked her hair, "I never said that. I'm touched that you are, but you don't need to be." Then I pulled her face to mine, crushing my lips against hers. "I'm yours, Christina."
"I know," she replied, "and I'm yours."
I stroked her hair, "I could apologize for my past indiscretions and promiscuity, for being a man-whore, as you told Lilian I was…"
"Sorry…" she mumbled, but I shook my head and I went on, "You're not wrong, but no amount of apologizing can change the past. So, yes, I did sleep with Emery, and others. But you are the only woman I want to make love to for the rest of eternity."

"How old were you the first time you had sex?" Christina asked.

"I was seventeen."
"Who was she?" she wanted to know.
I turned my eyes to the ceiling to recall the memory, "Her name was Ljudmila."
She nodded slowly. "Pretty name. Was she human?"
"She was."
"How did you meet?"
"We were living in Bulgaria at the time, and she was our next-door neighbor's niece," I explained.
"Was she your first girlfriend?"
"No," I denied, "you were."
She didn't respond to my statement, only went on with her question, "If she wasn't your girlfriend, how did it happen that you slept together?"
I cracked the knuckles on my left hand, "We were rather good friends, and it just sort of happened one day."
Christina seemed satisfied with the answer. "Did you… Do you want to know about my first time?" she asked.
I offered her a smile, "You don't need to tell me if you don't want to, love."
But she shrugged, "It seems only fair."
I nodded in acceptance, "Alright then. Go ahead."
She cleared her throat before she started, "I had just started university, about seven months in. His name was Matthew, and we had gone on a couple of dates before… you know."
Why the fuck did I agree to listen to this? I want to find this Matthew cunt and rip his fucking face off... But I restrained myself. "How long were you together?"
Christina let out a laugh, "That's the thing. We weren't. The sex was… horrible. I think I saw him again once or twice after that, and then I ended things between us."
I ran my hand up her leg, to her knee and back down. Then she continued.

"When did you sleep with Emery?" she asked, and for a moment I could not fucking remember,
"Uhm… 1980… something? Early 80's, I think."
"How many times?"

I dropped my head, “Only once. And she meant nothing to me. She still doesn’t. No-one does. Nobody but you.”
She kissed my cheek, “I know. That’s why it doesn’t bother me.”
“Were you really going to physically fight her?” I asked.
Christina nodded, “Hell yes. I was waiting for her to throw the first punch, and then I was absolutely going to kick her scrawny ass all the way up and down the High Street.”
“Why?”
She shrugged, “For talking about you like she knows you, like she owns you. And she doesn’t. You’re mine.”
I smiled, “I’ve never had anyone stand up for me that way. To know that you were ready to fight someone, for me, it just… melts my vampire heart.”
She smiled shyly, but she rolled her eyes and stuck her tongue out at me.
“There she is, my feisty little Gremlin,” I grinned, and she wrinkled her nose at me. *Moonlight hear me, I love this woman so much.*

I pressed her hand to my lips and kissed her palm, “What’s your next question?”
She cleared her throat and then she started, “I don’t care about the past, but I do need to know… who was the girl that you got pregnant?”
I cracked my knuckles and ran my hands through my hair, “Kat is a pest, so she figured it out on her own, but I have never said the woman’s name out loud to anyone but my mother…”
“Why?”
“Because… It’s a proper scandal, that’s why.”
She rubbed the tip of her nose, “Well, if you want to marry me, then I think you should be able to tell me. Even if it is as big of a scandal as you say.”
I sighed, “You’re right… Could I tell you her first name and leave it at that? I’m sure you’ll be able to fill in the blanks…”
Her eyebrows slowly went up, “Okay…”
I covered my eyes with my hand before I said the name, “Anne…”
“Anne Boleyn?” she gasped.
I lowered my hand and nodded once, and her jaw dropped even further, “What the flying Hell, Jonathan?”
I pursed my lips and pulled up my shoulders, “I told you I was a prick.”

Then she went quiet, and I started to worry. *This is not the kind of information that would make her leap at forever with me. Shit.*
"Is that… Is that a dealbreaker?" I asked, very carefully.
"No," she responded rather quickly, "I saw you rip a dude's head off with your bare hands, and I watched you guzzle a bag of A-negative just a few minutes ago and none of that fazed me, so no. You getting some snootch hundreds of years ago isn't going to put me off. It just makes you that much more interesting."
I pressed my lips together to prevent myself laughing out loud, "Even if she was married?"
Christina shrugged, "That part sucks a bit. You probably shouldn't have boinked her if you knew she was married. But that was Past You. You're not the same person now that you were back then, and I know you're not going to dip your dick in anyone else while I'm in your life…"
"Never," I said definitely, "I might not have cared about hers, but our relationship is the reason I'm even alive. So no, I would never do that."
She nodded knowingly, "Exactly my point. Besides, I give incredible head."
I shook with silent laughter.
"I understand why you didn't want to tell me, though," she went on.
"You do?" I frowned, and she nodded, "You're ashamed of who you used to be."
I dropped my head and looked up at her from underneath my eyebrows, "This is why I want to spend the rest of my life with you."
"Because I know you?"
I nodded slowly, "You see me."

Christina took a quiet breath, a half-smile on her lips, then she went on to her next question, "If I do marry you, if I marry the Black Prince, what does that make me?"
I mirrored her smile, "My wife, my queen, my everything."
"Would I have a title?" she asked.
I pondered for a moment, "Possibly. Her Highness, Lady Christina, Princess of Carpathia. Something along those lines."
Her eyes widened. Noticing the look on her face, I went on, "If you said yes, my mother would probably ask us to do some sort of an announcement, introducing you to the rest of the order as my wife."

I wanted to take her hand, but I wasn't sure if it was a good idea at that moment. My heart lightened when she turned to face me and straightened her legs to put her feet in my lap, "Next question, do Infinite royals have rules to abide by, like how to behave in public and stuff like that?"
I took one of her tiny feet in my hand and started massaging it, "No. You can run down the street arse-naked if you want to. I have. But there are certain Laws that we have to abide by."
Her eyebrows shot up in surprise, so I explained, "Ibiza, Truth or Dare. I made a choice, and I stuck to my guns."
"And then you and your gun went running down the street?" she queried.
I nodded, "Yes... I… Yes." That was where the story ended.
She grinned at me, "I'm sure it was an unforgettable night for many women."
My face wrinkled in embarrassment for a moment, and I covered my face with my hands.
"Go on, you were telling me something," she urged.

I went on, "Right. We have what we call the Laws of Night, which is the code of ethics that we live by, and a violation of the Laws is punishable by death if necessary."
She gulped, "What are these Laws?"
I explained, "The First Law of Night, 'Sacred is the blood of the innocent'."
"What does that mean?"
"It means we cannot feed on a living person and take their life. That's why we use blood bags to feed."
"Okay, but surely, after all this time, you've learned how to control yourself?"
I tilted my head, "Most have. But feeding from the source makes it difficult to stop, and the risk of killing the person you are feeding on is too great. Blood bags are easier, and safer, When it's empty, it's empty, and you stop."
"Have there been times when you were… unable to stop?" she wanted to know.
I nodded, "Once…"
"Tell me…" she urged.

I raked my fingers through my hair again before I responded, “There was a young lady in Poland… 20 years ago… and I forgot who I was, and she nearly died.”
“You mean…?”
I nodded, “I didn't mean to, but I fed on her, and I couldn't stop until it was almost too late. I nearly killed her.”
“What happened to her…?” Christina wanted to know.
I went on, “I didn't know what else to do, so I called my mother. Thank the Moonlight Dr. Woods was able to revive the woman and she woke up shortly after.”
“How did you explain to her what happened?”
I shook my head, “I didn't. My mother altered her memory, so she would have no recollection of ever meeting me.”
“Wow…” Christina breathed.
“That… That was the reason we left Poland, and also the reason I chose to remain celibate for so long. I didn’t…” I pinched my eyes shut, “I didn’t trust myself not to kill the next person I slept with. And then I met you, and you taught me how to trust myself again,” I opened my eyes to find her smiling at me.
“Did she know what you were?” Christina wanted to know, and I shook my head, “No, she was innocent in that sense.”
“Did you have feelings for her…?” she asked.
“No, she was a means to an end.”
“What end?”
“Satisfying a need,” I said.

She spoke again after a few quiet moments, “What defines someone as ‘innocent’?”
“Two types of people might be seen as innocent: Those who have done no harm to others, and those who have not seized the truth.”
“Okay, but what if you tell someone what you are? Can you feed on them then?” she asked.
“Second Law: Expose only that which is worth the risk. We have to keep our Infinity a secret, unless we have absolutely no other choice,” I clarified.
“Like when that nascent attacked us…” she said, “You had no choice. You had to show your truth.”
Nodding, I went on, “And the third Law: Blood begets blood.”
“Like ‘an eye for an eye’?”

"Justice be done."
"There has to be a line though, right? Surely you can't go around punishing every criminal for every single crime?" Christina asked.
"If an Infinite has spilled mortal blood with justifiable reason, then the First Law might not be applicable. It differs from case to case. Generally, we're not vigilantes, we don't involve ourselves in mortal crimes. It poses too much of a risk of breaking the Second Law," I explained.
"So I can never tell my mom everything without breaking any Laws?" she asked cautiously.
"I couldn't, but you could. You're not Infinite, you're not bound by our Laws. You could tell your mother anything you wanted to."

She was quiet for a few moments before she went on, "If we got married, where would we live? In which country?"
"That remains to be seen," I said, "I have a feeling my mother is going to want to move eventually. And honestly, moving back to Europe would be easier, from a business perspective. The time zones kill me sometimes."
"What about a job?" she asked, "I still don't have one."
I smiled, "You really don't need to work if you don't want to, love."
She gave me a blank look, "And what would I do? Just spend your money?"
I grinned and nodded, "Yes. Buy as many pairs of shoes as your heart desires."
Christina rolled her eyes and shook her head.
I winked at her, "Next question?"
She waited a moment before she spoke again, "Okay… What about kids? Do you still want kids?"
I nodded slowly, "If that's what you want, yes."
"But if I'm Infinite, then we can't have kids, right?" she wanted to clarify, and I nodded again, "Only if you are mortal."
The silence was so suffocating that I was waiting for her to hand me the ring back and tell me to go fuck myself.
"What if I say no, what about my mom? Will she be in danger again?" she asked.
"Your mother will always be protected," I assured her.
"What about me?" she wanted to know.

"Christina, darling," I replied, "You will always, always have the protection of the entire Infinite order, whether you agree to marry me or not."
"What about… my mortality? In case you forgot, I am still very much human."
I wiped a hand across my face, "I was dreading this question…."
"I haven't thought much about it until now, but now that you've asked me to marry you, I have to think about it. Are you going to turn me?" she wanted to know.
I turned my head to look at her. This reality had been scraping at the back of my mind since the first time she told me that she loved me. And now I couldn't ignore it any further, "If that's what you really want… I will."
"Does it hurt?"
I looked her in the eyes and nodded, "Yes. It does."
"How… how is it done?"

I rolled my neck, "There is a specific ritual that we have to perform, things that I have to say, things you have to say, an oath that needs to be taken."
"That's it?"
I shook my head, "That's just the beginning. Then I have to drain your body of blood almost completely. And just before you lose consciousness, you have to, voluntarily, take the Curse upon yourself. You have to drink my blood."
"What happens then?" her small voice asked.
I leaned forward and wrapped my arms around her legs and hugged them to my chest, "My cursed blood will bring you back from the banks of the River Styx. It will spread through your body, and change your DNA as far as it goes. It will break you, break every single bone in your body, more than once, and rebuild and heal you as an immortal."
Christina's face paled, and even though my voice came out strained, I kept going, "At some point, the pain will become too much, and you will lose consciousness completely.
And when you wake up, you will be Infinite."

Thick, silent moments passed before Christina spoke again, "Okay… Would I have any powers? Like Niki, or Kat?"

I nodded, "It is possible, yes, but we have no way of knowing if and what until after your transformation has been completed. Not everyone manifests abilities."
"Last question," she said then, "I'm your first girlfriend ever, right?"
"Yes. I've never been in a real relationship before I met you."
"Are you sure you want to marry me then? I mean, don't you want to date around first, see other people for a while?" she asked.
I frowned, deep, "Is that… Is that what you want? Do you want to see other people?"

Fuck.

I never considered the possibility. I knew she loved me, but she was so young, only 25. What if she wanted a break? I wouldn't be able to handle it if she said she wanted to see other people; I'd rip the head off the first man that dared touch her.
I almost puked in relief when she shook her head, "Fuck no. I was just worried that maybe that's something you want."
I shook my head, "I absolutely don't. I don't want anyone else. You're my first girlfriend, and I want you to be my last."
For moments that felt like hours, the only thing passing between us was thick, almost visible silence.
Christina took a deep breath and released it slowly, "This is a lot to take in…"
She slowly lifted her legs out of my lap and stood up, "I'm going to bed. I need to think."
I just nodded.

I waited until she was asleep to change my clothes and go outside for a walk, hoping, praying that she would say yes, that she would be willing and wanting to take on Infinity by my side.
But I realized that it might be wise to prepare my heart for the very real possibility that Christina was going to reject my proposal. She had so many questions, and a lot of them simply did not have the greatest of answers.
I wouldn't be able to sleep, so I spent a good part of the night strolling around the woods, just listening to the sounds of the night around me.

And when daybreak started rolling in, I went back to the cabin, kicked off my boots, and flopped down on the sofa. I lay there for a while, staring at the ceiling, and as the first rays of dawn lit up the inside of the cabin, sleep finally took me.

Chapter 61

Christina

I woke up alone.
The bed was empty and unslept-in next to me, and I frowned when I realized that Jonathan must have not come to bed at all.
The rest of the cabin was just as eerily quiet as the bedroom.
I took the jewelry box from the dresser and opened it.
I thought that Lilian's ring was the most beautiful ring I'd ever seen, but this, my ring… Oval-cut black fire opal, surrounded by black diamonds and set in gold that twisted into the symbol for 'infinity' on either side. Perfect choice, coming from the Black Prince. Black fire to match his own.

I closed the box and headed downstairs to look for him, and I breathed a sigh of relief when I found him fast asleep on the sofa. He'd kicked off his boots by the door, and he fell asleep in his clothes.
I wanted to kiss him awake, but his heightened senses must have alerted him when I crouched down next to him, and he opened his eyes.
"How are you so beautiful this early in the morning?" he asked in that incredibly sexy Early Morning Jonathan voice that I adored so much.
He sat up on the sofa and I took a seat next to him.
Time to give him my answer to his proposal.

Jonathan

"Jonathan…" Christina started, and an icy hand gripped my heart.
I didn't trust myself to say anything, so I let her continue.
She took a deep breath, "Our relationship has been great. We've had some amazing times, and I will cherish the memories forever. We've also had some really hard times, and those I will also never forget."
"Christina…" Her name was a prayer.
"Being with you and being your girlfriend has been great, even though it has been dangerous at times. I think being married to you would be even more dangerous than being your girlfriend. I have a feeling there's more going on with the vampires that killed Devyn than you're telling me.
And I know there's darkness inside you. And I think that darkness, that part of yourself that you call the Black Prince, is still very much a part of who you are. I saw it when you killed the nascent, I heard it in your voice when you had Owen pinned to the wall. And I know you said you'll keep me safe…" she went on saying.
She gave me a pained smile as she handed me the jewelry box, "I love you more than life itself. But, Jonathan, I'm sorry…"
My throat tightened and my chest caved in. *No…*
She went on, "There's no way your wife is going through Infinity helpless and dependent. You're going to have to train me."

I did a double take, "What?"
What the fuck?
What just happened?
"You… you're saying yes?'
She wrinkled her nose and giggled, "I'm saying yes."
Christina laughed at her own little joke… until a really vile Romanian curse word escaped my lips and she realized that I was shaking.
"What's wrong?" she asked.
"I thought you were saying no. I thought…" I gulped, "I thought…" I couldn't bring myself to say the words.
She shook her head, "No, of course not!"
I was frantic. I reached for her and pulled her onto my lap and into my arms, burying my face in her hair, "Don't play with me? Please, don't play with me?" I pleaded.

She stroked my hair, nodding, “I’m sorry, my love, I’m so sorry. That was a bad joke, I’m sorry. Jonathan, why would I say no to the biggest adventure my heart has ever been on?”
I pulled back and looked questioningly at her as I lifted her off my lap, “I’m going to ask you again, just to be sure,” I dropped down on one knee in front of her and opened the jewelry box, “Christina Elodie Miller, will you marry me?”
She bit her lower lip and nodded. “Yes, I will,” she beamed as I slipped the ring onto her finger.

I breathed a sigh of relief. Then I kissed her like I never had before. Christina cupped my face in her hands when I pulled back, “I love you, My Eternal Majesty.”
I kissed her again, “Don’t say that to me now, now is not the right time to get me hard.”
She laughed.
I ran my fingers through her hair, “I’ve actually asked you this before, but I guess you didn’t hear me then.”
She frowned, “Asked me what? To marry you?”
I nodded, and her jaw dropped, “When?”
My grin softened into a smile, “It was after we played that drinking game that you suggested, and I was putting you to bed.”
She blinked slowly, “Was that what you said?”
I nodded again, “I asked you to marry me.”
She rolled her eyes at me, “Yeah… In Romanian. Which I don’t speak.”
I bit the inside of my cheek and I shrugged, “I was practicing.”
My future wife wrapped her arms around my neck and hugged me tightly, “You can ask me any way you want, in any language, even the ones I don’t speak, my answer is yes. Always yes.”

Chapter 62

Christina

In the jet on the way back home, I couldn't stop staring at the ring on my finger. My engagement ring. *I'm engaged.*

I'd never seen a black fire opal before; I didn't even know they existed. The colors encapsulated in it were absolutely mesmerizing. Every which way I turned my hand, whichever way the light hit it, the stone seemed to catch fire and it glowed like a multi-colored rainbow in the night.

"How's the future Mrs. Langdon?" I heard Jonathan's voice float over to me from where he was sitting in the recliner next to me.

I smiled dreamily, "Mrs. Langdon… Now that sounds really good."

I looked over at him, and he winked at me, "It certainly does, darling."

"Hang on," I asked, "so your mom and I will both be Mrs. C Langdon?"

Jonathan chuckled and shook his head, "My mother uses her maiden name, Adelphi. You will be the first and the only Mrs. C Langdon."

Smiling, I tipped my glass of water to him, "I will drink to that."

"By the way," he said, tipping his glass back to me, "I have a confession."

I raised my eyebrows at him, "Oh?"

He nodded slowly, "Yesterday, when I told you Niki was asking about the vineyard we went to?"

"Yes…?"

He pulled up his shoulders, "That was a bold-faced lie."

I laughed, "I knew it!"

Jonathan pressed the tip of his tongue to his upper lip, "Sorry, love. But I couldn't tell you the truth, that she was asking if I had proposed yet."

My jaw dropped, “Niki knew you were going to propose to me this weekend?”
He chuckled and he nodded, “She did. My whole family knew, actually.”
I shook my head incredulously, “The deception…”
“She’s probably still waiting to hear what happened…”
“We can tell her now, if you want,” I grinned, and he smiled, pulling his phone from his pocket to call his sister.
Niki answered the phone really quickly, “Did you ask her? What did she say?”
“Hello, Donika,” Jonathan smiled.
“Yes, hello,” she replied impatiently. “Did you ask her or not?”
He chuckled, “I did, I asked Christina to marry me.”
“And?” Niki asked excitedly.
“Ask her yourself,” he responded and held his phone closer to me, “Hi Nix,” I smiled.
“Chris!” Niki shrieked, “Can someone please tell me what happened?”
I wrinkled my nose; Niki’s excitement was so cute.
“Book the spa dates, Niki-Nix, I’m marrying your brother!”
Niki took a deep breath… then she squealed. And hung up.
I laughed, “Someone’s excited.”
Jonathan smiled, “That was a bit rude of her, but alright. I think my whole family is excited.”
“Speaking of family,” I said, reaching for my phone, “can I call my mom? I want to tell her the good news.”
He nodded, “You don’t need to ask my permission, love.”
Grinning, I punched in my mom’s number, but my grin turned into a frown when it went straight to voicemail.
“No answer?” Jonathan asked, and I nodded, “I wonder where she is…”
He pulled up his shoulders, “If you want, we can stop by your house first.”

But my mom wasn’t at the house either. Her car was in the driveway, but there was no sign of her. I was baffled, “Where did she go?”
“Wherever she is, I’m sure she’s fine, love.”
“Maybe I should just stay here and wait for her.”
“Love…” he said, but I wasn’t having it and I shook my head.

I tried calling her again, but the line still went to voicemail and my stomach was starting to twist into knots. If anything happened to my mom… "Where is she?"

"You're assuming the worst," he said gently, and I whipped my head to look at him, "Can you blame me? I didn't hear from Devyn for a while and look what happened there."

The look on his face told me he knew I was right, but he said nothing.

"Let me just…" I said out loud, but my brain didn't bother to finish my sentence. I left Jonathan standing in the living room and I went to my mom's room to check… something. Her room was empty, but neat and tidy, no overturned furniture anywhere, and all her clothes seemed to still be there.

So I went back to the living room where Jonathan was still standing. "I don't know where she is…" I said, and my voice was starting to crack a little.

He opened his mouth to answer when my phone buzzed in my hand. My mom.

"Mom, where are you?" I answered.

"Sorry sweetie pie," I heard her smiling, "I'm running a few errands, I didn't even realize my phone was off."

"Okay, but when are you coming back?"

"I can't be sure," she said, and I frowned. *What does that mean*? She went on, "I have to go, I'll see you soon okay? Love you!" And she hung up before I got a word in.

I turned to Jonathan, "Well at least she's okay…"

He offered me a smile. "Do you feel better now?"

I raked a hand through my hair, "Kind of… But maybe I should wait for her."

He gave me a skeptical look, "Would you not rather come with me and pop a bottle of champagne at the house? We did just get engaged, after all."

A smile formed on my face, "Celebrating with my fiancé does sound like a lot more fun than sitting here alone."

Jonathan held out his hand for me to take, "Come along then, future Missus." My heart pumped melted chocolate. *I'm the future Mrs. Jonathan Langdon. I fucking love the sound of that.*

At the manor, Jonathan asked the staff to unload our luggage from the car as he led me up to the front door.

He kissed my cheek before he held the door open for me, and as I stepped into the foyer… The cork popped on a champagne bottle, and the entire foyer erupted in cheers and applause.

Celeste, Alastair, my mom, Magnus, Niki, Kat, and almost every member of the staff were standing in the foyer, applauding us as we made our entrance into the house.
Behind the cheering family members, draped over the railing of the landing at the top of the stairs, was a white banner with 'CONGRATULATIONS' printed on it in big silver and gold block letters, and the foyer was covered in silver and gold balloons.
Like the first day we met, Celeste was the first to pull me into a long, tight hug before she kissed me on both cheeks and then hugged me again. "I'm so happy to have you as a daughter," she beamed.
I didn't get a chance to reply before Alastair pulled me in for a hug, "Welcome to our family, dear one."

When he let go, I turned to my mom, "Mommy! I tried calling you, I wanted to tell you myself!"
My mom's eyes were brimming with tears, "It's okay honey, I knew it was happening," she assured me as she wrapped her arms around me, and my mouth gaped wide open, "Everyone knew except me!"
My mom laughed, "Jonathan asked me for my blessing weeks ago, when you were in New York with the girls."
I pulled back from my mom's hug and turned to look at Jonathan where his mom had him in a vise grip hug.
'Sneaky' I mouthed at him, and he just winked at me.
Kat grabbed my hand, "Let's see the bling," and gawked at the ring.
I laughed and turned to her, "Did you also know?"
"Pfft," she waved a dismissive hand. "Please, he's been calling you his wife behind your back for eons."
With a loud squeal of joy, Niki pulled me into a bear hug, jumping up and down, shrieking.
"And obviously you also knew your brother was going to propose," I accused.
Niki had a guilty smile on her face as she nodded, "I almost said too much at the spa."

Jonathan came over and wrapped an arm around his fiancée's waist. *It's me, I'm his fiancée.* "Why did I not know you went to the spa with my sister?" he asked me.
I smiled a small, sad smile, "It was just before Devyn died..."
Wordlessly, he nodded and kissed my temple.

Celeste ushered everyone into the family dining room which was lined with tables covered in black and silver tablecloths, and platters of savory and sweet canapes were waiting.
The smell of food found my nose. Everything smelled so good, and my tummy did a rumble. He was a few steps away from me, but he must have heard it because Jonathan's head slowly turned away from his father, and he looked at me. As did his mom where she was standing at the end of one of the tables.
"Christina, *koritsi mou*," Celeste called to me. My girl
"Here, eat something," she said as she came over and held out a plate of delicious-looking snacks to me.

I took the plate from her with a sheepish grin on my face, "Thanks... Mom."
Celeste's eyes seemed to light up, and she wrapped her arm around my shoulders and hugged me again, "Oh, you're going to make me cry."
I hugged her back, "Please don't, you'll set me off too." Then I pointed to the tables laden with food, "When did you do all this?"
She beamed a happy grin, "My son had the good sense to let me know early this morning that you had said yes. He knows I would have been very unhappy if he didn't give me enough time to plan a celebration."
Niki gasped, "Mummy, you knew she said yes?" I looked over my shoulder; I didn't even hear her approach.
Celeste nodded and winked at Niki, "I know everything."
From the other side of the room, the sound of silverware against crystal drew everyone's attention to where Alastair was standing, a glass of champagne in the air.
Jonathan came to stand behind me and wrapped his arms around me, resting his cheek against my hair, and I snuggled back into him.

"I will try my best not to talk too much, my wife instructed me not to be too cheesy," Alastair started, "but I shan't make any promises."

"Christina," he went on, smiling at me, "We consider ourselves incredibly lucky to welcome you into our little family. May you and Jonathan have a very long, very happy life together. Congratulations!"
The other guests echoed Alastair's congratulations, and Jonathan lowered his mouth to my ear and whispered, "*Carpe noctem,* darling."
I turned my head so he could kiss my cheek, "*Carpe veritatem* my love."
Alastair came over to us from the other side of the room to give me another hug.
"There's more I wanted to say," he said, and glanced over at Belinda where she was talking to Magnus a few steps away. Alastair lowered his voice to continue, "I will do so later," before he tipped his glass to me and Jonathan and strode over to join his wife.
"On the topic of later," Jonathan said, turning me around to face him, "I am not ready to let my fiancée go, so will you please spend the night with me?"
I put my hands on his neck, "Do you want to have a just-got-engaged pajama party with me?"
He nodded, smiling, "Absolutely."
I pressed a quick kiss to his lips, "Let me check if my mom has anything planned," I said before stepping out of his embrace to speak to my mom.

She was looking deep into Magnus' eyes as he was telling her a story from his travels. She broke eye contact with him to look at me when I approached.
"Hi, sweetheart," she smiled.
I hugged her, "Hi Mom."
"Oh, just so you know," my mom said, "I won't be home tonight."
"Oh?"
Magnus nodded in confirmation, "I'm taking your mother away for a few days. If you don't mind, of course."
I grinned, "Of course not, I think that's an inspired idea." *Guess I'm staying with my future hubby for a few more days then.*
That night, standing in the kitchen helping Celeste make *seada*, Niki's favorite Italian dessert of deep fried pastry ravioli stuffed with sheep's cheese and lemon zest, I took a moment to look around me, and I realized that this was a big part of what I said 'yes' to, Jonathan's family.

To Niki, where she was standing next to him, chopping vegetables for *caponata,* stopping every once in a while to flick little pieces of vegetable at him.

To him, where he was deveining prawns for the *brodetto*, flinging prawn poop at his sister, Niki shrieking indignantly at the assault.

To his father, standing by the stove, stirring the béchamel sauce for the lasagna.

There was so much happiness in my heart, knowing that I was going to be a part of this happy little unit for the rest of my life. For the rest of life, period.

"What I wanted to say earlier," Alastair said to me later at the dinner table, "was that your relationship with Jonathan has had its light days and its dark days, thinking of one incident in particular."

I smiled wistfully, but I put my hand over Jonathan's on the table, "More light than dark."

Smiling, Alastair continued, "I know that my son has put you through a lot, so I think I speak for the entire family when I say: We're very glad and very relieved that you said yes, instead of telling him to hit the road, as you very well could have."

"Father," Jonathan spoke up, "I hope you aren't under the impression that she said yes immediately?"

Alastair's expression was curious, "Oh?"

Jonathan pressed his lips together, "Not at all," he gave me a sideways glance, "I proposed on Saturday, after a lovely…" his eyebrow twitched slightly, "Dinner at the cabin."

I knew exactly what he was referring to, and I was sorely tempted to kick him under the table for hinting at what we got up to that night, but I just smiled sweetly at him and took a sip of my wine. *I'll kick his ass later.*

"But," he carried on with his story, "She left me hanging, and she made me sweat until this morning before she gave me an answer."

"Serves you right," Niki said, "You've put her through the wringer."

Jonathan dropped his jaw in mock indignation and turned to me, "You just got here, and already my entire family has turned against me," and the whole table burst out laughing.

After dinner, Jonathan had some work he had to finish on his laptop, and while he worked, I sat on the sofa with my arm over the back of it, watching him. There was nothing I needed to be doing immediately, and even if there was, I'd much rather watch him work, he was so damn pretty. After working quietly for a while, he smiled, "Are you having fun, sitting there, staring at me?"
"I'm not staring," I denied, "I'm observing."
"Yes, observing, of course. And what conclusion have you come to?" he asked.
I slowly shook my head, "No conclusion. I just have a question."
"Go ahead," he urged, his eyes still on the screen.
"How am I going to survive an entire lifetime of you being this gorgeous?".
Jonathan chuckled, but he took a deep breath and turned to me, "Are you ready?"
"For what?"
He gestured at himself, "An entire lifetime of me, and all of the things that go with that."
I smiled, "I think so. But I think maybe there's a lot more we would need to talk about as time goes by."
Jonathan nodded, "I believe so, yes."

He stood up from the desk, his hands in his pockets, and slowly strode over to lock the bedroom door before he made his way over to me on the sofa.
"Tell me more about these things that you say go with you," I asked him when he took a seat next to me on the sofa, and I moved in against him, tracing his collarbone and the lines of his chest and abs through his tank top with my fingertip.
"Danger," was his honest answer.
I kissed the crook of his neck, "What kind of danger?"
Jonathan raked his fingers through his hair, "I have a suspicion that there might be a long lost member of my mother's family roaming around, and that this family member was responsible for Devyn's death. Possibly Owen's as well."
All the blood drained from my face, "Shit…" I said softly, and Jonathan nodded, "But I don't know much more than that."
"Will you tell me if you do?"
He nodded again, "I will, I swear."

I planted a kiss on his cheek, "Thank you."

"How do you feel about marrying the Black Prince now?" he asked.
I thought about it for a moment, "The Black Prince scares me a bit, but I think over time I could get over that, morph my fear of him into some kind of healthy respect."
"So you aren't planning on running for the hills?"
I shook my head, "Not on your life."
I swung my legs over his and cuddled up against him in silence, just feeling him, savoring this quiet, peaceful moment of being wrapped up in his arms, the scent of his skin and the warmth of his body cocooning me. This would be mine, forever.

After a few quiet, blissful moments, I looked up at him, "Was Kat serious? Have you really been calling me your wife behind my back?"
He grinned and kissed my cheek, "I absolutely have. Since the first time we went to Prague. But I've thought of you as my queen for much longer than that."
My jaw dropped, "Duplicitous."
He kissed me then, "I've known that I wanted to spend forever with you since the first time you yelled at me in the street."
"I knew I loved you before I met you," I said, and he burst out laughing, "Now who's being a cheeseball?"
"So," I went on, the first twitches of a salacious little smile starting to curl around my lips, "Since you already locked the door, can I assume that your plan for the rest of the night involves full frontal nudity and a lot of moaning?"
Jonathan grinned and pulled me into a slow, lingering kiss, "Smart woman," he said when he pulled back. "By the way, I really am very happy that you said yes."
"Are you really?" I smiled back, and he nodded slowly, "I am. Tonight, I want to make love to my beautiful fiancée, and tomorrow morning, we can start training. If you want."
I took off my shirt and dropped it onto the sofa, "Let's start with the first thing you mentioned: the love-making. I like the sound of that."
He grasped my breasts in his hands and I moaned.
"Hmm," Jonathan hummed approvingly, "and I like that sound…"

∞

Waking up as Jonathan's future wife was a different kind of peaceful. My eyes still closed, I rolled over and reached for him, but when the bed next to me was empty, I opened my eyes and looked around.
I sat up and turned my head to look towards where I heard movement coming from the closet.
Jonathan was standing inside the walk-in closet, clad in a black t-shirt, his CK briefs, and a pair of white gym socks. And no pants.
My eyes were immediately drawn to the bulge in his briefs, and I bit my lower lip. I was very well acquainted with every inch of what was hiding there. Now if he'd just lower those briefs an inch or two…
"Darling, if you keep staring at me like that, my underwear might just start taking itself off," he said teasingly.
I pulled my knees up and wrapped my arms around my legs, "Sounds perfect, I will have to stare harder then."
He laughed, emerging from the closet holding the sweatpants that he had been searching for, and sat down next to me on the bed. He wrapped his arms around me and hugged me to him, kissing my temple.

When I pulled back I looked down at his muscular thighs and wiggled my eyebrows at him, "Babe, seriously, if I had legs like yours, I would probably walk on my hands all the time."
Jonathan laughed. I nudged his shoulder, "I mean it. Don't be surprised if you wake up one morning to me humping your leg or something."
Jonathan blushed and stood up from the bed, "So flirty so early in the morning. Whatever shall I do with you?"
"Kiss me, feed me, fuck me. Easy."
"In that specific order, or can I just start anywhere?" he asked.
I laughed.
"I feel so privileged," I smiled, watching him as he started putting on his pants, "I usually see you when you're all dressed up and put together, it is very rare that I get to witness the process."
Jonathan shook his head as he tied the drawstring on his pants, "Are you going to change into your gear? Or are you planning on hitting the gym in your pajamas?"
I sighed, but I got out of bed anyway, "Fine. You're so bossy today."

"Okay," I asked him once we were inside the gym, "What are we doing?"
He gestured toward the weights, "Some days we'll do weight training, other days we'll do cardio, other days we will do some combat training. But today we start here."
I looked at all the weights and all of the equipment in the room. It was intimidating to say the least.
"Do I have to come here every day?" I asked.
Jonathan started stretching, warming up, "You don't have to do anything, darling. But the more you train, the better."
"Alright," I sighed when we were done warming up, "Where do I start?"
Jonathan rambled off a bunch of exercise moves that had my head spinning: Dumbbell bench press, lateral pulldown, overhead dumbbell press, leg press, rope press-down, barbell bicep curl, and I blinked slowly at him in confusion, "I understand those words individually… But in that order, I have no idea what you just said."
He smiled, "I'll show you."

Chapter 63

Hunter

Something wasn't sitting right with me.
Ever since I joined the House of Apollo, I firmly believed that the First Family was evil. I was convinced that it was their scion, the one they call the Black Prince, that murdered my father.
I was very excited when the priest assigned me to keep eyes on the Queen and her husband, and I was determined to report back with intel on all of their unholy acts and evil doings.

I followed them when they flew into war-torn Syria, and I steeled myself to bear witness as they slaughtered innocent people just like my father had been exterminated.
The first thing they did was walk into a 'slave bazaar', and I thought this was it: I was going to capture evidence of them buying sex slaves. But then they ripped off the heads of the captors and freed dozens of girls, saving them from being sold and taken to other provinces or countries as sex slaves. And the Queen didn't take any money, didn't ask for anything in return. She didn't take them with her, didn't claim them as hers. She just… hugged them. Dried their tears. And let them go.

After they left Syria, they traveled through Iran, and they did the same thing again.
Emptied out brothels, took the young girls that were being held there to safehouses, and ripped the owners and customers to shreds.
The queen crushed their brains without laying a finger on them, and her husband flattened the buildings where these hell-holes stood to the ground with invisible blasts from his hands, not leaving one brick

on top of the other.
And then they were gone, before anyone could see or talk to them.

From Iran they went North, to Belarus, and they just did the same thing again.
I watched them get punched, kicked, even shot. But nothing deterred them from finishing what they started until they were soaked in the blood of evil men.
And each time they freed the captives–the small children, the desperate women who believed they had no choice and no hope–all they wanted in return was a smile. Nothing more. No media, no pictures. They sought no recognition, no fame. The Queen and her husband really had no ulterior motive. They were just… Helping. Helping those who couldn't help themselves, when no-one else had dared.

By the time I returned to Germany, I had nothing to report. The priest wasn't happy with my lie that I lost track of them, and that I spent my time abroad trying to retrace their steps. Actually, I was sure the priest knew I was lying. But that was a chance that I was willing to take. I was their first success story, and I commanded their legions; they wouldn't do anything to me, and they would just have to take my word. Blindly, just as I had taken the word of Apollo–for who knows how long–that the First Family was evil. That they were bloodthirsty, murderous monsters that had to be stopped.

Now, I wasn't so sure anymore.

Chapter 64

Kirill

I'd always liked London. I couldn't quite put my finger on why, but there was just something about it that resonated well with me. I didn't get to go there often, so I was quite glad that this contract, working as private security, brought me here. The work was easy. Almost too easy. The pay was really good, and all of my expenses would be paid for, so it felt like a mini-vacation.

And I needed that. After Devyn…
I thought about her a lot. Her laugh, her smile. And every time I closed my eyes, I saw her lifeless face before me and it made me angry all over again that her young life had ended so brutally. I wasn't sure why I thought of her so often, I didn't even know her all that well. I tried my best not to have regrets in life, but I did regret that I hadn't seen her more often or spent more time with her before she died. I would have liked to get to know her better; she could have been a really good friend. Perhaps she might even have been more than a friend, someday. Even if I would never have been able to tell her everything about myself.

Thinking of Devyn always led my thoughts to Christina. It must be very difficult for her to deal with losing her best friend, but Vanya would take really good care of her.
He has dealt with death and loss many, many times, so if anyone knew and understood what Nuchka was going through, it was Vanya. The rest of Vanya's family would also be there for Nuchka, and help her and support her in these dark times, but I was still worried about her.

She had become my friend too, and I didn't want my friends to be unhappy.
Perhaps I should stop by when this contract ends, check in on her and Vanya, see how they're doing.
I wonder if Vanya proposed yet? He'd been talking about it for a very long time. That would be nice, some good news would be very welcome.

I took another sip of my coffee. It was good coffee. *I should get some for Grigor. Grigor loves coffee.*
That reminded me, Grigor had been acting… strange… mysteriously disappearing from the house for days at a time, never able to talk about where he had gone, unknown numbers calling the house at all hours of the night. I mean, I was curious, but I wasn't going to pry. Not unless I received direct orders from her Majesty or Vanya. It seemed as if Grigor either had a new woman in his life that he was trying to keep secret, or he was up to no good.

Checking the time on my phone, I grimaced.
My lunch break would be over soon, and I would have to go back to the client. I didn't know the man; it was part of my contract that I didn't need to know the reason that my clients sought protection. I wasn't there to be judge or jury, but I was sure that if I knew too much about my clients' business, I might be tempted to be the executioner, and killing the person who was supposed to sign your paycheck was never a good idea. But I didn't like this man. Not that liking someone was a requirement for doing my job, but there was something about this man that reminded me of a snake… His face and his eyes had a distinct serpentine quality to them.

I sipped more coffee, gazing at the people passing by down the busy street that the restaurant I was sitting in was located on, when the voice of a ghost from the past brought my entire existence to a skidding stop. My eyes widened, my mouth ran dry and I sat forward, trying to pinpoint where it came from.
There it is again. That voice. I know that voice. But it can't be.
A couple walked past the restaurant, one of them a fairly tall, slender man with pale skin and long black hair.

Something about him seemed very vaguely familiar. I shook my head. Probably nothing. Strangers sometimes just look familiar.
But everything in my body ran cold when I saw the person accompanying the man. Arms linked, laughing and smiling at the long-haired man, was a lovely young woman, with long black hair… and eyes the color of wild honey.
She was the spitting image of my first love.
My *lastochka.*
Valentina.
The couple rounded the corner and I leapt to my feet. I didn't know why, but I followed them. I had to see for myself, I had to know. Was it her?
But when I rounded the corner, they were gone. Disappeared, like mist in the morning sun.
Scratching my head, I walked back to the restaurant and paid the bill before heading back to the client's office.
I shook my head at myself. It couldn't have been her. She would have been long dead by now.
I was just finally losing my mind, that would probably make more sense. *Maybe I'll stop by a liquor store on the way to the office... Fuck knows I need a drink.*

Chapter 65

Christina

"Are you sure you don't want to join us?" I double-checked with Celeste at the breakfast table. Jonathan and I were heading back to my house after breakfast to start wedding planning with my mom, and even though I asked Celeste to join us, she declined.

"Now, *koritsi mou*," she smiled, "wedding planning can be very overwhelming. You and your mother will have lots to discuss and lots to think about, and you don't need your mother-in-law in the middle of that."

"But I want my mother-in-law in the middle of that," I pouted.

Celeste laughed, "Oh, you're the cutest."

Jonathan nodded, "I know. That face gets me every time."

Smiling, she squeezed my shoulder, "I promise I will join you for the next round of planning."

I put my hand over Celeste's and nodded in acceptance, "I'd like that very much."

She excused herself from the breakfast table, and she ruffled Jonathan's hair when she walked past the back of his chair, "You need a haircut, sweetheart."

He ducked out from under his mother's hand, "Not yet, my wife said she likes it."

I really did. His hair was getting really long, and my ovaries were poised to explode if he ever put that glorious mop of black silk up in a man-bun.

"Darling," he sighed when he loaded my overnight bag into his car after breakfast, "I don't want to do this anymore."
I frowned, "Do what?"
He gestured to my bag, "Take you home, wake up without you. I don't want it. I just want you next to me, every moment of every day."
"We'll be married soon, and…"
"I don't want to wait until then," he shook his head, interrupting me. "Move in with me?"
I clasped my hands together over my heart, "Really? Are you sure?"
He smiled and nodded, "Of course I'm sure. We'd need to expand the closet, I don't think there's much space left. But that shouldn't take too long. Will you? Will you move in with me?"
I bit my lower lip and nodded, "Of course."
"Thank you," he murmured against my neck as he wrapped his arms around my waist and hugged me tightly, lifting my feet off the ground. "Come on," he said when he put me down and kissed my forehead, "let's go plan our wedding."

At my house, my mom and her list were waiting for us at the kitchen table.
"Okay lovebirds," she started after she poured everyone a cup of coffee, "first things first, have you chosen a date?"
Jonathan looked over at me and grinned, "How's tomorrow?"
"Hah!" I guffawed, "I love you to bits, but there's no way."
He chuckled then turned to my mom, "We haven't decided. But we can discuss other things first, if that's alright."
Nodding, my mom scribbled something on her sheet of paper, and then looked back at us, "What kind of budget are we looking at? Who is paying for which part of this auspicious occasion?"
Jonathan put his hand on my leg under the table, "Would it sound terrible if I said there's no limit on the budget?"
My jaw dropped, "You can't be serious?"
He squeezed my leg, "I am. Very serious," he said before he dug his credit card from his wallet and put it down in front of me. "Anything you want, love. Make your Pinterest board a reality."
"But babe…"
He kissed my cheek, "Please, darling, no buts. Let me do this? Let me give you your dream wedding?"
I grabbed his hand with both of mine, "What about your dream?"

Smiling tenderly at me, he ran his thumb across my lips, “You are my dream, Christina.”
My mom smiled, “Jonathan, that's very sweet of you, but you really don’t have to pay for everything.”
He nodded, “I fully understand that, Mum, but I really want to.”
I leaned over to him and rested my head against his shoulder, “You’re amazing. I’m going to rob you blind.”
He kissed my hair, “Go right ahead, love.”
“Next question,” my mom went on, “do you want a big wedding? Or are we thinking small and intimate?”
I looked up at Jonathan, “This one you have to decide, you know a lot of people.”
He thought about it for a moment before he replied, “I do, but everyone I know does not need to be invited to our wedding. I don’t know that I want a big wedding.”
My mom scribbled something again, then turned to me, “Christina, honey, have you given any thought to the bridal party?”
I smiled wistfully, “I always thought that one day when I got married, I’d ask Devyn to be my maid of horror.”
My mom just smiled while Jonathan squeezed my hand, and I went on, “But I think now, maybe I’ll ask Lilian. And I would like for Niki to be my bridesmaid.”
Jonathan smiled, “She’d be ecstatic.”
“No flower girl?” My mom wanted to know.
I shook my head, “No, that’s okay. Do you know who you want as your Best Man, babe?” I asked him.
He nodded, “Best Woman. Kat.”
I grinned, “My future-husband, the feminist. Nice. Do you think she’ll want to wear a suit?”
He chuckled, “I hope not, she looks better in a suit than I do. She’ll steal my thunder. Either Kirill or Nathaniel can be our ring bearer, if that’s alright with you.”
He went on when I nodded in acceptance, “The two of them can fight it out amongst themselves for who wants the job,” he said.
I glanced over at my mom’s list, “You can take ‘wedding website’ off the list, Mom, I’m not doing that.”
“Okay,” she shrugged, “and Jonathan, I’m guessing the ring is already insured?”
He nodded, “Taken care of.”

“We have to choose a venue,” I said to him then, and he nodded again, “We can drive around and see a few, if you want.”
“Actually, I was hoping we could have the ceremony in the chapel. Where Devyn’s funeral was held,” I said softly. He took my hand again, “That sounds perfect, love.”
I pulled my mom’s list closer, “For some of these things, the photographer, videographer, caterer, florist, and musicians… Babe, can we ask Kat?”
“Of course, that’s what she does,” Jonathan said, “I’ll ask her.”
“Great,” Belinda said as she jotted something down on her list, then she turned to me with a smile, “So about your dress…”
“Mom, wait,” I interrupted her, then I turned to Jonathan with a guilty smile, “I’m not trying to be a bridezilla, but I want to surprise you.”
He raised his eyebrows, “Are you politely asking me to leave?”
I wrinkled my nose, “Kind of… Sorry babe.”
He smiled, and pushed his chair back, “No problem, I understand. I think. If you’ll excuse me then, I shall take my leave.”

I walked with him back to his car.
“By the way,” I asked when he unlocked the doors, “do I need to sign a prenup?”
“What?” Jonathan snarled, and if I didn’t know any better, I could have sworn that the atmospheric pressure dropped.
Very slowly, Jonathan turned around to look me in the eye, and the look on his face almost made me take a step back. His face was calm and nearly expressionless, but his eyes were coal black, and anger seethed from his every pore.
“What did you just say?” he hissed through clenched teeth.
I gulped. *He’s mad at me.*
He’d never been mad at me before, not like this and I didn’t know what to do, “I’m just asking…” I said in a small voice.

He took a breath that shuddered through him and he expelled it in an angry huff, “Christina, I love you, and I have a world of respect for you, but darling… What the fuck kind of a question is that?”
I gulped again. I really didn’t know what to say. Why was he so mad? I was just asking a question.

Jonathan cursed under his breath, and shook his head. Then he raised his hands in surrender, "You know what…" he mumbled, "I can't do this."
"Can't do what?" I whimpered, "Talk to me?"
He lowered his hands, clenching his hands into fists at his sides. He looked at the ground, and when he lifted his head up to look at me, his fangs were out and my eyes widened. He really was angry.

He flung open his car door, "Right now, no, I can't. So I am leaving."
Tears welled up in my eyes, "Where are you going?"
What is happening?
He got into his car, slammed the door shut and started the engine, 'I don't know."
"Jonathan," I sniffed, "Wh… Are you coming back?"
He turned his head. He was looking me in the eyes, at least, "Of course I am. I love you, and I still want to marry you."
"Love you too," I managed to get out before he sped off, leaving screeching tires, exhaust fumes, and a completely baffled me in his wake.

I stood outside the house for a few moments in shocked silence. *This has never happened before and I have no idea how to handle Furious-With-Me Jonathan.*
"Honey?" my mom's voice cut through the silence.
I turned to my mom, and I could feel my lower lip trembling.
A concerned look clouded my mom's face and she held out her arms for me to step into a hug, "What happened?" she wanted to know.
"I don't know…" I mumbled.
My mom ushered me back into the house, "Let's go inside, I have wine in the fridge…"

Jonathan

I had no idea where I was going.
Why the fuck would Christina think it even necessary to ask me that? As if I gave a shit about money, as if I had ever considered that she wanted me for that.
As if I would ever leave her.
Ever-loving fucking Hell, if she ever left me she could take every last penny I had, I wouldn't give a fuck. All I wanted was her. And if, Moonlight forbid, the day ever came where she no longer wanted me, then nothing in the world would be worth fighting for anymore. Especially not money.
"Fuck!" I exclaimed loud enough for the driver in the next vehicle over at the traffic light to hear, and the man looked over at me in concern and consternation.
I raised a hand in apology, "Sorry about that."
The guy shook his head, "No sweat. Are you okay?"
I shrugged, "Probably. I don't know."
The man nodded slowly, "I feel that, dude. But hey, look, my mom tells me everything will work out the way it's supposed to, you know?"
The light turned green, and I nodded to the man in the car next to me, "Thank you, I needed to hear that. Take care," I said before I drove myself home.

On the way I put in a quick call and left a message for Nathaniel. There was something I needed him to take care of. Then I called Kat to drop by the house and portal us to London.
After speaking to Kat, I sent Christina a text:
I'm going to London with Kat
I love you.
I was fucking livid, but I wasn't going to abandon my wife.

"What are we doing here?" Kat asked me as we strode into a random little pub in London.
Rolling my eyes at her, I ordered a round of drinks, "Drinking, what does it look like?"

She replied slowly, "Yes, day-drinking, I can see that, but why here in London?"
I shrugged and slammed all three of my shots from the six that I ordered, "Why not London? It's a fine place to drink, in my opinion."
"Right..." she said incredulously.
A few more rounds later, she raised her eyebrows slowly at me, "Have you calmed down enough to tell me what pissed you off?"
I shook my head, "I need a new friend, mine knows me too well."
She chuckled, "Jonny-boy, I knew you were pissed off the moment you called me."
"How?" I raised an eyebrow at her.
She took another shot, "When you lose your shit, the air smells like ozone. I could smell it through the phone."
I tipped my head back and laughed.

"Pray tell, who or what pissed you off?"
I ruffled my hair, "Christina."
"What the fuck?" Kat was taken aback.
I smirked, "My exact words."
Kat made a beckoning motion, "Out with it, tell me the full story."
"She asked me if she needed to sign a prenup."
Silence.
"And...?" she said after a while.
"That's the reason I'm pissed. Because she felt that she needed to ask me that."
Kat didn't reply. She ordered us another round, and waited for the shots to be lined up on the bar in front of us before she spoke again, "You're overreacting. Signing a prenup is very normal. She didn't mean anything by it, and you know it. Get off your man-strual cycle and apologize to your wife."
I frowned, "Just like that?"
She took two shots and nodded, "Yes, just like that. You losing your temper and deciding to go day-drinking over a logical question was a massive dick-move on your part, and you owe her an apolo..." her sentence ended short, and her face twisted into a grimace.
I looked just past her shoulder at the short, burly fellow that had decided to slap and squeeze her arse, who was now grinning to his buddies about it.

I hissed out a breath, "I've been looking for an excuse to get aggressive."

I grabbed the man's wrist and yanked him away from Kat. One quick punch to the stomach, and then I slammed his face into the bar. Twice. He dropped to the floor, bleeding and groaning in pain. "Never touch a woman without her consent, you sack of shit!" I shouted. Movement from the corner of my eye drew my attention: one of the burly man's friends was storming at me, his face twisted in what appeared to be rage, balled fist at the ready. I heard Kat chuckle to my left, and I shot her a meaningful glance before I ducked out of the way of the pudgy fist and punched the man in the stomach. He doubled over in pain, and I let him drop to the floor before turning to the next advancing chump. I waited until he was close enough before stepping to the side and sticking out my foot to trip him up. I laughed out loud as he fell face first into the side of the bar. I looked up to see what Kat was doing, and I whooped when she slammed an elbow into the nose of another fellow. He fell backward onto a patron seated nearby, who was not at all happy about his beer being knocked over, and he shoved the man forward. "Watch what the fuck you're doing!" he shouted at Kat before joining the fray. He swung a fist at her face, but her fist hit his elbow from below and he hollered in pain.
Another fist flew at my face from the side, but I swiped the hand away and plunged my fist into the solar plexus of the man that had swung at me.

The bouncers were on their way over to us, and I thought now was as good a time as any for Kat and I to get the hell out of there.
"Kitty!" I called out to her, and she spun her head to look at me, but not before she slammed her forehead into that of another guy that had lunged at her. I didn't need to say anything else; she nodded and pushed her way through the brawling men, and made her way toward me. We shoved our way out, past the man that had groped Kat where he was still laying on the floor, and I got in one more swift kick to his head before I threw open the door and ran out of the pub with Kat in tow.

She squealed with laughter as we ran out onto the street and rounded the corner. We kept going until we were several blocks away from the pub before we stopped running.

We looked at each other in breathless silence… and Kat burst out laughing where she had flopped down on a bench, "That was a fucking riot."
I leaned forward, my hands on my thighs, "Arrogant son-of-a-bitch. I will never understand how someone that short has balls that big."
Kat laughed even harder, "I was going to kick his fat ass myself, but thank you for defending my honor."
I straightened my back, "Speaking of riotous behavior, are you up for… an unscheduled appointment?"
She grinned, nodding, "Fuck yes. Where are we going?"
I cocked an eyebrow, "Emery's apartment."

Chapter 66

Katalina

I'd never been to Emery's part of town. Never wanted to, never had any reason to go there. But there I was, standing next to Jonathan, waiting for him to call Emery to see if she was at home. I was not entirely sure that I liked where this was going, but I was willing to let it play out and see what he was up to. Up to a point.

"Your Majesty, good evening," Emery purred when she answered.
"Emery, hello," Jonathan replied, and the huskiness to his voice made me pull up my nose in disgust. He looked blankly at me before he continued, "I'll cut straight to the chase. Are you at home?"
Emery drew a breath in surprise, "Is this a booty call?"
Jonathan chuckled seductively but didn't reply, and I shuddered. *Gross, Jonny.*
She giggled, "I see… Well, then, in that case, yes, I am at home."
"Excellent. Are you at the same address?" he wanted to know.
"Yes, Your Majesty."
"Good. Do you mind if Katalina accompanies me?"
"Uhm…" she stammered and gulped audibly, "No, not at all. I'd be delighted to have both of you... over."
The innuendo wasn't lost on me, and I groaned inwardly. *What the fuck is going on?*
"See you soon." He ended the call.

When we arrived at Emery's apartment, I wanted to burst out laughing at the myriad of candles that she had set out and lit all over her apartment. She even put on mood music.

Jonathan gave Emery a solemn nod by way of greeting, and he strode right by her and started unbuttoning his shirt.
I didn't like what he seemed to be planning. Emery was an oblivious, chirpy idiot, because this wasn't the Jonathan that she was expecting. From the set of his jaw, to the streamlined way he moved and the way he spoke, I knew this was not Jonathan, this was the Black Prince. Be that as it may, I really didn't like what I was seeing.

Emery gave him a sultry smirk, and she beckoned the Prince closer. He moved toward her, and fury simmered in my belly. *I cannot believe he's about to fucking cheat on his fiancée. I'm going to kick his royal ass. Fucking prick.*

Still wearing that crooked grin, he stepped closer. Emery reached for him, and he wrapped his hand around the base of her throat… And he slammed her into the wall behind her with such might that it forced the air from her lungs, and his claws dug into the wallpaper.
"Did you really think I came here to fuck?" he snarled at her through his bared fangs, the seductive grin on his face replaced by a look of utter disgust, "Why would I ever want to fuck you a second time? Once was bad enough."
"Majesty…" she whimpered but he wouldn't let her speak, "Shut the fuck up and listen.
Do. Not. Ever. Threaten. My fiancée. Again," he bit out the words, and I was shocked at the venom dripping from his voice.
"Go near Christina, and I will cut out your fucking tongue. Do you understand?" he snarled, and I gulped. I could smell Emery's fear, surely he could as well.
"Do you understand?" he bellowed, and Emery nodded really fast, "Yes, yes I understand. I'm sorry."
The Black Prince let her go abruptly, and she crumpled to the floor in a pile of shivers and sobs.
He gave her one more look of disdain, buttoned his shirt and stormed out.

I was right behind him, and when we reached the street, I shoved him so hard that he staggered a few steps forward, "What the fuck was that?"

He spun around to glare at me, anger flashing across his face, "That vicious bitch had the audacity to call Christina my human plaything. Who the fuck does she think she is?" he barked at me, "And don't fucking shove me!"

"You didn't have to attack her for it!" I yelled back.

He turned his back to me and took a few deep breaths.

"Jonny," I said, as calmly as I could.

"I know, I know…" came his shaky response, "That's why I needed you to come with me. If you hadn't been there, I would have splattered her across the fucking wall."

I strode over to him, "If you needed an anger buffer, why didn't you just tell me?"

"I don't know… I'm sorry."

"That was cruel… You made Emery think you wanted her…"

"I wanted to see the look on her face when I crushed her hopes right in front of her," came his honest answer.

I cocked my head to the side, "And at what point did you decide that I needed to be there for this fuckery?"

For a moment, he didn't respond. Then he turned around to face me, "I don't have an answer for that. That…. That wasn't me. That was him. I'm sorry."

I glared at him for a moment. Then I went on, "I'm not the one you should be apologizing to."

His expression turned from contrite to incredulous, "If you think I'm going to apologize to Emery, you're out of your fucking mind."

"Who are you right now?" I asked, and he ran a hand through his hair.

"What does that mean?"

I gestured back towards Emery's place with an open hand, "You completely flew off the handle at Christina for asking you about a prenup, which is the most normal thing ever to ask before getting married. I've never been in a relationship and even I know that. I'm baffled how you, in all of your wisdom and knowledge, didn't know that and how you thought it meant something bad about her. And then you did that shit to poor Emery…"

"Fuck that!" he countered, "She deserved worse."

I groaned in frustration, "My point is, you are acting completely out of character. What is going on?"

He lowered his head and took a deep breath, "I don't even know…"

“Are you getting cold feet already? You regret proposing? To Christina?” I asked. Jonathan shook his head vigorously, “No, never.”
I gave him a pointed look, “Then what the fuck, Jonny?”
“It caught me off guard when Christina asked, because I thought she would know that we didn’t need a prenup… I… I couldn’t stand the thought of anyone ever thinking that she only wanted me for what I had in the bank…” he mumbled bashfully.
I folded my arms across my chest, “That is the biggest crock of horseshit I’ve ever heard in my immortal life. That woman loves you, and you should thank the Blessed Moon for her every day.”
He nodded, “I do, believe me.”
“Good,” I went on. “Then grow up, and act like the man she deserves.”
He took another deep breath and looked me in the eye, “That was egregious, wasn’t it?”
I nodded. “It really was.”
“Asshole,” I said before I ducked in under his arm and draped it over my shoulder, my arm around his waist as we started walking down the dark street, “For a moment I really thought you were actually going to fuck Emery, and I thought to myself ‘Jonathan, I swear, if you cheat on Christina, prince or not, I'll kick your fucking ass’.”
He pulled me closer and hugged me, “Never. I’d never, ever do anything that would jeopardize what I have with her. But that fierce loyalty is one on the many reasons I love you, you fucking psycho.”
“I know, that’s why I’m going to be your Best Woman.”
He frowned at me, “Who said I was going to ask you?”
I nudged him with my hip, “Pfft, please. Just try asking someone else, and I’ll show you psycho.”

Emery

His Eternal Majesty left my apartment hours ago, but I was still shaking.
I hate him.
Ugh, who am I fucking kidding? I don't hate him. I love him. I've loved him since 1975. And then we had one magical night together a few years later, and I hoped he would call me the next day to ask me out again. He didn't. But I held on to hope, even when he never spoke to me again and hardly greeted me. I waited, watching from the sidelines as he took other girls home without so much as a glance in my direction. I waited.

I'd heard he had a girlfriend, but I didn't believe it. He'd never had a girlfriend, not that I knew of, and I had always hoped I would be his first. I would be such a good girlfriend. I'd never argue with him, never challenge him. I would live to serve and obey him, and he would be my Prince, and I would be his Princess, and we would take on eternity together.
When I saw him walking towards me at the club my heart felt so light, and I thought he finally realized that I was what he had been looking for. But then he introduced me to her, and I couldn't believe he brought her with him to London. I was disgusted.

She wasn't even one of us. She was mortal. Weak. How could he want her over me? I was stronger than she was. She would never be able to keep up with his appetites in the bedroom the way I could. And she clearly had no respect for him; she didn't even bow to him when he got on the stage.

I was so happy when he called me tonight. I didn't care that it was a booty call, I didn't care that he wanted to bring his friend. I was just happy that I would be in his arms again, have him in my bed, have his beautiful cock inside me.
But then he slammed me into the wall, and….

Tears took over again as I recalled the violence in his eyes, the hate in his voice as he told me to stay away from her. From his fiancée. He was going to fucking marry her! And my broken heart shattered even further.

I hate him. I love him.

I hate how much I love him.

And he'll never be mine.

Chapter 67

Christina

It was the weekend of Lilian and Nathaniel's wedding, and my bags were packed and ready to go, but Jonathan hadn't been back since he lost his temper and stormed off a few days ago, so I wasn't entirely sure how I was supposed to get to London. The only thing I could do was wait.

I was tidying up the kitchen on Friday morning after my mom went to work, when the doorbell rang.

"Jonathan," I whispered, running to the door and flinging it open to see…

Three delivery guys, each holding a massive bouquet of red roses.

"Delivery for Mrs. C Langdon?" the first one said, and I almost cried from happiness, "That's me."

"Hang on, let me get your tip," I said to them on their way back out the door after they put the flowers on the kitchen table.

"That's alright ma'am," one of them denied, "already taken care of. Have a nice day now."

With a smile so big it could split my face in half, I sat down at the table to read the card that came with the roses:

My darling wife,
I horribly overreacted, and I am very sorry.
I hope you can forgive my disgusting behavior.
If you're ready to join me in London,
I will send Simon to take you to the jet.
But please call me when you get this.
I love you, forever and infinity.
Your husband

I clutched the note to my chest. *This is so sweet.* Then I looked at the roses and I shook my head. My rich boy.
A small bouquet would have been more than enough, but not for Jonathan. Oh no, His Royal Darkness sent me not one, not two, but three dozen long-stemmed red roses. The definition of overkill.

He picked up the phone almost immediately when I called.
"My darling, my love, my light in the dark, I am so sorry for acting like such a prick," he started.
"Hi love," I smiled into the phone. "Thank you for my gorgeous flowers."
"I miss you, are you coming to London?" he wanted to know.
"Of course I am. I'm the Maid of Honor."
"Is that the only reason? Do you not want to see me, even just a little bit?" he asked, and I could hear the pout in his voice.
"Only if you're going to be very naked."
Jonathan laughed, "I love you, woman."
"I love you. You can tell Simon I'm ready to go."
"Immediately, your highness."
I felt myself blushing, "Stop… I'm not a princess."
"Your pussy certainly tastes like one," he murmured and my blush deepened.
"Jonathan…" I admonished.
"Are you blushing?" he asked.
"Yes…"
He chuckled, "You are so cute when you blush, I could just eat you out."
I laughed, "Don't you mean you could eat me up?"
"I really don't," he replied and his grin was audible, "I said what I meant, I meant what I said."

When the jet landed at the air strip in London, the same wider-than-my-ears-grin found its way back onto my face when I disembarked, and the first thing I saw was Jonathan waiting for me with yet another giant bouquet of red roses.
He smiled that heartbreakingly beautiful smile of his, and I ran to him and leapt into his arms, letting him crush my body against him in a hug.

“I am so sorry,” he mumbled, his lips pressed against the side of my neck, “You asked me a simple question and I reacted like a complete moron. I am so sorry darling.”
I returned the hug, “It’s okay, it was a dumb question.”
Jonathan pulled back and kissed me. “It was not,” he said when the kiss ended. “It was sensible, and logical, and I had no reason to be mad at you for asking. I’m sorry.”
I cupped his handsome face in my hands, “I forgive you. You still haven’t answered my question, but I forgive you.”
Smiling, he shook his head, “No, you do not need to sign any kind of prenup. All that I have, all that I am, everything belongs to you.”
I kissed him again. He was too sweet, too cute, too hot for me to stay mad at him. I still couldn’t believe I was actually going to marry him.

“Did you drive here?” I asked when he finally put my feet on the ground and took my hand to walk me to the waiting car.
He shook his head, “No, I had the driver bring me. I wanted to be able to hold you all the way to our apartment.”
I bit my lower lip, “You said ‘our apartment’…”
He kissed my temple and nodded, “I did.” Then he scanned me up and down, “Please tell me you’re wearing that tiny little skirt for a reason…?”
I winked at him, but didn’t reply.
But he growled and instantly set my blood on fire, “*Cochetă…*”

At the apartment, he waited for the bellboy to carry my luggage inside, then he pressed a tip into the young man’s hand and ushered him out the door.
I knew why.
As soon as the door snicked shut, Jonathan kissed me hungrily as he hoisted me up onto the kitchen counter and stepped in between my legs.
I wrapped my legs around him and reached my hand down the front of his pants, and I heard myself moan when I felt how hard he was in my hand.
“Babe,” I murmured, nipping at his earlobe with my teeth, “hard for me already?”
He nodded and pressed his dick into my hand.

I kissed him, twining my tongue with his. When he reached in under my skirt, I tilted my hips to help him slip off my panty and drop it to the floor.
"May I?" he asked
"May you do what?"
He gave me a pointed look, "You know exactly what I want to do."
"I do," I replied, trying to keep my breathing even while his hands were exploring my breasts, "but like you said, for the intents and purposes of today's… activities, I'm going to need you to say it out loud," I quoted his own words back to him.
He raised his eyebrows, "Oh, so you want my filthy, ancient mouth, is that it?"
I bit my lower lip and nodded. It really got me wet when Jonathan talked dirty to me. That was exactly what I wanted. To be wet and to have his magnificent dick inside me.

He took a breath between his clenched teeth… Then he grabbed my left arm and looked at the inside of my wrist, "Darling what is this?"
I pressed my lips together as he lightly traced the outlines of my new tattoo.
"I forgot to tell you about that…" I'd been wanting a tattoo for a while, and though we'd never directly talked about it, once we got engaged I knew exactly what I wanted to get, and I didn't think he'd mind.
He looked up at me, wonder and astonishment written all across his face, "This is... this is the mantling from…"
"From your family crest." I completed his sentence and I nodded, "I thought it was appropriate."
I had originally thought of getting the family crest as is, but I eventually settled on just the mantling instead of the whole thing. The flourish of it struck me as a tad more feminine. "Since I am joining the family, I guess that makes it our family crest?"

"Babe…" I breathed softly when tears welled up in his eyes.
Jonathan pinched his eyes shut and wiped his eyes with the back of his hand.
"You're spectacular," he mumbled before his lips reclaimed mine.
He dragged my body to the edge of the counter and two fingers slipped inside me as his tongue found mine.

I groaned into his mouth and his thumb slid to my clit, "Fuck…" he whispered.
"I want you inside me," I said.
With a crooked smile, he gently pushed me over so I lay down on the counter, "I want to be inside you. But first I need to taste you."
My damn legs parted themselves. He took a step back and leaned down to press his tongue to the warmest part of my body and took a long, slow taste.
He closed his eyes and sighed, "You say you're not a princess, but with a pussy this delicious, how is that possible?"
Without waiting for my response, he leaned back down and absolutely went to town on me, tongue and teeth and lips and fingers, and before I even knew what was going on, my back was arching off the counter in primal rapture. When my orgasm ended, Jonathan picked me up off the counter and carried me over to the bed.
He was about to lay on top of me but I turned myself around and got on my hands and knees.
I heard him groan at the sight of me, on all-fours in front of him, my skirt up around my waist, "Do it again?" I asked.
"Do what again?" he acted innocent, "Eat you out? You want my tongue all over your pussy again?"
Fuck, this dirty mouth…
"Yes…" I muttered, "There too…"
"Oh, darling," he chuckled darkly, "You want my tongue on your arse?"
"Mm-hmm," I hummed in confirmation.
He ran his finger through the folds of my pussy, the tip of his finger flicking over my clit, "Say it."
"Babe…" I felt my face glowing red.
"Talk to me, Christina. Tell me what you want me to do."
Fuck it. If he wants me to say it, then I will. I pinched my eyes shut and I went for it, "I want… your tongue… on my ass."
"Yes, your highness," he said, and the next sound that left my mouth was his name, moaned from the deepest parts of my chest, when his tongue started at my clit and went up. And up some more, right over my ass. Again. And again. And again.
I'd never been comfortable with anything or anyone going anywhere near my ass, and I wanted him everywhere, but it still took me by surprise when the tip of his finger slipped into my ass… and I froze.

He pulled his hand back immediately and pushed my body down onto the bed, pressing his body down on mine, pinning me beneath him.
"How is every part of you this delicious?" he asked, snaking his hand around to the front of my body and in between my thighs to stroke my clit.
I was whimpering and breathless beneath him, but I turned my head to look at him, "You didn't have to stop."
He kissed the side of my neck, "Not today, love," he breathed next to my ear.
"Next time?" I asked.
"There's no need to rush," he replied. "When you're ready, when you're sure that's what you want, I will be more than happy to take your arse. And if you decide you don't want that…"
I gasped when I felt the tip of his dick pressing against the entrance to my pussy and he eased himself into me, unbearably slowly, "Then I will be more than delighted to have you this way, for the rest of eternity. My cock fits inside your pussy so well."
He pulled back and slowly plunged into me again, and I knew he was right: His dick was made for me.
His hips rolled into me until I shattered in climax, and he kept going until he came inside me.

"It is absolutely true what they say," I panted when Jonathan had rolled off of me, and I turned myself over onto my back, "make-up sex really is worth fighting for." It really was, and the whore in my heart savored the feeling of his cum dripping out of me.
Jonathan groaned as he stretched next to me and slowly sat up, "Be that as it may, I'd prefer not to fight."
"But babe, if we don't fight, how are we ever going to have make-up sex?"
He chuckled, "We'll pretend we had a fight, and just fuck really well anyway."
I started pulling my skirt back down, but Jonathan stopped me, "Wait... Open up for me, let me see."
"Fuck, babe…" I blushed, but I did as he said; I knew what he wanted to see.
He put his hands on my knees and I heard him hiss. I clamped a hand over my eyes, "Do you like what you see?"

"You mean, do I like seeing my cum dripping out of your pussy?" he asked and my face heated up even more, "Fuck yes."
"Jonathan," I complained, "I need to get cleaned up, before your cum goes everywhere. I feel like a fucking Twinkie…"
"Darling," he chuckled, "if I had my way I'd cover you in cum from face to shoelace, and then I'd take you shopping." Then he shook his head at me, "A Twinkie, really…"
I lifted my head and gave him a blank look, "You'd take me shopping, smelling like cum?" and he chuckled, "Absolutely."
I rolled my eyes at him, "I'm not even going to respond to that. I need to get cleaned up, please, before there's cum all over my skirt."
Jonathan shrugged, "Then I'll wash it for you. You should wear pants tonight, anyway."
"Why?" I frowned.
"I forgot to tell you, Nathaniel invited us and a few friends to join him and Lilian for a final bachelor-bachelorette celebration," he said.
"Are we going clubbing?"
"No, actually. Paintball."
I grinned, "Fuck yeah!"
"Are you excited?"
I nodded, "I'm scared of getting shot, because I heard it hurts like a bitch, but yes, I'm excited."
Jonathan's smile mirrored mine, "Can you shoot?"
I shrugged, "Not well, but I think I'll be okay. Obviously you can."
He shrugged as well, "I honestly prefer a sword, but I can handle myself around guns."

Pretty words, but a bare-faced lie, I quickly realized once again when we arrived at the outdoor paintball arena: Jonathan could do a lot more than just 'handle himself around guns'.
Even though they were just paintball guns and not the real deal, he held and handled them like they were part of him, extensions of his being.
At the start of the game, Nathaniel laid out some rules, one of the rules being that no Infinite abilities would be allowed. But Jonathan didn't even seem to need his Infinite skills.
Decked out from head to toe in safety gear, I was teamed up with Jonathan, because he wouldn't have it any other way.

I was awestruck at the effortless grace with which he moved through the course. Guns were firing, paintballs flying everywhere, players running and jumping and cursing, but Jonathan moved through the course, silently, fluidly, like a tiger on the hunt. His face was a mask of unfeeling focus, his body moved with military precision and proficiency, opposing players dropping like flies around us. He kept himself in front of me the entire course, using his body to shield me, and I barely got a shot in, but I was too wet to complain. It was incredibly fucking sexy to watch. My breath caught in my throat when he suddenly stopped, yanked me against him and spun me out of the way to take out two other players that had snuck up behind us.

When they dropped to the ground, he looked down at me, “Are you alright, love?”

I swallowed hard and looked up him, my lower lip drawn in between my teeth, “I am so fucking wet right now.”

He’d taken his off, but I was still wearing my mask and I couldn’t kiss him the way I wanted to. “I really want to kiss you right now,” he said before he lifted the gun and shot another player behind me without even breaking eye contact with me.

“You really are The Undeniable… You’re making me so hot for you,” I whispered.

He stroked my hair, “Feel free to show me how much… As soon as I’m done handing everyone’s arse to them.”

“I spoke to Lilian,” I said to him as we were walking hand-in-hand down the street in the dark, leaving the paintball arena, “she told me that Emery was disinvited from the wedding…”

“Good…” was his only response.

“Jonathan…”

He cocked an eyebrow, “Christina.”

I squinted at him, “What did you do?”

He pulled up his shoulders, “Nothing. And before you ask, I didn’t make them do anything, either. Whatever they chose to do, was their own decision.”

I rolled my eyes. He was such a fucking liar sometimes, “Do you really expect me to believe that you had absolutely nothing to do with that?”

He tilted his head from side to side, “I didn’t say that…”

I pinched his arm and he winced, "Ow! Gremlin."
"What did you do?" I demanded, and I stopped walking and tugged on his arm. He turned back to look at me and rolled his eyes, "Kat and I dropped by her apartment the other day and I told her to stay away from you, or else."
I stopped dead in my tracks, "Are you serious? You threatened her?"
He shook his head, "I reminded her of her place."
I folded my arms across my chest, "Tell me the truth, Jonathan. Did you threaten her?"
I was met with a facial expression set in steely resolve, "No, I warned her."
I pursed my lips, "What did you say?"
He cricked his neck to one side and I fought the urge to make an ugly face at him, "Tell me," I urged.
"I told her that if she went near you ever again, I'd cut out her tongue," he said with no expression on his face whatsoever.

A frown creased my brow, "Why did you do that?"
His eyebrow twitched, "Because I will not allow anyone to speak to my wife the way she spoke to you."
I took a slow breath, "I don't blame her, you know?"
He seemed confused, "For what?"
I pulled up my shoulders, "She's in love with you."
The look on his face told me that he was waiting for the rest of an explanation, and I sighed, "She's in love with you, and you don't love her back."
He shrugged, "Apologies, but I fail to see how that is my problem."
I rolled my eyes, "Did you know she had feelings for you when you slept with her?"
"No. But even if I did, what difference would it have made?"

Ass. Obviously he doesn't get it, and I don't feel like explaining it to him in the midnight streets of London. "Point is, unrequited love makes people do crazy things." I said as I took his hand and we started walking again.
"Would you really cut out her tongue though?" I asked.
He nodded, "I would. I have. Darling, I've done worse."
My eyebrows shot up, "Really?" and he nodded again, "World War II was an interesting time…"

I blinked slowly at him. I didn’t fully know what to do with that information.

A few steps further, Jonathan stopped walking and frowned all of a sudden, sniffing the air. He tugged me in behind him and motioned for me to be quiet. Very quietly, he pushed me back against a wall. My body stiffened. Clearly, there was something or someone dangerous nearby, and he wanted me to stay out of sight. I wasn’t scared, but I wasn't going to argue either and I pressed myself as flat as I could against the wall behind me.

Then he crouched and pulled out a knife that he had strapped to his ankle that I had no idea was even there, and my eyes widened.

Jonathan

The strong stench of sage took me by surprise. Clearly I was right about the House prowling the streets of London, but I was not sure what they were doing in this particular neighborhood. This area did not fit the criteria of the usual places they hunted in. Whatever the reason, they were here. And they were much, much too close to Christina.

"What is it?" she whispered.

"Send Kat your location, and stay here," I whispered back, "we're not alone."

Thank the Moonlight she didn't argue. She just nodded, did as I told her, and pressed herself back against the wall, trying to stay out of sight.

Blade at the ready, I took off into the dark to find the source of the smell.

I didn't need to look far. Only a few meters ahead of us, I found it. As I approached, the smell changed, and I realized that I'd stumbled upon one of the House's fully turned vampires. Tucking my knife back into my pocket, I smirked. *This is shaping up to be a good weekend indeed.*

It didn't notice me until it was too late and I dropped a kick to its spine that sent it staggering forward. Once it regained its balance, it spun back around and lunged at me, swinging a fist at my head. I ducked and plunged my shoulder into its solar plexus, knocking all the air out of its lungs before I jumped back a step and put my fists up. The vampire in front of me hunched over, gasping for air. I took advantage of the moment of weakness, pushing my body up into the air to land right on top of it, my elbow aimed at the back of its head. There was a satisfying 'thwack' at the moment of impact and the creature went sprawling to the ground. It was down for but a second before it hoisted itself back up onto its feet.

"That wasn't fair," it said, and I shrugged, "No-one ever said it was supposed to be."

I attacked.

I swung my right fist at its face in a laughably obvious move. It ducked out of the way of my fist, but it was too late to avoid my left foot that connected to its rib cage in a blow hard enough that I heard bones breaking. The vampire howled in pain, and I chuckled.
My right hook caught it off guard and it staggered again, a few steps to the left. I was just getting started. Grabbing it by its shirt, I slammed my forehead right into its nose, following up with a quick left hook to the gut.
Blood spattered from its mouth and I had to step aside to keep it from ruining my clothes. *I'd rather not go back to Christina covered in blood.* "Watch it," I issued a warning, "This is a brand new shirt."
"I didn't come here to fight," it said then, "but if that's what you want…"
I grinned. "It is."
Baring its fangs at me, the vampire pulled a switchblade from its pocket. I followed suit, wrapping the fingers of my right hand around the handle of my own blade.
I beckoned it closer, "Come on then, show me the power of the House."
With a snarl, it lunged at me, swinging the knife at my face. I kept out of reach of his blade and on the fourth swipe I transferred my own to my left hand and swung my right fist up into an uppercut that hit the vampire right on the underside of its elbow, and it cried out in pain again. I clamped my hand around its right wrist and slammed my blade into its side before I kicked the inside of its left knee. The joint crunched beneath my boot and bent into an unnatural angle that could only mean that it was broken. I shoved it away from me, grabbing my knife back and letting blood spill from the open wound before putting my weapon back in my right hand.
"Was that it?" I asked, "Was that the best the mighty Apollo has to offer?"
"You son of a…"
"Careful now," I cut it short. "Choose your next words very carefully. They will determine if your jaw stays on your face or not."
Seemed like it wasn't a complete idiot, because it didn't say anything further.

I was bored with the fight, and the vampire was apparently getting desperate, because it reached for the gun in the holster strapped to its trousers. Before it could get a shot in, I kicked the gun out of its hand, yanked it closer and spun it around to press my knife to its throat.
"You chose the wrong neighborhood, friend."
The vampire raised both its hands in surrender, "I mean no harm."
"And why should I believe you? After all the blood your House has spilled in these streets."
"That wasn't all me, but I'm really sorry about that. Am I speaking to the prince?" it responded.
"Indeed," I confirmed, "good guess."
"Not really a guess. It's weird… I can... I can feel it. It's like my blood knows who you are," it explained.
"Fascinating, I'm sure. What are you doing here?" I pressed the blade tighter against its throat.
"Your Majesty, is there a chance you can get the blade off my throat? I've actually been looking for you, I just had no idea you were even in London tonight," it said, and I considered the request for a moment, "Who's with you?"
It shook its head, "I'm here by myself, I swear."
I wasn't sure I could believe it. I kept my hand on its shoulder and extended my claws until I heard it wince. Then I moved my knife and pressed the tip of my blade against its lower back, right to its spine, "One wrong move, and I sever your spine."
"Duly noted, I'm not stupid."
I focused my hearing and my sense of smell, and when I detected no others around, I eased my grip on its shoulder ever so slightly, "Why were you looking for me?"
"I wanted to talk to you," it said.
"You found me. So talk," I pressed.

"Alright. My name is Hunter McCoy, I'm a former Navy SEAL. And, you probably figured out by now, I'm the House's vampire. One of them, at least."
I chuckled, "Yes, they finally scored a B at the science fair. Good for them. I still don't know why you were looking for me so you better talk, and fast, before my patience runs out."
"I was looking for you because I think… everything the House stands for is a bullshit lie."

I blinked slowly. *Didn't see that coming. If it's true, of course.*
"Go on…" I urged.
"They brainwash us, pump us full of these lies about you and your family… But I've seen what you do, what your family does… and I haven't seen you do anything that I would consider evil, or bad, or even selfish. I mean, what your mother did for those girls in Syria, and in Belarus…"
I pressed the knife forward until I felt flesh give way beneath it, and Hunter grit his teeth. "Why were you following my mother?" I snarled.
"I had orders to follow her, to find proof of her evil. But all I saw was good," Hunter explained himself.
"So what do you want?" I asked. *I want to get back to Christina, Hunter needs to get to the point and fast.*
"I want to help you take down the House of Apollo. For good."
I felt my eyebrows raise, "Do you now? And why should I trust you?"
"You don't have to. But I have access to all of their information, all of their plans, they trust me, I command all of the other vampires."
"How many are there?"
"139 and counting," Hunter said.
"Hmm," I mused, "more than I thought."
"Your Majesty, please. I know I've done some questionable shit. Like those hikers in Germany, my guilt fucks me raw everyday about that. But I want to make it right. Or at least try. Tell me what I need to do to prove that to you."

"Well… I need information on a man named Anthony Sutton," I instructed, "I have reason to believe he may have joined the House at some point during the past 20 to 30-odd years. I want to know if he did and what happened to him."
Hunter nodded, "Sir, yes sir. Consider it done."
"Come back to this exact spot a week from now. If you have what I need, I will consider your offer. This conversation is over. Now fuck off, really fast and really far."
I shoved Hunter forward. He staggered, but I didn't stick around long enough to see if he regained his balance. I turned around and made my way back to Christina.

"Good," I said when I found her standing in the same place that I had left her with Kat at her side, "I see the psycho found you."

Kat rolled her eyes and nodded, “I was in the area.”
I nodded, “Of course you were. Thank you Kitty.”
She winked and waved goodbye to me and to Christina before she disappeared into the dark.
Christina stepped away from the wall and flung herself into my arms, “Are you okay?” she asked, her voice strained with concern.
I kissed her hair, “Of course, darling. What about you? Are you alright?”
She nodded, “I’m fine. You can tell me what happened later, let’s go home.”

Christina

Back at the apartment, my hormones were wreaking havoc on me. It had been a confusing day. It started with international travel, roses and make-up sex, then getting turned on by Jonathan's military maneuvers at paintball, then the possibility of being attacked by something again, and then getting turned on again by him pulling a knife from a hidden holster strapped to his ankle.

While he took a shower, I was rooting around in my bag looking for my make-up remover, and my hand brushed against something cold. I pressed my lips together. I actually forgot that I packed a pair of handcuffs. Maybe tonight would be a good time to use them. *I'm sure I'll be okay.*

When Jonathan came out of the bathroom, I turned to him with a sultry smile, the handcuffs dangling from my forefinger, "How about it, stud?"

His dark eyes ignited, "Do you want me to handcuff you?"

I nodded slowly, "I do…"

A low growl rumbled in his chest, and he immediately dropped the towel that he had draped around his waist and strode over to me.

I looked him up and down and I sighed. Everything about him was pretty, even his dick.

Jonathan pulled me against him and I inhaled deeply, breathing him in. *He smells so good, so clean.*

Then he kissed me, his hands reaching around me to grasp my ass and pull me against him. I melted into him. His kisses always rendered me weak.

His lips not parting from mine, he laid me down diagonally across the bed, and when he pulled back, he had the handcuffs in his hands.

"Hands above your head," he murmured, his voice heavy and dark with desire.

I did as he asked, and he slung the handcuffs around the corner post of the bed and cuffed me.

Oh, shit. This is familiar.

I closed my eyes as he started to raise my shirt.

My breathing shallowed out.
It's okay. You got this, everything's okay.
He lowered my pants, and I felt my heart pounding in my chest.
Breathe, Christina.
I felt him kneel on the bed, his leg between mine.
It's okay.
He lowered himself and pressed his body onto mine. I couldn't move.
No. No.
Something inside me snapped, "No! Stop! Stop!"
I couldn't escape and my hands were tied and he was on top of me and there was nothing I could do and nowhere I could go and I started twisting and thrashing and kicking and trying to get him off and I heard something snap, and suddenly my hands were free and I bolted upright and I fought back and I hit and I slapped and I scratched and I screamed, "No! No! Get off me!"
"Christina, you're safe," a warm voice said.
I know that voice... and I went still.
"It's alright, my love, you're safe," the kind voice said again.
I became aware of warm, gentle hands cupping my face and I slowly opened my eyes:
Jonathan.

Kneeling in front of me, cradling my face in his hands, scratches healing on his face, arms, shoulders, and chest, his beautiful face wrought with worry, "It's alright my love," he said again, his voice so, so gentle. "Breathe, my darling."
I released a breath in a shudder.
"Good, breathe in, count of four… one… two… three… four…" he said, "And out… four… three… two… one…"
Again.
And again.
One more time.
My head dropped and I clasped my hand over my mouth, "I'm sorry," I murmured, "I'm sorry, I'm sorry, I'm sorry…"
Jonathan sat down next to me and held out his arm to me, but he didn't touch me. It looked like he was waiting for me, gauging my reaction.
I slumped over onto him, and he pulled me in between his legs on the bed, his arms wrapped tightly around me, and I collapsed against his chest.

And I cried.
"I scratched you, I'm sorry," I sobbed, "I'm sorry."
He shook his head, kissing my hair, "I was a strong baby, I can handle it."
"I can explain…" I sniffled, but he shook his head again, "You don't have to explain anything to me, love. All you have to do is to keep breathing. If you want, we can talk in the morning. If you don't want to talk about it, we don't have to."
I nodded, wiping my nose with the back of my hand.
Jonathan got up from behind me and opened the covers. Then he tucked an arm in behind my back, and the other under my knees, picked me up, and put me in bed. He kissed my cheek, then strode to the other side of the bed and got in next to me.
I lifted my head and looked up at him, "What happened to the cuffs?"
He reached toward the bedside table and showed me the pieces that were left of the handcuffs.
"You snapped the rivets?" I asked in disbelief. He shrugged, "I hope they weren't expensive."
He lay back down and held out his arms, and I was more than happy to crawl into the warm safety of his embrace, and that was where I stayed until morning.

∞

When I woke up, Jonathan was already awake, but he was still in bed next to me. My heart skipped a few beats when I opened my eyes and the first thing I saw was his stunning smile.
"Good morning my lovely," he smiled.
"Hi," I replied, and I wondered why my voice sounded so small.
"Did you sleep alright?" he wanted to know.
I nodded, "I did, but babe I'm really sorry about last night. I…"
He put his forefinger to my lips, "Hush, love," he said, "There's nothing that you need to apologize for or that you owe me any kind of explanation for."
I kissed his finger, "But I want to tell you…"
He nodded understandingly, "Then I'll listen. Let me make us some coffee, and then I will come sit right here next to you, and you can tell me. Alright?"

I sat up in bed and took a few deep breaths, and by the time he handed me my coffee and got back into bed next to me, I could only hope I was ready to talk.

"I've never told anyone about this," I began the story, "Not even Devyn. Or my mom, for that matter."

Jonathan didn't say anything, he just let me talk. I took another deep breath. Better to just blurt everything out and get it all out in one go, "It's not a long story. But here goes. When Owen and I were dating, there was one time, we were going to… you know… and he asked if he could handcuff me to the bed, and I was a bit skeptical but I said okay, we could try, but then I changed my mind and I asked him to stop, and to uncuff me but… he… he wouldn't stop and he just kept going, and I… just closed my eyes and…"

It felt like my chest was going to explode and I couldn't get out any more words.

Jonathan's face went pale.

In slow motion, he stood up out of bed, his fingers interlocked at the back of his head. Wordlessly, he crossed the apartment to the windows on the other side.

He uttered a curse word in Romanian, a seriously vile one, before he turned back and came back to me. He stood at the foot of the bed, and I gasped when his fangs lowered and his wings flared at his back.

He. Was. Furious.

"Are you telling me," he hissed, his teeth clenched, "that he forced himself on you? After you said 'No'?"

I just nodded.

Jonathan pinched his eyes shut, "Son of a bitch, I should have fucking killed him…" he mumbled.

Probably the biggest takeaway from my relationship with the vampire crown prince, was that there was a side to everyone that we all kept hidden. Like this aspect of him: the dark, violent, vengeful part of himself that he kept locked away.

But the longer I was with him, the more I realized that having that kind of darkness wasn't necessarily a bad thing. Sometimes, darkness was the only thing that could protect the ones we loved. Maybe I also needed to learn how to be just a little bit darker, to keep myself and the people I loved safe. Or maybe it was okay for me to be light. That way, I could shed some warmth on this man that I loved so much, and remind him that he was more than just the dark that lived within his soul.

Jonathan came up to my side of the bed, and dropped onto his knees, his hand on his heart, "I am so, so sorry that happened to you."

He lowered his head, and even his wings seemed to droop.

"It's okay," I muttered, "it was a long time ago."

He stayed on his knees, "I am so sorry, darling."

I swung my legs off the bed, "Hug me? Please?" I didn't want to talk about this, but now I did, and I was done, and I didn't want to give it any more space in my head than it already had.

Immediately, Jonathan got to his feet and swept me up in his arms as he stood up, lifting my feet off the ground and holding me tightly against him.

When he lowered my feet back to the floor, I pressed a kiss to his lips and smiled, "How about we put this dark shit behind us, and go watch our friends promise each other forever. What do you say?"

He smiled his trademark crooked smile at me, cupping my face in his hands, "I like the way you think, Mrs. Langdon."

Oh, I like the way that sounds.

Lilian and Nathaniel's wedding was Gothic perfection.

Jonathan was also part of the wedding procession, one of the groomsmen. Nathaniel said his vows in Irish, and though I didn't understand a word of it, the emotion behind it was obvious. As Lilian promised to love him until time stopped ticking, I looked at Jonathan. At the man I was going to marry, at the love eternal that I had said yes to.

I can't wait to be his wife.

Chapter 68

Christina

"Are you ready darling?" Jonathan asked me. It was my first time back at the cemetery since Devyn's funeral, and we were sitting in his car in the parking lot. The cemetery was empty, we were the only living souls there.
I readjusted the bouquet of yellow roses in my hands and I nodded, "I think so. I really want to do this."
Nodding, Jonathan put his hand on the back of my neck, "Do you want me to go with you?"
But I shook my head, a sad smile on my face, "It's ladies' night."

I took a deep breath, then I got out of the car and slowly made my way over to Devyn's headstone. The marble headstone was so clean, so plain, so simple, so contradictory to the vibrant person that lay beneath it. When I put the roses down against the headstone, my tears overwhelmed me, and I sank down onto the grass.

I looked over to where Jonathan was strolling mindlessly through the cemetery a little further away. He looked up and smiled reassuringly at me. I blew him a kiss, then turned back to Devyn.
"Hi Dev," I started through my tears. "Shit, I have so much tea to spill. So my mom has a new boyfriend, his name is Magnus, I don't know if I've ever mentioned him. He's friends with Jonathan's family. Everything in my life revolves around the Langdon family, it seems. Anyway, Magnus is Danish. He's almost as stupidly rich as Jonathan. But he's really good to my mom, she giggles like a teenager whenever he calls or texts.

They met at that casino night that Jonathan's mom had that I told you about. Do you remember? I wore that red dress and then Jonathan man-handled me right outside the bathroom?"

I chuckled at the memory, "I know you saw Jonathan handle a gun, but you should see him with a knife. Sheesh, talk about a panty-dropper. Oh, speaking of Jonathan, guess what?"

I showed my left hand to the headstone, "I'm engaged! Jonathan asked me to marry him, and of course I said yes. I would've loved for you to be my maid of honor. I wish you could have been here. But since you can't, I hope you don't mind if I ask Lilian? I think you would have liked her. I know she would have loved you. She's the girl that got engaged at that fancy club in London, remember? When that British bitch had a mouthful to say to me in the bathroom.

Lilian reminds me of you. I guess that's why I like her. She's a little bit like the heavily tattooed British version of the best friend I lost. Oh, right, and I also got a tattoo," I showed my wrist, "It's from Jonathan's family crest. My new family crest. He loves it."

I sniffled and wiped away a stray tear, "Oh, and random news of the day, Owen died. And before you say anything, no, Jonathan did not have him taken out. I asked."

I took a deep breath and slowly got to my feet, "I should get going. Jonathan asked me to move in with him at the manor, so I need to start packing. I miss you Dev. Love you girl."

I ran my hand across the top of Devyn's tombstone and I wiped away another tear before I started to make my way out of the cemetery.

On the way, another fairly-new headstone caught my eye. Owen Beaumont Stanford North.

BS. Nice.

I stopped. There was a relatively fresh bunch of flowers in front of the headstone. Someone must have visited recently.

"Here you are too," I said out loud. "I don't know if you know this or not, but you weren't a very good boyfriend. I don't know if you tried to be but didn't know how, or if you just didn't give a shit. Either way, you sucked at it.

That's neither here nor there. I don't know that I'm sad that you died, but I am sorry that your life ended the way it did. Killed in an alley. No-one deserves that. So, yeah. I hope you get whatever it is that you do deserve."

Then I headed back to Jonathan's car.

Jonathan

Christina walked past me on her way to the car. When she passed me, I gently took her by the wrist, "I'd like to say hi to Devyn too, if you don't mind."

She smiled and kissed my shoulder, "Not at all. I'll be in the car."

I waited until she got back in the car and closed the door before I walked over to Devyn's grave and crouched in front of it.

"Hello, Devyn. It's Jonathan. But you knew that, you know I'm never too far behind Christina.

I'm not sure I ever thanked you for taking care of her that night at the club. If it hadn't been for you, Moonlight only knows what could have happened. So thank you, thank you for looking after the love of my eternity when I wasn't there. And thank you for being such a good friend to Christina. She loved you a great deal. She still does, and I'm sure she always will. Oh, and by the way, you were wrong about me. I'm not a mob-boss," I said as I got to my feet, "I'm the future vampire king."

Then I winked at the headstone before I stood up and headed toward the grave where Christina had stopped on her way out.

I heard everything that she said to the person lying there, and I had my own piece to say.

I glared at Owen's name on the headstone, and I took a moment to formulate what it was that I wanted to say.

Then I started, "I don't share Christina's sentiment. I don't give a fuck that you died in an alley, and I should have ripped you apart when I had the chance. Scum like you deserve a much bloodier ending, and if you weren't dead already, Moonlight is my witness, I would have fucking killed you myself for what you did to her. If I could, I would resurrect you just so I could have the pleasure of ripping your fucking head off and pissing down your throat myself. Consider yourself lucky that someone else got to you before I did. You deserve nothing good, in this life or the next."

Then I hawked up a bogey, pulled it back as far as I could, and I spat on the grave, "Burn in Hell."

My mother would be ashamed of me if she saw me do that. But how else was I supposed to show my disrespect for the dead?

Then I went back to the car and got in behind the wheel.

"What was that about?" Christina wanted to know.

I smirked, "Not to worry, love."

She gave me a look of disbelief, "Right… Babe, I saw the look on your face…"

I chuckled, "My mother did say that I have a vicious tongue, but it's my face that needs deliverance."

She laughed, "The accuracy though…"

Belinda

"Life has certainly taken us on interesting turns this past year," I said to Christina over brunch.
"I know," Christina replied, refilling our mimosas, "A year ago I would never have believed that I would be engaged to Jonathan and on the verge of moving in with him."
I clinked my glass against hers, "To surprises, pleasant or otherwise."
She frowned, "What unpleasant surprise did you get, Mom?"
I took a big gulp of my drink and a very deep breath, "Oh, shit, sweetheart, I don't even know how to broach this topic."
She put her hand over mine, "I'm here for you, Mommy, you can tell me."
"I know, honey, I know, it's just… so hard to believe."
Christina smiled endearingly, "Try me."
I took another deep breath and I just blurted out the unbelievable truth, "Magnus is a vampire."

Christina said nothing.
"And… you already knew that," I said quietly, "Of course you did, you knew him before I did."
She gave me a guilty smile, "I knew… But I couldn't tell you, I'm sorry Mom."
I waved a dismissive hand, "Of course you couldn't, how would that conversation even have started?"
"How did you find out?" she asked.
"I opened the wrong refrigerator…" I said sheepishly, and Christina laughed.
"Wait…" I said then, "If Magnus is a vampire, does that mean… Jonathan's a vampire too?"
She shook her head slowly, "Mom, Jonathan isn't 'a' vampire. Jonathan is 'the' vampire. They call themselves Infinite, and Jonathan is the Infinite crown prince."
My jaw dropped, "Alastair is the king?"
"Celeste is the queen. Her Infinite Majesty, Sovereign Celeste Aricia Adelphi, Queen of Carpathia," she said.
"Holy heck. And Jonathan?"

Christina smiled, "This is the first time that I actually get to say his title out loud: His Eternal Majesty, Lord Jonathan Ambrose Langdon, The Undeniable, The Undisputed Son of Delphi, Black Prince of Carpathia'."
"The Black Prince… Why the Black Prince?" I wanted to know.
She took a sip of her mimosa, "That's a story for another time."
I nodded in acceptance, "Okay, sure. How did you find out about Jonathan?"
"This is what we had that huge fight about," Christina said.
"The truth, finally!" I whooped, "I've been wanting to get to the bottom of exactly what happened between you two for months. Can you finally tell me what happened?"
She laughed, "I'm so sorry, Mom. I really wanted to tell you, but I couldn't. Now I can."
I refilled our glasses, "I am all ears all over."

"Basically," she started, "an evil vampire attacked me, and Jonathan went into Infinite-mode and killed it. And I saw everything."
"And then you were so freaked out that you couldn't deal," I said, and she nodded, "That's the gist of it, yes. But you talked some sense into me, and Alastair and I had a chat about it when we went to lunch that day, and I decided to give Jonathan a chance to tell me everything. I love him and I wanted to be with him, Infinite or not."
"Because he saved your life?" I asked.
"Because he is my life." she smiled. Honestly, she didn't have to say it, I knew it.

"That night, when you saw him for what he was, were you afraid of him?"
Christina shook her head, "The nascent that attacked us freaked me out. That, and the fact that I actually knew nothing about the world, that vampires didn't exist only between the pages of a shitty teen romance novel. The truth scared me. But I was never afraid of Jonathan."
I smiled, "So how did it make you feel when you found out that the guy who stood in for your Crimson Count that first day was an actual vampire?"
Christina giggled, "Shocked and very turned on."
I could relate, and I blushed.

"Mom…" she asked, "Has Magnus shown you his fangs?"
My blush deepened, and I nodded.
"Hot, right?" she wanted to know, and I bit my index finger and nodded again, "Incredibly."
Christina laughed, then she squeezed my hand, "I am so happy for you Mom, you deserve to be happy. And I'm really, really glad I don't have to keep this a secret from you anymore."
I took another deep breath, "There's one more thing I need to tell you. And this is kind of huge."
She eyed me skeptically, "Should I be nervous?"
She had no reason to be, but I was nervous to tell her, and my daughter knew me well enough to know.
"Whatever it is, Mom, I can handle it."
"Okay…" I conceded, "I'm moving to Copenhagen."
Her jaw dropped, "What?!"

I nodded fast, "Magnus asked me to move in with him, and I know this sounds odd coming from someone my age, but I am very much in love with him, vampire and all. So I said yes. I am moving to Copenhagen. I already put in my notice at the school."
She was speechless for a moment. Then she jumped up from her chair and flung her arms around me, "That's amazing Mom! I am so happy for you!"
I returned the hug, "Really? You don't think I'm too old for this?"
Christina laughed, a happy tear rolling down her cheek, "I don't think you have any notion of what 'old' means, Mom. Ask Magnus how old he is."
I laughed, "And I suppose Jonathan is also quite advanced in years?"
She nodded, "Very much so."
"Then I guess us Miller-ladies are panthers by nature."

"When are you moving?" Christina asked when she sat back down.
"I guess as soon as possible. My two week notice period ends next week."
Her eyes widened and her face slacked the slightest bit, "Shit… that's really soon."
She's right… It is really soon. I probably should have told her sooner.
"I hope you're not planning on packing up the house by yourself?" she said.

I shrugged, "I was… should I not be?"
She shook her head, "Please, no. I'll ask Jonathan, they have a really good moving company. They can probably have everything cleared out in less than a day."
I nodded in acceptance, "That would be lovely, thank you sweetie."
"Is Jonathan coming over later?" I asked then, and she nodded, "Yes, his Royal Darkness is going to help me start my move to the manor, why?"
His Royal Darkness. I chuckled at the nickname before I took another sip of my mimosa, "Am I supposed to call him 'Your Majesty'?"
Christina burst out laughing, "Please do, I'd love to see the look on his face. He doesn't know that you know who he is. But only once, he'll be weirded out if you call him that all the time."
I chuckled, "Does he not like it?"
"Nope, not at all."
Shaking my head, I leaned back in my chair, "These are interesting times we live in, that's for sure."

Christina

When Jonathan rang the doorbell that evening, I hung back and let my mom open the door, and I nearly squealed in excitement. *This is going to be good...*

Jonathan greeted my mom with his perfect smile, and a very polite 'Good evening', and she took her chance. She bowed her head and curtsied deeply, "Salutations, Your Majesty."

I pressed my lips together to stifle my laughter when Jonathan's eyes widened and all the blood drained from his face.

He turned to me in utter confusion… and when my laughter exploded from me, my mom also burst out laughing.

"What is happening?" Jonathan asked, completely befuddled.

"It wasn't me," I said between giggles, "Magnus spilled the beans, he told my mom The Truth."

He blinked slowly, "Really…?"

My mom nodded, "It's so stupid, I'll tell you later."

Jonathan cocked his head to one side, "And you're just… fine with it?"

She shrugged, "Why wouldn't I be? I quite love who you are, what you are in addition to that doesn't matter. You could have been a hairy werewolf for all I care, you're family."

A smile plucked at the corner of his mouth, but he fought it, "Was that why you decided to prank me? Because I'm family?"

My mom held her arms out to Jonathan for a hug, "Sorry, I had to. You should have seen the look on your face. Hello, sweetheart."

His eyes still wide, he returned her hug, "Hello, Mum. It's.. uh… it's alright. Strange, but alright."

Then he pulled me in for a kiss, "Hello, beautiful."

"Hi handsome," I smiled back at him.

"I have an idea," my mom said as she headed back to the kitchen, "Jonathan, why don't you spend the night? You two can head to the manor in the morning."

"Sounds good, Mum," he replied. He looked at me and I wrinkled my nose at him, "Gotcha."

He didn't disagree.

We spent the evening cooking, relaxing, and spending time with my mom, and we started packing the next morning.
I didn't know that packing up the room I slept in for most of my life was going to be so hard, and quite so emotional. I was grateful that Jonathan didn't say anything every time I sniffled or blubbered over a memento or a teddy that had to go into a box.
By the time that all of my clothes and most of my personal belongings were packed up and loaded either into my car, or his car, my room was mostly empty, and I just stood there, staring at the emptiness.

Jonathan came up behind me and wrapped his arms around me, "Are you alright my love?" he asked.
"I grew up here, in this room. And now I'm leaving. It just feels... surreal, you know?"
He nodded slowly, "I know. You don't have to come with me tonight if you're not ready. You can stay longer if you need to."
I shook my head, "No, it's okay. I'm ready. A sunset is nothing more and nothing less than the backside of a sunrise."
"So I'm your knight in shining armor, and we're about to ride off into the sunset together?" he asked, and I turned my head and kissed his cheek, "More like my immortal goofball in tin-foil, but yes, something like that."

That night at the manor after dinner, Jonathan was taking a shower while I was unpacking my books. He moved many of his books off of the bookshelf in his room to make space for mine, and I thought it was very sweet. He'd even made a special spot on the shelf just for Dimitri, my rainbow bat plushie.
I was about to start on my second box of books when a document on the desk caught my attention. I sat down in the desk chair to look at it. It was the report from the surveyor on a property that Jonathan seemed to be interested in.
Report in hand, I opened up his computer and pulled up a few historical journals that I used for my dissertation. I wasn't even sure what I wanted to check. I was sure the surveyor did a good job, but the property was in Rome, and I was curious to see if it might have had any historical significance.

As I scrolled, I thought about how our relationship had grown and changed and progressed from when we first met, to now. We'd been having a whole hell of a lot of sex, but it was probably as much of a sexual awakening for him as it was for me. I'd never felt as confident in the bedroom as I did with him. And he seemed to be opening up a bit more and letting me see more of his kinks and preferences. He was finding more ways to show me how much he loved me. *And earth-shatteringly good sex has never been a bad thing.*

"See anything interesting?" Jonathan's voice next to me startled me and I quickly put down the report, "Sorry babe, I didn't mean to snoop."
He laughed, "Darling there's nothing on my desk that I don't want you to see. I was just asking out of curiosity."
I made a face at him and pointed at the report, "What were you planning on doing with the property?"
He looked at the document under my hand, "The usual: Develop it and sell it, as I always do. Why?"
I turned my attention back to the screen, "Can you hold off?"
He nodded slowly, "I could… if you can tell me why?"
"Well," I said pensively, "I feel like this property could potentially be a historical asset, but I'd need some more time to look into it."
He leaned in and read where I was looking at the screen, then he ran his fingers through my hair, "Alright, how much time do you need?"
I looked up at him in surprise, "Really?"
He nodded, "History is important and needs to be preserved as best we can. How much time do you need?"
"When were you going to start construction?"
He looked at the report again, "Next week. But I can easily postpone it. Would seven days be enough?"
Seven days was plenty, "Perfect," I smiled, "Thank you babe."
He winked at me, then his expression turned curious, "Have you found a job yet?"
"No…" I said quietly.
He grinned, "What would you say if I offered you a job as my Heritage Advisor?"
"Do you even need one?"

Jonathan nodded, "Yes, I do. I stumble upon historical properties more often than you think, and I don't like looking for new service providers every time. I prefer people I know and trust. So I've been thinking of appointing a heritage consultant of my own to manage construction and restoration projects on heritage sites, someone to provide guidance on heritage issues."
I gave him a skeptical look, "Don't you have property surveyors that do that for you?"
He shook his head, readjusting the towel around his waist, "A surveyor can only identify the boundaries of a particular property and inform me of any potential restrictions so that I can avoid legal problems. But they can't tell me anything about the historical significance of a property. You could."
I raised my eyebrows at him, "You're seriously offering me a job?"
Jonathan nodded, "I am."
"Because you think I can do it? Or because nepotism?"
He crossed his eyes at me, "Because I have faith in my fiancée. I'm rather sure that my father's company might also need your skills from time to time. You're welcome to freelance for them, but you're mine."
I laughed, "Of course I'm yours."
"What do you say? Will you accept my offer?"
"Hmm…" I thought about it, "How much are you going to pay me?"
His jaw dropped, "Is my love not enough?"
"Ha. Ha. Ha." I laughed mockingly, "Your love is more than enough, but I'm not going to work for free."
Smiling, he scribbled an amount onto a Post-it and showed it to me, and my jaw dropped, "Holy fuck. That much?"
He nodded, "That's about how much I would be willing to pay if I had to hire someone."
I stared at the amount. *That's a lot of zeros in one place*, "This is a lot of money, babe."
He smiled, "I pay what is necessary for necessary services. Take a few days, but please consider my offer. I would very much like it if you said yes. I will admit that I do have an ulterior motive: I would be really glad if you were no longer working at the escape room, so that I never have to travel anywhere without you ever again."
I pouted, "Aww, he's just a baby."
He chuckled and shook his head.

“And I have seven days to look into the property?” I asked, and he winked at me.

“By the way,” he asked as he started towel-drying his hair, “Do you have a specific date in mind for our wedding?”
Grinning, I picked up the calendar that was standing on the desk next to the computer and pointed at a date, “How about this one?”
Jonathan froze and he blinked slowly, “Any particular reason for choosing that date?”
I shrugged, “I don’t know. I was just flipping through the calendar and it was like this one spoke to me. Why?”
A small smile crept onto his face, “That’s my birthday.”
My eyes widened, “Wait… What? You're a Scorpio…? I mean of course you are, I should have known. You’re such a shit.”
He flashed me a look of surprise, “What did I do now?”
I tapped the date on the calendar with my index finger, “I’ve been trying to get you to tell me when your birthday is without asking you directly, because you somehow knew mine, but…”
He pursed his lips, “You could have asked my mother… or my sister…”
“No, but…” I started saying, but I interrupted myself. He was right, I could have. His mom or Niki would probably have told me with a smile.
“You’re right,” I admitted, though I had to ask. “Why didn’t you tell me, though?”
He shrugged, “I’ve been alive so long, I don’t celebrate it anymore. No-one in my family does.”
I frowned, “Seriously? The Langdons don’t do birthdays? Not even Mama Celeste?”
Jonathan shook his head, “We stopped after the first hundred.”
I stood up from the chair, “Well, I think getting married on your birthday makes it even more perfect. If you’re okay with that, of course.”

A wide grin on his face, Jonathan pressed his lips to mine in a long, slow, lingering kiss.
When he pulled back, his eyes darted to the desk where I had put down my engagement ring, and he picked it up and frowned at me, “Why are you not wearing your ring?”

"I don't want it to get damaged..."
Jonathan stuck his tongue out at me, "It's insured. If it gets damaged, then that is something that happened, and then I buy you a new one. Wear it."
"Fine," I gave a dramatic sigh. *Like I don't want to wear my stunningly beautiful engagement ring.*

He narrowed his eyes at me, then dropped down on one knee, "Christina Elodie Miller, will you give me the greatest gift I've ever received and marry me on my birthday?"
"My love," I smiled as he put my ring back on my finger, "I will marry you any day and every day."

Chapter 69

My blood coursed through my veins in pulsating, throbbing excitement.

From the moment we walked through the doors of the laboratory building, I felt it. Blood was about to be spilt, and I couldn't wait to feel it, to see it, to taste it.

I leisurely pushed the door open and let myself in, my queen right behind me.

"How can I help you?" the mousy little receptionist with her unimpressive hair color yapped when we entered.

Smiling at her, I summoned a ball of fire right into the middle of my palm and launched it right at her face.

I laughed when she screamed in agony as the flames engulfed her, and the smell of burnt flesh and hair filled the air. My queen cackled as the receptionist dropped to the floor screaming.

But only for a moment. Then she stomped on the woman's throat, and the screaming stopped.

We moved on to the next area, the laboratory. Exactly as I expected, everything about the place was clinical and sterile and white.

It held little interest for us; what we were after was deeper in the building. It had to be.

At least the little scientist lab rats, running and hiding, begging for their lives, made for a little bit of entertainment and refreshments.

I stood back and watched my queen work. She moved like lightning, flying through the air as if someone had picked up their shadow and tossed it across the room. She flitted quickly from one little piggy to the next.

When she landed back at my side, her face was smeared in fresh blood, and I licked it from her face with an eager tongue.
"Did you enjoy your snack, *malyshka*?" I purred before my tongue slipped into her mouth.
I winced and pulled back when she clamped her teeth down and bit my tongue, my blood spilling into her mouth.
She spat it out onto the dead face of one of the lab techs, frozen in their final scream before she had slit their throat.
"It was delicious, *zaichonok*," she leered.
I clamped my fingers around her throat, "Come, let's go claim our throne."
With little more than a gentle shove, I pushed the heavy steel doors to the back of the lab right off their hinges, and we strode through.

The priest's personal guard stormed at us from the front.
I laughed, "Look at you, you look so cute with your little guns."
I lazily turned my head to my queen, "All yours."
She licked her lips and kissed me before her face contorted in a psychotic grin, and she launched herself at them.
She grabbed the first guard by the wrist, snapping his forearm and turning his gun back on him. She pulled the trigger, and blood and brain matter splattered onto the face of the guard behind him.
She slammed her long fingernails into his neck and ripped out his throat. Slowly, she turned to the other two. "Hmm," she mused as she licked the blood from her fingers, "Who is going to die next?"
They cocked their guns, warning her to stop.
"Stop right there!"
"Don't move!"
"In the name of Apollo, don't move."
When she didn't stop, they fired.
She laughed at them as the bullets hit her and she kept coming toward them,
"*Eniky beniky eli vareniki, eniky beniky… klets.*" Her finger landed on the first guard as the nursery rhyme ended. "You," she grinned, "You die."
Before he could steady his weapon and shoot again, she had already torn his head from his neck and chucked it over her shoulder.
The last guard screamed and tried to run, scrambling to get away.

But then it was my turn. I couldn't let my queen have all the fun. And I needed this one. To make the necessary introductions.
In a few steps, I grabbed the guard by the back of his uniform and lifted him up into the air, "Now, now, little mutt. I'll make you a deal," I snarled, my tongue flicking against the guard's ear as I put extra emphasis on the l-sounds, "If you do a good job, maybe I will let you live."
"Please…" the guard begged, "I don't want to die. Are you going to kill me?"
I laughed, "I haven't decided yet."
Behind me, my queen wrapped her arms around me, "What are we going to do with this squirming little worm?" she asked
"Whatever we want…" I grinned, "But first he needs to tell us where we can find…"
I looked at her with a frown on my face, "What did they call him?"
"The priest?" she guessed, and the vicious grin on my face widened, "Yes, the priest!"
I slammed the terrified guard's face into the wall, "Where is he?" I barked
"In... the… th-the... holy room," the guard answered immediately.
I sighed in disappointment, "No loyalty. And I was so looking forward to bleeding the information out of you." I sighed again before I sank my fangs into the guard's neck.

I dropped the drained body onto the floor and gestured down the hall, "Shall we?"
She curtsied, and skipped ahead of me.
I smiled to myself as I walked. This was way more fun and so much easier than I imagined.
I could hear it: The voice of the priest, coming from the holy room. This was perfect. Perfect, perfect, perfect.
Quietly and carefully, I opened the door to the holy room, and I had to keep myself from bursting out laughing at the sight before my eyes. The doting believers bowed to the priest where he stood on a pedestal, his eyes turned to a holographic projection that, I guessed, was supposed to be the visage of Apollo.
I shook my head. Cheap parlor tricks and deception. Before I even had to tell her, my queen was already making her way to the projector room.

Mere moments later, blood spattered against the glass of the projector room, and she wiped it away to grin at me. It was time.

In the blink of an eye, I was right behind the priest. I grabbed the priest by the hair, and I spoke as the believers gasped and shrieked, "This day marks the dawn of a new era. The old gods are dead, the new gods have arisen!"

"Who… who are you?" the priest stammered.

"Who, me?" I asked, "I am the future."

Someone in the audience screamed as I sank my fangs into the neck of the priest and his blood stained the white ceremonial cloak in glorious crimson.

The projection flashed and flickered and disappeared at the same moment as the priest's lifeless body dropped to the floor, and I kicked it from the pedestal.

More screams sounded up from the audience, and someone cursed me, "Apollo will strike you down, foul beast!"

My queen took the unbeliever's head before I even needed to tell her.

"Listen to me, you worthless maggots," I spoke again.

"From this moment, you no longer serve Apollo. You serve me. I am your master."

My queen made her way between the trembling followers, and stepped up next to me, her arms snaked around my waist.

"Tell them who you are, *zaichonok*," she purred.

I grinned down at her, "Of course, *malyshka*."

I unfurled my wings and I summoned a handful of flame, letting it crackle in the palm of my hand. Then I turned my head away from my raven-haired queen to look at the followers of Apollo, cowering, groveling in fear before me, and addressed my new subjects:

"My name is Aris Adelphi, great-grandson of Ambrogio,
the First, the holiest of our kind.
Apollo is dead.
You are in the House of Aris now.
And I am your god..."

The third book of the Night Heir series is set for release in July 2024…

Acknowledgements

To everyone who had a hand in getting this book to this point, I appreciate you more than words can say.
To my absolute superwoman of a PA, Ann, for being my brain when my own is in dolphin-mode.
To Antoinette, for your unwavering support.
To Melanie, for always letting me think out loud and for helping me make sense of my head-thoughts.
To all my girls: Allison, Bianca, Anchal, Faith, Adrieanna, Anita, Shannon, Crystelle, Belinda, Maddi, Morgan, Simone, Kim, Chelle, Jessica, Lily, Erikka, Jordynn, Liza, Tiffany, Kristin, Robyn, Leanna, Samantha, Pricilla, Tina and Zara. You guys are the absolute best, thank you for everything.
To my husband for his support and silent fortitude when I need it the most.
The biggest 'thank you' goes to my dear friend Victoria. Thank you for the hours out of your life that you took to support me. Thank you for the in-depth look and for giving me a fresh new perspective on my writing that I would not have had otherwise. And thank you that I still get to call you my friend after all these years.
I will always be thankful to my late aunt, and everything I write will always be in her memory.

And to everyone else, for clicking the clicks, posting the posts and reading the reads.
Thank you. Thank you. Thank you

Moonlight bless you and keep you.

Love, Hannah J

Made in the USA
Columbia, SC
07 June 2025